# Somebody's Fool

# Somebody's Fool

RICHARD RUSSO

ALFRED A. KNOPF
New York
2023

THIS IS A BORZOI BOOK
PUBLISHED BY ALFRED A. KNOPF

www.aaknopf.com

Knopf, Borzoi Books, and the colophon are registered trademarks
of Penguin Random House LLC.

Library of Congress Cataloging-in-Publication Data
Names: Russo, Richard, 1949– author.
Title: Somebody's fool / Richard Russo.
Description: First Edition. | New York : Alfred A. Knopf, [2023]
Identifiers: LCCN 2022039308 (print) | LCCN 2022039309 (ebook) |
ISBN 9780593317891 (hardcover) | ISBN 9780593317907 (ebook) |
ISBN 9781524712495 (open market)
Subjects: LCGFT: Novels.
Classification: LCC PS3568.U812 s66 2023 (print) |
LCC PS3568.U812 (ebook) | DDC 813/.54—dc23/eng/20220902
LC record available at https://lccn.loc.gov/2022039308
LC ebook record available at https://lccn.loc.gov/2022039309

Jacket photograph © glasslanguage / iStock / Getty Images
Jacket design by Kelly Blair

Printed in the USA
First Edition

# SATURDAY

# Inheritance

THE CHANGES WOULD BE gradual, or that was how the idea had been sold all along. But no sooner did North Bath's annexation to Schuyler Springs become official than rumors began circulating about "next steps." North Bath High, the Beryl Peoples Middle School, and one of the town's two elementary schools would close at the end of the school year, just a few months away. In the fall their students would be bused to schools in Schuyler. Okay, none of this was unexpected. The whole point of consolidation was to eliminate redundancies, so education, the most expensive of these, would naturally be at the top of that list. Still, those pushing for annexation had argued that such changes would be incremental, the result of natural attrition. Teachers wouldn't be fired, merely encouraged, by means of incentives, to retire. Younger staff would apply for positions in the Schuyler Unified school district, which would make every effort to accommodate them. The school buildings themselves would be converted into county offices. Same deal with the police. The low-slung brick building that housed the police department and the jail would be repurposed, and Doug Raymer, who'd been making noises about retiring as chief of police for years, could probably get repurposed as well. His half-dozen or so officers could apply for positions within the Schuyler PD. Hell, they'd probably even keep their old uniforms; the left sleeve would just bear a different patch. Sure, other redundancies would follow. There'd be no further need for a town council (there being no town) or for a mayor (which in Bath wasn't even a full-time position). The town already purchased its water from Schuyler Springs, whose sanitation department would now collect its trash, which everybody agreed was a significant upgrade. At present Bath citizens were responsible for hauling their crap to the dump, or hiring the Squeers Brothers and letting their fleet of decrepit dump trucks do it for them.

Naturally, not everyone had been in favor of this quantum shift. Some maintained there was really only one genuine redundancy that annexation would eliminate, and that was North Bath itself. By allowing itself to be subsumed by Schuyler Springs, its age-old rival, the town was basically committing suicide, voting for nonexistence over existence, and who in their right mind did that? This melodramatic argument was met with considerable derision. Was it even possible for an intubated patient on a ventilator to commit suicide? For the last decade about the only thing Bath had any control over was its morphine drip, because its debt had become so crushing that the town budget allowed for little beyond its interest payment.

How had all this come to pass? Well, the recession the whole damn country was still in the middle of was partly to blame, but many argued that the town had been circling the drain long before that. Most people blamed Gus Moynihan and the damned Democrats, who, when they took power, just spent and spent and spent. Before that, Bath had been a model of fiscal restraint, its unofficial motto being: *No spending. Ever. On anything. For any purpose.* If there was a pothole in the middle of the street, drive around the fucking thing. It wasn't like potholes were invisible. The wider and deeper they grew, the easier they were to spot. Hell, it wasn't *that* long ago that the streets weren't paved at all. No, the fiscal crisis was due to a curious combination of hubris and self-loathing, the anti-annexers maintained, the inevitable result of Bath's attempts to emulate its rich neighbor. The Democrats, being Democrats, figured that if the town spent money like Schuyler Springs did, maybe it could have everything Schuyler had. You had to spend money to make money, right? Okay, sure, Republicans countered, but what the Democrats were conveniently ignoring was that Schuyler Springs, a lucky town if there ever was one, *had money to burn.* The city was flush. It was full of fancy restaurants and coffee shops and museums and art galleries. It had a thoroughbred racetrack, a performing arts center and writers' colony and snooty liberal arts college, all of which generated a veritable shitstorm of revenue. How was Bath supposed to compete with all that? Moreover, why would they even want to? After all, there were other ways of measuring wealth, other sources of civic pride. Schuyler might be lucky—its mineral springs still percolating up out of the ground more than a century after Bath's ran dry—but the historic drivers of its economy were gambling and horseracing and prostitution (a claim advanced by North Bath fundamentalist churches, though the only whorehouse of historical note had actually been located on their own outskirts), all of which explained why Schuyler was full of rich assholes and latte-drinking homosexuals and one-God-at-most Unitarian churches, a town where morally upright, God-fearing, hardworking people couldn't afford to live. That it hadn't gotten its comeuppance yet didn't mean there wasn't one coming. If potholes and second-rate schools kept taxes low and degenerates, atheists and Starbucks out, then let's hear it for potholes.

That was the other thing: taxes. If Bath was subsumed by Schuyler, how much longer would they remain low? Those in favor of annexation conceded that, yes, *eventually,* if Schuyler Springs assumed North Bath's debt, at some point all town property would have to be reassessed. Taxes might conceivably go up. Language like *eventually* and *at some point* and *might conceivably* had the intended effect of rendering these outcomes as *remote* and *possible,* as opposed to *immediate* and *inevitable.* Now, though, word on the street was that this reassessment of both residential and commercial properties would commence *next week.* Just that quickly *eventually* had become a synonym for *tomorrow.* So, yes, North Bath teachers and cops and other public servants could *apply* for their old jobs in Schuyler schools and the Schuyler PD, but if their property taxes doubled, how many of them could afford to keep living there? Sure, residents with the nicest houses in the better neighborhoods would make a killing and move away, but what about everybody else? Wouldn't they just end up in some other town like Bath that couldn't afford services like trash removal, except with a longer commute?

Birdie, who was the principal owner of Bath's venerable road-house, the White Horse Tavern, had followed the civic debate with interest, despite not really having a dog in the fight. The way she saw it, she was pretty much screwed either way. If the tavern was reassessed and her taxes doubled, then she'd probably lose not just the business but her home, since she lived in the apartment upstairs. Theoretically the property would be worth more, but that would also make it even harder to sell. While the tavern wasn't technically on the market, it was common knowledge that Birdie had been looking for an off-ramp for a while now. She'd recently turned sixty-three, and most mornings, including this one, she woke up feeling like she'd been rode hard and put up wet. She couldn't afford to retire, but how many more years of hard labor did she have in her? A decade ago the bar had kept her afloat during the winter, but not anymore. Summers were still busy, of course. She opened the main dining room around Memorial Day, hired seasonal waitstaff and cooks who pushed steaks and prime rib out of the crowded kitchen and into the expansive dining room, but all of that went away after Labor Day. She kept the kitchen open as a service, but mostly for burgers and pizza. The whole place needed a good sprucing up, and not just a fresh coat of paint, either. Every stick of furniture in the joint needed replacing, and she'd been putting off purchasing new point-of-sales equipment for years. She wanted to update her soft-ware, too, something her ancient computer wouldn't support. Face it. The Horse was, like the town itself, on a respirator. Maybe it was time to pull the plug. Put a merciful end to her misery. Before the recession she'd been hoping for—praying for, really—somebody from away to wander into the tavern and be both charmed by its historic vibe and blind to its present decrepitude. Someone capable of closing their eyes and seeing in the resulting darkness a bright future. A romantic fool, in other words. Unfortunately, people like that were more likely to invest in bookstores and B and Bs than roadhouse taverns.

Still, you never knew, which was why Birdie was paying particular attention to another rumor that was currently making the rounds: the one about the Sans Souci—the old hotel that sat in the middle of a large, wooded estate situated between Bath and Schuyler Springs. Of course the place had always been a rumor mill. Every few years there'd be talk that some downstate investor was interested, that the old hotel would be renovated yet again, a celebrity chef brought up from Manhattan to run its high-end restaurant, the extensive grounds converted into a golf course or maybe a music venue to rival Schuyler's performing arts center. Others believed that the state of New York would eventually step in, purchase the land and make a public park out of it. This new scuttlebutt was strikingly different: somebody already *had* bought the Sans Souci, and not some downstater, but a West Coast billionaire and movie studio owner who meant to tear the hotel down and build a soundstage in its place. That was last week's scenario. This week's purchaser was a Silicon Valley tech firm looking for an East Coast presence by replacing the Sans Souci with an entire campus built from the ground up, which would mean hundreds, if not thousands, of employees. Overnight the whole area would be flooded with new people, all of them looking not just for housing but for places to eat and drink. Could it be that for once in her life Birdie was actually in the right place at the right time? She never had been before, but where was it written that her luck couldn't change? Her old friend Sully had been as unlucky as anybody she knew until one day his luck turned with a vengeance. Why not her?

Birdie was contemplating this rosy possibility when she heard Peter Sullivan, Sully's son and one of her two minority business partners, letting himself in via the tavern's delivery entrance, as he did every

Saturday morning without fail. Peter seemed to believe he was a very different breed of cat than his father, which always made Birdie smile, though in some respects she supposed it might be true. College educated, he was white collar where Sully had been faded blue, and Peter was both well dressed and articulate. In other respects, however, he was his old man all over again. If you ever needed to know where Sully was, all you had to do was glance at your watch. At seven he'd be at Hattie's for his morning coffee. Eight-thirty would find him at Tip Top Construction, where Carl Roebuck, its owner, would let him know what disgusting job he'd lined up for him that day, one even Sully couldn't fuck up. Over the noon hour he'd drop by the OTB, where he'd bet his 1-2-3 exacta and shoot the shit with the other regulars there. Six o'clock or thereabouts would find him back home, in the shower, scrubbing off the day's grime (though he'd sometimes skip going home if the job ran long). By seven he'd be on his favorite barstool here at the Horse, where there was always cold beer and *The People's Court* or a ball game on the wall-mounted TV, not to mention the regular bar crowd—Wirf, Jocko, Carl and the others, all gone now, dead or moved away or drinking elsewhere—whose balls he enjoyed breaking. And there he'd stay, until midnight on weekdays, or last call on weekends, after which, if a poker game broke out in the back room, so much the better. He'd kept to that schedule pretty much right up to the end, even when the knee he'd injured years before got so stiff and painful that the few people who didn't know him assumed he had a prosthesis.

Peter seemed to believe that because he drank coffee at the Horse on Saturday mornings instead of beer there every night of the week and because he read the *New York Times* instead of watching *The People's Court,* he'd won some sort of victory over genetics. Birdie had her doubts. With each passing day he looked more like his old man, and while she wasn't privy to the details of his day, she knew its broad strokes—teaching at the community college during the week, on Saturdays slow-walking the ongoing renovations to the house on Upper Main Street that his father had left him, playing racquetball (whatever that was) or tennis at a fitness club in Schuyler on Sundays. Evenings? Every now and then he'd stop by the Horse for a martini (Birdie stocked his favorite high-end vodka), but he usually drank at that hipster bar in Schuyler, the kind of place where a glass of wine went for twelve bucks and you weren't supposed to mind the short pour. Peter's routines, in other words, were every bit as ingrained and regimented as Sully's had been, which was why Birdie foresaw that the DNA contest Peter imagined he was winning would end in ignominious defeat.

And how different he *already* was from the young fellow who'd arrived in North Bath back in the late eighties, his marriage in tatters, his family splintering. Shaken by having just lost his university teaching position but still encased in a protective layer of irony, he managed to convey to everyone that his life was a game he was playing under protest, one he expected to be upheld when his case was finally heard. Sure, he was stuck in Bath for the time being, but he'd made it clear that he wouldn't be staying a moment longer than necessary. A few years at most. Once Will graduated from high school, it was adios amigos. But then he began inheriting things. First, his mother's house, a modest, three-bedroom ranch in a once solidly middle-class neighborhood that was now in decline. Vera had been an iron-willed, congenitally unhappy woman who worshipped her father, a Yale Ph.D. who'd chaired the Classics Department at Edison College over in Schuyler. As far as Vera was concerned, the man could do no wrong, and consequently none of the subsequent men in her life ever measured up. Sully certainly hadn't, though what possessed her to imagine he would was a mystery. Enter Peter's stepdad, Ralph, a kind, good-hearted doofus and Sully's polar opposite. The poor man's heroic efforts to make his wife happy, or at least less *un*happy, elicited quiet contempt on a good day and wild-eyed rage on a bad one. And face it, Peter had ended up disappointing her, too. Yes, he'd become a scholar like his grandfather, but Vera could see his heart wasn't in it, and when he failed to get tenure at an undistinguished state university, she let it be known that he'd disappointed both her and his grandfather. Her only other demand had been that he forever bear a grudge against his own father for walking out on them, but it turned out he couldn't even manage that. Instead of moving back into his childhood home and finding respectable work when his marriage broke up, Peter had instead gone to work with (no, *for!*) Sully, and after a year or two in a rented apartment with his son Will, he'd actually moved into the house Sully had by then inherited from old Beryl Peoples. He hadn't meant that to be a slap in the face, Peter assured her, but really how else was she supposed to interpret it? Still, he was an only child. In the end, who else was she going to leave her house to?

Since Peter had no intention of living in his childhood home, his first thought was to sell the place for whatever it would bring. Later, when Will went off to college, Peter could use the money to facilitate his own escape. The problem was that the house, always neat and tidy when he was a boy, now needed a ton of work, both inside and out. After Ralph, his stepfather, retired, there hadn't been much money, and when he fell ill, keeping the place up had fallen to Peter, who'd done, he had to admit, the bare minimum. Yes, he'd taken care of the seasonal chores: mowing the lawn in the summer, raking leaves and shoveling snow in fall and winter. If an appliance fritzed or a pipe burst, he came over and fixed it. Otherwise, though, he steered clear, because of his mother. Vera's grip on sanity had always been relaxed, but over time her behavior was increasingly batshit. She viewed her son's continued presence in Bath as a betrayal, and the mere sight of him was often enough to send her over the edge. In her mind's eye she continued to see her son dressed like the college professor he'd once been—in chinos, a button-down oxford shirt and a tweed sport coat and loafers, whereas now when he showed up to mow the lawn or fix the burst pipe he was invariably dressed in work boots, faded jeans, a coarse denim shirt and, if you could believe it, a feed-company bill cap, as if he were announcing to the whole neighborhood that despite her efforts to make a cultured man of him, he'd chosen instead to be a common laborer like his father. "Take it off!" she shrieked at him one day when he came inside for a glass of water. "I can't bear it!" What she couldn't bear, it turned out, was the sight of him wearing a tool belt, a hammer dangling from its iron loop. When he appeared unexpectedly, she would usually make a show of going into her bedroom, closing the door and remaining there until he was gone. Other times she'd come busting out, wild eyed, and launch into one of her melodramatic tirades about how she'd much prefer that the sidewalks go unshoveled, the grass unmowed, than to see him looking like this. Let the burst pipe gush water. What did she care? Let her drown. Couldn't he see she'd been drowning for years? Let the whole house fall down on her. Just go ahead and finish her. Didn't he know that this was what she prayed for each and every night?

Well, if that's what she'd been praying for, by the time he inherited the house, it appeared to Peter that at least some of those prayers had been answered. Every window in the house needed replacing, as did the roof. The brickwork needed repointing. Inside, everything—appliances, countertops, kitchen cabinets—was dated. There was faded wallpaper everywhere. When it rained, the basement flooded. "Fix the place up yourself," Sully had advised. "It's not like you don't know how." Which was true. Working with his father, Peter had learned basic construction skills. He could frame and roof and throw up drywall and use a circular saw. He could also handle basic plumbing and even a little electrical. Better yet, he was, unlike Sully, patient. He could read a schematic and knew to measure twice so that he'd only have to cut once. (His father tended to measure once, incorrectly, and cut a half-dozen times, all the while muttering, "You motherfucker," when the board that had been too long a moment ago was now inexplicably too short.)

Perhaps because renovating Vera's house had been his father's idea, Peter was slow to warm to it. (He was more his mother's son than she knew; indeed it would've cheered her to know how deep his lingering resentment of his father ran and how often it flared up.) Not long after her death he'd gotten a part-time position teaching composition at Edison College, which gave him more than enough to do, and while his adjunct professor salary was meager, he had relatively few expenses. The rent his father charged him and Will was well below market, and there was just the two of them. Charlotte, his ex-wife, had remarried a couple years after their divorce, which meant an end to his alimony payments, and the small loans he'd taken out to help pay for college and grad school were by then paid off. But Sully was right. If he did the necessary work on his mother's house himself, it would bring a better price, and his Saturdays were mostly free. Why not spend them fixing the place up? If it took him a year to get it shipshape, so what? At least get started. If it turned out the work bored him, he could always hire others to finish up.

Except the work *hadn't* bored him. Quite the opposite, in fact. After grading papers all week, he found himself actually looking forward to Saturdays, to strapping on the tool belt that had so shamed and infuriated his mother. Sully, who was by now mostly retired, had offered to lend a hand, but Peter had told him thanks anyway. For one thing, his mother would turn over in her grave if she knew Sully was tromping around in there with his muddy boots muttering the word *cocksucker* under his breath, but it wasn't really that. In the end what it came down to was that with help, even Sully's, he'd finish sooner, and he didn't want to. Nor was it just that work was pleasurable after a week of lecturing and paper grading. Something else was going on that Peter was having a hard time wrapping his head around. Maybe his hadn't been what you'd call a happy childhood—his mother's various neuroses had seen to that—but it hadn't been an unhappy one either, thanks in large part to his stepfather, who'd treated Peter like his own flesh and blood. Surely Ralph deserved to have that kindness repaid. Also, not long after his mother's death, Peter had begun to imagine her suffering, something he'd never been able to do when she was alive. Okay, she'd always been crazy, and that made her mean, especially to Ralph, but Peter also suspected that she had never in her life been truly happy. He'd always believed she brought that unhappiness on herself, and maybe that was true, but what if it wasn't? Did she consider herself a disappointment to her adored father? What if, for her, happiness simply hadn't been in the cards? In the beginning the work Peter was doing in his mother's house felt almost vengeful, like he was paying her back for her undisguised disappointment in him. But gradually the renovations took on a different meaning entirely. Recalling her taste, her favorite colors and styles, as well as her many aversions, he began to take pleasure in doing things in the house that might've pleased her. What the hell was *that* about? Was he offering some sort of belated apology? He couldn't say for sure, but whatever the reason, he found he wasn't anxious for the work to end, and when it finally did, he was surprised to feel a powerful sense of loss. Whatever those Saturdays had been about, it apparently wasn't money, and when the place went on the market and sold for far more than he'd expected, he couldn't help feeling as if some sort of debt he hadn't even known he owed had been paid.

Turned out, Vera's house was only the beginning, because in due course Peter came to inherit his father's house as well. And when that happened, he was once again of two minds. Miss Beryl's old Victorian, which was how his father always thought of it, was a fine property in one of North Bath's best neighborhoods and, thanks largely to Will, who loved attending to whatever needed doing there, was much better maintained, so it was worth a lot more than Vera's house. On the other hand, Peter was superstitious about the place. He'd always seen it as tethering him to Bath, which he meant to flee as soon as his son went off to college, lest he end up his father's keeper. Will had certainly done his part. After applying to universities on both coasts, he was offered free rides everywhere (here, too late, was somebody Vera would've been proud of), and when he finally settled on Penn, Peter's own exit strategy came into sharper focus. Once Will was settled at Philly, Peter himself would look for an apartment in New York, only an hour away by train, but far enough that he wouldn't cramp his son's style. Better yet, New York area colleges and universities were all hungry for adjunct professors who could be hired cheaply. He could teach a course here, a course there, and maybe, over time, wangle something a bit more permanent. He'd never be eligible for promotion or tenure or even health care, but thanks to the sale of his mother's house he now had a financial cushion. For a while, he could make it work. At the very least he'd be out of upstate New York.

Okay, not completely. The clean getaway he preferred would require an additional four years because Will loved both his grandfather and the Upper Main Street house, and he was especially looking forward to spending vacations in Bath. He'd have no trouble finding a summer job and he could continue helping Sully out with house maintenance that required climbing ladders or going up and down stairs. For his part Peter would have preferred to remain in the city, but he had to admit that returning to North Bath for June, July and August made sense, for both of them, really. There would be fewer teaching opportunities in the summer, and New York would be a sauna. Also, he'd learned by renovating his mother's house how much he enjoyed physical labor. The other old Victorian homes on Upper Main were all getting snapped up, and their new owners were clamoring for carpenters and plumbers and others in the construction trade. He could probably make as much money there in three months as he made as an adjunct professor in the city the other nine, and the hard work would help keep him trim, which lately had become an issue. The clean getaway that he craved—from Bath and, yes, from Sully himself—would just have to wait.

Except that April, three weeks before Will was set to graduate from Penn, Peter had gotten the call from Ruth, his father's longtime paramour, that he'd been dreading. His father had been in an accident, she informed him. No, he wasn't injured, but he'd totaled his truck and—surprise, surprise—alcohol had been involved. And because this was his third accident in two years (*Wait, what? There'd been two others?*) his license was being revoked, which meant he could no longer make his usual rounds (to Hattie's, the donut shop, the OTB, the Horse).

"You're telling me he needs a keeper?" Peter said.

No surprise, Ruth had bristled at that. "I'm telling you he needs his son."

"Yeah, well," Peter said, also bristling, "there were times as a kid when I needed him, and where was he?" Hearing himself say this, it occurred to him that somewhere his mother was smiling her cruel, vindictive smile.

"Two words," Ruth told him. "Grow up."

Though this crisp advice—if that's what it was—had stung, it wasn't exactly unexpected. How many times over the years had he watched this same woman turn both barrels on his father and pull the trigger? Anyway, what would be the point of getting pissed off at her? It wasn't Ruth's fault he'd waited too long to fly the coop. And if he was honest, he probably wouldn't have lasted that much longer in New York anyway. Rising rents were quickly making the itinerant adjunct life, which had been crappy to begin with, unsustainable. And while it was true that his father hadn't been around much when he was growing up, it was Sully who'd thrown him a rope that long-ago Thanksgiving when he'd slunk back into town, his marriage in tatters, and no idea what to do next. Worse, after grabbing that rope, he'd unjustly resented Sully for the loss of the academic life he himself had so royally messed up. So, he called Ruth back the next morning and told her he'd wrap things up in the city as soon as he could and return to Bath. "Do me a favor, though? Don't tell him I'm coming?"

"Okay," she agreed. "Mind telling me why?"

"I do, actually." Because, for one thing, returning to North Bath would have a lot of moving parts—finishing his classes, turning in grades, severing ties with the various institutions where he'd been teaching, renting a van to transport the stuff he accumulated in the city, saying his goodbyes. Who knew how long that would take? More importantly, he was going to need time to come to terms with his decision. He didn't want to arrive back in Bath nursing a sense of grievance, resentful of the choice he was freely making.

To his surprise, things had gone more smoothly than he would've predicted, and it was less than a month later when he sauntered into Hattie's and slid onto the empty stool at the counter next to his father, who, absorbed in the newspaper's sports page, didn't immediately notice him. It hadn't been that long ago—only since Christmas—that Peter had seen him, but in the intervening months it seemed that the man had segued into advanced old age, his hair and wiry stubble mostly gray, his eyes rheumy.

Finally noticing who now occupied the adjacent stool, Sully folded the newspaper, set it on the counter and said, "You're just in time. You can give me a lift out to Rub's place."

If this hadn't been his father he was talking to, Peter might well have concluded that Ruth had broken her promise and alerted Sully that his son's arrival was imminent, but no, this was just his father's way. One of the many maddening things about Sully was that he seemed not to fully believe in the world outside Schuyler County. Despite Peter's absence, he didn't truly accept that his son had moved away and now lived in New York. Somehow he'd been right here the whole time and they just hadn't crossed paths. And now here he was, which proved him right. Therefore, no hello. No long-time-no-see. Just, *Here you are. Good. I've got a job for you.*

"You remember his wife, Bootsie?" Sully was saying. "She died last week. Did you hear?"

"I don't think it made the New York papers, Dad."

"She had a coronary getting out of the bathtub."

Peter remembered her. An enormous woman. Three hundred pounds, at least.

His father read his thought. "I know. How'd she get into the tub to begin with?"

"That's not what I was thinking," Peter lied.

"Sure, it was," Sully said. "You know what else you were thinking?"

"No, what?"

"That she must've made a hell of a racket when she went down."

Which was true. Peter had been thinking exactly that. Sully was now putting some bills down on top of the check so they could leave.

"You mind if I have a cup of coffee first?" Janey, Ruth's daughter, who now owned the place, had seen him come in and was already pouring him one.

"Look who's here," Sully instructed her, finally displaying muted surprise at Peter's unexpectedly materializing on the stool next to him.

Janey set down a steaming cup of coffee and nodded. "My personal favorite of all your children," she said, deadpan.

Doctoring the coffee, Peter said, "Has the funeral happened?"

"Yesterday."

"Poor Rub," Peter said. He'd always felt bad for the man, hapless as he was, the defenseless target of Sully's relentless ribbing. "How's he doing?"

His father shrugged. "How would you be doing?"

Again Peter pictured the woman in question, and again his father read his thought. "She was actually pretty nice when you got to know her," he offered.

"I don't doubt it."

"And being married to Rub can't have been easy," Sully added.

"You would know," Peter grinned. Because if Rub had been married to anybody these last thirty years, it was to Sully. Most nights he went home to Bootsie only when Sully told him to.

Sully was studying him now, apparently ready, finally, to address the fact of his presence. "Okay," he said, "what gives?"

"As in?"

"As in, why are you here?"

Peter took a sip of coffee. He was, he realized, enjoying this. "I live here."

"Since when?"

"Not long. A couple days. And not *here,* exactly. I rented an apartment in Schuyler."

Sully scratched his stubble thoughtfully. "Why?"

"I like it there? There's more going on? I might want to go to a movie or hear some live music." He lowered his voice. "Get a decent cup of coffee."

"Yeah, but you could live at Miss Beryl's for free," his father pointed out. Which never failed to make Peter smile. His father had owned the house for two decades.

"Compared to Brooklyn," Peter explained, "the place I rented is practically free."

"Suit yourself," Sully conceded. "I'm just saying. There's nobody in the upstairs flat. It's yours if you want it. Or, if you wanted the downstairs, I could move back there. Makes no difference to me."

Except it *did* matter, Peter knew. He'd moved downstairs reluctantly because the stairs had become too much for him.

"No, I'll be fine in Schuyler," Peter assured him. "Besides, I already signed the lease."

Sully nodded at him, suspicious now. "What changed your mind? I just seem to recall you saying that after Will went off to grad school you were all done with this place."

"I was. But then I heard you might need a chauffeur."

"Right," he said. "Somebody told you about my little accident?"

"I heard you had one. What happened?"

Sully paused, contemplating, Peter suspected, how best to make something that would happen only to him seem like it could happen to anybody. "You know how the parking lot out back of the Horse slopes down into the woods?"

Peter pictured this in his mind's eye. "Come on. There are concrete barriers."

"They tell me I went over one of those."

"You didn't see it?"

"I was facing the other direction."

Peter tried to make this work in his head. "That . . . would mean the vehicle was in reverse?"

"That's how *I* figure it," Sully admitted. "It would explain why the ass end of the truck was what hit the tree."

Peter massaged his temples. "Jesus."

"What? You've never made a mistake?"

*How about right now?* he wanted to say. *Coming back here? Letting myself get sucked back into Sully World? Would these qualify as mistakes?*

"Okay, so you're here," Sully continued. "What are you planning to do for work?"

"Teach."

"Where?"

"SCCC." He'd heard about the just-posted opening when he'd called a friend at Edison College to see if there was any chance of getting his old job back. This other position at the community college, being full-time and providing benefits, was better. "I'm the new chair of the English Department, actually."

"That would've pleased your mother."

"No," Peter replied. "Being named chair of the English department at *Yale* would've pleased my mother."

"How come you didn't tell me about all this?"

"How come you didn't tell me about the accident?"

Having no ready answer, Sully took out a couple additional dollars for Peter's coffee and tossed them on top of his check. Janey came back down the counter. "*Two* Sullivans now?" she said. "God help us."

Sully slid off his stool. "Tell your mother I'm going to want a word with her. Specifically about that big mouth of hers."

"I'll tell her, but I don't see it ending well for you," she said. She raised a questioning eyebrow at Peter, who agreed with her wholeheartedly.

Out front, Sully scanned the cars parked at the curb for one that might belong to his son. "This one here," Peter told him, electronically unlocking the Audi A6 he'd paid too much for at a used-car lot in Schuyler a couple days earlier.

His father got in, surveyed the car's interior, moved the passenger seat back so he could stretch out his bum knee. "I went to war with Germany, you know," he said.

"Yeah?" Peter said, turning his key in the ignition. "Who won?"

"I did," his father told him as the Audi's engine sprung to throaty life. "It was nip and tuck there for a while, though."

Eighteen months. Neither knew it, of course, but that was the amount of time remaining to them. Eighteen months before Peter would walk into Hattie's one morning and Janey would inform him Sully had gotten tired of waiting for him and limped up the street to the OTB to bet his daily trifecta. Peter found him sitting on the bench outside, studying the racing form. Or that's what he'd apparently been doing when his heart quit.

Eighteen months. Barely long enough for Sully to help Peter understand that it wasn't just Miss Beryl's house and his father's savings account he would be inheriting.

# Owning It

"So, how does it feel?" said Dr. Qadry, fixing Raymer with her pale blue eyes. "Yesterday was your last day, right?"

Right. In fact, his photo had made the front page of the paper, its headline reading: "The End of an Era." He was pictured at his desk, surrounded by cardboard boxes. Behind him on the wall was a framed quotation that was, unfortunately, readable: WE'RE NOT HAPPY, it said, UNTIL YOU'RE NOT HAPPY. Attribution? Douglas Raymer, North Bath Chief of Police, 1989.

The stated sentiment, of course, had been the exact opposite of what he meant. He'd been told by Mayor Gus Moynihan that he needed a campaign slogan, something pithy and short enough to fit on a business card, and *We're not happy until you're happy* was the best he could come up with. He still had no idea where that extra *not* came from. The printer swore that what they put on the card was exactly what he'd written. It was his responsibility to say what he meant, not theirs to figure it out. That had been his eighth-grade English teacher's position as well. (He'd been a well-intentioned but disorganized thinker and careless writer, a shortcoming that didn't seem to bother his other teachers but *did* bother Beryl Peoples. *Say what you mean!* she wrote in his margins. *Mean what you say! Don't assume! Proofread!*) As to the latter, the printer had given him the opportunity, though apparently he'd not taken full advantage. He remembered pausing briefly at the word *you're* and thinking, Should it be *your*? But no, *you're* was correct. (Miss Beryl again, correcting him over and over until he finally understood. *You're means You are. The apostrophe tells you that.*) Somehow, he just hadn't seen the extra *not*. Neither, alas, did the first fifty or so voters he'd handed cards to, but eventually someone did, and overnight, he was famous. People stopped him on the street, left messages on his home phone. There'd even been a small item about his gaffe on the editorial page of the paper. "Finally," said the snarky columnist, "an honest cop." Nor did people forget. Dr. Qadry herself remembered the incident a decade later when he started seeing her, and it was she who first suggested he get the quotation framed and hang it on his office wall. That way, she reasoned, he'd be owning it.

Dr. Qadry was big on "owning" things, actually. The word came up again and again in their sporadic therapy sessions. Everybody makes mistakes, she liked to say, but aren't you better off owning them? Owning a mistake effectively neutralized it, she claimed, taking away its power to wound. Moreover, he'd be telling the whole world he could laugh at himself, thereby short-circuiting other people's mockery. To Raymer's way of thinking, there were several flaws in this reasoning. First, not everyone did make mistakes. Take Dr. Qadry herself. In the decade or so Raymer had been coming to see her, he'd never known her to do or say anything remotely foolish. She seemed to have the ability to proofread even spoken words before they left her mouth. Second, was it really true that laughing at yourself dissuaded other people from having fun at your expense? Certainly not in Raymer's experience, which was considerable. Not that he'd ever do it, but if you really wanted people to stop laughing at you, wouldn't you be better off punching them in the face? *That* they'd remember.

Still, what did he know? Maybe Dr. Qadry was right. She was definitely a smart woman, and he knew she meant well. It was hard to say why he almost never took her advice, if advice was even what she was offering him. (She never said, *Here's what you should do,* or *Try this.*) Her suggestions were often highly theoretical. Not *Take it from one who knows,* which would have implied shared experience, a genuine understanding of folly. Rather, she seemed to be saying, *Here's something I read in a journal once. I've had no occasion to try it myself, but who knows? It could work?* Was that why he rejected so many of her suggestions out of hand?

His real mistake, of course, had been sharing her advice about having *We're not happy until you're not happy* framed with Charice, who'd immediately gone out and done it without telling him. "Don't you touch it, either," she warned him after hanging the framed quotation on the wall. "It's my gift to you."

"But . . . ," Raymer had begun.

"But *what?*" Charice said, hands on her hips, daring him to say something dumb, a dare he could never resist.

"But . . . if it's a gift, doesn't that make it mine? Don't I get to do what I want with it?"

Eyes narrowed now. "Like what?"

"Like . . . put it facedown in a locked desk drawer?" Because here was the problem in a nutshell. Most of what these two women wanted him to own, he himself would have preferred to *dis*own completely. There were times, in fact, when he would've liked to disown his entire self, were such a thing possible. The fact that they were so often of one mind about what ailed him and what he should do about it made him wonder if they were somehow in cahoots. Was it possible that after his therapy sessions, Charice called Dr. Qadry to find out what all he was banging on about now? This would certainly have been a violation of a good therapist's confidentiality rules, but the fact that they were so often in agreement did suggest they might be tag-teaming him.

"You know what I think?" Charice wanted to know one day when he expressed his conviction that most of Dr. Qadry's opinions were of the oddball variety. "I think therapy is wasted on you."

Nor did Raymer disagree. His sessions with Dr. Qadry were pleasant enough, but were they actually doing any good? The reason he kept going back was that he kind of liked her, and the town of North Bath picked up most of the tab. Also, it got him out of the office. Nor did he want to hurt her feelings by suggesting they weren't getting anywhere, when she seemed to think they were. Often, when they came to the end of their hour, she'd regard him seriously and say, "I think we made some progress today," to which he'd dutifully reply, "Me, too," though what he really wanted to say was *What progress, exactly?* Was it possible they really were making headway he was totally unaware of? Why couldn't she tell him what this supposed progress consisted of, so he could decide for himself?

"Instead of ignoring all her suggestions," Charice said, predictably taking Dr. Qadry's side, "why don't you listen to the woman? You've *got* this problem," she said, pointing at the framed quotation on the wall as evidence, "and she's trying to help you with it, but you won't let her."

"What problem?" he said, not because he didn't think he had any problems but because he was curious as to which one Charice was identifying with such confidence. That he needed to proofread more carefully? That he was, in general, his own worst enemy?

"Your *problem,*" she explained, "is you think you can control how other people see you. Can't *nobody* do that." She paused to let this wisdom sink in. Raymer knew Charice too well to suppose she was finished, though, so he waited for her to drop the hammer, which she did. "Least of all *you.*"

God, he missed her.

"Have you given any thought to next steps?" Dr. Qadry wanted to know. His future, she meant. Now that the end of an era had arrived.

"Not really," Raymer said. A lie. He'd thought about little else for weeks. It used to worry him that he lied so often during these therapy sessions. After all, what was the point of going to a doctor if you weren't going to be honest about your symptoms? Once he'd even raised the issue with Dr. Qadry herself, obliquely, by wondering how she was able to tell when her clients weren't telling her the truth, and her response had been surprising. It probably didn't matter, she explained, since untruthful answers could be as revealing as truthful ones, sometimes even more so. "It's not really important for me to know if you're telling me the truth," she'd said, making the whole thing less hypothetical. "It's important for *you* to." Which made him wonder, and not for the first time, what exactly he (and the town of North Bath) was paying her for. He could lie to himself for free.

"But working for the Schuyler PD is out?" she said. "Explain to me again why you don't want to do that?"

"Well, they already have an excellent chief of police," he said, which elicited a knowing smile.

"And do you need to be the one in charge?"

"Not necessarily." Though in this particular instance . . .

"Would you have trouble taking orders from a woman?"

"Of course not," he said, as if insulted by the suggestion. Though, again, in this particular instance . . .

Dr. Qadry smiled. Said nothing. Her way of reminding him, he suspected, that she hadn't been kidding. She really didn't mind him lying to her.

*Was* he lying, though? Hadn't he been equally resentful of Mayor Moynihan's incessant recommendations and interference in police matters even before the business card fiasco? And what about Judge Flatt? Hadn't Raymer chafed at every belittling comment offered by his old nemesis? "You know my thoughts on arming morons," he'd once remarked from the bench after Raymer, then a young officer, had accidentally discharged his weapon, the wayward bullet narrowly missing an old woman seated on her commode half a block away. "If you arm one, you have to arm them all. Otherwise, it isn't even good sport." When it came to authority, Raymer liked to think he was gender neutral, equally resentful of both men and women.

Though, now that he thought about it, maybe she was onto something. It was true that he didn't always recognize good advice when it came from a woman. In fact, he'd admitted as much when the subject of his mother had come up in one of their early sessions. (Of course it came up. Would therapy even exist without mothers?) Raymer's own had been a perpetually frightened woman who as a child had witnessed her father, a thief, being arrested and taken away by the police. She made no secret of her fear that Raymer had inherited this thieving gene and would in the fullness of time suffer a similar fate. Even his decision to go into law enforcement hadn't completely disabused the woman of the notion that he might be headed for a life of crime and end up cuffed in the back of a police cruiser like his grandfather. As a result, he'd learned from an early age never to trust his mother's advice. Was it possible his relationship with her had somehow bled over into subsequent relationships with other women? He thought again about Miss Beryl, his eighth-grade teacher, who seemed to intuit his many struggles, both in school and at home. She'd tried to help by gifting him books she believed would speak to him and perhaps make him feel less alone in the world. At the time he hadn't understood that she was simply being kind. Indeed, he'd been suspicious of every gift, convinced the old woman must have some ulterior motive, even though he couldn't imagine what it might be. Maybe it was the books she chose. Why give him *Great Expectations*? Was she trying to terrify him? Because that's what the book had done. The dark scenes on the marsh where the escaped convict Magwitch had so frightened young Pip? He'd had nightmares for a week. Convinced, even after Magwitch was taken away in irons, that he would return to menace Pip anew, maybe even turn him into a criminal as well, Raymer had quit reading and hidden the book in the back of his closet where his mother wouldn't find it and accuse him of theft. It was as if Miss Beryl had peered deep into his soul and concluded his mother was right. He would end up a criminal, so here was a Dickensian primer to help him on his way. Had such formative experiences with women permanently messed him up? Was he still, even as a middle-aged man, suspicious of smart women like Charice and Dr. Qadry?

"So," said the latter, "is going someplace new still on the table?"

"I don't know," he admitted. "I guess. There's nothing really keeping me here." Though, truly, everything was.

Dr. Qadry, appearing puzzled, paused to consider this, then

flipped back through her notes. "In our last session you said that it was probably time to move on, but I think you meant romantically."

*Okay,* Raymer thought, *here we go.* These days, now that he and Charice were no longer living together, these sessions always came back to their relationship. It hadn't been Charice but Raymer himself who'd suggested that a time-out might be in order. Even now he had a hard time explaining to himself—never mind to his therapist—what had possessed him. Charice had been offered the Schuyler job, and even though she'd claimed to be conflicted, he was pretty sure she wanted to take it. Until fairly recently her duties at the tiny North Bath police department had been mostly administrative, partly because she was so good at making the department run smoothly, but also because Raymer, even before he was able to admit his feelings for her, hadn't wanted her on the street. It wasn't that Bath was any more racist than the rest of America, but he couldn't banish the idea that if he let her out from behind her desk, it would only be a matter of time before she knocked on the wrong door or pulled over the wrong car, and then she'd be dead and it would be his fault. But of course his trying to protect her had been both wrong and insulting, and she'd chipped away at him until he finally caved and put her on the street, where she'd quickly become his best officer, her judgment cool and impeccable.

Asked to explain why he'd suggested they take a time-out that Raymer himself didn't want, he'd told Dr. Qadry that Charice needed some space to decide what she wanted to do. They weren't breaking up, he explained. Not at all. They were just taking a breather. *Breather. Time-out.* These terms were a safe haven, especially the latter. Didn't *time-out* imply that at some point play would resume? The problem was that with each passing week, it felt less like he was on the bench waiting for play to resume than in a locked penalty box. Not only had play not resumed, the other contestants had gone home, and the arena lights had been turned off. Sitting alone in the dark penalty box, it occurred to him that a *time-out* was also what you'd give a misbehaving child. *Had* he misbehaved? He had to admit that things between them hadn't been great for some time, though he couldn't quite put his finger on what was wrong. Maybe it was just that the first-blush excitement of their romance had begun to fade. His fear, though, was that Charice might be having second thoughts about him. That she was trying to figure out how to dump him without hurting his feelings. His having arrived so instinctively at such a conclusion was probably screwed up, but hadn't pretty much the same thing happened with Becka? Hadn't his wife, over time, come to see him more clearly and as a result fallen out of love with him? And then, when someone else—someone more appealing, whose interests and temperament aligned more closely with her own—came along, well, she'd moved on and left Raymer behind to wonder why. Could it be that to prevent this from happening again, he'd acted preemptively, leaving Charice before she could leave him? If so, stupid, but then again, maybe not. No sooner had he moved into his new studio apartment on the top floor in one of the big, subdivided old Victorians on Upper Main Street in Bath than Charice accepted the Schuyler job (apparently with Raymer gone the decision hadn't proved so difficult after all), and he thought, *Okay, that's that, message received.*

Though as messages went, this one was pretty mixed. "So," Charice said when she called to tell him she'd accepted the Schuyler job. "You gonna congratulate me or not?"

"Charice," he said. "I couldn't be happier for you." Which was both true and untrue. He *was* happy for her. Could he have been happier? He was pretty sure that was possible.

"Yeah?" she said, her voice full of challenge.

"Of course," he assured her, and it was on the tip of his tongue to say, *Why do you think I recommended you in the first place?* But that was something he'd promised himself never to divulge—that he'd been offered the job first. In fact, he'd never even told Dr. Qadry, just in case the two women *were* in cahoots.

"Okay, prove it," Charice said.

"How?" he said, hoping she'd say, *Move back in with me,* because by then he was more than ready to return, tail between his legs, if she would have him.

"Celebrate with me."

Okay, that wasn't what he'd been hoping for, but it was better than nothing. "Celebrate how?"

"I'll take you out to dinner," she said. "We can go to that fancy wine bar in Schuyler."

"Adfinitum?" Raymer said. His least favorite place in a thirty-mile radius. The one where Becka used to hang out with her artist friends.

"Infinity," she reminded him. For some reason he always got their screwball name wrong. "We'll order a ridiculously expensive bottle of wine."

Raymer had seen the wine list and knew that everything on it was ridiculously expensive.

"And afterward . . ."

"Do you equate those two things in your mind?" said Dr. Qadry, interrupting his reverie. "Finding some*body* new and moving some*place* new?"

"It might be easier if we weren't so close."

He'd been hoping that after their celebratory dinner at Adfinitum, Charice would say, *Let's go home,* but what she'd said instead was "Your place or mine?" quickly adding when she saw his disappointment, "Come on. Don't you want to show me your new digs? It's got to be better than the Moribund Arms, right?" The Morrison Arms, she meant, where he'd lived before moving in with her. The Arms had since been condemned and razed to make room for a new affordable housing project that still hadn't broken ground, or he probably would've moved back there. Anyway, they'd done as she suggested and checked out his new flat where they had a good laugh because even though he'd been there a whole week he still hadn't unpacked any of his boxes. There was a lot going on down at the station, he explained. Most nights he didn't leave the office until late, which was true. It turned out that shutting down a police department was almost as complicated as getting one up and running. But Charice seemed to suspect there was more to it than that. Being Charice, she probably even knew that the real reason he hadn't unpacked a single box was that he'd been hoping he wouldn't have to.

"Anyway," she said, putting her arms around his neck, "now for the *real* celebration." And he thought, Okay, after *that,* she'll invite me to come back home. But no, when they finished making love, she'd asked him if he wanted her help setting up his kitchen.

None of which he would confide to Dr. Qadry.

"We still run into each other a fair amount," he told her instead, making it sound like these were chance encounters he would rather have avoided. Actually, with Charice setting up shop in Schuyler and him gradually winding down his tenure in North Bath, there was a fair amount for the two of them to coordinate. A lot of it could be done on the phone, but most Friday afternoons they discussed logistics at Adfinitum. (The place was growing on him. He no longer expected to see Becka seated in the big corner booth with all her artsy friends.) Sometimes after the wine bar they returned to his place, where Charice gave him small "settling-in" gifts (a soap dish for the shower, a pitcher to hold his kitchen utensils). They never went to her place, which he couldn't help thinking of as theirs. Still, even though their Fridays left him disappointed, even depressed, he continued to look forward to them. Lived for them, actually.

He also knew that most other men would have envied him this new relationship with Charice. (*Wait. You're still having sex . . . and when you finish she goes home and leaves you to watch the ball game in peace?*) Raymer would have given anything to be such a man, but he knew he wasn't and never would be. So, he had to wonder: If they weren't going to end up back together, wouldn't it be better to just rip off the Band-Aid? (*No! That would mean no more Fridays!*) The previous week things had reached their nadir. Charice canceled Adfinitum, claiming something had come up, though she declined to say what. Nor had she called yesterday when the end-of-an-era story appeared in the paper. Which no doubt had pissed her off, because how could it not? He'd thought about calling to apologize. At the very least he should've given her a heads-up. Why hadn't he?

"So what are you thinking?" Dr. Qadry wanted to know. "Location-wise. Albany? Boston?"

"Possibly," he said. "Or Fiji."

Which elicited that smile she always gave him, the one that said: *I know you better than you know yourself.*

And she probably did. Why not rip off the Band-Aid? Because he loved Charice, just as he'd once loved his wife, even after it became clear that Becka no longer loved him. The whole Band-Aid concept was deeply flawed. The idea was that when you ripped it off, the pain might be intense, but only for a second, and then it would be over. Whereas in reality ripping it off would reveal that the wound had not healed. Underneath, it was still red and swollen and wet and angry, and the pain *didn't* go away. It hurt worse. And now, with the Band-Aid gone, you got to look at what lay beneath and pick at it and . . .

"I haven't ruled out Albany," he told her. Which was true. In fact, he'd been encouraged to apply for a position there, a job in administration. A desk job wouldn't be such a bad way to spend his last decade before retirement. The problem was he couldn't decide whether Albany was too far away or not far enough. Or if he wanted a desk job. Or even a job. That fall he'd qualified for his full pension, so he could just retire if he wanted. Go to Fiji. Why not?

Because he didn't *want* to, was why not. There was really only one place he wanted to be and that was the one he'd left of his own volition. Charice believed that his time-out idea was just what they needed and said so, over and over, lest he forget the idea had been his, not hers. *No!* he wanted to scream. *We don't need it! I don't need it. I only suggested it because I thought you'd say no! It was my dumbest idea ever! Far dumber than* I'm not happy until you're not happy.

Dr. Qadry continued to flip through her notes from other sessions. "So," she said, finding what she was looking for. "Do you ever hear from your old friend Dougie anymore?"

Fucking Dougie. He hadn't come up in a while and Raymer

had been hoping she'd forgotten about him. What had possessed him to tell her about him in the first place? Here was yet another what-in-the-world-was-I-thinking-type mystery. After Becka died, a decade ago now, his life became a clusterfuck of grief (she'd *died*), anger (she'd been about to leave him for another man), guilt (she'd slipped on the rug at the top of the stairs—a rug he'd promised to put a matt under and kept forgetting, and broken her neck in the fall), confusion (why had she stopped loving him?) and frustration (now that she was dead he'd never know the identity of her lover). Then, as if all this weren't enough, he'd actually—even now this was hard to credit—been struck by fucking lightning. And if he thought he was messed up before (he did), well, he didn't know the half of it, because now, in addition to dealing with grief and anger and guilt and confusion and frustration, he also had a voice in his head. He'd given that voice his own name (or a variation of it) because who else could be speaking to him with such uncanny, intimate knowledge from *inside his head*? Except the little bastard was also, emphatically, *not* himself. In fact, Dougie had been his polar opposite, cocky where Raymer was insecure, cynical where Raymer was trusting, arrogant where Raymer was self-effacing, confrontational where Raymer was, at least in public, polite, a bully where Raymer was given to mea culpas—a complete fucking asshole, really. Not surprisingly, this Dougie, whoever he was, had been singularly unimpressed with the man whose head he now, without invitation, shared. If Raymer thought Dougie was a dipshit, Dougie made no effort to conceal his opinion that Raymer was an idiot in dire need of a tough-love mentor.

Dr. Qadry's own conclusions about Dougie were expressed, as was her custom, as a series of leading questions. Was it possible that Raymer had created Dougie out of some subconscious need? Or, alternatively, had Dougie always been part of him, lurking in the dark interior of Raymer's psyche, just waiting to be released by that lightning bolt? What did Raymer make of the fact that Dougie was so good at the very things Raymer struggled with? This last was not a bad question, Raymer had to admit. Dougie might be an asshole, but he'd convinced Raymer of something that should've been obvi-ous from the beginning—that most people a cop encountered in the course of his duties should, in fact, be viewed with suspicion. In the eyes of the law people might be innocent until proven guilty, but in Dougie's experience, proving them guilty wasn't that difficult if you paid the fuck attention. He'd also taken perverse delight in forcing Raymer to ask questions he was embarrassed to ask, the answers to which usually led to truths he was reluctant to accept. Under Dougie's mentorship, he'd become—there was no way around it—a better cop.

Could it be, then, Dr. Qadry wondered, that Dougie represented aspects of his personality that Raymer didn't approve of, things that, until the lightning strike, he'd successfully suppressed? Well here, to Raymer's way of thinking, was where Dr. Qadry's leading questions ran aground. Suggesting that Dougie represented things about himself that Raymer disapproved of (cruelty, suspicion, vul-garity, cynicism and violence) implied there were other things about himself that he *did* approve of, and none sprung immediately to mind. Which was why he still preferred his own, simpler explana-tion for Dougie's sudden appearance—that being struck by light-ning had screwed up his circuitry. Dougie's gradual *dis*appearance he explained in the same fashion. The circuits fried by the lightning were over time replaced by healthy ones. That he liked his own amateur diagnosis better than Dr. Qadry's professional one only proved that Charice was right. Therapy was wasted on him.

So, *had* he heard from his old friend Dougie lately? Here at last was a question he could answer honestly. "Nah," Raymer said, try-ing to sound nonchalant. "I think he's gone for good."

The words were no sooner out of his mouth than he felt an elec-trical shock to his groin that made him jump. His cell phone in his pants pocket, he realized, set to vibrate. Either that or Dougie had decided his work in Raymer's head was finished and had moved south. Taking out the phone, Raymer saw that the call was from Miller, his former sergeant.

"Our time is nearly up if you need to take that," Dr. Qadry said.

She had a strict no cell phone policy during sessions, but since he was a public servant, she'd always granted him an exemption. Since yesterday was his last day on the job, however, that exemption no longer applied.

"Actually," he said, pressing DECLINE and returning the phone to his pocket, "I need to *not* take it." Miller, since transitioning over to the Schuyler PD a week earlier, had called Raymer several times. He couldn't quite seem to get it through his head that when he pressed CHIEF on his cell, Charice's phone should ring, not Raymer's.

"How would you feel about that?" Dr. Qadry continued. "If Dougie's voice was gone for good?"

Raymer was pretty sure where this question was designed to lead him. If Dougie was gone, Dr. Qadry's logic suggested, it followed that either he was no longer needed or he'd somehow been reintegrated into Raymer's fractured psyche. "I don't know," Raymer said, following her suggestion. "Relieved?"

Because, yeah, Dougie's disappearance was a relief. For a while there, he'd been convinced he was losing his mind. But he was also puzzled. Maybe even a little concerned. Because sure, it was possible Dougie disappeared because he was no longer needed, but it was also possible, given that Raymer took his advice even less frequently than he took Dr. Qadry's, that he'd concluded that Raymer was a lost cause. If his advice were summarized in two words, they would've been: *Man up!* (Dougie would've insisted, for instance, that Raymer rip off that Band-Aid.) Could it be that Dougie finally concluded he was wasting his breath?

"Were you afraid of him?" Dr. Qadry prodded.

"A strange voice in your head, telling you to do things you didn't want to do? Wouldn't you be?"

Dr. Qadry's expression remained carefully neutral. It wasn't her habit to indulge hypotheticals that encouraged her to imagine herself insane. "What's your biggest fear now that he's gone?" she said.

His biggest fear? Maybe that the newspaper headline was right and an era was in fact coming to an end. After all, it wasn't just his police department that was vanishing but the whole town of North Bath. For a time there, after Gus Moynihan was elected mayor, sweeping the old, moribund Republican machine out of power, it had looked like the town might actually have a future, like maybe the most famous of the banners that had been strung across Main Street—THINGS ARE LOOKING ^ IN BATH—might finally prove true. But it had all come crashing down, Gus himself a casualty. Raymer still remembered vividly the night he came upon the poor guy in the Schuyler hospital parking lot. His wife, Alice, had been taken to the emergency room earlier in the evening after swallowing a whole bottle of sleeping pills. She'd nearly died and Gus had—not without reason—blamed himself. In and out of the state mental hospital for years, the poor woman had slipped her tether about the time cell phones started appearing in Bath. Not having one herself and immediately recognizing their utility, she'd unplugged the receiver from the cord of her bedroom phone, thereby making it "mobile." Pretending to hear it ring in her purse, she'd take it out and have long conversations with imaginary friends in public, freaking people out. Having somehow gotten it into his head that it was these conversations with imaginary friends that were making her sick, Gus had taken the handset away from her, causing her meltdown. There in the hospital parking lot, explaining all this to Raymer, the poor guy had become so distraught that he'd purposely hit himself in the face with the phone, hard enough to draw blood.

Raymer had done his best to console the man, assuring him that the Utica doctors would get Alice's meds straightened out and she'd be home in no time, but Gus was inconsolable, convinced that the damage he'd done was irreparable. And apparently he'd been right. Once committed, Alice had remained in Utica, at least as far as Raymer knew. He'd never seen her around town again. Nor, after that night in the parking lot, had he seen much of Gus, who hadn't run for reelection the following year. He must have known his wife wouldn't be coming home again because he sold their big house on Upper Main and rented a small apartment in the old mill that Carl

Roebuck's crew renovated in downtown Bath, then mostly disappeared from public life.

So, yeah, the end of an era. Maybe the time had come for Raymer to disappear as well. Not wanting to give voice to a sentiment so rich in self-pity, he was glad when his cell rang again and this time pressed ACCEPT. "What is it, Miller?"

"Chief?"

"Nope. It's not."

A long beat of confused silence followed. Raymer, after a decade of working with the man, knew Miller's thought process almost as well as his own. The person who'd answered the chief's phone had said Miller's name, and his voice had sounded like the chief's, whose number he'd called, so it followed that the person he was talking to was, in fact, the chief. So, why was the chief claiming not to be who he was? Raymer seriously considered letting Miller work it out on his own, but the prolonged silence was too painful. "I'm not your chief anymore," Raymer reminded him for the umpteenth time. "If this is about business, I'm not the one you should be calling."

"I tried to call Chief Bond, but she's not picking up."

*Of course, she isn't,* Raymer thought. *She's got caller ID.* "Keep trying."

"Okay, but Chief? I think you need to get out here right away."

"Where are you?"

"At the Sans Souci."

"Why?" He'd heard a rumor that the place had been sold, but the estate was still closed to the public. So what was this about? More vandalism, probably. Kids tossing rocks through windows.

"Chief?" Miller said. "Please? Could you just come?"

The correct answer, of course, was no. He was no longer the chief of police. No longer even a cop. But unless he was mistaken there was real urgency, maybe even panic, in Miller's pleading request. He knew he shouldn't be calling Raymer and was calling him anyway, so this was probably not about kids busting windows. And . . . why not face it? He was curious. He could deny being a police officer all he wanted, but that didn't mean he wasn't one. Also, eventually

Miller would get through to Charice, and if the matter was indeed urgent, she'd end up out at the Sans Souci as well. Maybe he and Charice could work through whatever this was together. Maybe Charice would remember what a good team they made. Maybe in light of this she'd tell him it was time to come home.

"All right," Raymer sighed. "Tell me what's going on."

"There's a body."

It was on the tip of Raymer's tongue to say, *What do you mean, a body?* but the time repellent Dougie had spent in Raymer's skull had taught him to pause before giving voice to dumb questions. "Okay," he said, "I'm on my way."

# Sully's Ghost

THIS MORNING, in addition to the *New York Times,* Peter arrived at the Horse with the latest, hot-off-the-press issue of *Schuyler County Arts,* the alternative newspaper he'd started up a couple years earlier when the recession put a stake through the heart of the *North Bath Weekly Journal.* He placed a large stack of these on the bar along with a small paper bag from the donut shop, which Birdie knew to put behind the bar. "Bad idea," she said, for the record.

"Nah, it'll be fine," he said, though privately he had to admit she was probably right. Hanging his parka on the coatrack by the front entrance, he returned to the bar and slid onto a stool. Seeing him do this always made Birdie smile. His father had had a way of sliding onto a barstool that suggested he'd been put on earth to execute this very maneuver, and Peter had inherited Sully's very specific grace. Unfolding the *Times,* he said, "Is that coffee I'm smelling?" As if he didn't know. As if she didn't pour him a cup every Saturday morning.

Setting the coffee in front of him, along with cream and sweetener, neither of which his father had taken, she waited for him to engage and wasn't surprised when he didn't. Maddening, really, how quickly the man could become engrossed in a newspaper. Wasn't the ostensible purpose of their weekly State of the Horse meetings to discuss the tavern? For her to let him know if she needed anything in the upcoming week? The fact that most Saturdays the subject of the business never actually came up suggested to Birdie that her minority partner was, for reasons that mystified her, content for the Horse to continue circling the drain. If so, why had he invested in the first place?

As she studied Peter, who continued to be engrossed in the national news, ignoring both her and the coffee she'd just set in front of him, it occurred to Birdie, and not for the first time, that while the man might be more like his deceased father than he cared to admit, there were also several significant, character-defining differences as well. Sully's narrow bandwidth of interests had been strictly local. Having played a role on the world stage as part of the Normandy invasion, he'd returned home determined to shrink his geographical perimeter to a size that suited him—a small, familiar world that could be navigated drunk if need be. Whereas Peter, despite having stormed no beaches that Birdie was aware of, apparently believed that he belonged on the larger stage that Sully had gladly quit. Infuriatingly, Peter somehow managed to convey that, despite his intelligence and good looks and easy charm, he'd somehow been marooned in this place his father had miniaturized on his own authority. Nor did Birdie quite know how to feel about the aura of fatalism that trailed in Peter's wake. It was mostly annoying, but there were also times when it was oddly attractive. In her considerable experience as a bartender, most men had higher opinions of themselves than were strictly warranted. Part of Peter's allure—and women were definitely attracted to him—was that he seemed to have taken the world's measure, as well as his own, and couldn't decide which he was more disappointed by. Which was probably why, over the years, he'd grown on her. In particular, she appreciated how nonjudgmental he was. From the time she was a girl Birdie had always blamed herself when things went wrong. Her parents blamed her, too, and so did her older brother, as well as every single one of her teachers. Now here she was on the cusp of old age, unmarried, overweight, with nothing to show for a lifetime of dogged effort but a failing tavern and lower back pain that some mornings was simply not to be believed. Most days it took real effort not to see her life as an abject failure, although when she asked herself just what in hell she was supposed to have done differently, she had no answer. Take men. The ones who'd been interested were all lazy and feckless, and even though she enjoyed their company more than the company of women, the sad truth was that most men weren't worth the trouble. At the moment the only man who seemed even remotely interested in her was David Proxmire, who owned a towing service on the outskirts of town, but he had a fibroid cyst growing in his skull. He claimed the cyst was benign, but it was also inoperable and, as it grew, was exerting pressure on his brain. That the thing would one day kill him he knew for a certainty because his older brother Harold, from whom he'd inherited the towing business, had had an identical cyst and his killed him. Though Birdie had expressed no doubt that what he was telling her was true, David brought in some sort of magnetic imagery photos of his and his brother's skulls and laid them out on the bar. Sure enough, in both photos, nestled right up against each man's brain was a cloudy, ghostlike mass. In other respects David Proxmire wasn't a completely unattractive man, but Birdie found that when you learned about something like a cyst it was impossible to forget, and she just couldn't imagine taking on as a lover a man whose head might detonate. So, actually, no, *don't* take men.

Since Peter was still engrossed in the *Times,* Birdie picked up a copy of *Schuyler Arts* and skipped to the back where her ad for the Horse, which Peter ran for free, was always located. In Schuyler Springs the *SCA* was available in every coffee shop, as well as the supermarkets, but so far as Birdie knew, the Horse was the only establishment in North Bath where you could pick up a copy, though not many people did, despite its being free. She herself could never find anything of interest in the damn thing. This week Peter had an article in it that listed and discussed his ten favorite movies of the year, not a one of which Birdie recognized. It was as if Peter had done a careful survey of every single North Bath resident to find out what their interests were, and then made sure the paper covered none of them. No local politics, no sports, no letters to the editor, not even a police log, which was a shame, because the one in the old *North Bath Weekly Journal* had been a hoot. But of course that was before the Morrison Arms, which housed most of the town's derelicts and nitwits, and Gert's Tavern, where those same idiots drank and caroused, were condemned and razed. Maybe there weren't enough morons to justify a police log anymore, though it struck Birdie as unlikely that the world—certainly not this corner of it—had suddenly run low on fools. Her own regular clientele certainly suggested otherwise. Why wasn't anyone recording their high jinks?

"*So,*" she said, probably a little louder than she needed to, in the hopes of getting Peter's attention.

"Yeah?" Peter said, without looking up.

"About this Sans Souci rumor."

He lowered the paper ever so slightly to peer at her. "What about it?"

She raised an eyebrow. "What's your best guess? True or false?"

"I have no idea." Back to the newspaper. Infuriating.

"I understand that you have no idea," Birdie assured him. "That's why I used the word *guess*. Gut reaction is what I'm looking for."

Peter sighed and set the paper down on the bar. And in so doing finally noticed the coffee she'd set in front of him five minutes ago. Doctoring it with cream and sugar, he stirred it thoughtfully. "Okay, then, true."

Which was surprising. Birdie had been pretty certain Peter would dismiss the rumor out of hand. "How come?"

He shrugged. "I don't know. Timing? The place has been on the market forever. And there's all those back taxes. Half a million is the number I heard."

"So?"

"Well, a buyer would have to pay those up front."

Birdie squinted at him, still not following.

"Think about it," he said, as if she wasn't. "If the Sans Souci sold *last* month, when North Bath still existed as a township, where would all that money have gone?"

"To us?"

"Whereas now?"

"To Schuyler."

Peter picked up the paper again and disappeared behind it. "Which would be about par for Bath's particular course."

"So you're saying maybe the deal was kept under wraps? That it actually got done last month?"

"Or last *year.*"

Birdie snorted. "God, you're cynical."

"Hey, this is America," Peter reminded her, lowering the paper again. "What am I supposed to be?"

"You really think something that big could be kept secret so long?"

"When large sums of money are involved, there are always people who know ahead of time. Do you know what they're called?"

"Assholes?"

"No, rich."

"Doesn't that piss you off?"

Peter appeared to consider this. "I don't know, Birdie. It's a slippery slope. Expecting things to be fair? Next, you'll be demanding justice. Equal opportunity. One morning you'll wake up and discover you've moved to Denmark."

Birdie sighed, missing Sully, who, having fought for his country, was never glibly dismissive of it. Like his son, he had believed that the deck was stacked against ordinary people, but extolling the political virtues of frigid, socialist countries never would've occurred to him.

"Still," she said. "If the rumor's true? Could be a good thing for us?"

Peter gave up, folded the paper, set it on the bar. "Good for business, do you mean? Or are you thinking about selling?"

Not really. Maybe. Last Sunday she'd suggested she was thinking about it to David Proxmire, who'd casually mentioned on more than one occasion that he wanted to grow his own business beyond towing. In order to do that, though, he'd need someone like his brother's wife, who'd basically run the business side of Harold's Automotive World, leaving Harold free to concentrate on buying, fixing up and reselling the vehicles on his lot. He'd need, in other words, somebody like Birdie herself. Except that when she mentioned she was thinking about selling the Horse, he hadn't made the leap she'd been half hoping he'd make—that together they might restore Harold's Automotive World to its glory days, if that's what they were. Had he just been blowing smoke about wanting to grow the business? Worse, had she misread his joining her at the Horse on Sundays, his only day off, as evidence of romantic interest?

No need to share any of this with Peter, of course, so she just said, "Hey, I'm not getting any younger."

"If you sold, would you stay around here?"

She snorted at this. "Hell, no."

"Where would you go?"

"Not Denmark. Someplace hot and cheap. Belize? Costa Rica? Someplace with a swimming pool. And servants."

"Sounds good. Take me with you."

Birdie allowed herself to entertain, for about two seconds, the notion of her and Peter sharing a condo somewhere hot, then banished it and gave his coffee, which had to have gone cold, a warm-up. "You wouldn't be pissed off if I bailed?"

"Of course not. Why would I be?"

"You sunk money in the place."

"I had this idea that somebody would've wanted me to," he said, nodding down the bar at his father's stool. After his death, Birdie had affixed to that stool a small metal plate that said: DONALD "SULLY" SULLIVAN. It had not escaped her notice that it was the one stool Peter never sat in. "It was his money, not mine."

Well, technically it *was* his. In addition to the house on Upper Main, he'd inherited his father's savings, the contents of which had been surprising. For that matter, Peter had been surprised to learn that Sully even *had* a bank account. He'd always kept his money in a clip in his front pocket and paid for everything in cash. He'd died, so far as Peter knew, without ever having owned a credit card.

"Still, I would've had to close down if it hadn't been for you," Birdie said, adding, "and your friend Tina." Who showed even less interest in how the tavern was doing than Peter. Strange, but back when Birdie had reluctantly accepted their help—in the process making them minority partners—she'd fretted they might interfere with how she ran the business. What if they encouraged her to spend money she didn't have sprucing the place up, or made dumb suggestions about the menu? As it turned out, she needn't have worried. Their hands-off approach was so comprehensive it suggested indifference, which, when she thought about it, was borderline insulting. As if they knew right from the start that the money they'd invested might better have been pounded down the nearest rat hole.

"Speaking of Tina," Birdie continued, "I ran into her on the street one day last week, and I don't think she even knew who I was." Though with her usual blank expression and that wonky eye of hers, who could even tell what she was looking at.

Peter nodded. "I've been meaning to drop in on her, actually."

Tina Purdy was yet another on the long list of people his father had asked him to check on from time to time. Exasperating, really. Right to the bitter end, Sully had assumed that Peter was back in Bath for good, that he'd learned his lesson living in New York City. Every time Sully suggested he was now a Bath lifer, Peter had corrected him, not that it did any good. Particularly galling, a year and a half after his father's passing, was the possibility that he'd been right. Because really. Had anybody ever made a slower getaway? As to Tina, why had Sully imagined she would require looking in on? Although it wasn't common knowledge, she was one of North Bath's wealthier inhabitants, a successful, if hermitic, businesswoman. Admittedly, appearances did suggest otherwise. She lived in the same shabby old house at the edge of town that had belonged to her grandparents. Her Grandpa Zack, a lifelong scavenger, had owned what he called a salvage business. (Ruth, his wife, referred to it as the town's second, unofficial dump.) For forty years the man had gotten up at the crack of dawn to canvass neighborhoods all over Schuyler County, loading onto the back of his flatbed truck whatever people put out on their front terraces to be carted off. He also was a regular at area flea markets and weekend yard sales, where he would purchase anything that, as he put it, you could buy for fifty cents and later resell for a dollar.

Because his wife had insisted on a fire wall between her business (Hattie's Lunch) and any dim-witted enterprise her husband might be involved in, they each had, in addition to their shared personal checking account, a separate business one. Ruth had no interest in Zack's—which he referred to as the Tina Fund—because (1) she thought of his business as a hobby, and (2) how much money could possibly be in it? Actually, she'd snuck a peek (he kept his passbook in his sock drawer), so she knew the answer: just a few hundred dollars.

The Tina Fund. One of the few things she and her husband agreed on was that their granddaughter was going to have a rough life. She had that wandering eye—the one that two expensive surgeries had failed to correct when she was young—which made her the butt of much cruelty among the neighborhood kids. But really, the eye was the least of it. The child hadn't learned to talk until she was three (either that or she chose not to), and immediately fell behind at school. Everyone assumed she couldn't read until one day Ruth noticed the girl's lips moving as she examined a picture book Ruth had bought the day before and hadn't yet read to her. "Hey, Two-Shoes," Ruth said, sitting down next to her granddaughter on the sofa. (Two-Shoes was her favorite nickname for the child; Janey, her mother, called her Bird Brain.) "Can you read?" But the child just stared up at her blankly, as if she didn't know what the word *read* meant. Later that evening, after the little girl had been returned to her mother, Ruth was still mulling the possibility over. "You're not going to believe this," she told her husband, "but I think that child can read."

For his part, Zack, whose own lips moved when he read a restaurant menu, didn't doubt it. Weekends, he let Tina tag along when he went to yard sales, and even though she had just the one good eye, he'd often noted that this eye didn't miss much. In fact, Tina often noticed things that other people, even adults, missed completely. Maybe you couldn't tell what she was thinking, but something was clearly going on in that little noggin of hers. Though he'd never really explained exactly what he was doing at these yard sales and flea markets, why he bought certain things and left others alone, the child seemed to understand. Sometimes when he picked something up to examine it more closely, she'd shake her head no, and he'd put it back. Other times she'd pick something up and hand it to him, and he'd think, *Really?* But since the items she selected were never things she'd want for herself, if it was cheap he'd buy it, and guess what? He was usually able to resell it in a day or two. Noting this pattern, whenever he couldn't decide whether or not to buy something, he'd hold it up to Tina and say, "What do you think?" and she would nod or shake her head, though other times she'd just stare at him, as if to say, *You're asking* me?

"She's Grandpa's little adviser," he told Ruth, who, happy to play along, replied, "Of course she is," never suspecting that her husband was speaking literal truth.

The other thing both Ruth and Zack noticed was that the child forgot exactly nothing. When something went missing, either in the house or out in the shed, where her grandfather kept most of what he referred to as his inventory, they'd ask Tina where it was, and instead of telling them, which would involve the use of her vocal cords, she'd go to wherever the missing thing was and stare at it. *"You,"* Ruth would say whenever she did this, "are one spooky kid."

All of which begged a fairly obvious question: Was the child miles behind other kids her age, or miles ahead? Neither grandparent could be certain. Ruth's theory was that her granddaughter was suffering from trauma. Roy Purdy, her father, had been a petty criminal who spent half his time in jail and the other half punching Janey, her mother, in the face, his preferred method of getting her to stop finding fault with him. How many times, Ruth wondered, had the child walked into a room and seen Janey laid out on the floor, bleeding from mouth and nose, but otherwise still, as if asleep, her father, wraith-thin and shirtless, standing over her with a balled fist. As a result, violence, or the perceived approach of something too scary for the child to contemplate, caused her to shut down, to go to some dark place where whatever frightened her couldn't follow. Ruth thought of it as her own private psychological bomb shelter. Once there—wherever *there* was—she'd await the all clear, a sign (for some reason her grandfather's voice usually did the trick) that it was safe for her to return to the real world, where in her absence order had somehow been restored (her father arrested for assault and then, since he could never make bail, returned to the county jail to await trial, after which, with luck, a good long stretch somewhere downstate). What scared Ruth was that each time Tina went away like this it was harder to bring her back.

Over the years the Tina Fund—and how much was in it—had become a game between Tina and her grandfather. "I bet you'd like to know how much is in there, huh?" he would inquire, though money—what its use might be—was something the girl seemed to have trouble grasping. Usually she just shrugged, her bad eye wandering off, as if in search of something that *did* interest her and whose value she *did* understand. "Okay, I'll give you a hint," he'd prod, and then, as if to prevent Ruth from overhearing, he'd whisper, "More than you think."

"When do I get it?" Tina would sometimes ask.

"When the time is right," Grandpa Zack always replied enigmatically, winking at Ruth.

"I wouldn't get my hopes up," Ruth advised her granddaughter. Not that the girl ever did. In fact, she seemed to *have* no hopes, which was what most concerned both her grandparents.

What Ruth didn't know was that her husband's bank account, the one in his sock drawer that had only a few hundred dollars in it, was a deep fake. There was another that she never once suspected the existence of at a bank in Schuyler, and it was in this account that her husband stashed his real profits. Bizarrely, at least to Peter's way of thinking, the only other person he told about the second account had been Sully.

One day, out of the blue, Zack handed him his savings account book from the Schuyler bank. "What's this?" Sully wanted to know.

"I been saving," Zack, looking downright sheepish, explained. "That's the total, down there at the bottom."

Sully read the figure, blinked, then put on his glasses, certain there had to be a mistake. "Ruth doesn't know about this?"

"The restaurant's hers and I don't interfere. This here don't concern her."

"Maybe not," Sully said, "but she's gonna be madder than a wet hen when she finds out."

Which she had been, though mostly at Sully for keeping her husband's secret for so long. "You *knew* about all that money?" she hissed as Zack's casket was lowered into the ground. He'd apparently come clean about the secret account on his deathbed. Also, that Sully knew all about it. (She and Sully had their dirty little secret all these years? Well, two could play that game.)

"He made me promise not to say anything," Sully had replied weakly.

"*Made* you," Ruth repeated.

"He said it was none of your business," Sully shrugged. "He had a point."

"And what point was that, exactly? Explain it to me."

A far-better idea, to Sully's way of thinking, would be to change the subject, so he said, "Where is she? Tina." She wasn't there at the cemetery and hadn't been at the church, either.

"Still down her rabbit hole," Ruth replied. "I don't know who's going to call her back, either, with Zack gone."

Janey, Tina's mother, stood a few feet away, shooting daggers at the two of them. It wasn't bad enough they'd been lovers all those years. Now here they were still kibitzing over her father's grave. "Have you told *her* yet?" Sully inquired. About the second account? About the fact that the money in it had all been left to Tina, not Ruth? That neither of them would come in for a share?

Ruth snorted. "You think *I'm* pissed? Wait till *she* finds out."

All Sully's life he'd made a point of avoiding female wrath whenever possible, so for a good, long while after the funeral, he'd steered clear of the diner. By the time he judged it safe to return, Janey had had new T-shirts made. HATTIE'S LUNCH, they said on the front. And on the back: MY DAUGHTER GOT THE MONEY AND ALL I GOT WAS THIS CRUMMY RESTAURANT.

One of the many things Peter would've liked to ask his father, now that it was no longer possible, was who in fact finally *had* gotten through to Tina after Grandpa Zack's death. Who had coaxed her back to the land of the living? Could it have been Sully himself? It was a crazy thought, but hadn't it been Sully who'd gotten through to Will so long ago when Peter and Charlotte brought their boys to North Bath that momentous Thanksgiving, the one that changed all their lives? Back then the poor kid had been frightened of his own shadow, and it was Sully who'd somehow intuited what the boy needed. Even now Peter couldn't help smiling when he remembered the stopwatch Sully had given his grandson so he could time himself being brave, a cockamamie idea if ever there was one. But Will had carried the thing with him everywhere and had gone to sleep with it ticking away on his bedside table each and every night. Had Sully worked a similar miracle with Tina? Or was there some other reason she'd landed on the list of people he'd wanted Peter to look in on?

===

"HERE'S SOMEBODY WHO might know," said Birdie. Flipping through *Schuyler Arts,* she'd come across Toby Roebuck's full-page Spa City Realty ad.

"It's possible," Peter admitted, glancing at Toby's smiling, CoverGirl-fresh face, the photo shot as if through gauze. If anybody had the lowdown on the Sans Souci, it would be Toby. Years earlier, after divorcing her husband Carl, Toby had gotten her real estate license and immediately become a mover and shaker at Coldwell Banker. Not long after that, she'd opened her own agency and quickly cornered a sizable chunk of Schuyler's high-end market.

"Are you two still——"

"Nope," Peter said, nipping this line of inquiry, he hoped, in the bud. It was true, though. He and Toby seldom saw each other anymore. The last time they'd crossed paths Peter had been scoping out a new Schuyler restaurant. He'd been about to call for his check when the bartender set a fresh glass of wine in front of him. "On the lady," she said, pointing to a nearby table. Peter hadn't immediately recognized Toby, who'd let her hair grow out, which he regarded as a good omen. Since her divorce, she'd had affairs with both men and women. Peter's working theory was that you could tell which gender she was most interested in just then by the length of her locks. Regardless, she was still, he had to admit, a knockout. Not many women in their late forties could get away with not wearing a bra.

On his way out of the restaurant, he'd stopped by her table to thank her for the drink, and she'd followed him outside. "Office Christmas party," she said, lighting up a cigarette. "Thanks for the rescue. Stay a minute while I smoke this?"

"Sure."

"I never see you anymore," she frowned. Was it disappointment he was hearing or accusation? He couldn't decide. "Why is that?"

"Your husband doesn't approve, is one reason."

"I'm not married," she reminded him. "I don't have a husband."

"Whatever you say," Peter smiled agreeably. Since losing his construction company, Carl Roebuck had become a car salesman. That whole enterprise being borderline fraudulent, Carl had proven a natural. He was, in fact, the one who'd sold Peter that Audi when he returned to Bath from New York.

"We have an arrangement, Carl and I," she continued, inhaling deeply. "He's free to fuck whoever he pleases and so am I."

He might be *free* to, Peter thought, but *free* wasn't the same as *able*. Carl's bout with prostate cancer a decade earlier had left him sadly diminished, or so Peter had heard. Proof, according to all the husbands he'd cuckolded down the years, that karma was real. "I'm the one guy he seems to object to for some reason," Peter told her. "He always seems to know when we've been together, too."

His hypothesis, actually, was that Toby herself was informing him. Nor would he have blamed her. Carl had cheated throughout their marriage. Now that the shoe was on the other foot, why shouldn't she keep him apprised of her own amorous activities?

"Poor Carlos," she sighed. "I've explained that it's just sex with us, not intimacy."

"That kind of hurts my feelings," Peter told her, though it didn't, not really.

She'd reached out then and touched his breastbone with a bright red fingernail. "You have actual feelings in there?"

He probably shouldn't have been so taken aback by the remark, but he was. Before they split up, Charlotte, his ex-wife, had accused him of surrounding himself with an emotional moat, a complaint that had been echoed by subsequent women. He'd always associated these accusations with breakups and hurt feelings, but maybe something else was going on. That tough-as-nails, unsentimental Toby Roebuck should offer the same observation so casually on the sidewalk outside a hip restaurant caught him off guard. Recalling the incident now, seated on a barstool at the Horse, Peter massaged his breastbone where she had touched him with that long, painted fingernail. Did lust count as a feeling? he wondered. It should.

From outside came the sound of heavy boots stomping, which could mean only one thing. "You mind?" Birdie said, but Peter was already sliding off his stool. When he unlocked and opened the front door, Rub Squeers was on the other side with his knuckles raised to knock. "Morning, Sancho," Peter said, stepping out of the way so Rub, frowning at the nickname he'd always hated, could come inside.

Of all the people Sully had wanted Peter to check up on, Rub had been at the top of the list, and even now it was terrifying to contemplate how close Peter had come to botching his father's prime directive. How long was it? Two weeks? Three? A whole month after Sully's funeral before it occurred to him that he hadn't seen Rub around, and neither, when he inquired, had anybody else. Had he even been *at* the funeral? Half the town had turned out, but Peter had no memory of Rub being there. At the time his undivided attention had been on Will, who—no surprise—was taking his grandfather's death hard. Still, how had he managed to forget Rub completely?

And so, one dark afternoon, hoping there might be something he could do to make it up to this man who'd barely left his father's side for a good three decades, Peter drove out to where Rub had lived with his wife Bootsie until her own death eighteen months earlier. The ramshackle house looked dark and uninhabited when he pulled into the empty drive. Had Rub left town without telling anyone? With his best friend gone had he decided he didn't want to remain in Bath where he'd be reminded, every day, of the man he'd squired so faithfully? It was possible. In fact, Peter half hoped—more than a little guiltily—that this might be the case, because if Rub was gone, that meant one less obligation.

Climbing the rickety porch steps, Peter pulled the screen door toward him so he could knock on the inner one. Though he hadn't yanked it hard, the door came free of its bottom hinge and dangled there from the top one. Rapping on the inner door, he waited, then rapped again, harder this time. When no one answered, he put his ear to the door and listened for sounds of stirring inside. Silence. Feeling an ambient dread in the pit of his stomach, he went around to the back of the house, hoping to see a light on in one of the rooms on the second floor, but it was dark up there, too. Remembering a story his father had told him about Rub climbing up into a tree that stood next to the house in order to prune a bothersome limb and somehow managing to strand himself up there, Peter went over to the tree in question and peered up into its web of dark branches, half expecting to see Rub up there, too embarrassed to admit he'd gone and done it again. But no. He was about to give up and head back into town when he happened to glance at the kitchen window, and there, framed in it, was Rub's pale orb of a face. Peter waved. Was it a trick of the light, or was the man's face streaked with tears?

Going back around to the front of the house, Peter again climbed the porch steps. This time when he knocked, Rub answered. He was wearing big rubber boots and his parka over what looked like pajamas. His eyes were, in fact, rimmed with red. He looked, in a word, ruined.

"Sancho?" Peter said. "You okay?"

Rub shrugged. "I thought you were him."

"My father?"

"His ghost," Rub explained. "You weren't limping."

"I'm not sure I follow," Peter admitted.

"I figured he'd come to tell me that being dead wasn't so bad. That his knee didn't hurt anymore."

Peter peered around the man, trying to get a better look inside. "Dark in there," he said. "Why don't you put a light on?"

"They turned off the electricity."

"How come?"

"I guess I didn't pay the bill."

"You guess?"

The other man frowned. "No money."

"I don't understand, Rub."

His eyes started to leak again. "I quit my job."

Peter started to ask why, then remembered that back when Sully died Rub had been employed by Hilldale Cemetery. *Dear God,* he thought, the whole thing making a kind of crazy sense now. After digging Sully's grave, Rub had quit the cemetery and simply gone home. He'd been here ever since, waiting, unless Peter was mistaken, for a life he was no longer interested in living to be over. Seeing what he believed to be Sully's ghost, he'd concluded that his own time had come. He was, Peter realized, disappointed to be wrong.

"Here's an idea," Peter said. "What do you say we run over to the Horse?" This was, he was pretty sure, what his father would've suggested, and he himself had no better plan.

"Why?"

"Why not?" he said, again channeling his father. "I'd suggest putting on some pants, though. Birdie won't let you in in pajamas."

Rub looked down and appeared surprised to discover that he was in fact wearing pajamas. "Can't I just stay here?"

Peter shook his head.

"How come?"

"Because," Peter explained.

"Okay," Rub said, for some reason accepting the verdict without protest.

"I'll wait here while you change," Peter told him, not wanting to go inside. Not wanting to see how the man had been living.

When Rub closed the door, Peter sat down on the steps to wait. He could hear Rub banging into things in the dark, searching, no doubt, for pants and a shirt. After a few minutes, the door opened again and Rub reappeared. When Peter rose to his feet, the other man said, "How come you're here?" Not, *Where have you been all this time?* Not, *Why did it take you a whole month to miss me?* No, what he wanted to know was why Peter had remembered him at all.

"I should've come before," Peter admitted. "I forgot about you. I'm sorry."

When he turned his key in the Audi's ignition, the screen door in that same second came loose from the top hinge and rattled to the floor, the timing so exact that the two events appeared linked by cause and effect, though Rub reacted to neither.

They barely spoke on the way into town, Rub staring out the window as if he were seeing this all-too-familiar terrain for the first time. It being the middle of the afternoon, there was nobody but Birdie at the Horse when they arrived. She was behind the bar, as usual, watching a soap. She turned it off when Peter entered with a comatose Rub in tow. When Rub just stood there in the entryway, making no move to remove his parka, Peter said, "You can take that off. It's nice and warm in here." When Rub did as instructed, Peter heard Birdie gasp and saw why. "Good Lord, Rub," she said, taking him in. "You look half starved. When was the last time you ate?"

Rub regarded her blankly, clearly unable to remember. (He would later confide to Peter that when he ran out of money he'd gone through what was in the fridge and pantry and then just thought, *Okay, there's no more.* As if he'd just eaten the last can of pork and beans on the whole of planet Earth.) "Haven't really been that hungry, I guess."

"Rub," Birdie said, trying to focus his attention. "Look at me. You need to eat."

"Okay," he said, as if this were an abstract proposition that, if agreed to, need not be acted upon.

"Come over here and sit down," she said.

Rub did as he was told, but paused, as if flummoxed by the array of barstools. Which one did she mean for him to sit on? Only when Peter slid onto one and patted the seat of the adjacent stool did Rub climb aboard.

"I'll make you something to eat," Birdie said. "Tell me what you want."

The old Rub wouldn't have hesitated, but this one did. Finally, he said, "A burger?"

Hearing this word come out flawlessly, Birdie and Peter had shared a quick, surprised glance. For as long as Peter had known him, Rub had been afflicted with a terrible stutter. Words beginning with the letter *b* were particularly problematic. (He was forever wishing for a buh-buh-big ole buh-buh-burger). Out at Rub's place, Peter had been so surprised by Rub's hollowed-out appearance that he hadn't paid much attention to how different he sounded.

"Anything on it?" Birdie said, eyeing the man suspiciously now, as if he might be an impostor.

Rub considered her query the way you would an equation that involved imaginary numbers. Solve for *x*. "Bacon?" he guessed. It was as if, like Lazarus, he'd returned from the dead and was having a hard time remembering how this whole life business was supposed to go, having gotten used to its absence.

"Anything to drink?"

"A beer?"

"What kind?"

"Budweiser?"

Birdie shook her head, mystified. "Rub?" she said. "What happened to your stutter?"

Rub just regarded her blankly, as if to say, *What stutter?* Except for his conversation with Peter back on the porch, this was the first time he'd spoken to a soul in the month since Sully's death. Having concluded that he'd never be required to speak again, he had no further use for his stutter or it for him. It was simply gone. How was he supposed to know where?

===

WHILE RUB ATE his burger, Peter got on the office phone, first calling Niagara Mohawk to get the electricity turned back on, then the heating oil company to schedule an emergency delivery for later that afternoon. He thought about calling Spectrum and ordering a basic cable package but decided against it for now. Tomorrow he'd go to the mall to pick up a cheap Trac cell phone. All of this took the obligatory forty-five minutes, and when he returned to the bar, Rub's barstool stood empty.

"Men's room," Birdie explained. His half-eaten burger sat on the bar. "I think he's throwing up in there."

Peter nodded. "This is my fault," he said. "I should've checked on him sooner."

Birdie shook her head. "He's a grown man, Peter. You're not his keeper."

"Actually, I am. My father made that pretty clear."

"You think he was intentionally starving himself?"

"It's possible. More likely he just ran out of food."

"How much weight do you figure he's dropped?"

"I don't know. Thirty pounds? More?"

"Impressive," Birdie said. "Losing thirty pounds *and* a speech impediment."

When Rub finally returned from the men's room, he looked

even more pale and shaky than before, and he wanted to know if they could go back home.

"Sure," Peter said, "but I thought we'd stop at the store on the way."

"What for?"

"Couple days' worth of groceries?"

"Can't I just . . . ?"

"Nope."

At this, Rub's brow furrowed deeply, making him look like a disillusioned bulldog. "How come you're, like, the boss now?"

"I just am," Peter informed him. "Is that okay with you?"

Rub considered this for a long moment before saying, "I guess."

Later, when they pulled up in front of Rub's place, the heating oil truck was in the drive. On the porch Peter handed Rub the bag of groceries and leaned the busted screen door against the wall. "I'll come by in the morning," he told him. "You gonna be okay until then?"

"I don't know what to do," Rub admitted.

Peter nodded. "We'll figure it out."

"We will?"

"Why not?" Though he could think of a hundred reasons. "Might be a good time to sell this place," he suggested. "Maybe find an apartment in town?"

"Okay," Rub said, though it was Peter's distinct impression that if he'd suggested now might be a good time to move to France, he'd have said okay to that as well.

Later that night, at home in his own bed, he thought again about Rub looking out his kitchen window and mistaking Peter for his father's ghost. For some reason the idea that Sully might actually be haunting North Bath didn't seem all that far-fetched.

═══

"YOU KNOW WHAT I wished?" Rub said listlessly, after hanging up his parka and joining Peter and Birdie at the bar.

That Rub was at long last wishing again Peter took as a hopeful sign. It had been a long road back, but he was looking better these days. He'd gained back some of the weight he lost during his month of solitary grieving and what Peter took to be existential despair. His color was better, and he was looking slightly less lost and abstracted, more willing to resume the burden of his life, though Peter did sometimes wonder if he regretted having been pulled back from the brink. Unloading his and Bootsie's ramshackle house at the edge of town had helped, though Rub had made no money on the sale. Every time they needed cash Bootsie had refinanced the place, which meant they had zero equity. Still, Rub seemed happy that it was gone, and the small in-town studio apartment above what had once been the Rexall drugstore seemed to suit him. Peter had also found him part-time employment on the grounds crew of the community college, which meant he was more or less solvent. And he seemed to look forward to Saturdays, which the two of them spent slow-walking the renovations to Miss Beryl's house on Upper Main.

"Let me guess," Peter said. "You wish I'd quit calling you Sancho."

"Not that," Rub said, though he did, in fact, wish Peter wouldn't call him Sancho and had said so many, many times.

"That it was July and not February?" Birdie said, getting into the act.

"No," Rub said, though, yeah, he wished this, too. What he really wished was that he could remember to just *tell* people what he wished instead of *asking* them if they knew, because the latter was an invitation for them to just keep guessing, piling one conjecture on top of another, so that by the time they finally gave up and said, *All right, go ahead and tell us,* he'd forgotten.

Today, though, Birdie took pity on him. "Tell us all about it, Rub. What do you wish?"

Which of course made his wish feel puny. "That you sold donuts here?" he admitted sheepishly.

"Well, you can quit wishing that, because we don't," she told him.

"I know," Rub frowned, frustrated by her predictable response. He *knew* she didn't. That was why he *wished* she did.

But then she reached under the bar for the bag Peter had given her earlier and set it in front of him on the bar. "We sometimes give them away, though," she said.

At this Rub perked up. Opening the bag, he peered inside. A jelly donut. His favorite. And just that quickly his eyes were full.

"Ah, Jesus, here we go," Birdie said, shooting Peter an I-told-you-so look.

"What do you want from me?" Peter said, though of course she was right. The donut had been a bad idea.

"Rub," she said sternly, returning her attention to him.

"What?" he said, barely able to get the word out, his throat having constricted.

"You know the rule."

His first thought was *What rule?* but then he remembered: *No crying in the bar.* Which he was doing, there was no denying it. Over a donut. A donut he *had,* not one he didn't. But that was the thing about wishes. When they came true, you realized that what you really wanted was something else entirely. It hadn't always been that way. Back when Sully was alive and he wished for a big ole jelly donut, that was what he'd actually wanted, or pretty close. Or maybe it was just that Sully was there to share his wish with. Maybe it was the fact that he already had what he really wanted—Sully's companionship—that made the donut so satisfying. Since Sully's death, Rub's wishes were invariably revealed as frauds, mere stand-ins for something else, and he knew what that something else was: for things to be like they used to be and would never be again. He wished, and could not stop wishing, that Sully hadn't gone and died like he did. He wished it first thing every morning and the last thing every night.

"You want me to go outside?" he offered.

"No, I don't," Birdie assured him. "I want you to quit crying in my bar. Do you know why?"

Rub shook his head pitifully. That such a rule should exist in the first place baffled him utterly.

"Because," Birdie explained, "any minute now I'm going to start crying myself."

Rub decided to risk taking a quick peek at her to see if this could possibly be true, and damned if it wasn't. A big ole tear was sliding down Birdie's puffy cheek. Surprised, he glanced over at Peter to see if he was crying, too, but he wasn't. In fact, he was shaking his head as he slid off his stool.

"What the hell is wrong with you people?" he said, though he privately wondered if maybe this was the wrong question. Watching Rub blubber, he thought again of Toby Roebuck's painted nail touching his breastbone, her questioning whether he harbored actual feelings in there. If he didn't, maybe that was for the best. His companions of the moment certainly suggested this.

"I can't help it," Birdie said, clearly ashamed of herself. "Other people crying makes me cry, too, that's all."

"Yeah, but enough, okay?" Peter said, heading for the coat-rack and struggling into his parka. "He's crying over a donut and you're crying over him crying over a donut." Returning to the bar, he offered to pay for his and Rub's coffees, but she waved him off, like she did every Saturday. "You should start charging people for stuff," he suggested.

Tossing Rub his coat, he said, "Are you done crying? Can we go to work now?"

Rub swallowed hard. He thought he was finished, but it was hard to know for sure. He took several breaths, each a little deeper than the last, searching for the stray sob that might still be lurking somewhere inside him, but none came. "Okay," he said, sliding off his stool.

"You all set for the week?" Peter thought to ask on their way out.

Birdie said she was, thinking, *Right. Another State of the Horse meeting duly dispensed with.* And her with nothing to show for it.

In this, however, she was wrong. When the door closed behind them, she saw that Rub had gone off and left his cried-over donut on the bar. She took it out of its paper sack and observed its tiny purple anus. *Jelly,* she thought. *Grape.* Her least favorite.

She ate it anyway.


Outside, Peter unlocked the truck, got in and leaned over to unlock Rub's door. Framed in the truck's rearview mirror was the tavern's expansive, empty parking lot at the edge of which was the long row of concrete barriers that marked the pavement's boundary. His father, it occurred to Peter, was probably sitting right here the night he emerged from the Horse with his usual snootful and somehow backed his truck all the way across the lot, over the concrete barriers, down the slope and into the woods, thereby setting in motion Peter's return to North Bath, a place he couldn't quite seem to escape. Adjusting the mirror, he caught a quick glimpse of himself. The man looking back at him from the narrow rectangle had his father's signature widow's peak and broad forehead. The eyes, though, were courtesy of his mother, and they seemed just then to be trying to tell him something. Probably, knowing Vera, that he had all this coming.

Putting the truck in reverse and backing out, Peter once again considered his inheritance, which included, in addition to Sully's widow's peak and savings account and the house on Upper Main Street, Rub himself. He had little doubt that once their renovations were complete, he'd be able to sell the house. If the rumor about the Sans Souci were true, he might even make a killing, after which he would finally be able to execute his long-delayed getaway. It wouldn't be a clean one, though, that much was clear. He told himself that all the people he'd promised his father he'd look in on would be fine. To them, Sully had been in some strange way essential, the mere fact of his continued presence in their lives somehow reassuring. Peter himself would never be that, for any of them. Yes, Rub was better now than he was when Peter found him, half starved, in his and Bootsie's house on the edge of town, but the man was still a mess, as this morning demonstrated. He'd probably never be his old self again. When Peter moved away, he would continue to struggle with depression and crippling loneliness. He might even retreat from the world again, this time into the even-smaller confines of his apartment above the Rexall. Still, Peter had done what he could, right? How much more could reasonably be expected of him? The problem was that despite everything he'd inherited from his father, Peter wasn't Sully and never would be. In Sully, Rub had had not just a friend, but a parent, someone to tell him what to do and why. Peter had been kinder and more considerate to Rub than Sully was, but he'd gradually come to understand that it wasn't kindness and consideration that Rub really needed. What he needed was, well, everything, and Peter, if he was honest, knew he didn't have that, or anything like it, to give. With Will gone, he wasn't sure he had it to give anybody. Maybe that's what Toby Roebuck was acknowledging when she touched his heart with her bloodred fingernail. No, all Peter had to give Rub was the occasional jelly donut and a few more months' worth of Saturdays. After that he was going to have to figure life out for himself, and so were all the other people—Ruth, Janey, Tina, Birdie—his father had wanted him to check up on.

*One more year,* he thought, turning onto Upper Main Street, *then freedom.* At the end of this long, wide street was the house his father hadn't wanted, but that his landlady, for reasons of her own, wanted him to have, the same house that Will would forever think of as home. And then, farther up the street, the entrance to the Sans Souci, which was also part of his genetic history. Big Jim Sullivan, his grandfather, had been the estate's caretaker at one point, and after the hotel closed, he'd supplemented his income by renting out rooms to friends for assignations. There'd also been a tragic accident there involving a boy who'd lost his grip climbing over the tall iron fence that surrounded the estate, impaling himself on an iron spike. If Peter was remembering the story correctly, Big Jim had been chasing the boy and shaken the fence as the kid scrambled over, causing him to lose his grip. The spike had entered the soft spot beneath his chin and exited through the boy's mouth, and he'd hung there by his jaw until he could be cut free. Had he died, that kid? Peter couldn't recall, but Big Jim had been fired shortly thereafter, and the family had spiraled into economic decline. Had Sully, himself a boy at the time, actually witnessed the event? Peter couldn't remember that either, but he knew it had haunted his father, perhaps as profoundly as the horrible things he'd witnessed during the war. He wondered, and not for the first time, if there was such a thing as a genetic memory, if this one might be part of his own dogged determination to put Schuyler County in his own rearview mirror as soon as possible.

For some reason, when they pulled up in front of Miss Beryl's house, there was an ancient canary-yellow Cadillac with West Virginia plates, a real beast, sitting in the driveway. "Whose car is that?" Rub wondered out loud, glancing over at Peter.

"Wild guess?" Peter said, turning the engine off. "I'd say it belongs to the fellow sitting up there on the porch."

Unlike the vehicle, the man in question *did* look familiar. Rub squinted at him, trying to figure out how he could both *be* and *not be* Sully's grandson. "He looks . . . like Will."

"That's because they're brothers," Peter explained. "You mind waiting here a minute?"

Rub did mind, in fact. On the drive over he'd been thinking about the fact that he'd cried over that jelly donut. It was Sully who'd always bought him jelly donuts, so when Peter did the same thing every now and then, it reminded him that Sully was gone and would always be gone. But lately, even though his first thought every morning and his last thought every night was of Sully, there were now long stretches of each day, especially on Saturdays, when Sully was absent from his thoughts. Would he wake up one morning and *not* think of Sully? Would he go to bed one night and realize he'd forgotten Sully for the whole day? Lately he'd begun to wonder if Peter was gradually taking Sully's place.

So when Peter asked him if he minded remaining in the truck, the answer was *Yes, he did,* though Peter hadn't waited for him to say so. He'd just gotten out and left Rub sitting there, which, now that he thought about it, was exactly what Sully used to do. He'd always hated having to share Sully with his other friends, and now here he was hating to share Peter. It was Saturday, and Saturdays were supposed to be just the two of them. Okay, maybe they didn't talk to each other like he and Sully used to. Rub never poured out his whole heart and soul like he used to with Sully, but still. On Saturdays he had someone he could call his own, even if it wasn't the person he wanted but who did look like him, who made it easy to pretend that the person he wanted was still there.

Rub rolled his window down for a better view of what was about to transpire. Odd, he thought, that the man on the porch stayed seated as Peter came up the walk, stayed seated even as Peter mounted the porch steps. When the man who looked like Will but wasn't finally did get to his feet and extended his hand, Rub half expected there'd be a gun in it and he braced for its discharge. But of course there was no gun, and Peter took the man's hand and said something Rub couldn't quite make out. It sounded like *Whack her*. But that made no sense.

# A Pile of Teeth

T HE MAIN THOROUGHFARE through the Sans Souci estate was closed except to foot traffic and bicycles. Since Raymer no longer had access to the electronic remote that raised and lowered the guardrail, he instead ignored the DO NOT ENTER! signs and bounced up the deeply rutted service road, parking out back of the old hotel next to Miller's Schuyler PD cruiser. At the far end of the lot sat another vehicle, a rusty old hatchback with a two-tone paint job. Was it possible, he wondered, that it belonged to whoever lay dead inside? His working theory was that the corpse would turn out to be a vagrant, somebody who'd forced his way in and then . . . what? Suffered a stroke and died? Because if the body belonged to a local, wouldn't he or she have been reported missing? Then again, now that Raymer thought about it, maybe not. Back in the fall, when the Morrison Arms was condemned and razed, it had displaced some of North Bath's poorest citizens, many of whom had no place to go. It was possible that whoever lay dead inside had been living in the rusted-out hatchback until winter's bitter cold had made that untenable. If such a person went missing, would anyone even notice?

Thinking about the Morrison Arms caused Raymer to recollect Mr. Hynes, the old Black man who'd lived there during Raymer's own bleak tenure. He'd spent most days in a folding lawn chair on the terrace waving his tiny American flag at passersby. Raymer and

Charice had argued about the man actually, Raymer claiming that for reasons he couldn't begin to fathom, the old man was patriotic, whereas Charice had argued he wasn't celebrating America at all, but rather protesting it, saying, *Look at me. Take a good look, and then tell yourself that all men are created equal.* Their disagreement had been unexpectedly heated and upsetting enough that Raymer had made a mental note to ask the old man who was right, but before he had the chance, Mr. Hynes, by then in his midnineties, had died. Whoever lay dead inside the Sans Souci, it wasn't him but some other poor, desperate soul.

Turning off the ignition, Raymer just sat for a moment, wishing, now that he was here, that he hadn't allowed Miller to talk him into coming.

It'd been years since he'd personally set foot on the Sans Souci grounds, and he was surprised by how badly the place had gone to seed. At least a dozen ground-floor windows were shattered, and the parking lot was littered with shingles blown off the roof. Last he'd heard, the property was owned by a dysfunctional New York City family whose siblings, after the patriarch's death, couldn't quit squabbling over whether to sell just the hotel or the whole estate. Once upon a time there'd been money set aside in trust for a full-time caretaker and a grounds crew. Until recently the expansive, manicured lawns had been a popular place for picnics in warm weather and sledding in the winter. But at some point the money had run out, and now the grounds, which had been allowed to go wild, were studded with NO TRESPASSING signs. Though the property abutted Schuyler Springs, it was, preannexation, part of North Bath, which meant that every night when the park closed Raymer had a cruiser swing through, mostly to discourage teenagers who liked to party in the surrounding woods. The hotel itself had been shut up tight for years.

Staring at the massive structure, Raymer found himself thinking about those squabbling New York siblings, who they were, what their lives were like. Imagine owning something so grand and letting it drift into ruin. Who would do such a thing? He knew what

Charice would say if she were here. *People so damn rich they can afford to, is who.* Before Charice, Raymer had never given much thought to rich people. Obviously, they existed. They blew into Schuyler every August for the racing season, expecting the locals to get out of their way and stay out. As a kid he'd always assumed that the wealthy must know some secret that poor people didn't. They had to be smart, or how else could they have gotten so far ahead of everybody else? In school he'd been taught that hard work was what led to riches, but most of these people didn't look like they worked at all. Charice, who hailed from rural North Carolina, had a whole different take on wealth and saw it as her duty to puncture Raymer's naïveté on the subject. "Show me a fortune," she liked to say, "and I'll show you a crime. Hell, I'd be rich, too, if everybody in my family'd enslaved people for two centuries." The first time she'd made this observation Raymer had pointed out that the people who invaded Schuyler County every August were mostly New Yorkers, not southerners. He doubted they, or their families either, had ever owned slaves. "Maybe not," Charice conceded, "but they owned the ships that brought them here."

Raymer didn't mind her sharing such opinions with him. Back before they started dating, when he was the chief of police and she was his employee, he'd gotten a kick out of listening to her when she got a righteous head of steam up. At the time he suspected she said such things because she knew they were outlandish and enjoyed seeing him rise to the bait. But later, after they started going out, it became increasingly clear that these were actual convictions and she didn't consider them outlandish at all. The more he listened, the less outlandish they seemed to him as well, which was, in its own way, even more unsettling. Moreover, the idea that injustice and inequality might be systemic cast police work in a whole new light. Seeing Charice get so upset over old Mr. Hynes and his tiny American flag reminded him how he'd felt as a boy when Miss Beryl had given him that copy of *Great Expectations*. Rather than confront the things in the book that had frightened him, he'd hidden it. Which was what he would've liked to do with Charice's often incendiary views, especially now that she was Schuyler's chief of police. It was one thing for her to share her convictions with Raymer, who was nuts about her, but he hoped that given her new, exalted and very public position, she was being more circumspect with others, who might not be. Schuyler was more progressive than Bath, but Raymer worried that the city's liberal politics might not always be a reliable barometer of what people actually thought. Despite the city's higher per capita wealth, there were pockets of extreme, pre-dominantly Black poverty, and the last two summers, there'd been unrest. That was one reason the city council had been interested in hiring a Black chief of police, someone who might be able to keep a lid on that population's smoldering resentment, which the recession had only exacerbated. And though she'd never said it in so many words, Raymer was pretty sure that improving the relationship between the city and Schuyler's Black community was one of the reasons Charice had wanted the job.

A sudden rap on his window caused Raymer to just about jump out of his skin. Sergeant Miller, his face deathly pale, had material-ized just outside his vehicle and was staring in at him. How had a man like Miller, who had no stealth mode, managed to sneak up on him like that?

"Chief?" he said. "What're you doing?"

Raymer rolled down his window. "Thinking."

"Aren't you going to get out?" He pointed at the hotel. "It's in there."

*It.* The body of a dead human being, he meant. "I'm trying to decide."

Miller swallowed hard. "You're going to need a handkerchief." He pulled his out of his pocket to illustrate. "Or a mask."

"I don't have either."

"The body is . . ." He searched for words.

"Decomposing?" Raymer guessed.

When Miller nodded, Raymer caught a whiff of something ran-cid. Was it possible, at such a distance, that he was actually smelling a corpse inside the building? But then his brain kicked sluggishly into gear, and another explanation offered itself. Miller had materialized so suddenly because he was already outside when Raymer pulled in. He must've been on his hands and knees behind the privet hedge. What Raymer had caught a whiff of was vomit.

"Is it a man or a woman?" he asked.

"Man," Miller said, though he sounded less than certain.

"Good," Raymer replied, surprising himself. After all, a human life was a human life. And yet, somehow, a woman would've been worse, promising additional layers of horror.

"His teeth . . . ," Miller continued, again swallowing hard.

*Teeth?* "What about them?"

"They're in a pile on the floor."

Raymer blinked, trying to visualize what Miller was telling him. He'd never seen it himself, but he knew that at some point in the decomposition process, usually a month or so postmortem, fingernails and teeth began to fall out. But . . . in a pile on the floor? "I don't under—"

"And his eyes. They're all . . ." Here Miller held both hands up in front of his face as if each contained an invisible baseball.

"I don't understand what that means," Raymer confessed.

"Because of the rope . . ."

*Rope?* Raymer rubbed his temples. "Miller? Are we talking about a suicide here?"

The other man's shoulders were hunched and his head was bobbing up and down. Raymer couldn't tell if each bob represented a yes, or whether collectively, along with his hunched shoulders, they meant he might throw up again. Raymer leaned away just in case. "You're telling me the man in there hanged himself?"

Miller opened his mouth to speak, then cupped one hand over it and darted back behind the hedge, where Raymer heard him retching. When he paused, Raymer called to him. "Have you gotten through to Chief Bond?"

"She called me back right after I talked to you," Miller panted.

"Has anybody notified the coroner?"

"Chief Bond said she would—" More retching.

When his phone vibrated in his pocket, Raymer took it out and glanced at the screen, which said CHARICE. Somehow their speaking her name had conjured the woman herself. Pressing ACCEPT, he said, since Miller was within hearing distance, "Chief Bond."

And then, there was her voice on the line, causing his heart to lurch, his eyes to tear up. And really, how messed up was that? Him feeling a surge of happiness at the sound of her voice when just inside the old hotel a man apparently dangled from a rope, his teeth in a pile on the floor, his life extinguished.

If the sound of *his* voice was making Charice happy, she gave no sign. "*Chief Bond?*" she said. "See, now that right there is classic passive-aggressive behavior."

"Charice? Didn't you used to call *me* chief?"

"That's a whole different situation and you know it."

"Actually, they're identical—"

"*You're* the one who said I should take the damn job in the first place, remember?"

"And I'm glad you did. You deserved it."

"Damn *right* I deserved it. But who gets their damn picture in the paper? Me when I take a job or you when you quit one?"

"I didn't quit my job, Charice. My job quit me."

"*The end of an era?*" she continued, as if he hadn't spoken. "You want to talk eras? How 'bout the beginning of one? First Black chief of police north of Albany? Ever? No story there?"

"Yeah, but it's not like *I* wrote the damn thing."

"True, but somebody who looks like you did."

It occurred to Raymer then that his happiness in hearing Charice's voice was not unalloyed. Once upon a time it had been, but not anymore. In the beginning it'd been just the two of them. A woman and a man. But then, almost immediately, the world had begun to intrude. What were their arguments over old Mr. Hynes and rich white people but the world intruding? Before they knew it, they'd become a *Black* woman and a *white* man, roles neither seemed able to escape. They became more aware of people staring at them in public spaces, trying to figure out if they were a couple, and, if so, why? Raymer, middle-aged and looking like he and the Pillsbury Doughboy might have a common ancestor, Charice younger and good-looking, but Black. Raymer found himself wondering what all these gawkers were thinking. *What does she see in him? What does he want with her?* It was impossible to tell. All he could do was hope everything would work itself out, but of course it hadn't. Did the world really have it in for them? It was possible. But it was also possible that they were somehow failing each other, not measuring up. How, though? They'd barely spoken in a week, and here they were already at each other's throats.

"Charice?" he pleaded. "Do I get to call 'over the line' on that last remark? Someone who *looks* like me?" When she declined to respond to that, he said, "Can I ask you a question?" "Why are we having this conversation over the phone?"

"Because I'm in Albany."

Which was news to Raymer. "Why?"

"What do you mean, why?"

"I don't know. You just didn't mention anything about going there, I guess."

"I'm attending a convention, okay?"

"Of Black police chiefs?"

"*Now* who's over the line."

"You're right. I'm sorry."

Silence again until—"What's that sound?"

"Sergeant Miller," he told her. "Barfing into a bush."

"Why?"

"Why is he barfing or why into a bush?"

"Both."

"Apparently it's a pretty grim scene in there."

"In there? So . . . where are you, exactly?"

"Out back of the hotel. I just got here. I wasn't sure I should go in without your permission."

"By *grim* you mean what? The body's decomposing?"

"That," he said. "Also? It's . . . hanging."

"Wait, what?" she said. "Hanging? Like . . . from the neck?"

"By a rope, yes. I'm guessing not by the ankle. Like I said. I haven't been inside yet."

"Miller," she said, her voice rich with wonder and frustration. "He calls to tell me that there's a dead body at the Sans Souci but fails to mention it's hanging."

"He does have a habit of burying the lede," Raymer conceded.

"Why did I let you talk me into bringing him with me to Schuyler, is what I'd like to know."

Raymer understood her frustration. Still, as cops went, Miller was far from the worst. He was loyal and honest. He took his duties seriously. Was never aggressive on the street. But there was also an innocence about him that verged on cluelessness, which for a police officer was the eighth deadly sin. Despite having memorized the handbook, he still didn't really understand the nuances of the job he'd been doing now for a good decade. In many ways he reminded Raymer of himself when he first joined the force. Did the man need what Raymer himself had once required? To be struck by lightning? Did he need a Dougie of his very own to take up residence in his head for a few months? Sort him out?

"Okay," Charice sighed. "Consider yourself deputized. I'll finish up here and come straight back. I appreciate your taking this on."

Her voice had softened and Raymer knew this was probably a good way to leave things, at least for now. So why couldn't he? Rolling up his window so Miller couldn't overhear, he said, "Charice? Before you go? I've been thinking. Are things improving? Between us? Should we quit pretending we're ever going to get back together? Just rip off the Band-Aid?"

She was quiet for so long he wondered if she'd hung up and he'd somehow missed the click. "Look," she said finally. "I haven't been completely honest with you."

*Okay,* he thought, feeling the Band-Aid tug up and away from the tender, inflamed wound. *Here it comes. There's someone else.* Because give Dougie this much credit. Right from the start he'd warned Raymer how this would go. Back when they were sharing space in Raymer's skull, Dougie had offered a steady stream of unasked-for advice about how to deal with women in general and this one in particular, advice that Raymer generally ignored, though he did sometimes wonder if maybe—just as a thought experiment—he should try some of it on for size. The guy might be a dick, but he wasn't always wrong. By convincing Raymer that most people a police officer encountered in the normal run of his duties should be viewed with suspicion, Dougie had made Raymer a more effective cop. The problem was women. Dougie believed they deserved the same careful scrutiny as suspects in criminal investigations and for the same reason: because they were mostly up to no good. Okay, maybe your average woman's behavior wasn't, strictly speaking, criminal, but emasculating the men in their lives, Dougie believed, was the prime directive of their gender mission statement. And Charice, he warned, was no exception. She was playing Raymer like a fiddle. *She's that wife of yours all over again,* he warned.

Which was completely unfair, right? The two women could not have been more different. Except, well . . . "There are two or three things about me," Raymer had conceded, "that irritate her."

*Right,* Dougie had snorted. *And those things are you, you and you.*

Him, him and him. And now here he was and here *it* was—the I-haven't-been-completely-honest-with-you moment he'd been dreading. *He* wasn't going to yank the damn Band-Aid off. *She* was. Feeling his throat constrict, he heard himself say, "There *is* someone else, isn't there."

Which elicited what Raymer could only describe as a cackle, though never in his life had he heard laughter so steeped in sadness. "In a manner of speaking," she said.

"I'm not following."

Yet another long silence. Finally, she said, "Look. I should've told you. Jerome is back."

"Jerome," he repeated. Because this was not at all what he'd expected. "Your *brother* Jerome."

"Do we know another Jerome?"

"But that's wonderful!" Raymer exclaimed. If Miller hadn't

been on the other side of the hedge, he'd have gotten out of the car and danced a jig. Jerome? Jerome he could deal with.

"Why is it wonderful?" Charice wanted to know. "Do you even *like* my brother?"

Well, he did and he didn't. Yes, her brother had been a bone of contention between them even before Raymer discovered it was Jerome that Becka was about to run away with when she slipped on that rug at the top of the stairs. Still, that was a decade ago, and you could stay angry at somebody as messed up as Jerome for only so long. And in his own way he'd tried to make amends, right? When it became clear that Raymer and Charice were serious, hadn't he given them the generous gift of his absence by quitting his job at the mayor's office, selling his condo in Schuyler and returning home to North Carolina? That couldn't have been easy for him. After all, until Becka, Jerome and Charice had been the most important people in each other's lives. Until Becka, it had been Charice who helped keep his debilitating OCD from completely taking over his life, and after her death it had been Charice, with Dr. Qadry's help, who had arrested Jerome's downward spiral and nursed him back to health. So, no, Raymer wasn't thrilled to learn that Jerome, a wide chasm of need, was back. Still, the other scenario he'd been imagining, Charice with a brand-new lover, was much, much worse. Also, Jerome had always seemed to like Raymer, to consider him a friend. A friend he'd betrayed. A friend he could no longer look in the eye. A friend he was hoping might forgive him one day.

"I like Jerome fine," he assured her. "It's just . . ."

"Just what?"

*Good question.* "Well," he said, stalling, "how long has he been back?"

"Does it matter?"

"Kind of?" he replied. "You said it yourself. You haven't been honest with me. How long have you been keeping this secret?"

"A month, okay? He's been here a month."

So . . . much of their time-out, then. "Whoa," he said.

"See?" she said. "Now you're mad at me."

"I'm not," he protested, which was true. He might have been mad if he believed her, but how could he? If Jerome had been back a month, why hadn't their paths crossed? Why hadn't anybody *else* seen him and reported his return? After all, Jerome had been a well-known figure around town. Tall, slender, Black, good-looking, he stood out. And if Jerome *was* back, why hadn't Charice herself come clean? Why would she allow Raymer to assume the worst—that she'd found somebody new? Had Jerome sworn her to secrecy? To what purpose? It wasn't the kind of secret they could keep, even if they wanted to. "You're telling me he's been in Schuyler this whole time? Where's he living?"

"With me."

"With you," he said. "Where *I* used to live."

"Look, he was in bad shape. How could I say no?"

*You've had no trouble saying no to me,* Raymer thought but didn't say. "What kind of bad shape?" Because since leaving Schuyler Springs and starting over down south, Jerome had supposedly put his life back together. He had a new job as head of security at a small predominantly Black college where, Charice claimed, he got along well with both students and staff and was even teaching a class in law enforcement. She'd been to visit him several times, and after her most recent trip she said he'd bought a new red Mustang—he'd had another when he lived in Schuyler—and was even starting to get his old swagger back. Raymer was actually sorry to hear about both the swagger and the Mustang. One of Jerome's favorite things had been to pull up to a screeching halt in front of Raymer, unholster his weapon, point its barrel at the sky in the iconic pose and say, in a British accent, *The name is Bond. Jerome Bond.* "You said he was doing great. What happened?"

Charice sighed. "Same as before. He fell in love."

"Who with?"

"Some painter. An adjunct professor at the college who had a side gig as an art therapist."

"A what?"

"I know," she said. "Don't start. Apparently, the idea is to use art to relieve anxiety. The one therapy he hadn't tried. Anyhow, he got hooked."

"On it or her?"

"Both? But I'm guessing more her. To me, it sounded like Becka all over again. Zero to sixty in two seconds flat. He meets her, and just like that, he's cured. No more OCD."

"Just tell me she didn't fall down the stairs and break her neck."

"No, she just broke up with him, and now he's wrecked again. Back to square one. He barely speaks. Refuses to leave the apartment. He's up all night surfing the net. Sleeps through the day."

Raymer tried to picture this, to reconcile this new information with the man who'd once fancied himself a Black James Bond. "If he's in such bad shape, shouldn't he be in a hospital?"

"He says I'm all he needs."

Amazing. Just that quickly the elation Raymer had felt moments earlier, when he learned that Charice hadn't fallen in love with somebody else, had dissipated completely. Fucking Dougie. That was the other thing he'd warned Raymer about: that if Charice ever had to choose between him and her brother—her *twin* brother—she'd choose Jerome.

"You're killing me here, Charice. You know that, right?"

"I'm sorry," she said, and she did, he had to admit, sound sincere. "Let's talk when I get back, okay?"

"Can I ask you one thing?"

She sighed. "Okay, but then I really have to go."

"Do you still love me?"

Again, the line went quiet. Finally, she said, "It's the wrong question? But . . . yeah, I do."

And then the line really was dead.

Raymer sat quietly for a long beat, but then, feeling his spirits, yo-yo-like, soar again, he shouted into the phone, "Did you hear that, asshole? She *said* she loves me!" When he realized it was Dougie he was shouting at, he quickly hung up. Because Dougie was born of and dwelled in electricity and might actually be on the line. When he put the phone back in his pants pocket, there *was* a voice in his head, just not Dougie's. "So," he heard Dr. Qadry say. "Do you agree?" In one of their early sessions, he'd confided to her that Dougie had warned him how things would end with Charice.

"I don't know," Raymer confessed at the time. "I think he just enjoys giving me a hard time."

"Okay," she said, "but is it possible that what Dougie *says*"—she paused here to remind Raymer that she didn't believe Dougie was real, that he actually spoke—"is what you *think* deep down?"

Which he should've seen coming. As well as what came next.

"And if so, shouldn't you own it?"

====

MILLER WAS ON his feet again, unsteady, his arms akimbo, like he was balanced on a surfboard and anticipating a wave. Finally, his equilibrium restored, he came out from behind the hedge and over to Raymer's SUV. "Chief?" he said, when Raymer rolled the window back down. "I don't know if I can go back in there."

"It's okay," Raymer said, getting out of his SUV. "I've got another job for you. I want you to make your way around the perimeter of the hotel and check for signs of forced entry. Can you do that?"

Miller nodded but made no move to carry out this request. "Chief?" he said. "Does this mean you're back in charge?"

"Only until Chief Bond gets back."

Miller nodded, his brow knit with struggle. "It's not that she's a bad boss," he said.

"I'm sure she's a good one."

"And it's not that she's . . . you know . . ."

"Black?"

"African American," he said, causing Raymer to suppress a smile. Miller had a problem with calling Black people Black, as if the word were a pejorative. To him the term *African American* was a refuge. He was pretty sure you couldn't be criticized for using it.

"No," Raymer said, "I'm sure it isn't."

"It's just that . . ."

"Miller," Raymer said. "Maybe we can discuss this later? Right now I need you to check the perimeter. Find out how our guy got inside. Can you do that?"

When he nodded, Raymer said, "Okay, go."

Then, hoping there might be something in the SUV that he could use for a mask, he went around back and popped the tailgate. Inside were two enormous beach towels that had been there since last summer. No other fabric of any description. Not even an oily rag. Sighing, he chose the towel that wasn't pink. He also grabbed a roll of yellow crime-scene tape and a handful of evidence bags. Only when he finished shaking the sand out of the towel and closed the tailgate again did he realize that Miller was inexplicably still standing there.

"It's just that," he continued, "down at the station . . . some of the guys . . . I don't like how they talk about Chief Bond when she's not around. If *you* were chief again . . ."

*This,* Raymer knew, was why he didn't mind having Miller around. Cluelessness aside, the man's myriad struggles never failed to cheer him up. Here he was in his midthirties, married and a recent father, but in many respects still back in middle school, worried about cliques, about what he should do about crude locker-room talk. "I don't think me being chief again is the best solution to the problem you're describing."

"What should I do, though? When they say things?"

"Try this," Raymer said, putting on his most serious face. "Next time somebody says something about Chief Bond that you think is inappropriate? Shoot him."

Miller's eyes got big, then he saw that Raymer was joking and became sheepish. "It's just . . . it's not right. Calling her—"

"Nope, it's not," Raymer interrupted, not really wanting to know what Charice was being called. "But Chief Bond is a big girl. You and I together probably couldn't take her in a fair fight." Though in truth, he was now mentally running through the list of the slurs that the guys at the station might've used and trying not to seethe. Whether she could handle this kind of crap was one of the things he'd been asked, actually. Because in order to hire her, the city council would have to pass over some white officers who probably thought they were in line for the position. Would Charice be able to win them over? And what about others in the rank and file who might resent taking orders from a Black woman? It was all well and good for him and Miller to joke about them not being able to take Charice in a fair fight. But the fight, if it ever came to that, wouldn't *be* fair. He knew that much without Charice or anybody else having to tell him.

Indicating the nearby service entrance to the hotel, he said, "Is that the way you came out?"

Miller nodded. "I think the door locked behind me, though."

"Doesn't matter," Raymer told him. "I can go around. Who all is in there?"

"That guy Franklin?" Miller said. Schuyler's town manager. Raymer had been introduced to the man but didn't really know him. "And the people he was showing around when they found the . . ." He seemed to be searching for a term like *African American* that he might substitute for *corpse,* an expression that wouldn't offend the dead man or his friends and relatives.

"How many of them are there?"

"Two. A man and a woman."

"That's it?"

Miller nodded.

"Okay," Raymer said. "Off you go."

Watching Miller finally depart, Raymer took a deep breath to steel himself for what lay ahead. Unfortunately, that breath filled his nose and lungs with the scent of suntan lotion from the beach towel, which in turn conjured up a vivid, bittersweet memory. That first year he and Charice were together, they'd taken a week off after racing season, driven to Cape Cod and checked into an old inn. The weather and ocean were still warm, so they spent most days at the beach, Charice stunning in a one-piece, canary-yellow bathing suit. Nights, they ate out and later, back at the inn, made love (and again in the morning before going down to breakfast). Had they suspected even then that what they had couldn't last? Was that why they'd been so hungry for each other? Because, admit it, Raymer thought, as he made his way around the old hotel over the crunchy snow, shivering in the February cold, they weren't going to make it. He was suddenly sure of it. Yes, the last thing she'd said before hanging up was that she still loved him, but it was the other part of her response that now seemed more important—that he'd asked her the wrong question. What, then, was the right one? He had no idea, which had to bode ill. Not having answers was the sort of thing a man might be forgiven for, whereas not even being able to formulate the right question suggested a degree of obliviousness for which there might well be no remedy. And hadn't he been, his entire life, just this sort of man? On Cape Cod, he now realized, he'd been deluding himself. Just as Jerome had believed that falling in love with Becka had cured his recurring, debilitating panic attacks, his myriad obsessive-compulsive rituals, Raymer had conned himself into trusting that with Charice at his side he would know how to *be* in the world. Somehow, he'd put the old hapless Raymer in his rear-view mirror for good. Since Becka's death, he'd grown, matured, maybe even evolved into someone new, someone with the experience and confidence to excel at a job he'd once despaired of mastering, and in so doing won the respect and, yes, love of a woman who, unlike his wife, actually seemed to enjoy his company. For the first time in his life he'd been able to imagine a happy future.

Had it all been a lie? He didn't want to think so. Life since Charice had been mostly good, right? He'd been reelected time and time again, serving both Democratic and Republican mayors. Yes, he was still gaffe-prone, but people seemed to agree that he was honest and mostly competent, that the words he'd had printed on that now-famous business card were in fact the opposite of what he'd meant. He *did* want the people he served to be happy. And hadn't he, in fact, manned up, just like asshole Dougie advised? Maybe. But then again, maybe not. Maybe that was part of the lie he'd been telling himself. He now recalled Dr. Qadry's earlier question: What was his greatest fear now that Dougie was gone?

That his time—his era—had passed, he thought. But it was more than that. Lately, what he really feared most was that he'd begun to regress, to backslide. Since he and Charice had agreed to their time-out, the Douglas Raymer he saw in the mirror each morning increasingly resembled the one he'd imagined he was shut of. What if *that* Douglas Raymer—the clueless one—was staging a come-back? Or, put another way, what if the new, improved Raymer of the last decade was merely an illusion? What if he was, now, what he'd always been? A man who had only a beach towel when what was required was a handkerchief or a surgical mask? Dear God. Did he need to be struck by lightning *again*?

Jerome really had been here a whole month? Seriously? How many times during that period had he and Charice had drinks at Adfinitum and gone back to his flat afterward, sometimes even making love there? All those opportunities to come clean, and not once had she let on that she had a new roommate. He'd believed her little housewarming gifts were evidence of her continued affection, proof that he remained in her thoughts when they were apart. Whereas actually, he now saw clearly, they were parting gifts.

Coming around the side of the hotel, he spied Bert Franklin, the town manager, standing on the steps of the hotel's main entrance, waving to a departing Range Rover that no doubt contained the VIPs who'd been touring the hotel when they came upon the hanged man. Raymer wondered again if they were here to inspect a property they'd already purchased or one they were thinking about purchasing. He supposed the absence of a realtor suggested the former, but who knew? They might have to be interviewed at some point, but probably not. When they were gone, Franklin turned on his heel and headed back inside without noticing Raymer's approach. There was only one other vehicle parked out front, a nondescript tan sedan of the sort leased by the city, probably Franklin's. Which was good. It meant that nobody else, not even the coroner, had arrived since Miller went out the rear door to barf. The last thing they needed was a crowd, at least until the scene had been secured.

Arriving at the steps that led up to the lobby, Raymer stalled, visited by a powerful premonition that he was about to make a mistake. For some reason he recalled the rusted-out old beater parked out back. Why hadn't he checked it out? If it belonged to the man who'd taken his life inside, it was probably unlocked, because why would a man intending suicide bother to lock his car? His vehicle registration was probably in the glove box, and that would reveal who the poor devil was, where he was from. There might even be a suicide note on the dashboard. Should he go back now and see? No, he decided. He was just stalling, looking for a reason not to do the awful job that shouldn't have fallen to him in the first place. When Miller finished the task Raymer had given him, he'd have him check out the hatchback.

And so, since the door to the hotel stood open, an invitation, Raymer took another deep breath full of suntan lotion and erotic memory, climbed the steps and entered the dark lobby, where he was promptly greeted by a blinding flash. It took only a second to restore his vision, but in that instant he understood his mistake. The beater in the parking lot didn't belong to the man who'd died by suicide, but rather to a newspaper photographer, who'd probably been listening to his police scanner and overheard Miller being dispatched to the Sans Souci and wondered what was up. Either Miller hadn't thought a photographer worth mentioning, or the man had come around to the front and entered through the lobby as Miller exited the rear. Didn't really matter which. What *did* matter was that Raymer's photograph (and not Charice's) would in all likelihood grace the front page of the *Schuyler Democrat* tomorrow, a man in a winter parka with a powder-blue beach towel draped around his neck, looking like God's own fool.

He also knew the question he should've asked Charice earlier. Instead of asking if she still loved him, he should've asked if they were finished. When she said that, yes, she still loved him, she was no doubt telling him the truth. It just didn't make any difference. Time to own it.

*Hey, Little Bro—*

*You don't mind me still calling you that, do you? I hope not.*

*Anyhow, guess what? I'm here! Didn't I tell you the Yellow Submarine would make it? Three hundred and fifty thousand miles on the old girl, but she ran good the whole way. One measly quart of oil was all she burned. You believe that? A thirty-year-old vehicle? That's what happens if you take care of something, I guess. Anyhow, I just want you to know I'm here and everything's going according to plan.*

*Better, actually. You should've seen the look on his face when he pulled up and saw me sitting there on that front porch of his. He knew it was me, right off, I'm pretty sure. You're always saying how much I look like our brother, and maybe I do, but just one look and he knew it wasn't his precious Will sitting there. Hah! Just one look! Remember that song? Mom used to play it when we were kids? I forget which cassette it was on—she only had five or six—but it went,* Just one look . . . and I knew . . . knew . . . KNEW. *You remember? How we all used to shout on that last* knew? *Probably not. I don't have that many memories from when I was as young as you were then. I think Mom might've been going out with Dickweed, but it was definitely before they got married. Men. She sure could pick 'em, couldn't she? Remember how we used to argue about Dickweed? You thought he was an improvement over some of the others, but I said no fuckin' way, he was the worst of the lot. Care to debate that anymore, Little Bro? I don't think even Mom would anymore. If there was any way out, she'd take it. Not that there is. Not at her age. Messed up as she is these days? Who'd want her? I know, I know. You don't like me to say things like that. And you're right. She's not the one to blame. But true is true, whether you want it to be or not.*

*I actually thought about her a lot on the trip here, all those hours alone in the Sub, nothing to do but think. She did try her best to cheer us up when shit happened, right? Remember that time we were being evicted? I'm pretty sure it was the first apartment, the one we were living in before her and Pop split up, but maybe it was one of the others. Anyhow, me and you were all worried about what we'd do and we kept bugging Mom about it, asking her where we were going to live, and she started singing, "We'll all live in the yellow submarine, the yellow submarine, the yellow submarine," and then me and you joined in. Remember?*

*Hell, it wasn't all bad until Dickweed showed up, right? We tried to warn her that he was a complete douche. Remember how we used to tease him about the Great Dick Divide, how nobody born after 1950 was called Dick but him? That was back when you could still tease him. Before they got married. Could be it was just me giving him shit. I don't remember. You were too smart to do it to his face after that one time. I was the slow learner and I got the scars to prove it, right?*

*Sorry. Kinda got sidetracked there, didn't I. Happens a lot these days, and not just when I'm drinking, either.*

*So. Where was I? Oh, yeah. The look on Pop's face. I wish you could've seen it. Him just sitting there at the curb in his pickup truck, the engine still running, like he's not sure if he wants to get out. Like if he stays right where he is, maybe I'll disappear. Or he can just drive off and when he comes back I'll be gone.*

*But wait. I know what you're thinking. Pickup truck? Yep. You heard right. Can you believe it? Our old man—Mr. College Professor?—driving a pickup? I shit you not.*

*Anyhow, he finally turns the engine off and gets out. Comes up the walk. Me just sitting there, not moving, just watching him. Maybe grinning a little. When he gets to the top step and I finally stand up, he holds out his hand and says, "Wacker." And I say, "Don't nobody call me that anymore." I say the words slow and make it sound all dumb-ass West Virginia, and he makes this face and says,* Don't nobody? *And I say, "You want me to sound more like you, you should've stuck around."*

*So, I hear you wondering. Did I shake his hand, right? Well, I did. I won't lie. I did, Little Brother. Mostly because I haven't figured out exactly how this should go yet. I mean, I know how it all ends. What we agreed has to happen. But I'm still working on the details, you know? The sequence? It has to be perfect. Can't be no rush job. I hope that's all right with you.*

*And see? I barely got started and already I've got things in the wrong order, talking about* him *recognizing* me *right off. Because when he pulled up at the curb, I was the one who didn't recognize him. Part of it was the truck, but he also had this weird-looking guy with him, not somebody you'd expect Pop to hang out with. He looked like those guys you see over by the dumpsters in the Walmart parking lot, waiting for somebody to come along and offer them a half-day shit job for minimum wage. Pop must've told him to stay in the truck, because he didn't get out. Fucker just sat there giving me the stink eye. Like he's already decided I'm bad news. Even when Pop finally gets out of the truck, I'm still not sure if it's him. You remember how he used to dress, right? Shirts with button-down collars. Khakis? Loafers? This guy coming toward me's in jeans and work boots and a denim shirt, and who he reminds me of is—get this—Grandpa Sully.*

*Except wait. Do you remember him at all? Probably not. You were just a baby. To be honest, I don't remember him that great myself. Mostly how he walked with a major limp because he fell off a ladder or some dumb shit like that. And his clothes were always super filthy, like he was a professional ditch digger or something. Anyhow, back then he was about the same age Pop is now, so that could be why he's coming back to me a little, our grandpa Sully. Brother Will was his favorite. That I do remember, but he always did draw the long straw, didn't he? Brother Will? Which means me and you got the short ones.*

*So you gotta be wondering about just how long that straw was, right? This place where our brother grew up and we didn't? The town itself is mostly how I remember it. Nothing special, but not so bad, either. Pop's neighborhood is the nicest. Bunch of big old houses and a few B and Bs set back off the road. Pop's is actually one of the smaller ones, but it's still pretty big and real nice, a lot nicer than anyplace we ever lived in. Two-story job. He asked if I wanted the nickel tour, so I said sure, and he signaled to the weird-looking guy in the truck that it was okay for him to get out now, so he did. Hopped out like a dog would that was waiting that whole time for somebody to whistle. Kind of pitiful. Anyhow, when he joined us on the porch, Pop says to me, "Okay, if nobody calls you Wacker anymore, how should I introduce you?" So I say, "Well, you named me Thomas, so how about that?" "Not Tom?" And I say, "Nope." It was on the tip of my tongue to say, No, only my friends call me that, but I didn't. "And this is Rub," Pop says, meaning the weird-looking guy, and I say, "Good to meet you, Rob." And Pop corrects me. Like it's important his name is actually Rub and not Rob. Like we gotta clear this hurdle before the next thing can happen. "Rub," I say, getting it right this time. "What kind of name is that?" And Pop just shrugs and says, "His." The whole time this Rub character is looking at Pop, like it's his job to explain this shit.*

*Anyhow. Inside we go, the three of us. It's like what you see in a magazine when you're stuck someplace that doesn't have any good ones and you pick it up because there's nothing else. Fireplaces. High ceilings. Dining room separate from the kitchen. Bedrooms with deep closets you can walk into. Except for the front room, there's no furniture anywhere. They've moved it all in there so it's out of the way. Turns out Pop and this Rub guy are renovating the place so Pop can sell it later. "Then what?" I asked him. "Where you planning on going?" But he says he hasn't figured that part out yet. I'm thinking, Someplace me and you won't be able to find him, but I don't say it. Instead, I go, "Well, jeez. Good thing I came when I did, then. Otherwise, I never would've got to see where Will grew up, and I always wanted to."*

*That landed, you could tell.*

*The whole time he's telling me all this, Rob or Rub or whoever he is is paying real close attention, like maybe Pop's plans are news to him, and he doesn't like it. Pop tells him to go on upstairs and finish up tiling the guest bathroom, and he doesn't like that either, being told to go away, which makes me wonder even more who he is and how he fits in. I can see now that the plan me and you cooked up was based on what we knew, which wasn't that much.*

*Anyhow. Guest bathroom. That kind of gives you an idea of what we're talking about. Growing up, did we ever once live anywhere with more than one bathroom for the four of us? This place has two upstairs and three down. Our brother had his own, is what I'm saying, and twice the size of the crappy little ones we shared.*

*He asked about you, Pop did. I told him you were good. Made it sound like, why wouldn't you be? He said he was glad to hear it. Not super glad, like you were real important or always on his mind. Not that kind of glad. More like he was glad you weren't in jail or in Afghanistan.* Too bad I didn't bring you along, *was how he put it. Like it was a shame you didn't get to see what you missed out on your whole damn life because the two of us drew that short straw. But anyway, he did ask after you. Wanted to know what you were doing with your life, what your plans were. So I made up some stuff about how you were taking some courses at the community college. How you just started a new job, doing I wasn't sure what, exactly. The kind of thing I figured he'd want to hear. He also wanted to know if you had a girlfriend, and I said no, you were gay, just to see how he'd react, then told him I was only kidding. He asked those same questions about me, of course, including the one about girls. I told him I got one in trouble a couple years back, but we'd taken care of it, so there was no need to worry. As if he might've, otherwise. Then I told him that wasn't true either, which I'm pretty sure he'd already figured out.*

*You probably don't remember this, but Pop never really laughs, at least not like me and you. Even when something's really funny he just smiles and nods, and it's not even that big of a smile, it's more . . . damn . . . What's the word I'm looking for? Wry. That's it. It's like there's something in him that just won't let him crack up like a normal person. Which is weird to watch. I mean, there I am, busting his balls pretty good, and the whole time he's giving me that half smile of his, the one that says,* Okay, I get it. *Like he's in on the joke. Or like he knows just how I feel, because he felt the same way, back when he was my age. He claims things were pretty much the same between him and Grandpa Sully. Growing up, Pop was always giving him grief about never being around. How his always being AWOL made Pop feel. Which is how he knows how I feel about* him *being AWOL. Like, if I'm pissed off, he can show me right where the line forms. "Except there's a big difference," I said. And he goes, "Yeah? What's that?" And I point out that when he was growing up Grandpa Sully was right here in Bath, in this very house, in fact. Whereas me and you were five hundred miles away, in a whole other state. Which he had to admit was true. But then he gave me that professor look of his, the one that says* Listen up. This *next part is, like, really deep. "Distance," he says, "isn't just measured in miles." And I'm thinking, Gee whiz, Pop. I never thought of that. Explain it to me, will you? Which he does, without me even having to ask. Sure, he admits, Grandpa Sully was just a few blocks away, on the other side of town. He wasn't, like, completely gone. Sometimes Pop would spot him on the street even, outside the pool hall or the place where you can gamble on horse races, but he claimed that just made things worse. 'Cause he was both there and not there. That's the part I'm not supposed to understand, I guess. This other way of measuring distance. So I go, "Fine, if you say so," but what I'm really thinking is,* Bullshit. *I mean, would it really have been worse for me and you if Pop and Will had been living down in West Virginia, instead of up here, when we were growing up? All those times when things got bad between Mom and Dickweed? How would it not have been better to have someplace safe to go until things blew over? And I'm thinking about you even more than me, because you always take things to heart more than I do and Dickweed already suspected something.*

*He asked about Mom, too, more out of curiosity than concern. Mostly he wanted to know if she knew I was coming up here. Whether she tried to talk me out of it. I told him no, I hadn't let on that I was headed up this way. Said I didn't really see that much of her anymore since getting a job and moving out. When he said he was sorry to hear that, I said, "Why?" And he just shrugged and said, "Well, she's your mother," and there's a bunch of things I could've said to that, but instead I just told him I didn't think me and her had that much in common anymore. He wanted to know if she was still married and I said, yeah, she was, and he said good. He was glad to hear it worked out. I about busted a gut at that. Basically, I think talking about her gave him the chance to explain his side of things, give us his version of how we ended up estranged. I kid you not. That's the word he used.* Estranged. *Which apparently means something different from* how come I abandoned you and your brother. *He did admit it wasn't all her fault. He was the one who fucked up by getting involved with that woman at the college where he taught. He didn't blame Mom for being pissed off when she found out, or for not forgiving him or for wanting to get back at him. He guessed he had that coming. But he wanted to make sure I knew it was her that insisted he was no longer welcome in our lives, that he'd forfeited the right to have anything to do with me and you.*

*And get this! He says he sent us presents. Christmas and birthdays both. Claims Mom sent them all back with some sort of fuck-off note. How long did this go on? I asked—figuring maybe he was lying—and he admitted not long. Just the first couple years, because what was the point of him sending us things if she was going to just send them back? Anyhow, it turns out that maybe you were right. Remember that time when we got home from school and there was a package on the kitchen counter with your name on it, with a New York postmark? You got all excited because the next day was your birthday and you figured it was a present from Pop, and I said it couldn't be because I hadn't gotten one on my birthday and why would he send you one and not me? And then the package disappeared and when you wanted to know where it went Mom said she didn't know what you were talking about, that you must've imagined it.*

*So . . . what do you think? Is it true? That she sent our presents* back? Stuff we probably needed? I don't know. I guess I can kind of see it her way. The things he sent us were probably nicer than anything she could afford, and she probably didn't want us comparing his presents to hers.

Anyhow, it was right around then that she took up with Dickweed. Pop says she wrote to tell him how she was getting married again, and her new husband was all the father we'd ever need and the best thing that could happen to me and you would be to forget he ever existed. Which sounds like her. He says he tried to call, but the phone had been disconnected, and when he wrote, his letter was returned with no forwarding address. Anyhow, that's his version. I'd ask her about it except these days, messed up as she is, she doesn't even know what fucking day it is.

Anyhow, when the house tour was over, Pop says, "So, what brings you up this way?" Like he's thinking, okay, this is where I'm going to put the touch on him. Why else would I be here, except to ask for money? So I came up with some lame horseshit about being on my way to Montreal. Told him I'd never been to Canada and thought I'd see what was up. Like wanderlust is my biggest problem in life. Like I'm forever just packing up and going new places. We're back out on the porch now and he looks over at the Yellow Submarine and says, "You think that thing'll make it up and over the Adirondacks?" I told him not to worry. If there was one thing the Sub was used to it was mountains, and he said yeah, he supposed that must be true.

Which reminded me. He did visit us in West Virginia that one time, remember? Him and Will? It must've been about a year after they split up. Before Dickweed. Why, though? Was he hoping to patch things up? Was he worried about us short straws? Man, there's a lot I don't remember. Did he warn Mom they were coming, or did they just show up at the door? How long did they stay? Where? Not with us. I would've remembered that. So . . . a motel? Or did they just head straight back to New York that same day they arrived? Mostly what I remember is Mom screaming at him and him telling her to calm down and her just getting more and more pissed off. Remember how they sent *the three of us outside? Like we wouldn't be able to hear them shouting out there?*

*You remember that backyard? How it was all bare ground and weeds? It had that rusty old swing set with no swings? Just the chains dangling? I remember Will taking it all in. He'd changed a lot. Remember how much bigger he'd got since we'd last seen him? But it was other stuff, too. I noticed how the clothes he had on were nicer than ours. How we needed haircuts and he didn't. And that silver stopwatch. You remember? The one Grandpa Sully gave him? How proud he was of it? Man, I wanted that watch. Okay, maybe* wanted *is the wrong word. I mean, what was it even good for? Fucking thing didn't even tell the time. You just watched the seconds tick away. I didn't want it for myself. I just didn't want him to have it, you know? It was like, as soon as I laid eyes on it, I could see how things were going to go. That our brother was going to have everything his little heart desired and me and you were going to have to scratch. Remember how he didn't even want me to touch it at first? Like I might ruin it somehow? But I kept after him, saying, "Ah, come on. I just want to look at it." You could see he didn't trust me, but he's thinking maybe I'd changed, too. He kind of knows better. Deep down, he's got to know I'm the same kid that used to torment him. But he finally says okay, I can look at it, and hands me the watch. Remember what I did? How I didn't even look at it? Just put it in my pocket? Jesus. The look on his face. Panic, right? I figured he'd just run inside and tattle to Mom and Pop like he used to. Sure, he was a year older than me and bigger now, but I figured he was still a pussy. The last thing I expected was for him to fight.*

*Not that it was a real fight, at least not at first. More like a game. Him trying to get the watch out of my pocket, me laughing and spinning away so he couldn't. Even when he tackled me and we were rolling around on the ground, it was still more like a game than anything. You thought we were just horsing around, right? But then things got serious. Back on our feet. Pushing and shoving. Hard. Then harder, until I caught him a good one. It was his chin I was aiming for with the heel of my hand, but I got his nose instead. I can still see him standing there, blinking at me. Surprised. Blood gushing out of his nose. Good, I thought, that's that. Then all of a sudden I was on my ass. I remember just sitting there, thinking,* What? *Because I never saw that punch coming, Little Bro. I blame you for that. Soon as you saw the blood, you started bawling, like it was your nose bleeding, not his. I must've looked over at you. That's the only way I can figure it. Not seeing that punch. Anyhow, there I was on my butt, him standing there over me with his hand out for the watch. And me just giving it to him. Funny, but I was kind of proud of him. How he'd fought for what was his. Wondering when had he learned to do that? Also how? It couldn't have been Pop that taught him. I mean, back when we were all still a family and I would pinch Will or punch him on the shoulder, and he would tattle, Pop would just shrug and say, "Punch him back," but he never would. So, somebody else must've taught him. Grandpa Sully is my guess. I mean, who else was there?*

*You remember what happened next? How Will just stood there staring at the stopwatch like he didn't recognize it anymore? Like maybe I'd pulled a switch on him? Substituted a crappy watch for his good one. And then he just hands it back to me. Says, "Here. You can have it." Remember the look on his face? I do. It was pity, Little Brother. Or maybe shame. It was like, now that we'd fought, he understood what it all meant. The fight. The watch. The weedy backyard. The whole shebang. How Grandpa Sully had given it to him and didn't give me anything. It was like he knew Mom shopped for our clothes and other stuff at the thrift store. How we didn't get regular haircuts. It was like he'd just figured out that when Mom and Pop split up, there were winners and losers, and we were the losers. That's what the watch meant. That me and you were the losers. Remember how I slapped it away when he tried to get me to take it? Said, "Fuck you"? I'm pretty sure that was the first time I ever used that word, and it was my own brother I said it to. And him just trying to be nice. You gotta admit, that's pretty screwed up, right?*

*Anyhow. After the house tour I told Pop it was time I got back on the road. He wanted to know what's the hurry, I just got here. Why not stay over for a day or two? There's plenty of room. I shit you not. That's what he said. Plenty of room. And I'm thinking,* Oh, yeah? Since when? *By now Rub-Not-Rob is back out on the porch with us and he's giving me the stink eye again, like it's his bedroom Pop's offering and now he'll be out on the street. So like I said, he's one of things I need to figure out. Who this guy is and how he fits in. And something else weird, too. While we're standing there on the porch, here comes this flatbed truck down the street.* GRANDPA ZACK'S TREASURES *written on the door. It slows down, the driver rubbernecking us up on the porch. Somebody Pop knows, because he waves, and for a minute I think the truck's going to pull over, but it doesn't. It just keeps on going. I say, "Who's that?" and Pop says, "Oh, just somebody." Well, hell, I know it's somebody. Everybody's somebody.* Who *was what I was asking. So, I'm getting ready to shove off and telling Pop thanks for showing me around, when here comes that same truck again—Grandpa Zack's Treasures—this time headed in the other direction. The window's rolled down now and I see the driver is a girl and she's staring at us, this weird look on her face, like she's seen a ghost. Then I realize it's not us she's staring at, just* me. *I shit you not, Little Bro. And it kinda freaks me out, you know? Like I show up and this chick I've never seen before gives me the once-over and somehow figures out why I'm here. Just one look, and she knew, knew, KNEW! I'm thinking this time she'll pull over and I'll find out what's up, but nope, she drives right on up the street, just like she done before.*

*Okay, I'm guessing you already got this figured out, right? I do, too, but it took me a minute, because, like I say, it freaked me out. But then it comes to me. Whoever this chick is, she thinks I'm Will. An old girlfriend of his, maybe? Who knows, but it's something else I need to figure out, right? Who's this chick? How does she fit in? Like I said, I want this to go perfect. We waited a long time, me and you. No way I'm going to fuck this up.*

*Anyhow, whoever she is, she's gone and Pop's saying he's glad I came by and why don't I stop again on my way back from Montreal. I tell him thanks but no, I don't have that long off of work. Maybe some other time, I say, now that I know right where he's at and not just his general location. And he just shrugs, as if to say,* Okay, fine, whatever.

*You remember that shrug of his? Weird, but it's what I remember most about him from back when we were all together. That shrug. Like, to him, everything is one big whatever.*

*Here's the part I'm ashamed of, Little Brother. As I'm leaving, I'm thinking, Hell, that wouldn't be so bad, a night or two in the house where our brother grew up. Maybe get an even-better sense of what we missed out on. Got cheated out of. Might even make things a little easier. But then it came to me that I was being tempted, so instead of saying, Yeah, I might just do that, I said, all casual, like it just that second occurred to me, "What's Will up to these days? Where's he at? Still in New York?" Nope. Turns out our brother isn't even in the country. He's in London, England, on a Fulbright, Pop tells me. And I say, "What's that?" So he explains the whole Fulbright deal. I'm not really listening though. Just watching his face. And him trying not to let on how proud he is. At least one of the three of us turned out okay, is what I figure he's thinking. Which I guess means that his "whatever" shrug doesn't apply to Will. Just to me and you. Like always.*

*And I thought to myself, Okay then. That was a close call. He almost had me.*

*Sorry to go on for so long, Little Bro. I got a fair amount to sleep on. I still plan to wrap this up quick as I can and head on back. There's a bunch of cheap motels out on the highway, so tonight I'll just check into one of those. Make it an early night. Or maybe drive into this Schuyler Springs place and check it out. There's a racetrack there, I hear, and some other stuff. Main thing is to not let things get too out of hand. Not get hammered. Which is pretty tempting. I gotta admit, seeing Pop after so long knocked me sideways a little. I kind of wish I hadn't remembered about that fight between me and Will all those years ago. What I can't get out of my head is how scared you were. How hard you cried. How I told you to quit blubbering like a damn baby. That there was nothing to cry about. I shouldn't have done that. There was a lot to cry about and you were still this little guy who didn't understand. What was happening to us. Why Mom kept screaming at Pop inside. Why Pop and Will were there in the first place. You'd just got used to them being gone, and now here they were again. And everybody was shouting and fighting. You couldn't figure it out. Which is why I do wonder sometimes. Did we fuck you up that day, me and Will? Fighting like we did? Probably not. Probably that's just me being crazy. Hell, I bet you don't even remember that fight. Still. Crazy or not, that's what I wonder sometimes. If maybe it was me and him?*

# Proctologist

R**UTH WAS IN** a funk. As she sat in the corner booth at Hattie's Lunch, waiting patiently for her granddaughter to pick her up, her thoughts had drifted to the subject of men, specifically to that period in her life when she decided she'd be much better off without them. Roughly a decade ago that had been. The three men who'd been front of mind when she arrived at this out-of-character conclusion were the two in her own life—her husband, Zack, and Sully, her longtime paramour—and the one in her daughter Janey's, a genuine fuckwad by the name of Roy Purdy. But all men, really. Lord, what filthy creatures they were. For starters, they were gassy, every single one of them. Nor was that the worst of it. They tracked dirt into the house and set things that were coated with grime on the kitchen counter and then just walked away. They had to be told to go wash their hands, and when they returned, they still had black under their fingernails. They left bathroom towels dark with smudges, the sink streaked with brown, the rim of the toilet spotted yellow. Even worse was the raw sewage that so many carried around in their heads. Better to be shut of the lot of them, Ruth had concluded. Go somewhere warm and clean, the Caribbean maybe, someplace where she could swim in the ocean and take long showers under one of those big, rainfall showerheads. With no men around, maybe she could get clean.

Now that all three of the men she'd been thinking about back then were gone and she was surrounded by women—her daughter, Janey, and Tina, her granddaughter—Ruth was no longer so sure. Yes, the air was fresher and the bathroom towels stayed clean longer. The toilet's porcelain rim remained snowy white, not to mention the nearby floor. But there was something so *knowable* about men. If you paid attention, even a little, you could figure them out—what they wanted, what made them tick—even if they themselves couldn't. Admit it, she kind of missed them. Well, not her son-in-law, of course. Ten years earlier Roy Purdy had beaten her into a coma, and on cold damp days like this one, every bone in her aged body ached, especially her jaw and left cheekbone, both of which he'd fractured with his fists. Awake, she never thought about Roy anymore, but every now and then he would find her in sleep. Her own damn fault. Most nights, the last thing she did before switching off the light on her bedside table was to roll over onto her side or stomach. It was always when she fell asleep on her back that Roy came calling, his knees pinning her elbows at her sides so he could pummel her face with his fists, his own twisted visage, blurry but rapturous, floating above her. She never felt those dream blows land. It was his being on top of her, her inability to free her arms from beneath his weight, that was so frightening. When she woke up from other nightmares, her sheets and blanket would always be tangled from her thrashing. When Roy visited, though, her arms would be motionless at her side, just like they'd been when it happened for real, and it would take a moment for Ruth to realize she had command of them, that he wasn't really on top of her, making movement impossible. "Get off me, Roy," she'd tell him then, though not actually speaking out loud. "You're dead and we both know it." Which was true. By the time Ruth had awakened from the coma Roy had put her in, he himself had met a grizzly end and was no longer a danger to herself, or Janey, or Tina, though Ruth suspected he visited their dreams as well.

Sometimes she dreamed about Sully, too. Those dreams weren't disturbing like the recurring Roy one. Seeing him always made her smile. But in the end the dreams where he made an appearance were strangely dispiriting. They'd been lovers for most of their adult lives, but toward the end there they'd sworn off sex, at Ruth's own insistence. It was the right thing to do, she'd informed him. She could no longer pretend that their carrying on was a secret, or that it ever had been. Everybody in town knew, including her husband and daughter. Nor could she pretend their affair hadn't damaged her family, Janey in particular.

She'd expected Sully to protest, though, and when he didn't, her feelings had been deeply wounded. And later, after her husband died and there was nothing to prevent them from picking up where they'd left off, he'd hurt those feelings again by expressing a belated moral reservation of his own. He hadn't minded going behind her husband's back when Zack was alive, but now that he was dead, it occurred to Sully that they'd been friends all along, which made it feel wrong. Ruth might've been able to accept this if she hadn't suspected that it wasn't the real reason, that Sully was offering this excuse because he couldn't bring himself to tell her the truth—that he no longer found her desirable. She'd never looked the same after what Roy did to her. She knew this. She'd undergone several surgeries, but the swelling in her face never entirely went away and her shattered cheekbone was now asymmetrical with its mate. She couldn't really blame Sully. It still broke her heart, though, because Ruth knew she'd always been a homely woman. One of the reasons she'd loved Sully was that he, more than any other man, had been able to look past that, and she hated to think that the beating Roy gave her had made her so unlovely that even Sully was repulsed.

In other respects, Sully had remained as devoted as ever, dropping by Hattie's just about every day, inviting her to join him at the Horse for dinner or drinks. Plus, she owed him. Boy, did she ever. It had been Sully who'd magically appeared in the nick of time to keep Roy from killing her, and Sully's had been the last face she'd seen before slipping into blessed oblivion. And except for the nurses in the intensive care ward, his had been the first face she saw when she returned to consciousness two days later. By coincidence, he himself had been admitted to the hospital with congestive heart failure, and fresh from surgery to implant a pacemaker, he'd somehow walked the length of the emergency room corridor, pulled up a chair beside her bed, fished under the blanket for her hand and held it until she opened her eyes. That had somehow given her the idea that when she actually *did* die his would be the last face she'd see, but no, he'd gone and messed that up by dying first. Eighteen months without him now, except for his occasional dream visits, and even those were regrettably chaste. Apparently, their decision to swear off sex was still binding.

Ruth did not dream of her husband at all, perhaps because her waking life was still so full of the man. She still lived in the house he'd inherited from his mother when she finally got around to dying. "Mother Ruthless," Ruth had called her, because her name was also Ruth and because she'd never bothered to disguise her disdain for the girl her son decided to marry. Even after the old woman had moved into a nursing home, the house had somehow remained hers, and in all the years they'd lived there Ruth had never not hated it. When she confessed this to her granddaughter, who now owned the house, as well as her grandfather's salvage business, Tina had proposed buying her a condo in Schuyler, or even one of the overpriced Old Mill Lofts in downtown Bath. "Let her, for Christ's sake," Janey had advised. "I wish she'd buy me one." But Ruth had declined the offer. It wasn't the cost. She knew Tina could afford it. The problem was that Ruth considered Tina's money to be her husband's, even though it was Tina who'd made a real success of his business. What Ruth couldn't get past was the fact that Zack had kept all that money a secret for so long, hidden away in a savings account she never knew the existence of until his passing. All those years of scrimping, and him sitting on all that cash. They could've gone places, done things, lived entirely different lives.

Here again, though, she had no one but herself to blame. Zack had had his reasons for keeping that secret. She'd never taken his business seriously, never even acknowledged that the long hours he spent rescuing broken, discarded crap from the dump and people's front terraces *was* a business. Hattie's Lunch? *That* was a business. It had a name (even if it was the previous owner's) and a cash register and employees and regular hours. Unlike her husband, Ruth paid rent and taxes that funded local schools and filled potholes. What her husband had, she maintained, was a hobby. In the end, though, what it really came down to was that by not taking his business seriously, she hadn't taken *him* seriously. *That* was why he'd never told her about the secret account. So no, she couldn't let Tina buy her a condo. If Zack hadn't wanted her to have the money in life, then he could keep it in death. Tina had never pressed the idea, which suggested to Ruth that her granddaughter felt the same way. It was Grandpa Zack, not Ruth, who'd been her special friend. She'd been the oddest of kids, and he, more than Ruth, or even Janey, had accepted that oddness, maybe even valued it. No wonder she'd loved him and always took his side. Took it even now, causing a rift between her and her mother that seemingly could not be bridged.

Anyway, the question Ruth had to ask herself was: Would she, in hindsight, have done things differently? And the answer: probably not. Should she have broken off her relationship with Sully sooner? Probably, but *should* wasn't the same as *would*. Her husband's hobby, business—whatever you called it—had kept him out of her hair. If he hadn't been out scavenging, he'd have been sitting at the counter at Hattie's, driving away her regular customers.

"She's late," Janey said, sliding into the corner booth and interrupting her reverie.

Glancing at the clock, Ruth saw that her daughter was right. It was three-thirty. The last of the malingerers at the lunch counter had left, and Janey had flipped the OPEN sign on the door to CLOSED.

"Should I give you a lift home?"

"Let's give her a few more minutes," Ruth said, "unless you're in a hurry?"

It was strange, though. Tina was usually punctual about fetching her at three. Ruth didn't come into Hattie's every day because she hated to take up a booth. There'd been a time when she could be of more use, but those days were gone. Arthritis had finished what

Roy started, making a cripple of her. On good days, she required only a cane, on bad ones a walker, so no more running around behind the counter or trips to the walk-in, and there was only so much you could do sitting down. You could make silverware roll-ups, refill salt and pepper shakers, the ketchup and maple-syrup bottles, wipe down the menus. She'd purchased a cheap laptop so she could help her daughter keep the books and do inventory, but that was about it. She spent three days a week at the diner, but that was mostly for a change of scenery and because, with her daughter and granddaughter mostly on the outs, she wouldn't have seen Janey, otherwise.

"You looked lost in thought just now," Janey told her.

"I guess I was." It happened more and more, actually.

"Sully?"

"And your father." No need to mention Roy. "Do you have plans for tonight?"

"One of the waitresses out at the Horse called in sick," she said. "Birdie called to ask if I wanted the shift. I don't, but I could use the money. After that, if I'm not too whipped I may head out to the Hand."

The Green Hand was a cop bar out by the racetrack in Schuyler. Janey had a new man in her life. Del, his name was. Conrad Delgado. Ruth had disliked him even before she found out he was a cop, but then she never liked the men her daughter was attracted to. Every single one of them seemed to have a mean streak. When she'd shared her reservations with Janey, her daughter had defended the man, saying he was just going through a bad patch. When Schuyler's police chief resigned last year, Del had thought he'd be a shoo-in for the job, but he'd been passed over and was still angry about that, and he was also going through a particularly acrimonious divorce. His second, Janey admitted when pressed. She hadn't admitted to sleeping with the man yet, but of course she was. She'd always been oversexed, which, Ruth had to admit, she came by rightly. Like her mother, she wanted to be wanted, needed to be needed. Tina, Ruth suspected, was the same way, but also different. The requisite physical urge was there, but her emotions were more closed off. In high school she'd fallen hard for Sully's grandson Will, who'd been kind to her, but Ruth was pretty sure there'd been no one since. When she and her granddaughter were together, she noticed that Tina would find excuses to drive past the house on Upper Main where Will had lived with his father. History repeating itself? Ruth hoped not. She'd tried to tell her granddaughter that *Sullivan* was a synonym for *heartbreak,* but the poor girl had been too far gone. There were reasons to believe she still was, a decade later.

"You look worn out," Ruth said, studying Janey now. Hard to believe her daughter was in her midforties, but she was.

Janey shrugged. "I look like you used to. Rode hard and put up wet." When Ruth didn't deny this, her daughter stared out the window, as if she, too, might be wondering where the years had gone. "I wish Daddy were still alive," she continued, "so I could kill him."

"Janey—"

"Don't Janey me. I'm serious. Giving her everything and me nothing?"

"He didn't leave me anything, either."

"Yeah, but he had a reason for that." Sully she meant. "What the hell did *I* ever do to him?"

"That's not what he was thinking," Ruth assured her. "He knew you were strong, like me. He knew you'd be okay. It was Tina he was worried about."

"Except it turns out she's stronger than you and me put together."

"Yeah, but he didn't know that. And besides. You should be happy for her."

"Yeah, I love always being the hind tit."

"I'm not saying—"

"How come people like us can't ever get ahead, is what I'd like to know. You worked seventy-hour weeks your whole life and what'd it get you?"

"I never minded the work."

"You were exhausted the whole time."

"I never minded the exhaustion."

"Yeah? Well, I *do,*" Janey said. "Isn't working hard supposed to get you somewhere? Wasn't that the deal?"

"There was a deal?"

"Wasn't there? That's what they taught us in school." She shook her head. "Del says the deck's stacked against us."

"Who's *us*?"

Janey didn't bother to answer. "Rich people get to pass their money on to their kids. We get to pass on our poverty."

"Some people figure it out. Manage to make a go of it."

Janey made a face. "Oh, great. We're going to talk about Tina now?"

Ruth shrugged. But, yeah, it was Tina she was thinking about. The success she'd made. Like her grandfather, she had a gift for knowing what she could turn a profit on. But Tina's gift was greater. She seemed able to look at a thing and assess its intrinsic worth, which might not be the same as knowing what she could sell it for. Unless Ruth was mistaken, she had a similar instinct for assessing people.

"That was Daddy's doing and you know it. If he'd given me all that money, I might've come out smelling like a rose, too."

It was on the tip of Ruth's tongue to say that she doubted it, but she loved her daughter and so held her tongue.

"Did I ever tell you about the proctologist?" Ruth asked her.

Janey just stared at her. Proctologist?

Ruth hadn't thought about the episode in decades. Its memory was suddenly just there, the details vivid. Late morning, the breakfast rush over, there'd been just one customer at the counter, a quiet well-dressed stranger reading the newspaper. Normally Ruth would've been behind the counter herself, but she needed to restock the fridge for the lunch crowd, so she'd taken advantage of the lull to visit the walk-in cooler. She returned to see her husband doing what she wouldn't have permitted had she arrived in time to prevent it—that is, sliding onto the stool next to her lone customer. How many times had she begged him not to bother people? Zack, of course, refused to believe he was doing any such thing. The way he saw it, he was simply being friendly. Because he hated being alone himself, he naturally assumed that other people would be happy to have company, even in those cases where it was clear—to Ruth, at least—that they wouldn't.

The man reading the newspaper that morning had looked up, clearly startled, and why not? There were empty stools up and down the counter.

"Zack," Ruth said, coming over to where they sat. "Give the poor man some space."

Ordinarily, when addressed in this tone of voice, the one that indicated his wife was in no mood to be messed with, Zack did as instructed. This time, for some reason, he was undaunted. Indeed, instead of adopting the hangdog posture of a man caught doing something he knew he shouldn't, he nudged the fellow's elbow, as if they were coconspirators. "My wife," he confided, as if to say, *Women. What can you do?*

"Zack?" Ruth repeated. "He's reading the newspaper. You're interrupting him."

"No problem," the man said genially, offering Zack his hand. "I'm Dennis."

"See?" Zack said, and damned if he didn't meet her eye, something he never had the courage to do when they were arguing. "No problem."

And just that quickly, it was two against one, and she the one.

"So, Dennis," Zack continued, ignoring the fact that Ruth was still standing there, glowering at him, "what line of work are you in?"

*For the love of God,* Ruth thought, though she shouldn't have been surprised. Intrusive, personal questions were her husband's favorite opening conversational gambit. As he'd often explained to her, most people liked to talk about themselves, especially what they did for a living. Better yet, Zack figured, after they told you about themselves, they'd sometimes ask what *you* did, and then you could launch right in, tell them all about the stuff people put out on their terraces to be hauled off, stuff they thought was worthless but wasn't. How, if you understood a thing's value, you could take it home and fix it up and sell it. Make yourself a tidy profit. Hell, the town dump was full of treasures, too, if you knew what to look for.

"No, it's fine," the man assured Ruth, before turning to Zack. "I'm a physician, actually."

Encouraged, Zack pressed on. "A doctor? What kind?"

"Well, for a long time I was a general practitioner, but now I'm a proctologist."

Zack nodded, slowly processing this new information. "Isn't that the kind that—"

"Yes, it is," Dennis smiled, picking his newspaper back up. To Ruth, he had the look of a man who knew from experience that he'd just delivered a gold-plated conversation stopper. After all, how did one respond to such an announcement? *Gee, that must be interesting work?*

Zack mulled it over, unwilling, Ruth could tell, to let matters lie there, but unsure just how to proceed. She understood, of course, exactly what her husband wanted to ask. Why would somebody who got to examine the entirety of the human body want to specialize in its least attractive feature?

"So . . . ," he said finally, "how come you switched?"

"Well, here's the thing," the man said. "There's real money in shit."

"Hah!" Janey said, clearly delighted when Ruth delivered this punch line. "And what did Daddy say to that?"

Strangely, Ruth couldn't remember. What had happened next was simply gone, as if a shade had suddenly been drawn and the scene, so bright and vivid a moment earlier, had inexplicably gone dark. Was it her memory starting to fail, like everything else, or did the drawn shade mean that the story was somehow over, that whatever happened next was of no consequence? For that matter, why had the long-forgotten incident returned to her in the first place? Then suddenly Ruth understood. Back then she hadn't known about her husband's secret bank account, about how much money was piling up in it. Which meant she had no more way of knowing than the proctologist himself that he was speaking to a man who was uniquely qualified to understand him. Who knew better than Zack that there was money in shit? No sooner did she think this than an even-stranger thought came to her. At the time Ruth had viewed the man as speaking to her husband, but what if in some strange, cosmic way he'd been sent there to deliver a coded message to *her*? Could it be that this was the universe's way of playing fair? Because had she been paying attention, she might've comprehended the metaphorical wisdom the proctologist was imparting. It also occurred to her that if the man had actually been speaking more to her than to her husband, then Zack was also, in a sense, speaking more to her than to his new friend. Sure, he was always trying to chat up strangers, but what if his intended audience was really Ruth? When her husband steered conversations to his business, trying to get people to understand what he did and why he did it, what if he was having with them the very conversation she herself had stubbornly refused to engage in? She'd always assumed that his purpose was to get these strangers to see him as someone important. But what if it was Ruth herself he'd been trying to impress? What if he was trying to tell her that, deep down, he knew the terrible truth—that she was ashamed of him? And her refusing to listen. She'd always assumed that *he* was the one who never picked up on things, who was oblivious to life's signals. But what if *she* was the one?

"Mom?" Janey had taken her hand and was looking at her with real concern. "Are you okay?"

Ruth was, she realized, crying. She could feel the tears tracking down her cheeks.

"Can you tell me what's the matter?"

"I don't know," Ruth told her, though that was a lie. Everything was the matter. The world was a place where signals that might have saved you never made it through the noise. But mostly this: she'd lived too long.

# BlackBerry

───────

L ORD," CHARICE SAID, massaging her temples with her thumbs, "what a day. Times like these I miss cigarettes."

"I didn't know you ever smoked," said Raymer, surprised.

"I didn't. That doesn't mean I can't miss it."

Raymer disagreed. To his way of thinking, that was exactly what it meant.

In the parking lot out back of the Sans Souci, though it was still late afternoon, darkness had fallen almost completely. As they leaned up against their vehicles, mentally exhausted from the long, dispiriting afternoon, it occurred to Raymer that the woman standing before him wasn't the one he'd been picturing lately. For some reason, since they put their relationship on pause, the Charice he'd been conjuring in his mind was the one he'd fallen in love with a decade earlier, back when there was still a place called North Bath and he was its chief of police and Charice was running the station. How full of sass she'd been then, forever busting his balls over every little thing, even as she playfully conveyed that, yes, she cared about him and had a higher opinion of him, perhaps, than he had of himself. What a mischievous long game she'd played back then. Claiming to have a tiny butterfly tattoo on her buttock, she'd warned him that if he didn't let her out from behind that desk soon it would turn into a pterodactyl. "Why did you tell me you had a butterfly?"

he asked later, after they finally became lovers and a thorough examination had revealed no such tattoo. "Made you think about it, though, didn't I," she chuckled.

What happened to that girl? he wondered now, and immediately felt guilty. If Dr. Qadry were here, she'd no doubt ask him if this was the right question. Had it occurred to him that his remembering Charice's younger self so fondly might be less about her than him? That maybe what he was really expressing was his preference for how things had been when *he* was in charge and she had to do what he said? He would pooh-pooh that idea, of course, and remind her that even when it had been his job to issue orders and hers to carry them out, Charice had regarded his instructions as mere suggestions she was free to pick and choose among. His therapist, of course, would buy none of that. She'd just give him that smile, the one that said, *Are you listening to yourself right now?* After which she'd quickly be off on some new tack. *Why do you think she told you it was a butterfly?* Like he was supposed to know? *She could have invented anything. Why a butterfly?* One leading question after another until he arrived, exhausted, at whatever cockamamie destination she had in mind. *Do you think it's possible she wanted you to understand that butterflies are meant to be free, not stuck on the end of some man's phallic pin?* God, he hated psychiatry.

Anyway, they'd somehow made it through the long afternoon, and for the time being, there was nothing further to be done. Virgil Canfield, the coroner, and his crew, had been and gone. Klieg lights had been brought in and photos of the scene taken. The body—what was left of it—was on its way to the morgue. Like most guys in his line of work Virgil didn't like to speculate until he'd had a chance to do a thorough autopsy, but he'd mostly confirmed Raymer's own conclusion—that there was no reason to suspect foul play. Whoever the poor devil was, he'd climbed the stairs that led to the balcony, secured one end of the rope to the iron railing and the other around his neck. It wasn't even a real noose, just the kind of knot you'd use to tie your shoes. Somehow it had held when the man climbed over the railing and leaped. Nor, even more amazingly, had the knot unraveled in the interim, which Virgil estimated to be any-where between six and eight weeks. It was February now, so prob-ably December or early January. "Some people just can't handle the holidays," Virgil had observed wryly.

"Look," Raymer said. "I'm sorry about . . . in there."

Charice frowned at him, clearly not following.

"With Franklin," Raymer explained. Though Charice had made clear that she and not Raymer was in charge and despite the fact that Raymer had tried to stay in the background as she ques-tioned the town manager about how they'd come to discover the body, the other man's eyes kept flickering in Raymer's direction, as if to acknowledge that *he,* a white man, must be the one who was *really* in charge. "I think my being there made your job harder. You had it covered."

"Welcome to my world."

Raymer consulted his watch. Four forty-five. Way too early for dinner, but he hadn't had anything to eat since breakfast. "You hungry?"

"I shouldn't be," she said, "after spending the afternoon with a rotting corpse, but I am. And a debrief might not be a bad idea. Where should we go?"

Raymer didn't care where they went, so long as it wasn't their separate ways. When Charice finally arrived at the Sans Souci at noon, he'd half expected her to send him away. After all, he wasn't officially a cop anymore. But she'd said, No, stick around, so he had. She'd stationed Miller out front at the main entrance to the hotel with orders not to let anyone in, especially not the press, while the coroner's crew worked the scene. "Doesn't matter to me," Raymer told her. "Want to try the Green Hand?"

She narrowed her eyes at him.

"What," he said.

"No, I just find it amazing that you would suggest the very last place on the entire planet that I'd want to go to."

"Why?" Raymer had never been there, but he'd heard the Hand was a favorite hangout for Schuyler cops, and his thought had been that she might enjoy being among friendly faces. On the other hand, if the rank and file drank there, maybe Charice wouldn't feel comfortable. What was it Miller had told him that morning? That he didn't like how some of the guys down at the station talked about her? At the time he hadn't wanted to know about that. Now he wished he'd let Miller elaborate.

"Actually," she said, ignoring his question, "let's avoid Schuyler altogether."

They settled on the Horse, which would be quiet and where they could talk without being overheard. Raymer, who seldom ate out, hadn't been there in forever, but the place was just as he remembered it, the same sad strand of Christmas lights strung along the backbar, and he was pretty sure the woman who greeted them—what the hell was her name?—was the owner. He'd heard a rumor a while back that the place was about to go under, but that hadn't happened. The dining room was completely empty, though, not a good sign on a Saturday, despite its still being early. When they were shown to a cozy two-top, Charice asked if they could have the half-moon booth on the far side of the room. When they slid in, the woman handed them two small, laminated menus. "Limited options, I'm afraid, this being the off-season. Mostly burgers and wings and pizza."

"Just drinks for now," Charice told her. "There might be three of us." This was dispiriting news to Raymer, who'd been looking forward to having Charice all to himself. Who had she invited to join them? Did she not want to be alone with him? They'd taken both their vehicles from the Sans Souci, and when he'd checked his rearview to see if she was still behind him, he could see she was on her cell. His first thought was that she must be talking to somebody at the station, but for that she probably would've used her radio. He'd checked twice more, and both times she was still on her phone. She'd hung up only when they made the turn into the Horse's parking lot. He'd considered asking who she was talking to, but then thought again. Had he asked Dr. Qadry's advice—why would he?—he had little doubt she'd ask him why he wanted to know. Was it possible that *this* was why Charice had needed more space? And anyway, as long as it wasn't Dr. Qadry herself that Charice had invited to join them, he supposed he could bear up. His idea of hell would be for those two smart women to tag-team him over dinner.

"Do you sell beer by the pitcher?" he inquired of the woman—*Birdie!* her name fluttered back to him on the frail wings of memory—who'd just seated them.

"Little-known fact," she said. "The beer pitcher was invented right here on these very premises."

Charice cocked her head. "Little known because it's not true?"

"That could have something to do with it," Birdie admitted. "Large or small?"

"Large," Raymer said. Especially if there was going to be three of them.

"Just a Coke for me," Charice said, adding, when Raymer arched a brow, "After today, if I start, I'll never stop."

"Then don't," he said. Alcohol had been known to make Charice frisky, and they hadn't frisked each other in nearly a month.

"I need a clear head. I hope you don't mind me inviting Jerome?"

"Jerome," he said.

"See? There you go again."

"What?"

"Every time I say my brother's name you repeat it."

"I'm sorry."

"And then you say you're sorry."

"I'm *not* sorry?"

She was smiling at him now. "No, you're definitely sorry," she told him. "I just thought maybe he could help us think all this through."

"There's something to think through?"

Because the man, whoever he was, had clearly taken his own life. The only question was why, and they were unlikely to determine that until after they learned his identity, which they would, eventually. Raymer had noticed a rectangular outline in the dead man's back pocket. He'd figured it was probably a wallet, but instead it was a cell phone, an early model BlackBerry, the kind where the QWERTY keyboard took up half the device. The battery was dead, of course, but as soon as the phone could be recharged, they'd probably know who they'd just spent the afternoon with. Strange, though, that the man's other pockets had all been empty. No wallet. No keys. Had he wanted to remain unknown to those who discovered him? Had he been embarrassed that it had come to this? When Virgil remarked that some people just couldn't handle the holidays, he'd been joking, but what if it was true? What if the man had killed himself at the Sans Souci to spare a wife or child from coming home to a spectacle? A picture would emerge, eventually. When the phone got recharged, it would probably be full of heartbreaking voice messages and emails. *Dad, where are you? How come you aren't picking up?* Or maybe threats from his credit card company. *Your account is three months past due. Call us at your earliest convenience to avoid having your account turned over to a collection agency.*

"I need to coax him back into the world," Charice was saying, still on the subject of her brother. "Get him outside his own head."

"Actually?" Raymer said. "I was kind of looking forward to a couple hours with just the two of us."

"Well," she said, rising from the table, "you'll probably get your wish. He said he'd think about it, but these days that's Jerome for no. Anyway, I need to hit the ladies'. Order us some wings?"

"Okay."

"Don't eat them all."

"How long are you going to be gone?"

"I might be a while. I been holding it since I arrived at the Sans Souci."

In other words she had to call the station, get brought up to speed on what had transpired in her absence. When Birdie returned with his pitcher of beer and Charice's Coke and set them down in the center of the table, she wrinkled her nose. "What's that smell?" she said.

There were times when Raymer wished his old nemesis Dougie were still around. Dougie would've told her, *Eau de cadaver.*

=

WHILE CHARICE WAS in the ladies', Raymer scrolled through the pictures he'd taken with his phone back at the Sans Souci. The investigation's official photos were taken by a police photographer, but lately Raymer had gotten into the habit of snapping a few of his own. He'd come to think of them as context photos, an attempt to capture a more macro experience. He found that the more pictures he took, the less he had to rely on written notes. Later, after the investigation concluded, he would delete most of the photos, though he always kept one or two. What had struck him most forcefully today, what he didn't want to forget, was how surreal it had all felt, like something out of a mostly forgotten dream. Bert Franklin, the city manager, had arranged with the utility company for the electricity to be turned on throughout the building, but for some reason that hadn't happened. The power was on in the lobby, but only a few lamps were lit, leaving much of the space in semidarkness. The room had been full of draped furniture, as were several other rooms they'd passed through. The cavernous ballroom, however, was lit only from the outside, pale, wintry light streaming in from the dirty second- and third-story windows. It had put Raymer in mind of a cathedral from which the altar and pews had been removed, leaving an architectural husk that was simultaneously sanctified and unholy. Unlike the other rooms they'd come through, this one was completely empty. Had the furniture and accessories all been sold off? Or had its contents for some reason been removed and stored elsewhere? Whatever the explanation, the resulting emptiness made the man hanging from the second-floor balcony appear that much more lonely, as if he'd been left behind by whoever had removed everything of value. A rickety card table had been set up near the entry, on top of which sat a Phillips-head screwdriver and a half-used roll of packing tape. The walls were pockmarked where the lighting fixtures had been removed, the dusty floor bare except for a small pile of broken-down cardboard boxes, a broom with a broken handle, a plastic dustpan and, inexplicably, a telephone handset minus its cord.

The most disturbing of today's photos was the one he'd taken from the balcony. What had possessed Raymer to go up there in the first place? Had he been trying to stay out of Charice's way? Letting her do her job? Whatever. As he peered over the railing, it had taken him a moment to grasp what he was looking at. From above, the hanged man seemed to be wearing a rust-colored skullcap. How, Raymer wondered, had it managed to stay on the top of his head when he leaped? Except it wasn't a skullcap. Something—a rodent?—had scrabbled down the rope and chewed its hungry way into the man's skull.

Sitting comfortably in a warm booth and drinking cold beer, Raymer wondered if maybe the time had come to walk away from such grizzly details. At what point did their cumulative effect become trauma and do permanent injury to the psyche? Was there such a thing as violence porn, and was this photo an example? If so, maybe he should take that desk job in Albany. Preserve what was left of his sanity. If his old friend Dougie were still around, he would no doubt advise Raymer to man up, to quit being such a wimp. Compared with big-city cops, who witnessed human depravity and unspeakable violence on an almost daily basis, his own life in North Bath law enforcement had been relatively benign. He'd glimpsed true evil on one or two occasions, most recently in the form of a grinning, sleepy-eyed young man who'd trafficked in poisonous reptiles, an encounter that had nearly cost Raymer his life. But mostly the job had required him to bear witness to a seemingly endless parade of baroque, small-town folly—barroom brawls with cue sticks for weapons and dim-witted erotic experiments that ended in visits to the emergency room, but not the morgue. All things considered, he'd been pretty fortunate.

On the other hand, not many big-city cops had been struck by lightning in a cemetery and, as a result, woken up with a chatty malignant sprite in their heads, one who, for all Raymer knew, might still be in his head somewhere, waiting for Raymer to scuff across a thick carpet in his socks and touch the refrigerator door's metal handle, thereby completing the circuit of static electricity required for his reappearance—*Zzzzzzt! Here's Dougie!* Maybe the best way to prevent that eventuality was to find a new line of work, leave policing to those who were temperamentally cut out for it, who could look at a photo like this one and not be haunted. Why not put this part of his life behind him before it was too late? Unless, of course, it already was. Was this what Charice was having such a hard time conveying to him—that he was already a borderline wacko? He didn't think he was, at least not yet, but if your head was messed up, you yourself wouldn't necessarily be the best judge, right? Your brain was what you used to identify and fix things that were broken. If *it* was broken, weren't you fresh out of tools?

When he looked up from his screen and saw Charice returning, he quickly switched off the phone so she wouldn't see the grizzly photo he couldn't quit staring at.

"I didn't say you had to wait," Charice said, indicating the steaming plate of wings that had magically appeared in the center of the table while his mind was back at the Sans Souci. "I just wanted you to save me some."

Five minutes earlier he'd been hungry, but when he saw that the sauce the wings were slathered in was the exact same rust color as the dead man's skullcap, Raymer's stomach lurched. "You may have to eat them all," he told her.

If she heard this, she gave no sign. "Jerome will not be joining us," she said, and the violence with which she stabbed the wings on the big plate onto her own smaller one suggested that she might be imagining stabbing her brother. *Good,* Raymer thought. Excellent, in fact. If she was mad at Jerome, then she wasn't mad at him.

"I'm sorry," he said, an outright lie.

"Probably just as well," she said. "Have you ever watched Jerome eat a chicken wing?"

"I haven't, no."

"He uses a knife and fork."

Seeing this in his mind's eye, Raymer couldn't help smiling.

"It's not funny," she insisted, still fuming.

"No," Raymer agreed. It was hilarious. Also pathetic. And very, very Jerome.

"I've never been as angry with him as I am right now," she said, which buoyed Raymer's spirits even further. "I actually hung up on him."

"I'm sorry," Raymer repeated giddily.

If she was really listening to him, she gave no sign. "Promise not to repeat this?" she said, pointing a half-gnawed wing at him. "Awful as that was at the Sans Souci? It was a relief to have something besides him to think about."

"He's really that bad?" *Tell me all about it.*

"He barely leaves his room. Remember his meltdown after Becka died?"

As if he would ever forget. Drunk on a toxic cocktail of grief and guilt, Jerome had become convinced that Raymer had known all along about his affair with Becka, that he was only pretending innocence. At one point he'd become so untethered from reality that he actually believed Raymer was sneaking into his condo when he was away so that he could torment Jerome by subtly moving his things—the TV remote on the coffee table, his shampoo in the shower, the creamer in the fridge. That Raymer would exact this sort of revenge actually made sense to him. Still, if Jerome had been losing his mind, he'd had company. Raymer, too, had been drinking liberally from the same goblet of guilt and remorse. In Dr. Qadry's professional opinion, it had been the anguish over Becka's loss, not the lightning strike, that had caused asshole Dougie to take up residence in his head and wreak havoc there. And when a scratch on Raymer's palm became infected, the resulting fever had caused him to hallucinate so vividly that he feared he, too, might be cracking up. He and Jerome had both ended up in the same hospital, where, until the antibiotics Raymer was given finally kicked in, it was impossible, according to Charice, to tell which of them was more bonkers.

It was clear which of them she'd been more concerned about,

however, and this had caused Dougie to do a celebratory victory lap around the inside of Raymer's skull. *What have I been telling you?* he crowed. *Who did you* think *she'd choose? You?*

"Jerome is her *brother*," Raymer had foolishly attempted to explain. "Her twin. It's natural."

*Natural?* Dougie hooted. *There's nothing natural about those two. You should come right out and ask her sometime. See what she says.*

Raymer knew better than to follow up on this oblique reference, but he couldn't help himself. "Ask her what?"

*Don't pretend you don't know what I'm talking about,* Dougie had replied with a nasty chuckle.

"Ask her what?" he insisted, though God help him he *did* suspect what Dougie was about to say.

*If she and her brother ever did the nasty.*

Thank God, Raymer thought now, he'd had the good sense not to share Dougie's revolting suspicion with Dr. Qadry, because that would've been one more thing she'd have recommended that he own. (Though apparently he'd done exactly that, because here he was remembering it.)

"I don't know how much longer I can be there for him," Charice was saying, "and also deal with everything at work."

"Everything, as in . . . what, exactly?" He was hoping to sound innocent, merely curious, but he saw immediately that this was not how his question landed.

"Okay," she said, her eyes narrowing at him. "Give. What've you heard?"

"Nothing," he said, not wanting to throw Miller under the bus. "Bullshit."

"Charice," he said. "You know how busy I've been closing up the station. And I promised when you took the Schuyler job, I'd keep my nose out of your business there, remember?"

"Which you have," she admitted, and it pleased him that she sounded at least a bit contrite. "But people gossip."

"About what? You might as well tell me. I can't help you if you don't."

"Doug," she said. "Trust me. You can't help me if I *do*."

"Sounds like maybe it's *you* who doesn't trust *me*." She wanted to. He could see that much, but something was holding her back. "Look," he said, "you know I'll be on your side, right?"

"That," she said, "is exactly what worries me."

"Whose side *should* I be on?"

"Oh, you should definitely be on mine. But being on my side means knowing you can't fix this problem. That's up to me. You need to believe that when they hired me, they hired the right person."

"I told them you were the right person at the time," he assured her.

"Wait," she said, her eyes narrowing at him again. "Told who? When?"

"Charice. You thought they'd hire you without asking your former boss what kind of employee you'd been?"

"I *knew* it," she said. "They offered you the job first, didn't they."

No. Well, sort of. Not exactly. They'd called to see if he was interested and been disappointed when he wasn't. "Charice," he said, determined to finesse the matter. "Why would they be interested in an old white guy limping toward retirement?"

"You're not old."

"I'm fifty-two."

"Fifty-two is only old when it's you."

"Thanks, but my point is it's you they were interested in. They liked your administrative experience, the way you made things purr along in North Bath. Hell, you even made me look good." He waited for her to crack a smile at this, but she didn't. He continued, "They also liked the fact that none of your fellow officers had a bad word to say about you, despite your being, as Miller would say, an African American–type individual."

This didn't get a smile, either. "Uh-huh. Everybody agreed I was heaven-sent. Is that what you're telling me?"

"No," he admitted, because of course she was right. There *had* been reservations expressed. However, with Charice in such a stew, he had to be careful how he related these. "They wished you had a bit more street experience, but I assured them that you were my best officer, by no small margin."

"Go on. What else?"

"They worried you might be stepping too far up in class." *Okay, that hadn't come out right.* "From a small-town department to one that was more . . . metropolitan."

"Metropolitan."

Raymer realized he was beginning to sweat. "Bigger," he explained. "More moving parts, was how they put it. Serving a population that was more . . . homogenous."

"Right," she said. "Code for African American–type individuals."

Raymer sighed. "Okay, say you're right—"

"Oh, I *am* right," she assured him.

And she was. Of course, she was. He'd known at the time that the job wouldn't be easy. Schuyler's Black residents, quite a few of them recent immigrants, here on seasonal visas, were concentrated in the city's cramped North Side, and the last several summers there'd been demonstrations over wages and rents. The neighborhood might be predominantly Black, but its landlords and employers were predominantly white. The protests were mostly peaceful, but they'd become increasingly heated. The summer before Charice was hired there'd been a confrontation between police and protesters who had neglected to get a parade permit. In order to disperse the crowd, pepper spray had been used, and several marchers had required medical attention. It being August and racing season, an Albany TV crew had been nearby and caught the whole thing on film, bringing into sharp focus the increasing hostility between North Siders and the city's mostly white law enforcement. Had Raymer been wrong to encourage her to take such a job? Wrong to recommend her for it?

Rule Number One: When you find yourself in a hole, stop digging. Raymer found he couldn't. "Look," he continued. "I'm not saying you're wrong. But things actually worked to your advantage, right? Sure, they wanted somebody the Black community would trust, but it wasn't only that. They were looking for somebody who could talk to all sorts of different people—rich and poor, college professors and hotel maids, locals and summer people. I told them that was you in a nutshell. I said we hired you and you had everybody wrapped around your little finger in no time, including me."

"You said that?"

"No," he admitted, "but it's true. You did. Still do, in fact."

At this, Charice closed her eyes, as if at the advance of a migraine. "I hate it when you do this."

"Do what?"

"Say things like that. It's not fair."

"What's not?"

"We're in the middle of an argument—"

"A discussion."

"A *heated* discussion. A discussion *you* can't win without cheating—"

"How am I cheating?"

She lowered her voice to a whisper. "By telling me you love me."

He lowered his, as well. "I *do* love you."

"I know that," she said, her voice returning to its normal register, "but it's irrelevant."

Raymer rubbed his temples. "Charice. You want me to beg? Okay, I'll beg. Please tell me what's going on."

She paused, considering, then finally said, "Put it this way. You were saying before how nobody had a bad word to say about me down at the station? That's no longer true."

"Go on," Raymer said, again recalling what Miller had told him this morning and feeling his blood begin to boil.

"The main problem is an asshole named Conrad Delgado."

"Let me guess. He was in line for your job." If so, no surprise. Raymer knew there'd been several in-house candidates, and the union was in favor of promoting from within. "And he got passed over when they hired you."

"Yeah, but it's a bit more complicated than that. See, before I took the job, Jerome suggested I talk to some North Side residents—"

"Jerome suggested."

"I asked his advice."

"Not mine."

"He had experience there from when he worked in the mayor's office," she reminded him. "Told me who I should talk to."

"And?"

"Everybody I spoke with felt the North Side was overpoliced. Too many patrol cars. Too many people stopped and questioned without probable cause. Other times, though, the police were strangely absent."

"For example."

"Okay, a couple summers ago some redneck in a pickup truck with its license plates removed went roaring through the neighborhood, honking its horn and flying a huge Confederate flag. This happened several times, actually. Yet, when people reported the disturbance, it always took half an hour for cruisers to respond, and by then the guy was gone."

"You think the cops—"

"Doesn't really matter what I think. It's what people in the community think. See, nobody recognized the driver of the pickup, so people speculated he had to be from away, maybe even invited by the cops. Otherwise, how can he be driving around with no license plate and not get stopped? And here's the thing. Of all the cops they know by sight and name, it's Delgado and his partner they have the most problems with. So, when I took the job I thought I'd do a little poking around, and what jumped out at me was how many North Side incidents, especially ones where there were accusations of excessive force, involved the two of them. Which was weird because they're senior officers, detectives, so why were they hanging around there? And the stories were all the same. The two of them making traffic stops for minor infractions—expired tags or a broken taillight or an air freshener dangling from a rearview mirror, and somehow these traffic stops escalate into arrests that involve injuries."

"So," Raymer said. "A couple of bad apples?"

"So I took Delgado and his partner aside and asked what was

going on, why they always seemed to be the first guys on the scene and why so many neighborhood people were scared of them. They claimed they were just responding to calls like any other officers would and wanted to know if I had a problem with that. I told them I had a problem with the use of force as a first option and instructed them to stay out of the North Side. If there were problems, to let other officers respond. His partner didn't have much to say, but Delgado got chippy with me, claiming I was overstepping my authority. What if other officers on the scene called for backup and they were in the area? Cops were supposed to be a team, all of us united. United against who he didn't say, but it was clear enough. Anyhow, the mayor got wind of it and called for a meeting. Long story short, a compromise was arrived at that made exactly no one happy. If dispatch was calling for all units, then fine, Delgado and his partner could respond. Otherwise, they were to steer clear of the North Side. Couple days later, there's a problem on the street—a couple teenagers in a shoving match—and guess who's first on the scene?"

"Right."

"Anyhow I ended up suspending Delgado, pending an investigation. He appealed, figuring the union and his fellow officers would have his back."

Which they probably would. Closing ranks was what cops did, Raymer knew all too well, by both instinct and training.

"In the meantime, I put in a call to Delgado's old department in Philly, and it turns out he had a history of excessive force there, too, mostly against minorities. He was—how did they put it?— encouraged to look into other opportunities in law enforcement. When I reported this to the mayor and council, Delgado dropped his appeal and promised to stay out of the North Side. Next time he shows up there, he's history."

"Maybe he'll see the writing on the wall and move on," Raymer said. "That's what he did before."

Charice shook her head. "He had a white male boss before. I think this time his plan is for *me* to move on, not him."

"Then he doesn't know you."

"Jerome thinks I should, actually. Just cut my losses and find something better to do with my life."

Fucking, fucking, *fucking* Jerome. "Like what?"

"He wants the two of us to go back home to North Carolina. Start over. He's after me to go to law school. In his opinion Black police officers are like plantation overseers. Their job is to make sure the system works like it's designed—to make sure the cotton gets picked. He believes I was set up to fail. By hiring me and then withholding their full support, the mayor and town council get to say, 'Look, we tried.' Then everything can go back to how it was."

"What do *you* think?" Raymer said, because if she agreed with her brother, then didn't it follow that he, as part of the system that had set her up to fail, was complicit? *Was* he?

"I'm not there yet," she said. "But I inch closer every day."

"I'm sorry," he said, this time meaning it. Though, if he was honest, wasn't he as sorry for himself as for her? For the past month, hadn't she basically shut him out, substituting her brother's counsel for his own? He thought again about their long-ago argument about old Mr. Hynes. Had she decided right then that the chasm between them could never be bridged? Was she being completely honest with him even now? Had Jerome returned to Schuyler because he needed rescuing, or had she asked him to come because she had no one else she could trust?

"What you have to understand about Jerome?" she said, melancholy now. "He's no longer the man either of us knew. He's withdrawn, lethargic, depressed. I think . . . he's basically given up."

"It sounds like he needs professional help."

At this, Charice broke into an unexpected grin. "Am I hearing this correctly? Douglas Raymer is recommending therapy?"

"I must've lost my head," he admitted sheepishly, because, yeah, that *was* what he was suggesting. Along with an aggressive regimen of strong meds. And if those didn't work, shock treatments and, if that didn't, a padded cell.

In the half hour since they'd arrived at the Horse, the place had gotten busier. A bunch of loud Con Ed workers had taken over the bar and two other parties had been seated in the dining room, where a waitress Raymer recognized from Hattie's (Jessica? Janine? Janey?) now worked the floor. That's the way things were, what with the recession. People were doubling up everywhere, trying to make ends meet. When she cleared their wings, Raymer's appetite returned and they ordered burgers. "Anyway," Charice said, pulling out a notebook, "enough about Jerome. Where are we with our suicide?"

Raymer, who had been hoping they were through talking business, closed his eyes and forced himself to return to the Sans Souci's ghostly ballroom, cold winter light streaming through the dirty upper windows, a badly decomposed corpse hanging from the balcony railing, its teeth and fingernails littering the floor.

"What're we thinking?" Charice said. "Is he local or from away?"

"I'm leaning local."

"Me, too, but let's talk it through. Say he's from away. Who is he?"

"Not who I thought at first," Raymer admitted. "I figured he'd turn out to be a vagrant. Some poor devil who'd come to the end of the road. Maybe he stumbled on the Sans Souci and thought it was probably as good a place as any. Found an unlocked window and climbed through. Except our guy isn't dressed like a vagrant. It's February now, so if he's been there two months, that means December, and a vagrant would've been wearing some sort of winter coat. Also, how did he get in? Miller swears all the ground-floor windows were locked."

Charice shrugged. "Maybe one was unlocked and our guy climbed in and locked it behind him?"

"I suppose it's possible," Raymer conceded. "But why would somebody intent on taking their life go to the trouble?"

"Force of habit?" she suggested, but then made a face that said, *Yeah, okay, pretty weak.*

"If he's not from around here and he isn't a vagrant," Raymer continued, "then you have to wonder if he's somehow connected to the Sans Souci."

"I had the same thought. Somebody who could let himself in. A lawyer, maybe? An employee?"

"Possibly," Raymer said. "But for all we know it could be one of the crazy siblings who have been fighting over what to do with the place."

Charice made a note. "We can check. But why would somebody from New York City drive all the way up here to commit suicide when he could've just jumped from the roof of any building in Manhattan?"

"Maybe he wasn't thinking about suicide until he arrived. Maybe he got some bad news."

"A call from his doctor," Charice riffed. "Stage four metastatic lung cancer. Figures if he offs himself up here, his wife won't be the one to find him."

"Except," Raymer objected, "when he didn't come home, she'd have reported him missing."

"Maybe he didn't tell her where he was going. Maybe she *did* report him missing, and everybody's been looking for him in the city. Also, if he drove up here, or flew into Albany and rented a car, where is it? It'd be parked outside, right?"

Raymer shrugged. "Could've been towed?"

She made another note. "We can check the impound lots."

"Or it could be sitting in the parking lot of the hotel where he was staying."

"For two months?"

"It's not impossible. In August, when parking is at a premium, hotel lots all get checked regularly, but not in December. This time of year the whole county's one big empty parking lot."

Charice was shaking her head. "Except that after a snowstorm or two, the vehicle would get plowed in. It'd be in the way. Also, if our guy had a car, why would he walk to the Sans Souci?"

"He didn't know the way? Decided to take a taxi? But look, I agree. It's not tracking. It makes more sense if the guy's local."

"Maybe," Charice said, "but not a whole *lot* more. You say Franklin had a key?"

Raymer nodded. "Probably not the only one, though. The property's been on the market forever, which means at least one listing agent. A broker would probably have multiple copies. Hell, at one point *we* had one down at the station, remember? And wasn't there a big renovation a few years back? That would mean workmen—plumbers, carpenters, electricians. They all would have needed access."

"Okay," Charice said, "let's say he's a contractor. Go."

"The recession hits and he loses his business. One day he's cleaning out his desk, which he discovers is full of unmarked keys." Raymer himself had discovered this about the top drawer of his own desk at the station just last week. "He recognizes the one to the Sans Souci because it was old and he'd had a devil of a time getting the copy made. He thinks to himself, okay, if he does it there at least he'll be found by someone who doesn't know him."

"All well and good," Charice said, "except that now we're back staring at the same old problem. If our contractor's been hanging there this whole time and he's local, then two months before that, he went missing. The wife he didn't want to find him would've reported it. All this time we'd have been looking for him. This morning when we heard about a suicide at the Sans Souci, our first thought would've been, Okay, mystery solved."

"You're right," Raymer sighed. "It doesn't add up either way. What are we missing?"

"Okay, start over. We don't know his identity, but what do we know *about* him?"

"Balding. Sweater vest. So probably an older guy."

"Chinos, loafers, corduroy jacket. Who dresses like that?"

"Insurance agents? Small business owners?"

"Also, academics?" Charice ventured. "Guy's up for tenure, gets turned down, says goodbye cruel world?"

"Again, his disappearance gets reported."

"Not if he's here on some kind of visiting gig. Regular faculty person falls ill. Replacement hired for fall semester only. Come December he turns in his grades, says goodbye to his friends. Nobody's expecting to see him again, so he doesn't get reported missing."

"Okay, but you just kicked the can down the road, right? If he was visiting, then home is somewhere else? People *there* would be expecting him home for the holidays. Why didn't *they* report him missing?"

"Maybe we're giving him friends and family he didn't have. The world is full of lonely people."

"But if he doesn't have anyone, then why doesn't he just do the deed at home? The reason we had him deciding to kill himself at the Sans Souci was that he wouldn't be found by a loved one. We can't just subtract that loved one now because it's inconvenient."

"Here's an idea," she said, returning her notebook to her bag. "How about I hand off this investigation to you?"

A joke, surely. "Me?"

"Why not? I don't want Delgado and my other guys anywhere near it."

"Except," he pointed out, "yesterday was my last day as a cop, remember? The end of an era?"

He expected this to get a rise out of her, but it didn't. Instead, she studied him quietly. Finally she said, "Come work for me."

*Him. Work for her.* And just that quickly he was back in Dr. Qadry's office. *Would you have trouble taking orders from a woman?* And her, smiling that maddening smile, the one that implied she could see right through him. *Of course not,* he'd told her, offended. Or had he just been pretending to be? He couldn't remember. Dear God, how exhausting it all was.

"As a consultant," Charice was explaining. "I have a small discretionary fund I can draw on. I don't need anyone's permission."

Raymer knew exactly what Dougie would say if he were here. *Fine. Go ahead. Humiliate yourself. See if I care. Isn't that where your whole sorry life has been heading?*

"I know it's a lot to ask," she continued, meaning, Raymer presumed, the role reversal. *Her* being the boss now. "But maybe there won't be much to do. When the guy's phone is charged, it'll probably tell us who he is. After which, it's all about tying up a few loose ends."

"Can I see it?" he said, suddenly curious, but also stalling for time.

"*See* it?" she snorted, pulling the cell phone out of her bag and handing it over. "You can have it."

Raymer studied the device, a BlackBerry 6710. How quickly these gadgets were all changing! This one was less than ten years old, but it might've been a relic from another century. The new iPhones and Androids all had large screens and touch pads and cameras and massive storage capabilities. Would this one even have a contacts list? A log of recent calls? Where would he even find a charger for the damn thing?

Holding the phone in his palm, Raymer felt his spirits plummet, as if its owner's despair were being absorbed through his skin. Whoever the man was, he'd come to the Sans Souci without a wallet or keys or anything else that might have led to his identity, which meant, unless Raymer missed his guess, that the device had probably been wiped of its data, maybe even returned to its factory settings. Why had the man even brought it with him? To make one final call? To whom? For what purpose? To say goodbye? Or had he brought it with him in the hopes of *receiving* one last call, maybe from the one person in the world capable of convincing him that life was worth the effort of living? Raymer found that possibility inexpressibly sad. Charice was right. The world was full of lonely people, but the more he thought about it, the more convinced he became that, in the end, this wouldn't be about loneliness. The man who'd taken his life wasn't Eleanor Rigby, who died and was buried along with her name. No, this man's death reeked of shame. Of humiliation. He hadn't wanted to just end his life. He'd wanted to do it violently. He was standing in judgment, a study in self-loathing. He believed he deserved to leave this life in the worst way imaginable. Had he known that some sharp-toothed thing would gnaw its way into his skull after he was dead, the thought would not have deterred him. And yet, he did seem to have chosen the Sans Souci out of consideration for someone else. There'd been someone he wanted to spare. Which meant that when the man was identified, this other, unknown person's suffering would commence. Charice was assuming that discovering who the owner of the BlackBerry was would close the loop, but what if the exact opposite proved true? What if what they learned was that suffering begat further suffering, world without end, amen?

"You know what?" Charice said, and Raymer was surprised to see that her eyes were full. Before handing him the BlackBerry, they hadn't been. "I've missed you."

At this, his heart leaped, and he set down the phone, more than ready to sever the psychic connection to the dead man, whoever he was. *Really? She did?*

But *hold on,* he told himself. Better to not let himself get carried away. Yes, the fact that Charice missed him was encouraging. He would allow himself that much. And, yes, it was good to know that she didn't think of him as just one more problem to be dealt with in the coming days—that he wasn't in the same category as Conrad Delgado, or her endlessly needy brother, or the rotting, unidentified corpse in whose company they'd spent the afternoon.

But *how* had she missed him, exactly? As a colleague? Their two brains working in concert toward a common understanding, as they'd just been doing? (If that was all she meant by having missed him, he'd be disappointed, but he supposed he could accept it.) Or had just seeing him again cheered her up, like laying eyes on her always did him? (Because that would be better.) Did she miss him in her bed, a warm body next to her own? (Better yet. Much better.) Was it the middle-aged man smiling at her from across their half-moon booth that she missed, or the younger version of himself who believed her when she told him there was a butterfly tattooed on her buttock? (It would serve him right if this was the case.)

But wasn't it also possible she missed him in *all* those ways? And wouldn't that mean she still loved him? Again, his unruly heart leaped and again he told himself to *stop, just stop.* Because much as he wanted this to be true, what were the odds? Hadn't there been both surprise and sadness in her admission that she missed him? And didn't those suggest that something had been permanently, not temporarily, lost? That love had already been relegated to memory? If so, then what she was feeling for him was the sort of fondness that lingered in the vacuum created by departed passion. She was probably tearing up now because she understood that even if she did her best to let him down easy, he'd still crash-land in terrain that was all too familiar, having been there before with Becka, his bafflement complete and profound—desperate to know exactly when and how he'd failed yet another woman.

"Look," Charice said, taking his hand now. "I know how hard our being apart has been for you."

*No, you don't.*

"And I know you want everything to be like it was."

*Yes, yes, yes, yes.*

"I wish it could be, too."

*Why can't it?* Because if it couldn't, then how could he ever reconcile himself to what he knew came next: *This isn't about you. It's about me.*

She was squeezing his hand now. "If you really want to help . . ."

"No need to beg," he assured her. "I'll do it. Like you said, there probably won't even be that much to do. Once the phone is charged—"

"Actually?" she said, giving him a pained look. "There's something else I need from you."

"Else?"

"Something difficult."

"What?"

"And you get to say no, because it's totally unfair of me to ask, and I know you really aren't going to want to."

Okay, well, this *was* getting a little scary. "Charice," he said. "Just tell me, okay?"

But when she opened her mouth to do just that, they both became aware that the noisy bar had gone quiet, and looking up, they saw why. In the entrance to the dining room stood a tall, slender, clearly agitated Black man who was carrying two very large matching suitcases, and though he'd paused in the entryway, he set neither suitcase down. To Raymer, he looked like an escapee from an all-Black production of *Death of a Salesman*. The last time he'd seen Jerome he'd been clean shaven, but now he had a full, unkempt beard that was flecked with gray. His hair was not only longer now, but weirdly asymmetrical, bushier on one side than the other. He was wearing a faded cardigan sweater that for some reason looked familiar.

And taking him in, this wreck of a man that Jerome had become, Raymer knew—of course he knew—what Charice wanted and needed him to do. And she was right. It wasn't remotely fair for her to ask it and he really, really *didn't* want to do it. She claimed he could say no, but she was still holding his hand, which meant that, no, he couldn't, not really. "Okay," he heard himself say. "I'll do it."

Why? Because, fuck Dougie. Really, just fuck him.

# Russians

---

THE WINE BAR WAS heaving when Peter arrived, every table occupied. On the far side of the horseshoe bar, there was one lone, unoccupied stool, so he made for that. Arriving there, he found that the adjacent seat was unoccupied as well, though someone had left a set of keys next to a wineglass with a couple of sips left at the bottom, signaling their intention of returning. Maybe, Peter thought, the timing would be good and whoever the keys belonged to would settle up and leave as Toby was arriving. Probably not, though. She was habitually and chronically late, which this evening actually suited Peter just fine. In truth, he was still reeling from his son's visit that morning. The totally unexpected sight of Thomas sitting there on the porch, looking like grim reckoning personified, had thrown him for a loop. He had to wonder: Had Sully felt the same way when Peter himself had suddenly reappeared in Bath, full of grievance, that long-ago Thanksgiving? When he saw who had pulled over onto the shoulder of the road to offer him a lift into town, did he think, *Of course. How could I* not *have foreseen this day?* Probably. And unless Peter missed his guess, his father had reacted much as he himself had done with Thomas today, by pretending to be delighted to see his son and not at all troubled that what *goes* around does indeed *come* around and that payback is, in fact, a bitch. All afternoon, as he and Rub finished retiling the upstairs guest bathroom, Thomas's strange visit had played on a loop through Peter's brain, its details paradoxically implausible and inevitable. Could it be true that Thomas had been headed to Canada and decided on the spur of the moment to drop in on his father? It seemed unlikely, but if the real purpose of the trip was visiting Peter, then why had he been in such a hurry to leave? None of it made any sense, and rather than spend the whole evening obsessing, he'd called Toby Roebuck and invited her out for drinks.

As he settled onto his stool, Alan, the regular Saturday-night bartender, who'd seen Peter enter, broke free of a conversation on the other side of the bar and came over. "I've got something new for you to try," he said, holding up an uncorked bottle of red wine.

"Okay," Peter said, though he'd actually been looking forward to a stiff martini to quiet his nerves.

"You like Syrahs, right?" Alan said, pouring him a small taste. Bartenders at Infinity were all trained to hold the bottle by the bottom, an affectation that would've invited Birdie's scorn had she been there to witness it. She grabbed all bottles by their necks, as you would a live chicken.

"I have no idea," Peter admitted, swirling the wine in his glass. "Do I?"

Alan stepped back and presented the bottle's label. "Fantastic, right?"

Peter took a sip, set the glass back down and pushed it forward. "It's fine." He liked Alan, but it was impossible not to mess with the man.

Alan's shoulders sagged melodramatically. "You're so *mean* to me."

"No, it's good."

"Really?"

"Yep," Peter said, pointing at the glass, giving him permission to pour.

But Alan was now in full pout mode. "It's Spanish," he pleaded, pointing at the spot on the label that announced this fact.

"Well," Peter said. "There you go."

"I'm just so *wasted* here," Alan lamented theatrically, finally delivering the short pour that every Infinity bartender was trained to execute, just up to the tiny asterisk on the glass and not a hair over. At the end of the evening, though, one glass would usually be free. Peter had no idea whether that was the establishment's policy or Alan's. "I never should've left New York."

"Why did you?" Peter asked. Though he himself often felt the same way, the assertion, coming from Alan, sounded preposterous.

"Love," Alan sighed. "Why else?"

"What's her name?" Peter said, keeping, as best he could, a straight face.

Alan regarded him for a long beat, then leaned closer and lowered his voice, suddenly serious. "Did you hear about the Sans Souci?"

"I heard a rumor it sold, if that's what you mean."

"No. About the b.o.d.y."

"Why are you spelling the word *body*?"

Alan lowered his voice even further. "It was a s.u.i.c.i.d.e."

"Why are you spelling *suicide*?"

"And get this." Alan continued. "They found it in the ballroom. Whoever it was tied one end of the rope to the balcony railing and the other end around his neck. And leaped." He paused to let this gruesome image sink in. "I mean . . . *ouch*, right?"

"Where did you hear this?"

"It's all over town. Apparently, the new owners were touring the place. They walked into the ballroom and *surprise*!" Here he lifted one arm in the air, made a fist of it around an imaginary rope, then cocked his head at a radical angle, to suggest a broken neck.

"Wow," Peter said. "Do we know who this person was?"

"That's the best part. There was no ID on the b.o.d.y. It could be anyone."

"Well, not really," Peter pointed out. "It's not you, for instance. Or me."

"*That's* why I was so glad when I saw you come in."

"Because otherwise you thought maybe I fit the profile?"

"Well, you never really know, do you?"

"I know I'm going to withhold belief until I read it in the newspaper."

Alan shook his head. "Who'd invent something like that? It's too creepy." When Peter just shrugged, Alan put both hands over his mouth. "Don't say it! I know what you're thinking. Tim Burton."

"Why would Tim Burton commit suicide in the Sans Souci?"

"No, I'm saying he's the sort of person who would imagine something creepy like that. And I agree with you about *Coraline*."

Peter had listed the movie in this week's *Schuyler Arts* as one of the year's ten best so far. "Except," he pointed out, "that's not a Tim Burton movie."

"Are you sure?"

"Very."

"If you say so," Alan shrugged. "But speaking of creepy things . . ."

Peter followed Alan's glance to where Carl Roebuck was just then emerging from the men's room. He appeared more than a little unsteady on his feet and it took two tries for him to successfully mount the barstool next to Peter. His eyes were rimmed with red. Peter tried to think whether he'd seen Carl since Sully's funeral. "I might have known those were yours," he said, indicating the key ring and the nearly empty wineglass that had been sitting there since he entered.

"Yeah?" said Carl, who didn't seem terribly surprised to see him. "How?"

"You're the only man I know who has to get up to pee every twenty minutes and requires another twenty to actually do it."

"Yeah? Well, have prostate surgery and see how often you have to pee." They clinked glasses. "Anybody ever tell you you look more like your old man every day?"

"No one needs to. There's a mirror in my bathroom."

"Must be discouraging."

"A little," Peter admitted.

"What brings you to this snooty establishment?"

"I need a reason?"

"No," the other man said, grinning at him drunkenly now. "I just thought you might be meeting somebody."

So, Peter thought. It was as he'd suspected. Yet again Carl had somehow managed to suss out what was up, this time before it happened instead of after. "A reasonable deduction. People have been known to meet in bars."

"She and I might be getting back together," he said. "Did she mention that?"

"You and *who* might be getting back together?"

"Me and the woman you're meeting."

"No, I hadn't heard that."

"Turns out she's still in love with me. Turns out, after me, no one quite measures up."

"I hadn't heard that, either."

"You smile," he said, "but it's not impossible."

"Really? It kind of is?"

Carl seemed to consider this second opinion seriously. "Okay, maybe she's not in love with me," he conceded, "but she's not in love with you, either."

"True."

"Funny how things run in families," Carl observed. "Your old man was in love with her, too. Did you know that?"

"I think it was more like a crush," Peter told him, but Carl was right. His father definitely had had a thing about Toby.

"God, it was pitiful to watch," Carl recalled nostalgically. When Peter had no reply to this, he consulted his watch. "She's late."

"Only ten minutes."

The other man reached into his pocket, pulled out a thin wad of folded bills, peeled one off and slapped it on the bar. "Twenty bucks says she stands you up."

"Done," Peter said, picking up the bill and putting it in his pocket. Because there in the entryway stood Toby herself, surveying the scene. Spotting Peter and her ex, she made her way among the tables, turning heads as she went, even the heads of much-younger men. Peter and Carl both rose to greet her.

"I see you found each other," she said, giving Carl a peck on the cheek.

"I was just telling Peter about how we might be getting back together," Carl said, apparently daring her to contradict him.

"Poor Carlos," she replied, sliding gracefully onto her ex-husband's barstool. When Peter slid back onto his own, it took Carl a moment to realize that he'd just been dismissed. Alan seemed to understand as well. Picking up Carl's tab on the way by, he took it directly to the register.

"Okay, then," Carl said. "You two kids have a swell time." Then he called down the bar to where Alan was ringing up his tab. "Good night, your gayness."

"Lord, he's drunk," Toby said, watching her ex-husband weave among the tables.

When Alan returned, Peter took out Carl's twenty and reached for the tab, but Toby was too quick. When she put a credit card on the plastic tray, Peter caught a glimpse of the total, which was over a hundred dollars. No wonder the man had been unsteady on his feet.

Alan was pouting at Toby now. "Really? You're going to let him skate on his tab?"

"It's a small price to pay for his absence," she assured him.

"Fine," Alan said. "Whatever. What are we drinking then?"

She eyed Peter's glass. "What's that?"

"Swill," Alan replied. "I wouldn't go near it."

"My usual, then," she said.

When Alan scurried off and she met Peter's eye, he was surprised to see there were tears in hers. "Poor Carlos," she repeated, this time with more affection. "He got fired this morning."

"What happened?" Peter said. "I thought he was the dealership's top salesman."

"He didn't say, but I can guess. He's used to *being* the boss, not having one. I hear he has mounting debt. Did he hit you up for a loan?"

"No, but your timely arrival may have prevented that. Here's what I find puzzling, though. He seemed to know we were meeting here. Has he somehow managed to tap my phone?"

She smiled. "I may have let the cat out of the bag. He called right after I hung up with you, wanting money. I can always tell when that's what he's after because he begins the conversation by asking who I'm sleeping with."

"Odd strategy."

"Then he wants to know if I'll marry him again."

"No less odd."

"I think he figures that when he finally gets around to admitting it's money he's after I'll be relieved and give him some."

Alan was back again and he set in front of Toby the chilled martini that Peter himself had been about to order before Alan appeared with the Syrah. They clinked glasses. "I'm still unclear," Peter admitted. "If he called right after you hung up with me, how exactly did I enter the picture?"

"Well, when he asked who I was sleeping with, I said nobody at the moment, but that I was having drinks with you this evening, which could lead to sex."

"In that case I'm glad I called."

"I said *could.* Not would."

"No, but I'm still encouraged."

"Your turn, now. How did I enter *your* picture today after not hearing from you for months?"

Not wanting to answer truthfully, that he'd been looking for a distraction, any distraction, after his son's unsettling visit, he said, "I was wondering if you knew anything about that Sans Souci rumor I keep hearing. That the place has sold?"

She gave him her coy, real estate look. "I heard the same one."

"And?"

"You forget. I'm in residential, not commercial."

"Still."

She shrugged. "Put it this way. If I were you and Birdie, I wouldn't make any big decisions based on rumor. It's a complicated situation that just got more complicated. I assume you heard about what happened out there today?"

"Just now," he said, nodding in Alan's direction. "I guess finding a corpse on a property you're buying *would* be off-putting."

"You think?"

"Still, how would it complicate a real estate deal? Unless the two are somehow related?"

"That doesn't appear to be the case."

"So . . . if I'm the buyer and I wanted the property before, don't I still want it? It's not a three-bedroom ranch. There aren't a hundred others. I don't say to myself, I think I'll buy the other one we looked at over on Lark Street, the one without the dead body."

Toby's nails were painted bloodred again. He noticed because she was tapping thoughtfully on the surface of the bar, as if trying to decide whether to explain exactly how and to what extent his logic was flawed. "Imagine," she said finally, "that you've come to agreement in principle to buy the estate. The land, the hotel, everything. Say the deal has been in place for a while, but you're in no hurry. The holidays are bearing down and anyway what's the rush? You'll close after the first of the year. Then you look up and—Wow!—it's February already. Let's sign the documents and make this thing official. There's only one thing left to do before that can happen. You've never actually seen the property, and you think that might be a good idea."

"Wouldn't I have done that before agreeing in principle to the purchase?"

"Normally, yes. But maybe for you that hasn't been practical. Maybe you don't live around here."

"Right," Peter said. "Maybe I live in California. That's the whisper I heard."

"Anything is possible," she said, with added emphasis on the word *anything*.

"Wait," Peter said, catching—maybe?—her drift. "I'm not American?"

She shrugged. "Like I said, I'm in residential, not commercial, but I do know that in the present economy American real estate is particularly attractive to foreign buyers, and there are always people out there with money to park. The question is where to park it. London? Manhattan?"

"Schuyler Springs seems a bit out of the way."

"Maybe out of the way is what you're looking for," she said, now raising her empty glass in Alan's direction. Peter made a mental note not to try to match Toby, drink for drink. Alcohol seemed to have no effect on her.

"So . . . ," he said. "I have all this money to park, but I'm actually less interested in what I'm buying than in avoiding scrutiny and publicity?"

"Who knows? Maybe you plan to flip it later."

"Which would make the money I'm spending now somehow . . . clean? Jeez. You're making me sound almost . . . Russian."

She cocked her head to study him. "Hey," she said. "You do look like a bit of a thug at that. I never noticed before."

Alan arrived with her fresh martini, which she raised in a toast. *"Nastrovia!"*

They clinked glasses. "I hope my thuggish appearance doesn't alter your plans for later in the evening."

"I guess we'll have to see," she said, picking up a menu, and signaling thereby that she'd said all she was going to say about the Sans Souci. "Should we see if we can get a table, or just order small plates here at the bar?"

"Why go to a table?" Alan said. "If you stay here, you get to talk to me."

"A table, I think," Peter said.

"He's *so,* so mean to me," Alan complained to Toby, his shoulders slumping again, but he motioned for the hostess, pointing first at a small table that was being bused, then at Peter and Toby.

They were gathering their drinks when Peter happened to glance at the backbar mirror just as a big, canary-yellow beast of a Cadillac slid by in the street outside.

# Normal

B Y TEN O'CLOCK, when Janey finished up at the Horse, she was so exhausted she considered doing the sensible thing and just heading home. She'd promised Del she'd come by the Green Hand, though, and knew he'd get bent out of shape if she didn't. That afternoon, when she called to tell him that Birdie had offered her a shift—her regular waitress having called in sick—he said, "Now why the fuck would you do that? It's Saturday night."

"See?" she said. "You answered your own damn question." Del went quiet then to let her know she'd pissed him off. According to her mother, it was the same mistake she'd been making her entire life: running her big fat mouth. Nor, admit it, was she wrong. For some reason she just couldn't seem to get it through her thick skull that men—pretty much straight across the board—didn't appreciate being told off. When she used to sass Roy, if he happened to be in a good mood, he'd say, "Why do you always have to be such a mouthy cunt?" If he was in a bad one, he'd just haul off and smack her. No warning, either. Just *whack!* Del didn't hit. At least not yet. He just went perfectly still, almost priestlike, as if he was offering her the opportunity to repent being such a bitch. Somehow, when she thought about it, that stillness was even scarier than Roy's fists.

"Friday and Saturday nights are where you make your money,"

she explained, hoping, since mouthing off hadn't worked, to elicit his understanding or, failing that, forgiveness.

And in truth, her shift at the Horse had been only so-so. A few tables had tipped decently, but thanks to the deepening recession people were cutting back, twenty percent tips becoming fifteen, fifteen becoming ten. It was the same at Hattie's. To make matters worse, Birdie always removed the expensive entrées—steaks and prime rib and seafood—from the dinner menu during the off-season, which meant you were getting ten percent of an already reduced tab. Worse, when she got to the Hand, Del would ask her how much she made and she'd have to decide whether to lie. If she inflated the amount she'd earned to win the argument, he'd say, Good, you can buy the drinks tonight. If she told the truth, he'd say, *What did I tell you? You'd've been better off here, having some fun.* Very little that Janey did seemed to make sense to Del, who was forever advising her to quit "her job" at Hattie's, claiming he could get her on at the Hand. He'd said it again this afternoon.

"And I keep telling you I *can't* quit on account of it's not a job. I own the fucking place."

"Sell it, then."

"I can't."

"Why not?"

"Because it's all I've got, Del. I know it's just a shitty lunch counter, but it's mine, okay?" And just that quickly she'd been on the verge of tears. "Can we not fight? Please?"

"Okay," he'd told her, relenting a little. "No need to get your knickers in a twist. Just don't change your mind later. I don't want to hear about how tired you are after working a double you could've turned down."

She promised she wouldn't.

"It's Saturday night," he said again.

"I know what night it is."

She also knew what his reminder really meant. For some strange reason Del equated Saturday night with sex. It wasn't that he didn't feel the urge on other nights, but on Saturday night he felt entitled to get laid. Another man would be disappointed but figure Sunday would be just as good. Not Del. Sunday wouldn't be as good for the simple reason that it wasn't Saturday. How long had he *been* like this? Janey wondered. How exactly had a particular night of the week and the need for sex gotten tangled up in that screwball brain of his? Was Saturday night when his parents had done it? Being Italian, he was raised Catholic and they had all kinds of batshit rules—Mass on Sunday, fish on Fridays—so maybe that was it. If they kept seeing each other, maybe she'd get him to explain. She didn't expect them to last, though. They were together for now, but after Roy, Janey was dead set on not remarrying, and Del had been equally clear that when his divorce from his second wife became final, that was it for him. What they had was fun and, when it stopped being fun, sayonara.

Outside, in the Horse's parking lot, Janey climbed in behind the steering wheel of her aging Jetta and inserted her key in the ignition. It would take her about fifteen minutes to drive out to the Green Hand, which was good. She could use the time to decide whether to mention she'd waited on Charice Bond, Del's boss, at the Horse. Her and Doug Raymer and, later, a tall Black man who, according to Birdie, was Charice's brother, Jerome. He'd showed up a good forty-five minutes after they did, carrying two large suitcases and looking like some kind of hobo. Del would want to hear all about it, especially what Charice and Raymer had talked about. They'd kept their voices low, but Janey was pretty sure she'd heard Charice say Del's name. Which wouldn't please him, convinced as he was that she was trying to get him fired. It might be best not to even bring the subject up, now that she thought about it. It *was* interesting, though, that she and Doug Raymer, who'd been Bath's chief of police until recently, were a couple, or had been once upon a time. Birdie said she heard they weren't together anymore, but they certainly looked like one tonight. They hadn't engaged in any public displays of affection, but still, you could tell. Janey didn't share Del's unshakable conviction that interracial relationships were "unnatural," but she had to admit these two were tough to figure—him overweight, white and older, her Black and good-looking. Del, of course, would never admit that Charice Bond was attractive. In his opinion a woman couldn't be both Black and good-looking, except for Halle Berry, who he claimed was basically white. Being a boob guy, Del was willing to cut her some slack. He freely admitted that Janey's boobs were what first caught his attention from all the way across the room, and she was pretty sure they were what kept that attention even now. He never seemed to tire of pawing them. Not that she minded, really. She'd always known that it wasn't her face that men were attracted to. When her make-up was right, she was plain-looking and borderline homely when it wasn't. There'd been a time when that bothered her. Back when she and Roy first started going out, she'd told him she knew she was on the plain side, hoping he'd tell her no, she was pretty enough, but instead he'd said not to worry about it. "Nobody's gonna look all the way up there anyhow."

Her face, her boobs and her big mouth—all three inherited from her mother, thanks a ton. She'd gifted her own daughter that same chest and face but somehow not the mouth, which she supposed was a good thing, though in truth she'd always found her daughter's long stretches of silence, even as a child, unnerving. How were you supposed to know what somebody was thinking if they wouldn't tell you? Why would you not *want* people to know what you thought? Well, okay, in Tina's case Janey kind of understood. The poor girl had grown up listening to her mother say the wrong thing and watching her father punch her in the face for it. The lesson there was pretty clear, and Tina had apparently learned it. According to Ruth, that vividly recollected violence was the reason Tina wanted so little to do with Janey now, why she refused to even enter Hattie's, the scene of so much childhood trauma. Nor could Janey really blame her. She herself still had flashbacks. On the other hand, Roy was gone. He'd *been* gone for ten long years, and to Janey's way of thinking the best way to make sure he stayed gone was to reclaim the emotional landscape he'd defiled. God knew, there were times Janey hated Hattie's herself, days when she would've liked nothing better than to burn the place to the ground, but most mornings when she woke in her apartment, which was attached to the restaurant, her first thought was *Hey, asshole*—meaning Roy—*look who's still here and look who's still fucking dead*. A similar thought would sometimes enter her head on Saturday nights with Del: *Look who's fucking me now, Roy, and guess who never will again*. There was satisfaction in all this, and she wished she could make her daughter understand that.

Janey was about to turn the key in the ignition when she remembered promising to call her mother when she got off at the Horse, so Ruth could bring her up to speed on Tina, who'd finally arrived at Hattie's that afternoon, forty-five minutes late. They had a regular baton-passing routine. Tina would pull up in front of the restaurant and toot the horn to signal her arrival. By the time Ruth managed to pull on her parka and make her way outside, Tina would have the passenger door open and the step stool positioned so that Ruth, with Tina's help, could hoist herself up into the cab. Today, though, when Tina pulled up, instead of tooting she just sat there, staring off into space. From her window seat inside the restaurant, Ruth could see that something was amiss, and grabbing her cane, she'd begun the arduous process of extricating herself, cripple-fashion, as she thought of it, from the booth.

Janey had offered to lend a hand, but Ruth said no, she'd handle it, her implication clear, that Janey would only make whatever was wrong worse. That had pissed her off, of course, though her mother was probably right. Oh, but it still hurt, because there'd been a time when Tina was little and Roy was downstate serving time, that she and her daughter had been inseparable, when Tina had insisted she be close enough to touch. How quickly that had changed. After she entered school, her daughter spent more time with her grandparents than with Janey, who told herself that this wasn't so unusual, and even if it was, what choice did she have, working all the time like she did? Grandpa Zack didn't mind Tina's company on his travels, and he had an almost magical calming effect on the child. Later, after his death, Tina had transferred much of that attachment to Ruth, which of course hurt Janey's feelings all over again. She'd hoped against hope that all would be well once Tina became an adult and started working herself. Maybe then she'd understand and find her way back to her mother. But that hadn't happened. Would it ever? When Ruth died, who would be left for her daughter to cleave to but Janey?

Listening to her mother's phone ring, Janey felt her resentment rise, like it always did these days, and when Ruth answered, she just dove right in, fuck the preliminaries. "So, what gives?" she said, not bothering to conceal the annoyance in her voice. "Is she okay?"

"Hang on a minute," Ruth said, and Janey could hear her rustling around, probably searching for the remote to mute the TV. When she came back on the line, she said, "I haven't been able to get much out of her. She claims she's fine."

"Good. Maybe she is. Did you ever think of that?"

"No, something upset her. I think . . ."

Janey waited, then waited some more. "What? What do you think, Ma? This is like pulling teeth here."

"What are you? Double-parked?"

"No, I'm heading out to the Hand."

"Fine. Go."

"First tell me what you're not telling me."

"I could be wrong."

At this Janey couldn't help snorting. "That goes without saying, Ma."

"It may have been one of her spells."

At this, Janey let her forehead rest on the steering wheel, thinking, *No, not this again.* "Ma. It's been years."

"I know. But remember what she was like, coming out of those?"

Dazed. Disoriented. Blinking. Scared. Yeah, Janey remembered. And worst of all, the expression on her daughter's face, like they were calling her back from a really nice place to a shitty one, and why couldn't they just leave her where she was? "Okay, go back and start at the beginning. After you left the restaurant."

"On the way home, she wanted to go past Sully's house."

"Sully's dead."

"I'm aware of that. She kept saying, 'He's back.' Over and over. It was all I could get out of her."

"Who's back?" Sully? Had her daughter lost her mind completely?

"I'm getting to that. So, we drove up Main Street past the house, but there was nothing to see. They're doing some renovations, but nobody was around. 'Right up there,' she said, pointing at the porch. 'He was right up there.' Like, it was herself she was trying to convince. Anyhow, we kept going up the street and I figured we'd head home, but instead she made a U-turn and headed back the way we came. This time she pulled over to the curb and we just sat there staring at the house. Finally, she said, 'He's really changed, but it was him.'"

"Yeah, he's changed. He's dead."

"Jesus, Janey, forget Sully, okay? This isn't about Sully."

"Then what the fuck *is* it about?"

"You don't remember Will?"

"Will who?"

"Will Sullivan. Jesus, Janey. Try and keep up. Sully's grandson. Remember the crush Tina had on him?"

What the *fuck* had possessed her to make this call? Janey wondered. Why hadn't she just driven on out to the Hand? "Ma. That was a decade ago. Fucking high school."

"She hasn't forgotten him."

"She *told* you this?" Her daughter, who wouldn't say shit if she had a mouthful?

"Look," Ruth said, sounding embarrassed now, "we share a computer, okay?"

The one in the kitchen, she meant. A couple years earlier, when it became clear that Ruth could no longer manage the stairs, Tina had had the first floor remodeled so Ruth could have a bedroom and bath down there. Tina would move into the large bedroom that had been her grandparents', or anyhow that had been the plan, though in the end she'd preferred the smaller bedroom that had been hers when she was little and stayed overnight. And anyway, these days, according to Ruth, her granddaughter spent most of her time in the shed.

"I can see where she's been," Ruth was explaining. "She Googles Will constantly. Follows him on Facebook."

"Okay, so what? They were friends. Everybody follows friends on Facebook." Not that Janey did, herself. Most of her own friends had moved away and were living better lives than hers. Why would she want to know about their better jobs and expensive vacations?

"We're talking every single day, Janey. She's constantly hitting refresh."

"Does she know you're snooping?"

"I'm not. If I was sneaking into her bedroom and reading her diary, that would be snooping. Her browsing history is right there."

She was ashamed of herself, though, Janey could tell. "So, if she's still infatuated with Sully's grandson, how come she's never said a word about him to me."

"When was the last time you two even had a conversation?"

"Thanks, Ma. Thanks for reminding me. It's you she talks to. You're the one she loves. I'm the one she hates. I really needed to hear that tonight. I *was* going to just drive out to the Hand and have some fun, but then I thought, No, I'll call Ma. She always cheers me up."

"This isn't about you, Janey."

"Yeah, but guess what? It never is. That much I can count on. It's always about her or you or Sully."

"There's no reason to bring Sully into this."

"I didn't, Ma. You did. You're the one who said Sully's house. He's dead and gone. Does he have to haunt every single conversation we have?"

"Now who's blaming?"

"*Me,* Ma! This is me, blaming you, okay?"

"You get to blame me, but Tina's not allowed to blame you?"

"You know what? Fuck this. I'm gonna go on out to the Hand and kick up my heels, okay?"

"Do that," Ruth suggested.

"I'm going to. You know why? Because I'm sick of everything being my fault. Her father beats the shit out of me, and she's still blaming *me*? How is that *my* fault?"

"You kept taking him back, is how she sees it."

"Okay, but it was me he beat on, not her. I got the scars to prove it."

"I know you do, Janey," Ruth said, adding, "so do I."

"Wonderful," Janey said. "Throw that in my face while you're at it. You took my beating."

"I was glad to take your beating."

"Yeah, yeah, yeah. Saint Fucking Ruth."

They were quiet then, and because the quiet seemed to give her permission, Janey began to cry. Finally, she said, "Where is she now?"

"Out in the shed." Which was what they called the massive structure—ten times the size of the adjacent house—where Grandpa Zack's treasures were stored.

"For the love of God," Janey said. "It's ten o'clock on a Saturday night. What is she doing out there?"

"She's out there most nights."

"Alone?"

"As far as I know. I don't go checking on her."

"No, you're snooping on the computer," Janey said.

Ruth ignored this. "She's fixed it up nice. She's got a sofa-sleeper in there and a TV. A small fridge."

"But why?"

"I don't know, Janey. You're not the only one she doesn't have a lot to say to."

"And now this Will is back."

"That's the thing," her mother said, embarrassment creeping back into her voice. "He's not. He's somewhere in England. On some sort of scholarship. It was on his last Facebook post. Also? He's engaged."

"Poor Tina," Janey said, crying harder now. *Poor little girl.* Because that's the way she still saw her grown daughter. "So, you're saying she's losing her mind."

"I'm worried."

"You think she's hallucinating."

"I don't know. Like I said. The house is being renovated. Maybe it was a worker she saw, somebody who just reminded her of him."

Janey stifled a sob. "Why can't she just be normal?"

"Well, that doesn't exactly run in the family."

"I'm normal," Janey managed to choke out.

"Right."

"I *am,* damn it. As soon as I hang up, I'm going to drive out to the Hand and I'm going to laugh and dance and listen to loud music. And after that I'm going to go over to Del's place and let him fuck me silly. And don't tell me that isn't normal, because that's what you and Sully did every time Daddy wasn't looking."

"The difference was Sully and I liked each other."

"I like Del just fine. You're just jealous because I'm still young and I've got somebody in my life and you're old and you don't."

It was the most hateful thing she could think of to say, and it was an exit line if ever there was one, but Janey surprised herself by not hanging up, and neither did her mother. For the longest time they kept the line open, as if there was something left to say. But if so, neither mother nor daughter seemed to know what it was.

# Black Tooth

ALL I CAN SAY IS, I better get this listing," Toby Roebuck re-marked after they had the sex Peter had been hoping for when he invited her out. A pretty funny line, he had to admit.

Leaving the wine bar, he'd hoped Toby might offer her nearby condo, but she said she was anxious to see how the renovations were coming on the Main Street house. They'd taken both cars and he'd worried the entire way that when they arrived back in Bath Thomas's yellow Caddy would again be in the driveway. It wasn't, though, which Peter hoped meant his son was telling the truth about being on his way to Canada. If so, then the reflection he'd glimpsed in Infinity's backbar mirror belonged to another vehicle entirely.

When they arrived, Peter poured them both a brandy and gave Toby a tour of the first floor, including the new chef's kitchen, which he was particularly proud of. The old kitchen had been small and cramped, the adjacent dining room large and formal, so he and Rub had removed two non-load-bearing walls to open things up. In the center of the newly created space they'd installed a long butcher-block island that could accommodate half a dozen barstools. Above each, individual lights dangled from the ceiling. "Wow!" Toby said. "You did all this yourself?"

"Except for the electrical."

She ran her painted nails over the butcher-block surface. "Well, whatever you spent, you'll make it back and more. It's all about kitchens and baths these days. Can we go upstairs?"

"Let's not," he suggested. "It's all torn up." Which was true. Both upstairs baths were being retiled, and except for the master bedroom, which was closed off, there was dust and debris everywhere. Also, with sex in the offing Peter found her enthusiasm for real estate unnerving. Even now that the sex was over, her immediate return to the subject was mildly off-putting. "You know," she said, staring up at the ceiling, as if her realtor vision allowed her to see right through it, "if you hired more help, you could probably get the place on the market by June. Why miss the season?"

For some reason, this pragmatic suggestion caused Peter to reflect upon his earlier conversation with her ex-husband. Was it possible that Carl had been right about Sully having had a serious crush on Toby? The possibility prompted further speculation: If his father had ever been lucky enough to coax her into the sack, would the experience have broken the spell she'd cast over him? He doubted Sully would've been disappointed in the sex itself, but Toby's ability to immediately segue to mundane subjects mere moments after the final shudder of pleasure might well have rattled him. Despite being a realist about most things, Sully was, Peter suspected, a closet romantic. Having nursed a crush for years, he would've expected transcendence, and here was yet another dissimilarity between them. Sex, though pleasurable, generally didn't overwhelm Peter, though he did enjoy its afterglow, especially if it could be enjoyed in dark silence.

Toby, he realized, was now up on one elbow, staring at him. "What's *with* you tonight?"

"What do you mean?"

"You've been acting like you're somewhere else."

"I'm sorry," he said. Nor was the irony of each lamenting the other's lack of focus lost on him. Should he come clean about Thomas's visit? He'd actually been on the verge of doing so during dinner, but the wine bar had been too noisy, the music too loud. He'd imagined this postcoital moment as a better opportunity for intimacy, but now that the moment had arrived, the urge seemed to have passed.

Perhaps sensing this, Toby said, "Fine. Be that way," and slipped out of bed. "Don't go anywhere, though. I may not be finished with you."

When the bathroom door closed behind her, Peter rose and went over to the window, where he parted the curtain and peered into the dark street, again half expecting to see the yellow Caddy glide by or, worse, be sitting in the drive. As much as he wanted it to be true, Peter didn't believe his son's story. Somehow sex with Toby had clarified his thinking on the subject. Thomas's unexpected appearance on the porch this morning had been no spur-of-the-moment decision. When he left West Virginia, Bath, not Montreal, had been his destination. The yellow Caddy he'd glimpsed in the wine bar mirror was Thomas's.

Also coming into sharper focus was why the conversation with his son had been playing on a loop in his head all evening. On the surface his visit had been pleasant enough, but something Peter wasn't able to put his finger on at the time had felt off about it. How was it that Thomas appeared to hold no grudge about how things had worked out? About him and his little brother growing up with their mother in West Virginia, estranged from himself and Will up here in Bath? How could he *not* be bitter? When Peter himself was Thomas's age, he'd never missed an opportunity to needle his father about having opted out of his own young life. Sully's defense had been that he figured Peter was better off without him, especially after Vera remarried and Ralph proved such a good stepfather. Unwilling to accept this lame excuse, Peter had been determined to make Sully understand that his boyhood, while safe, had still been full of terrible longing and wrenching doubt. For this, Vera was partly to blame, of course. She'd made Sully feel like an unwelcome intruder in her home, but Peter still hadn't been able to understand why his father had given him up without a fight. The only conclusion he could come to was that he must not be a boy worth fighting for.

Wouldn't Thomas harbor similar resentments? Why hadn't he demanded to know why, when Charlotte ordered Peter to stay out of their lives, he'd gone along as if hers had been a reasonable demand? Okay, maybe Thomas had gently mocked him (*I never would've got to see where Will grew up, and I always wanted to.*), but where was his righteous anger at the injustice of it all? How could he not resent the fact that he and his little brother had missed out—on a nicer place to live, on a doting grandfather, on the opportunity for a better education? Thomas had made it sound like he was merely curious about Will's life up north, but he would've been more than curious, wouldn't he? He'd have been sick with envy. To triumph over such resentment, you'd have to succeed in life in a way that rendered your older brother's unmerited good fortune irrelevant. If Thomas had started his own company, then sold it to Amazon and bought a yacht with the proceeds, sure, he could afford to be cavalier about all of Will's advantages, but clearly, nothing like that had happened. The way he dressed, together with that beast of a car he drove, proved it. Why, then, wasn't Thomas seething?

The more Peter replayed their conversation in his head, the more he wondered if Thomas's end of it had been a well-rehearsed performance. Only when he seriously entertained this possibility did he recall how peculiar some of the details of their interaction had been. For instance, when Peter had informed him that Will was currently in England on a Fulbright, hadn't Thomas's left eye visibly twitched? And later when he'd invited him to stick around for a day or two, assuring him that there was plenty of room, hadn't that eye twitched again? And what about Thomas's facetiously reporting that his brother Andy had turned out to be gay? (Had he?) *Had* Thomas actually gotten a girl pregnant, as he'd joked about having done? At the time Peter had written off these bizarre declarations as bungled attempts at humor, but wasn't it also possible that they served a darker purpose: to illustrate that Peter didn't have the faintest idea who Thomas and Andy were, or what their lives had been like?

But slow down. Even if all that was true, wasn't he still jumping to conclusions? If Peter was indeed clueless about his son's life, could he really say with any degree of certainty that Thomas hadn't somehow managed to grow up decent and forgiving? Maybe he too had benefited from having a kind, loving stepfather. What if he actually *was* better off for Peter's absence? What if Peter was just projecting onto Thomas his own recollected anger at Sully, his own sense of injustice? It was possible. And yet. Peter actually *had* been in Thomas's place, and not that long ago. The myriad resentments he'd felt where Sully was concerned had taken him most of his adult life to work through, and in the end he hadn't so much banished them as brought them under control, allowing Sully, a man who was as charming as he was feckless, to grow on him, to gradually enter his affection. Whereas Thomas, if their conversation today was taken at face value, had skipped that entire process. Was that even possible? Peter wanted to believe so. That morning, when Thomas inquired after Will, he'd thought, *Good.* Maybe time had in fact healed some very old wounds. As boys they'd been constant antagonists, forever bickering, always at each other's throats, and the collapse of his and Charlotte's marriage had only exacerbated matters. Just how badly, Peter hadn't realized until he and Will had made that ill-fated trip to West Virginia after the divorce. He'd hoped that by then Charlotte might have surrendered a few of her grievances or, failing this, that they could arrive at some sort of accommodation. From the moment they walked in the door, however, it had been clear that Charlotte's hatred had calcified. When she wasn't spitting venom at him, she was bragging about how many men she'd slept with since they separated, how every single one of them had been better in bed than Peter, how she wished their marriage had come apart sooner, so they wouldn't have wasted all that time. Was she actually wishing away their children? Peter couldn't tell, but one thing was for certain. His ex-wife had become someone he no longer recognized, both irrational and unhinged.

"Admit it," she'd raged at him. "You want me dead. I know you do, because that's how I want you."

Every attempt he'd made to calm her down had caused the conflagration of her rage to burn hotter. She'd even mocked his plan to have Thomas and Andy spend the summers with him and Will so the boys wouldn't completely lose touch.

"What do you care if they do?" she'd sneered at him. "You got the one you wanted, right?" Peter could still feel the force of that thrust, the truth of it. Because yes, Will had been his favorite, a kind, sweet boy.

At some point during that awful visit, they'd sent the boys outside so they wouldn't have to listen to so much acrimony at full volume, but somehow conflict had followed them out into the weedy backyard. There, Thomas and Will had gotten into a fistfight over the stopwatch Sully had gifted his grandson, a fight that, to Peter's amazement, Will had actually won. It was the only time he'd bested his younger brother in any sort of physical contest. But if Peter was proud of him, Will himself was clearly ashamed. When Peter and Charlotte emerged from the house, Will had run to him and sobbed into his shirtfront. Little Andy, also wailing, had gone to his mother, and Thomas, one eye already closing and turning color, had joined her as well. Peter could picture him even now, his small face a mask of profound resentment, his mother's face in miniature. It was the face of a boy determined never to forgive or forget.

"Wow," Toby Roebuck said, having materialized at his elbow. "You really are a mess tonight."

Since there didn't seem to be any point denying this, Peter didn't. She stroked him hopefully, having apparently decided in the bathroom that indeed she was not through with him. When it became clear that her efforts were to no avail, she dressed and left.


Peter was generally a light sleeper, but the combination of alcohol, sex and emotional exhaustion from the day's events plunged him into a profound slumber, so when the upstairs toilet flushed, his first thought was that the sound had to be part of the strange dream he'd been awakened from. Had Thomas been in it? *Go back to sleep,* he told himself, but no sooner had the thought registered than he heard, directly overhead, the sound of muffled footsteps. *Thomas?* Had his son belatedly decided to take Peter up on his offer to spend a few days in Bath? But that made no sense. How would Thomas (or anyone else for that matter) have gotten in without a key? When would he even have arrived? After Toby left? Could Peter have been sleeping so soundly that he hadn't heard someone enter the house, climb the hall stairs and let themselves into the upstairs flat? Groggy, he rose, went over to the window and parted the curtains, convinced, though it made no sense, that this time Thomas's yellow Caddy would be in the driveway. But again, no.

*So, okay,* he told himself sternly. Whoever was upstairs, it wasn't Thomas. The fact that he'd been dreaming about his son when the toilet flushed did not mean that Thomas was the one who'd flushed it. But if not him, then who? The only other person with a key to the front door was Will, who was in England. And even if he'd flown home early, hoping to surprise his father, he wouldn't have gone upstairs. He'd have claimed his own downstairs bedroom. The place had been locked up tight when he left for Schuyler and was locked when he returned with Toby. Later, when she left, the door would've locked automatically behind her. The seldom-used rear door was always locked, the only key to it on Peter's key ring. Which meant . . . what? He massaged his temples, trying to reason it through. There had to be a simple explanation.

But if so, it eluded him. In fact, he couldn't even come up with a complicated one that made any sense. If whoever was up there had no key, then that person had broken in, either by picking one of the locks or forcing a ground-floor window. But seriously? On Upper Main Street in Bath? Pulling on a pair of jeans and a T-shirt, Peter made his way through the dark downstairs flat, looking for evidence of an intruder—a half-open window, an overturned chair—but there was none. No one *could* be upstairs, but apparently somebody was. Stopping at the hall closet where Will stored his sports equipment, he grabbed an aluminum bat, thinking, *Just in case.* But in case of what? Out in the hallway, he checked the front door, but no, it was locked, just as he knew it would be. He considered turning on the hall light, but decided—again, *just in case*—not to signal his approach. At the foot of the stairs, however, he stalled. He had, he realized, two working hypotheses for what he would find upstairs, the first ludicrous, the second batshit crazy. Neither seemed to require the aluminum bat he was gripping.

*Thomas.* Ridiculous though it was, Peter simply couldn't banish the notion that the intruder would turn out to be his son. There were a fair number of moving parts in Peter's life, but only one—Thomas—was new. And if it *was* Thomas up there, it followed that his purpose would be dark. Otherwise, the yellow Caddy would be parked out front. There were only two reasons to break into someone's home. You either meant to steal something or do someone harm. If the intruder was Thomas, then theft could pretty much be ruled out. Just that morning Peter had taken him on a tour of the house, so his son knew it was basically a construction site up there. Nothing much worth stealing unless you were in the market for a circular saw. On the other hand, maybe the intruder had been *down*stairs when Peter and Toby showed up. Had he scurried upstairs to avoid detection? But that would mean he'd been up there for the last two hours, which also made no sense. A thief would've slipped out of the house while he and Toby were otherwise occupied. By the same token, though, anyone bent on doing Peter harm would have come downstairs and done so as soon as she left. But who would've wanted to harm him in the first place? The only person he could think of who'd ever truly hated him was Charlotte, and that was a long time ago. Did she still? Possibly. Though Vera's hatred of Sully had been impotent, she'd nursed it all the way to the grave. Maybe Charlotte's rage wasn't impotent. Maybe hers was the rage that hell hath no fury like. Had she managed to instill that same black hatred in Thomas?

But no, it was a fever dream. Admit it, he'd been sick with guilt since pulling up in front of the house and recognizing Thomas on the porch. In that moment it had come home to him that he'd done to Thomas what Sully had done to him. Probably worse. There was no way to sugarcoat it. Peter had not fought for his kids. Yes, he'd provided a good, safe life for one of them, but the other two he'd abandoned to the care of a crazy woman. Even on that ill-fated trip to West Virginia, there'd already been evidence of his absence. Despite his alimony and child support checks, Thomas and Andy were dressed shabbily and looked undernourished compared with Will, who was the picture of health. What was Charlotte doing with the money? Drinking it? What right did he have to even ask? Later, he'd been relieved to learn she intended to remarry. Maybe her new husband would improve things for all concerned. "It's possible," Sully said, when Peter shared the welcome news. "But shouldn't you go down there and check this guy out?"

"It's none of my business who she marries, Dad," Peter told him, though he'd considered doing exactly this.

"No, but your sons are," Sully replied, which was rich, coming from him. "You want me to go?"

"No," Peter assured him. "I want you to butt out."

He should've gone himself, though. That much was clear. This afternoon, when he and Thomas were on the porch and he'd wondered if his son's ancient yellow Caddy would make it to Montreal, Thomas had smiled and assured Peter it would. That smile had revealed a black, rotten tooth. How long had it been like that? Peter wondered. Was it a recent occurrence, or evidence of a life spent without access to dental care and who knew what else? The wave of guilt he felt at the latter possibility had made him weak in the knees. Worse, tonight, his guilt appeared to be morphing into something truly ugly. He was actually imagining that one of the sons he'd abandoned had driven all the way from West Virginia bent on violent revenge. To prevent this, he'd armed himself with an aluminum bat, which he apparently meant to use on the boy he'd failed. Feeling his stomach turn over, he leaned the bat up against the wall.

*Think*, he told himself. He needed to reconcile two seemingly unreconcilable facts. Whoever was upstairs was (1) *an intruder,* despite (2) *not sounding like one.* What he sounded like was someone who lived there. Who belonged there. Someone so familiar with his surroundings that he could navigate them in the dark, as Peter himself had just done downstairs. Someone for whom the place was, well, *home*. The problem was that no such person existed. Well— and this was where his second working hypothesis took wing—no such *living* person. If, however, one was open-minded (lunatic) enough to include the dead, then it was obvious who was upstairs. It was none other than Sully himself and, to Peter, the notion that his father had this night returned from the dead felt strangely plausible, despite its utter impossibility. For one thing, if Sully had grown weary of the grave and decided to return to the land of the living, Miss Beryl's house was definitely where he'd come, and unlike any living person Peter could think of, he'd go straight upstairs, where he'd lived above his landlady for much of his adult life. Moreover, if his father *could* return from the dead he definitely *would*. The most single-minded of men, Sully had left Peter a to-do list, and it was just like him to want to check on his progress. In fact, lying there in his grave with nothing to do but think, Sully had probably come up with a few other duties to add to the list, lest his son cross out the last item on the original and finally make his long-delayed escape from North Bath. There was also, though it pained Peter to admit, another possible reason for Sully to return today, of all days. Maybe, just maybe, he'd come to lend a hand, to offer advice, to acknowledge that with Thomas's return, Peter was in over his head.

Thankfully, in addition to its fundamental lunacy, there were other reasons to discount the theory that Sully had returned from the dead. Start with internal logic. Such a return would render him a ghost, and what need would a ghost have of a toilet? Would the footfalls of a spirit be audible to the living? And if they were, wouldn't those footfalls sound more like Sully's, whose gait in life bore more than a passing resemblance to Captain Ahab's?

One thing was for sure. He wasn't going to find out who or what was upstairs by remaining downstairs, so up Peter went. At the top of the stairs he again paused to put his ear to the door. From within, silence. When he tried the knob, the door swung open. Inside, the only light came from the street. If someone, alive or dead, came toward him in the darkness, would he be able to detect the movement?

Again Peter paused to listen and, from the far end of the apartment, the bedroom that had been for decades his father's, there came a resounding fart.

===

"I SHOULD'VE KNOWN," Peter said when he switched on the bedroom light and saw Carl Roebuck, clad only in his boxers, stretched out on the bare mattress. He seemed to have sobered up some since leaving the wine bar, but his eyes were still webbed with red. Peter was actually more relieved to see him than he cared to admit. His rationality having suddenly returned, he felt positively buoyant, better than he'd felt all day, including when he was having sex with Carl's ex-wife. "I'm a little confused about how you got in, though."

On the bedside table, next to his wallet and cell phone, lay the key ring that earlier had sat on the bar at Infinity. Carl picked it up and found the key in question. "With this," he said. "You forgot. I used to live here."

He was right. Peter had forgotten that. There'd been a period of two or three years when his father was living in a trailer he'd parked out back and Carl had rented the upstairs flat. "But that was a decade ago."

Carl nodded. "I have to admit, I was pretty surprised when the key still worked."

"Okay if I come in?" Peter said. He was feeling a little awkward, standing in the doorway.

"Hey," Carl said with a sweeping gesture. "*Mi casa, su casa.*"

"*Es verdad,*" Peter replied. Unless he was much mistaken, the two men had pretty well exhausted their Spanish. There was a paint-splattered step stool leaning up against the wall, so Peter unfolded it and took a seat. On the floor at the foot of the bed lay a copy of the *Schuyler Democrat,* which people in Bath referred to as the *Dumb-o-crat* because of its left-leaning opinion page. Picking this up, Peter used it to fan the air, which was still rich with Carl's flatulence. "So . . . you've been up here this whole time?"

Carl met his eye. "You mean the whole time you were screwing my wife?"

"I feel like I should say—for the record?—that she divorced you fifteen years ago. If you still think of her as your wife, you're the only one who does."

"Also for the record?" Carl replied. "I'm *not* the only one. There's also God, before whom we swore an oath. Till death do us part."

"Fascinating that this is the part of the ceremony you should fixate on," Peter smiled. "Anyway, I'm sorry you had to listen, even if it does serve you right. I hear you've had a rough day."

"Day?" Carl snorted. "Try week. Month. Six months."

Peter tossed the newspaper back on the floor, the air somewhat less polluted now. "What's been going on?"

"That's the weird part. Until recently, I never really understood the allure of gambling."

Peter couldn't help chuckling at this. Part of Carl's charm, or perhaps its entirety, derived from his being so completely full of shit. "I seem to recall you were one of the regulars at the poker game in the back room of the Horse."

"True," Carl admitted, "but I never really considered that gambling. Playing cards with your old man and the rest of those dimwits was more like a lucrative hobby. Games of actual chance are completely different. They're designed for suckers who believe you can beat the house, and you can't. If you could, there'd be no casinos."

Peter nodded agreeably. He'd heard this same sermon from any number of compulsive gamblers. "Okay, so what changed?"

Carl scratched his groin thoughtfully, as if the answer to this question might be located in his boxers. And why not? The majority of Carl's problems had always been located there, not to mention a few of Peter's own, if he was completely honest. "I'm not sure," Carl admitted. "Divorce? Prostate cancer? Losing my old man's construction company? I think at some point self-doubt may have crept in."

Peter shook his head in wonder. If ever there was a man who stood to benefit from self-doubt, that man lay stretched out before him.

"On the other hand," Carl continued, "maybe it was simple boredom. Long story short? I discovered online poker."

"And now you're fucked."

"If by fucked you mean broke, jobless and homeless, then, yeah, I guess."

"That's what I meant," Peter nodded.

"Also, my car was repossessed."

"When it rains."

"And tonight," he said, "on my way over here? Something else occurred to me. I have no friends. Which didn't use to be the fucking case."

"Are you sure?" Peter asked, because he knew most of the men Carl used to hang around and they mostly just tolerated him. Sully had liked Carl more than most, and even he frequently wanted to murder the man.

"And the really unfair part?" Carl went on.

"There's more?"

"The really unfair part is that your old man warned me, more than once, that all this would come to pass."

"You didn't believe him."

Carl made a pained face. "Why the fuck would I? The guy was a compass that pointed due south. Whenever he told me I was going to end up truly fucked, I had no choice but to conclude my luck would hold." Clearly, the man could still find no flaw in this logic even now. "Anyhow. Thank God he's dead. At least I don't have to listen to him saying I told you so."

"Sounds to me like that's exactly what you're doing," Peter said. "Also, you're wrong about being homeless. If you don't mind living in a construction site, you can camp here until you find something else."

"Seriously?"

"Well, you seem to have a key."

Carl was studying him now. His eyes narrowed. "You're not doing this out of the goodness of your heart," he said. "You just feel guilty about screwing my wife."

"If you say so," Peter said agreeably. "There's one stipulation, though. Rub and I will be working here on Saturdays. You'll have to find someplace else to go."

Carl smiled sadly. "How is old Rubberhead? Still in mourning?"

"Pretty much."

"Tell me something," Carl said. "Do you still think about him? Sully?"

"Are you kidding? Living in *this* house? When I heard the toilet flush up here I smelled his aftershave."

"I think about my old man, too," Carl said wistfully. "Kenny Roebuck. Now there was a man who had friends. For all the good they did him."

"What do you mean?"

"He still died."

"Well . . . ," Peter said.

"No, I mean really. Think about it. You do everything right. You never fuck up. People respect you. Love you. Then one day you wake up dead. Couple days after that, you're in the ground next to somebody who never did anything right and couldn't even be bothered to try. Same result. What's it all supposed to mean?"

"You're asking me?"

He shrugged. "I keep thinking about that poor bastard out at the Sans Souci. You ever consider doing what he did? Just be done with all of it?"

"Nope."

"Never?"

"Never."

"Me neither," Carl said, perhaps a little too quickly. "What does that make us?"

"Alive?"

"Okay, that. But here's what I'd like to know. Why are you still here?"

Peter squinted at him. "You mean still alive? Here in Bath? Or here in this room talking to a crazy person?"

"The middle one," Carl said. "I mean, I know you enjoy fucking my wife every now and then, but that can't be what's keeping you here."

Peter made a sweeping gesture that took in the entire upstairs flat. "As soon as I finish these renovations and put the place on the market, I'm gone."

Carl was grinning at him now. "I got a thousand bucks says you'll be right here ten years from now."

Given Carl's bluesy mood, Peter was relieved to learn that he was thinking in ten-year increments. "Except you *don't* have a thousand bucks."

"I *would* have, if you'd take the bet."

Peter was curious about something. "Were you serious before? About you and Toby getting back together. That's what you want?"

"I don't know. Lately I've been wondering if maybe she was my good luck charm. Maybe if I got her back, everything else would fix itself?"

"When was the last time anything broken ever fixed itself?"

Carl blinked. "Now just hold on," he said. "Back up. You're suggesting I should fix things myself instead of waiting for my old dumb luck to return? *That's* your advice?"

"You're right," Peter agreed. "Dumb idea. Forget I said anything." Going over to the closet, he pulled out a set of sheets, a blanket and a pillow, all of which he tossed to Carl. "Get some sleep," he suggested.

He was halfway out the door when he heard Carl chuckle. "You and your old man are two peas in a pod, you know that?"

"How so?"

"He was a soft touch, too. Back in the day? When Toby would get pissed off and toss me out of the house, I'd come over here and sack out on the sofa until she cooled down."

"How many times did that happen?"

"I lost track. A dozen? More? You think maybe that's why I keep waiting for her to take me back again?"

"Could be."

"You in love with her?"

"Nope."

"You sure?"

Peter nodded.

"Excellent," Carl said, placing the pillow under his head and stifling a yawn. "Good night, John-Boy."

Back downstairs in his own flat, listening to his new tenant snore overhead, Peter tried to remember if Carl had been on the original list of people his father had asked him to check on. It probably didn't matter. He was apparently on it now. Which made Peter wonder if Sully's ghost really had paid him a visit.

# Lie Detector

WHEN JANEY ARRIVED at the Green Hand, Del was holding court at the large round table the Schuyler cops always commandeered on weekends. Tonight, he had an attentive audience of a dozen or so officers and their spouses and dates. She saw him notice when she entered and glance at his watch so he'd know how much shit to give her later on, then went back to the story he was telling. Like most of Del's stories, this one—about how he and the cops at his old Philly precinct would mess with guys in the drunk tank on slow nights—was cruel but also, she had to admit, pretty funny. Everybody always howled at the end, never mind the fact that most of them had heard the story before. Janey didn't know what to make of Copworld, as she'd come to think of it, the way these officers saw no contradiction between their stated duty—to maintain law and order—and their unstated conviction that to do their jobs effectively meant bending every single rule in the book and breaking the ones that wouldn't bend. Was this why Charice Bond had it in for Del?

Since the story was a long one and the Hand's lone cocktail waitress was taking drink orders at another large table, Janey stopped at the bar and ordered a shot of tequila and a beer chaser. Hah! Just like that she'd decided what kind of night this would be. Amazing, really, how truly gratifying making the first bad decision of the night could be. She was getting a late start, but that was the good thing about the Hand. Come closing time, the door would be locked, but if you were already there, you would continue to be served. No need to worry about getting raided, not with all the guys who would've conducted the raid already there and fully complicit. Looking around, Janey wondered if maybe Del was right. Eleven o'clock and the joint was hopping. Maybe she should just go ahead and sell Hattie's. She'd probably make more money waitressing here and, God knew, there'd be fewer headaches. If she sold the restaurant, its attached apartment would have to be part of the deal, but that was fine by her. She could rent someplace here in Schuyler. It would be more expensive, but with money from the sale of the restaurant in her pocket, she could probably swing it. Putting North Bath, which technically didn't exist anymore, in her rearview mirror, along with lingering memories of her ratfuck husband, didn't seem like such a bad idea. It would mean her daughter and mother would be in one place and she in another, but so what? Would they even miss her? Fifteen minutes ago she'd been crying her eyes out to think of her daughter alone on a Saturday night, pining for a boy who probably hadn't thought of her once in the last decade, but really, what the fuck was Janey supposed to do about it? How were you supposed to comfort somebody who wanted nothing to do with you? Who blamed you for her pitiful, sorry-ass circumstance. Tina was unhappy? Wake up, little girl. There was a lot of that going around. If she was having her spells again, well, she just was. Janey's being close by wouldn't prevent them. Saint Ruth was right there on the premises, and she couldn't do anything about them, either.

And speaking of sorry-ass circumstances, what about Janey's own? Once again, she allowed herself to reflect upon the injustice of how things had worked out—her daughter inheriting her grandfather's scrap-heap business, which to everyone's surprise was worth a small fortune, while Janey got Hattie's which, even before the recession, had been circling the drain. How was it fair for her daughter to be in financial clover while Janey herself was forced to pick up extra shifts at the Horse and wonder if the tips she earned there would even cover her bar bill? Del had made clear that he couldn't afford to pay her tab, not as much as she drank, not when he was in the middle of a divorce. The divorce was probably just an excuse, though. The way Del saw it, women were an expense that shouldn't be allowed to get out of hand. He knew this because he'd allowed it to, not once but twice. Janey could buy her own damn drinks.

At the far end of the bar Janey noticed a guy about her daughter's age, borderline good-looking, if a bit on the scruffy side. He had the look of a man who'd decided hours earlier to get positively shit-faced and had made excellent progress toward that straightforward goal.

When she arrived at the cop table, everyone scooched closer together so she could sit next to Del, who didn't even break stride in his story when she set her tequila and beer down on the table and settled in beside him. The lie detector story he was in the middle of was one of his favorites. Nights like tonight, when he had a rapt audience, Del's stories all stretched out like taffy. In this one Del and his partner have pulled an old Black guy out of the tank and taken him to an interview room. There they explain that they're hooking him up to a lie detector, though all they're really doing is attaching a splint, the kind sold in medical supply stores, to his index finger. They tell the dumb *mulignan* that there's a microchip embedded in the metal, that the whole thing is wireless. (Del referred to Blacks as *mulignans,* which, according to him, was the Italian word for eggplant—*Ever see a white one?* Janey didn't know how to feel about this. To his credit, Del never came right out and used the N-word, but how much better was this?) He explains to the *mulignan* that they're going to ask him a series of questions, and if he lies to them, they'll know. The guy's a little suspicious at first—can this be true?—but these are cops he's talking to and what the fuck does he know? Not much, including the fact that they've rigged a buzzer underneath the table.

They begin by asking him questions they already know the answers to. Is your name Lamar Jones? *Yes.* Are you sixty-one years old? *Yes.* Do you live at the Prospect Gardens apartment complex?

*Yes.* Do you work at Dunham Financial Group? *Yes.* Are you the night security officer at their downtown office building? *Yes.* This is where things get interesting. Del asks Lamar Jones if he's ever engaged in an illegal activity while performing his duties at Dunham. When he says no, Del activates the buzzer and the *mulignan* just about jumps out of his fucking skin. Mr. Jones, I think you just lied to us, Del informs the man, who could pass for white now, that's how fucking pale he's gone. *No, sir, I didn't,* Lamar protests. *Maybe,* Del suggests, what you did wasn't illegal, strictly speaking. Maybe it was just something you'd rather your boss didn't know about. *Okay, okay,* Mr. Jones gives in. Some nights he buzzes a few friends into the building so they can watch the 76ers on the big flat screen in the back room. He keeps all the other monitors on like he's supposed to and checks them all, every single one, during the commercials to make sure no unauthorized persons have entered the building, which never happens anyhow.

When Del asks him if alcohol is ever involved, Mr. Jones says, "No, sir," and Del can tell just by looking at him that he's fucking lying. *Bzzzt!* Off goes the buzzer. Again Mr. Jones startles at the sound, but not like before. He's expecting it this time, lying sack of shit that he is. *Okay, okay,* Mr. Jones admits. Some beer, but no hard stuff. How about drugs, Mr. Jones? Del asks him, and this time—*Bzzzt!*—he activates the buzzer before the *no* is even out of the *mulignan*'s mouth. Fucking guy comes unglued right there. *Ima lose my job, ain't I?* Lamar Jones begins to cry uncontrollably. At this point Del and his partner usually come clean and admit to the hopeless *mamaluke* (more Italian, Janey has learned) that he's the victim of a joke. They never just come right out and tell the guy, though, because where's the fun in that? Instead, they ask him a question that's simple, clear and straightforward, something there'd be no reason for the guy to lie about, and when they hit the buzzer on the guy's truthful response it finally dawns on him that he's being fucked with, that the thing on his finger is just a drugstore splint and that no, you dimwit, you're not going to lose your job. So this is what Del is expecting. "One last question, Mr. Jones," he says, and it's all he can do not to bust out laughing. "Have you ever had sex with a man?" The *mulignan* is so outraged that he flies out of the chair and pounds his fist on the table. "No!" he screams. "Never!" *Bzzzt! Bzzzt! Bzzzt!* The buzzer screams back at him. For a long moment Del and the *moulignan* are nose to nose, until finally Lamar Jones collapses back into his chair, his head in his hands. "Okay," he admits. "Once."

And now, though Del's audience has known all along that this punch line was coming, the whole cop table erupted in laughter.

The story had a moral, too, and Del never skipped it: "Can you believe we let these fuckwads *vote*?"

Only after delivering it did he turn and acknowledge Janey. "Hey, babe," he said, "what the fuck kept you?"

From this point the evening unspooled in predictable Copworld fashion. More war stories. More drinking. Lots of rowdy, boisterous laughter. Around closing time, or what would've been closing time in any other Schuyler bar, somebody shouted "Ramblin', gamblin'!" and Bob Seger thundered onto the sound system. Tables got pushed back to create a dance floor. Del never danced, nor did most of the other cops, though a couple female officers enjoyed cutting loose, along with some of the spouses and dates. Normally Janey did, too, but not tonight. Despite the tequila and her determination to have some fun, her thoughts kept drifting back to her daughter and, yes, her mother, especially that last hateful thing Janey had said. Ruth wasn't going to be around forever, a fact that Janey knew but couldn't seem to remember when she was angry, which was nearly always. Still, she couldn't help noticing how played-out her mother looked these days. She hadn't been the same, really, since Sully's death, a fact that made Janey both angry and, yes, jealous, too. Aside from the fact that he'd wrecked her parents' marriage, she didn't have anything against the man. What baffled her was that her mother couldn't seem to get over him. Experience had taught Janey that men were mostly interchangeable. Sure, you needed one, but did it really matter which? If Ruth was right and Tina was carrying a torch for a boy she'd never even dated, well, that was beyond pitiful. Unless, of course, Janey had it backward. Maybe *not* knowing the person you were in love with was what made such devotion possible. After all, wasn't it getting to know the men in her life that had taught Janey how interchangeable they were?

*Fucking tequila,* she thought. It was the sneakiest booze ever, no question. When her spirits were already high, tequila elevated them further, beckoning her to climb up on top of that table and dance and howl. When they were low, like tonight, it turned her inward, made her morose. She'd tried her best not to let it show, but finally Del said, "The fuck's wrong with you tonight?"

"Nothing," Janey told him, not wanting to go into it. "Don't you ever get blue?"

He snorted. "The fuck is *blue*? What does that even mean?"

"I don't know, Del. Ask a blues singer. I worked two shifts today. I'm tired."

"Yeah, but remember earlier? How I told you not to come out here whining about how tired you were."

"No, Del, that's *not* what you said. What you told me was to come here no matter how fucking tired I was, and here I am. And don't tell me it's Saturday night. I know what fucking night it is."

Okay, maybe men were not completely interchangeable. If it had been Roy she'd just said that to, she'd be sitting on the floor now, tasting blood. She glanced at Del's hands to see if they were balled up into fists, like Roy's always were a split second before he punched her, but they were flat on the table. Still, she was surprised when he said, not without tenderness, "Hey, now. Don't be like that." Which—*fucking tequila!*—pissed her off even more, because it reminded her of her father, how he used to plead with Ruth when she was angry at him. *Come on, now. Don't be like that.* And Janey wanting to scream at him, What's point of saying, *Don't be like that,* when *that* was clearly how she was and always had been and always would be? Was that how Sully had been different? Had he accepted her mother for who she was? Was that what she herself was looking for and never finding? A man who wouldn't say, *Don't be like that,* which was, after all, the same as saying, *Don't be you?*

She was about to say that maybe she'd just head on home when there came, from somewhere behind her, a loud bang, followed by a woman's scream. Perhaps because the room was full of cops, Janey's first thought was that the bang must've been a gunshot, and when she turned to look, sure enough, someone was stretched out on the floor, not moving, at the end of the bar. It took her a moment to realize it was the guy she'd noticed when she entered. Coming out from behind the bar, the bartender knelt down beside the man and slapped him gently on the cheek. "Come on now, fella," he said. "Wake up."

"That's the damnedest thing I ever saw," said the woman who'd screamed. "The dude leaned back on his stool and just kept going."

"Passed out," the bartender said.

"Should we call an ambulance?" the woman said. "He hit the back of his head awful hard."

"No ambulance," the bartender said. No need to explain why. The Hand was supposed to have closed an hour ago. "He's not bleeding. He'll come to in a minute."

"Drunks don't generally hurt themselves when they fall," Del agreed. He and the other cops had formed a circle around the fallen man. "It's their superpower."

"I should've seen it coming," the bartender admitted. "He's been downing shots all night."

"And you kept serving him?"

"How was I supposed to know how drunk he was? He didn't say two words to me all night. Just pointed at his shot glass."

"Well," said Bobby, Del's partner, "we can't just let him lie there."

"Hey!" the bartender shouted, slapping the man's cheek harder now. "Wake up!"

Del shook his head. "Nah," he said. "He's out cold. Tell you what. The station's on my way home anyhow. I'll drop him off there and he can sleep it off in one of the empty cells."

Nobody else seemed to have a better idea, so Del and three other cops each grabbed a limb and together lugged the comatose stranger outside.

"Back seat?" said Bobby.

"Fuck, no," Del told him, popping open the trunk. "You think I want him hurling on my back seat?"

"It's okay if he hurls in your trunk?" Bobby said.

"Not really, but I'm willing to risk it."

Back inside, people finished their drinks and called for their checks. By Hand standards it was still relatively early, but after all the excitement, everybody seemed ready to call it a night. The other cops all wanted to say good night to Del before leaving. "Don't forget that asshole's in your trunk and drive home," one of the female officers warned. "You come out in the morning and find him frozen to death in there and you'll be even farther up Shit Crick than you are now."

"She's right," one of the other cops agreed. "Char-Easy would do the happy dance."

"Fuck Char-Easy," Del said, and something about the way it came out made Janey wonder if his hatred of the woman might be more complicated than he let on. Had he in his head made the same exception for Charice Bond that he'd made for Halle Berry?

"What the hell's got into you?" she said, when they were at the door, struggling into their heavy coats. In addition to paying his own tab he'd grabbed hers and paid it, too.

"Beats me," he admitted. "Just don't think I'm going to every time, 'cause I'm not."

Outside, Janey told him she was fine to drive, but he said no, she'd been drinking tequila. She could ride with him and they'd retrieve her car in the morning.

"Should we check on him?" she said, meaning the man in the trunk.

"What? You mean to see if he's still in there?"

"No, to see if he's still breathing. What if he chokes to death on his own vomit?"

"You worry too much," he said, unlocking the sedan's driver's side and then hers. She supposed he was right. She'd done nothing but worry all night and for what?

The only other vehicle in the lot besides Del's and hers and Gary the bartender's was a huge, bright yellow Caddy that had to be twenty-five years old. Janey figured it must belong to the guy in the trunk. When they swung by, Del's headlights illuminated the vehicle's West Virginia plate. "Huh," Del said. "He's a long way from home."

# SUNDAY

# Roomies

WHEN RAYMER WOKE on Sunday morning, he was surprised to find his new roommate seated at the kitchen table, dressed in the same clothes he had on the day before and squinting at the screen of a laptop. His two suitcases still sat near the front door, right where he'd set them down the night before. Raymer tried his best to make some kind of sense of this. The laptop had to have been in one of the two suitcases, which meant that at some point Jerome had removed it. Why would he have closed the suitcase up again and set it back by the door instead of bringing it and its companion into the spare bedroom where he'd be staying? Was he trying to convey to Raymer that he was playing this whole match under protest? That he could change his mind at any moment and leave? The last thing Charice had warned Raymer about before leaving the two of them together was that his world was about to change and not for the better. Very little of what was in store for him with Jerome was going to make much sense. Best to just roll with it.

The night before, when Jerome arrived at the Horse with those same two suitcases, his stated intention had been to have Charice drive him to the airport. From there he would fly back home to North Carolina. He seemed to regard the luggage as evidence of this intent. In Charice's view, contravening evidence—Jerome's well-documented flare for melodrama, together with the fact that evening flights out of Albany's regional airport were nonexistent on the weekend—had been more compelling. "I'm sorry I yelled at you on the phone," she told him. "But this"—here she indicated the suitcases—"is crazy."

At the time the three of them were standing in the middle of the dining room. Everyone else in both the restaurant and bar was watching, a few pretending not to, but most not bothering.

"We've discussed this," Charice reminded her brother. "You can't go back home till you're right. I hope you're not going to stand there and tell me you're right, because we both know you're not."

Raymer had expected Jerome to dispute this, but he didn't. Instead, he just stood there with the two suitcases, looking like Willy Loman. "How did you even get here?" Charice wanted to know.

"I summoned a taxi."

Raymer couldn't help smiling at this. Other people called taxis. Only Jerome would summon one.

"Well, you wasted your money," she said. This whole time Jerome had still not acknowledged Raymer's presence. "Aren't you going to say hello to Doug?"

Jerome shrugged. "He hasn't said hello to me."

"Hi, Jerome," Raymer said.

"He hates me," he told his sister, as if Raymer had not spoken.

"I don't hate you, Jerome."

"He does," Jerome insisted, again to Charice.

"Nope."

This time the other man looked down at his shoes. "Really?"

"Really. I don't hate you."

At last Jerome ventured a quick glance at Raymer, who put on what he hoped was a sincere-looking smile.

"See?" Charice said. "What did I tell you? This is all in your head."

Jerome shrugged, as if to concede that in fact there was a fair amount about the contents of his head that he didn't understand.

"We've got burgers coming," Charice said. "Do you want to sit down and have dinner with us or do you want to just stand there looking like a crazy person?"

"I've already enjoyed a small repast."

"That doesn't mean you can't join us. There's plenty of room in the booth. See?"

Jerome glanced over at the booth in question, which was, as advertised, large enough for three.

"Join us," Raymer said. "Please."

At this, Jerome finally set down the suitcases, went over to the booth and slid in, stopping in the middle, a deft maneuver, Raymer realized. Now Charice would have to sit on one side of him and Raymer on the other, a geometric shape that, unless Raymer was mistaken, probably reflected a new reality. Or, if odious Dougie was to be believed, an old one that Raymer refused to acknowledge. Charice slid in next to her brother and patted him on the knee. Which left Raymer in the center of the room with Jerome's suitcases. He lifted these—they were surprisingly heavy—and set them down out of the way, before joining them in the booth. A moment later their burgers arrived. The waitress also brought an extra beer glass, which Raymer filled from the pitcher for Jerome.

"And I boxed these up for you," she said, setting the wings Charice hadn't eaten in the center of the table.

"There now," Charice said when it was just the three of them. The other diners had mostly returned to their food and their own conversations. "Isn't this better?"

If Jerome had an opinion, he declined to share it. Instead, he pulled the cardboard box toward him, opened it and peered inside. "They're all yours if you want them," Charice told him.

Hesitating, he looked over at Raymer, who said, "Knock yourself out."

When Jerome continued to stare at the wings without making a move to take one, Raymer intuited the problem and slid back out of the booth. From a nearby table he filched a plate and a silverware roll-up. When he set these down in front of Jerome, the other man removed the cutlery and tucked the paper napkin into his shirt collar. Raymer considered grabbing another roll-up so Jerome would have a second napkin for his sticky fingers, but then remembered what Charice had told him earlier. Despite having been prepared for what came next, he was still amazed to see Jerome go at the wings with a knife and fork.

What on earth had he been thinking? Raymer asked himself. The last thing he needed was a roommate, especially this one. So why, why, why? Love, he supposed. What else? Charice needed him to do this and so he would. For a whole month she and her brother had been cooped up together and they both needed a break. Charice was clearly at her wit's end. And yet, watching Jerome saw away at those chicken wings with a knife and fork was truly terrifying, and Raymer, feeling his resolve buckle, wondered if it was too late to renege. If he did, Charice would understand, wouldn't she? Because she was right. It *was* completely unfair of her to expect this of him. He opened his mouth to tell her so, but saw that she was tucking into her burger with genuine appetite. To Raymer, she had the look of someone who'd been carrying a piano and had just set it down. *He's yours now,* she seemed to be saying. *Bring him back when he's fixed.*

Raymer sighed and took a bite of his burger, which somehow, despite bacon, cheese, ketchup and several thick slices of pickled jalapeño, tasted of ash.

==

"WHAT YOU'VE GOT in this place," said Jerome, not bothering to look up from his laptop, "is some seriously antediluvian Wi-Fi."

Raymer, puzzled, scratched his stomach. "How did you manage to log on?" He hadn't written down the log-in info anywhere.

"It took me all of three tries to guess your password, Dawg," Jerome replied.

When had he started calling guys "Dawg"? Raymer wondered. Or was he purposely mispronouncing Raymer's first name?

"I hope your credit cards are better protected."

"Card," Raymer corrected. "I only have the one."

"And your bank accounts," Jerome added.

"Same deal," Raymer admitted. "Just the one."

Jerome still hadn't looked up from the screen. "Checking or savings?"

"Checking."

"Where?"

"What do you mean, where?"

"By *where* I mean what people usually mean by that word. As regards a particular place or location. Which bank, is what I'm asking."

"Why do you want to know?"

"I bet I could hack your account."

"Then I'm definitely not telling you."

"Give me a day or two and I bet I could steal your whole identity. I could *become* you, Dawg."

"Why would you want to become a guy with antediluvian Wi-Fi?" Though, for the time being at least, that's exactly what he was.

"I could use the money in your bank account to make improvements. You need to get yourself a good French press, for example. Nobody drips coffee anymore. Only drips drink drip coffee."

"Then I guess I'm a drip," Raymer said.

He'd awakened this morning, as he did most mornings, with an urgent need to pee. Grabbing his cell phone off the kitchen counter, he went into the bathroom, shutting the door behind him. He'd promised to call Charice when he woke up, so as soon as he'd relieved himself, he did. She answered on the first ring. "How is he?"

"I'm fine, thanks," he said, taking a seat on the commode, and reminding himself to flush as soon as he hung up. "How are you?"

"I'm sorry," she sighed. "How are you?"

"Too early to tell. You don't sound great."

"Just woke up with an upset stomach, is all. How is Jerome?"

"Chatty. He insulted my Wi-Fi."

"That's good."

"How, exactly?"

"He's talking."

Raymer supposed this was probably true. He'd said next to nothing during dinner last night, even when he himself was the subject of their conversation, how this new living arrangement would work. Later, after they'd arrived at Raymer's flat and he'd showed Jerome the spare bedroom that would be his for as long as he stayed, Jerome had gone in and shut the door behind him, leaving his suitcases in the entryway as if they contained nothing he was likely to need, and leaving his sister and Raymer alone in the living room. Charice, staring at the closed door, said, "This is going to be even worse than I feared."

"We'll make out somehow," he assured her.

"No," she said, "you won't. It's going to be a shitshow." In fact, she told him, if they managed not to kill each other, they'd likely both emerge from this experiment profoundly damaged, maybe even requiring some sort of institution that served meals and had extensive grounds with high fences where, on sunny days, the two of them could take long, medicated walks.

"He says it took him only three tries to guess my password," Raymer told her.

"*Not happy?*" she said. "I'm surprised it took him that many. The underscore must've thrown him off."

This, of course, was what came of taking advice from your therapist. He'd chosen *not_happy* because Dr. Qadry had suggested he own the famous we're-not-happy-until-you're-not-happy business card. Also, it was easy to remember (this was true of humiliation generally). In fact, he used *not_happy* for just about everything that required a password. "So, you guessed it too?"

"Chief?" Charice said. She mostly called him by his first name these days, but every now and then she'd revert, especially when she had something particularly derisive to say. "Anybody who's ever seen your high-school-yearbook photo could guess it."

"That's just plain mean," he told her. Also, where had she seen his yearbook photo? Not wanting to be reminded of high school, he'd thrown his own copy away. Were such things online now?

"You could probably guess my password, if you thought about it," she said.

"Why would I even want to know your password?"

"So you could check up on me? Find out all my secrets?"

"I respect your privacy," he said. *What secrets?*

"That's very sweet," she said, "though I'm not sure it's the best profile for a cop."

She was probably right. Despite Dr. Qadry's attempts to probe his mind for hidden motivations and Dougie's cynical attempts to make him more suspicious of his fellow man, Raymer did tend to believe what people told him, even when their stories didn't track. "He also says I need a French press."

"I'll bring ours over later. It was the first thing he made me buy when he moved in. He says only—"

"—drips drink drip coffee. I know. His suitcases are still sitting by the front door."

"It's going to take him a while to settle in."

"He's still in the same clothes he was wearing last night. That sweater looks familiar."

"He found it in the back of your closet."

*Lord,* Raymer thought. What if Jerome really did intend to become him? "I don't think he's even used the bathroom."

"He doesn't like to share facilities."

"He expects his own bathroom?"

"It's just going to take him some time to wrap his mind around things."

*What about my mind?* "Does he think he can hold it?"

"That's exactly what he thinks."

"And when does that change?"

"When he can't. Try not to overthink this. By the way," she said, "what's with that sign out front?"

"What sign?"

"There's a FOR SALE sign on the lawn. I noticed it on the way out."

Raymer had forgotten all about it. The sign had appeared the week before, after his downstairs neighbors moved out. Since the recession, half a dozen houses on Upper Main had come on the market. "People put those there when they want to sell their property," he told her.

"You should consider buying it," Charice suggested.

*I don't want to own a house of my own, Charice,* he thought. *I want to move back in with you.* Instead, he said, "I no longer have a job, remember?"

"Yes, you do. You work for me. You're going to find out who killed himself at the Sans Souci. You're also on Jerome duty. That's two jobs."

"Which reminds me. We haven't discussed salary for either position."

"Let's see how things go," she suggested. "What are your plans for the day?"

"I thought we'd go get some breakfast, then see if I can find a charger for that BlackBerry."

"I doubt he'll leave your apartment."

"There's nothing to eat here."

"He's very stubborn."

"Which will occur to him first, do you think? That he has to eat or take a shit."

"Jerome doesn't shit," she reminded him. "He defecates."

There was a knock on the door. "I can hear every word you're saying in there" came Jerome's voice from just a few inches away.

"Okay," Raymer said. "Thanks for telling me."

"I need to get in there, Dawg," he said. "Really, really bad."

Raymer stood. "Ooops," he told Charice. "Gotta run."

"Go," she said, hanging up.

When he opened the bathroom door, a panicked Jerome burst past him.

Out in the hallway, Raymer allowed himself to smile, but a split second later there was a shriek from inside the bathroom. He had forgotten, Raymer realized, to flush.

*Me again, Little Bro—*

 *Remember that pact we made when we were little, me and you? After Mom took up with Dickweed? How we swore never to lie to each other? How we sealed our oath with blood? I'd wanted to do it like in a movie, where you'd use a knife on your palm, but you were too little and after that fight I got into with Will—the one over the stopwatch—blood freaked you out, so we decided on a pin instead. We used the stove burner to sterilize it, remember? And you still got scared and wanted to back out when the pin glowed red, but I said I'd go first to show you how easy it was. So, I jabbed the pin into the tip of my index finger and when the tiny bead of blood formed, I handed it to you and told you to do like that. Except you wouldn't stick yourself hard enough to draw blood. You said we should just swear the oath. We didn't really need the blood part. But I said, No, you can't have a blood oath without it. Remember? So, finally, I went, okay, fine, just forget it, and I held out my hand for the pin so I could put it back in Mom's pin cushion. But as soon as you gave it to me, I quick grabbed your hand and stuck your finger with it, and right away a nice bead of blood formed and we put our fingers together and smeared my blood into yours, you crying the whole time, right? But afterward you were as proud as me. You told everybody what we'd done and you had this big smile on your face. You even told Dickweed, and he called us morons.*

*Back then I don't think it occurred to me that our swearing to always tell each other the truth started out with a lie—me promising to put that pin back in the cushion and sticking you with it instead. But here's the funny part. We never did lie to each other after that. We were serious about our oath. I mean, we sure couldn't trust either Mom or Dickweed to tell us the truth about anything, but me and you played it straight. At least I did. If you ever lied to me, I don't want to know about it.*

*So I'm not going to lie to you now, Little Bro. I fucked up last night. After telling you I planned to make an early night of it? Well, I didn't. I don't really count that as a lie, because at the time I meant what I said, no bullshit. I know I don't have to explain how that works. How you can really mean something and then, an hour later, it's like you aren't the same person who made the promise? I mean, you are, but you also aren't. To most people that wouldn't make sense, but I know you understand. It's kind of like those dreams where you can fly? You're soaring above the clouds and looking down at the earth and you think to yourself, This is so cool! How did I forget that I could do this? Why have I been walking everywhere? So in your sleep you just fly and fly and it seems so real, and then you wake up and you know it was just a dumb dream and you can't fly at all, and that's when you kind of give up, partly because you can't fly but more because why would you, of all people, be able to do something that cool? If they were handing out wings, would you be one of the lucky ones to get a pair? Fuck, no. Our brother Will, maybe, but not me and you.*

*I think now that it must've been seeing Pop again that did a number on me, made me want to drink the well dry. Him inviting me to hang out for a few days. Not for the rest of my life or anything, just a couple days. Like maybe he could stand having me around that long. And the worst part, me kind of wanting to, I'm ashamed to admit. I don't know. Maybe I'm just making excuses. Anyhow, I drove around this Schuyler Springs place, looking for the right spot, somewhere I wouldn't stand out, but the joints on the main drag all looked expensive and you just knew they'd be full of assholes. And I don't have to tell you how I get when I'm around certain kinds of people and listening to how they talk and it doesn't even matter what they're saying, I just want to punch their freakin' lights out. What I had in mind was to just drink and not talk to anybody. Maybe listen to some country music. The good kind, you know? Hank. Waylon. Merle. Not this new shit. Anyhow, I get off the main drag and I see this place called the Green Hand and I can tell from the vehicles in the parking lot that it won't be full of rich assholes, so in I go.*

*I find myself a seat at the end of the bar, close to the men's room, because I'm thinking beer, which I can drink pretty much all night, but then I think again and order a shot of Jack and let me tell you, Little Brother, old Jack never knew what hit him. He slid down my throat like velvet, right into the grave. Slow down, I told myself. Just cool those jets, pardner, or you're never gonna last the night. Also, I can't get so carried away that I wind up flat broke. I got just about enough money for one more night in the motel and gas for the trip back after I've done what I came to do. I'm pretty sure I know what that is but, like I said before, not every last detail.*

*So, here I am in this Green Hand joint, getting my bearings, you know? People are talking and laughing and I don't see anybody I might want to punch out later, which is good, because usually I can kind of tell if there's going to be trouble just by looking around. There's this one big, really loud table, mostly guys but a few women, and it turns out they're all off-duty cops. I kid you not, Little Bro. I'm in a fucking cop bar. But I think, Okay, good. One more reason to behave myself.*

*Here's where it gets interesting. Fast-forward a couple hours, maybe three, and four or five more Jacks. It was crowded before but now the place is really hopping. The cop table is getting louder and louder. The door opens and in comes this woman who looks kind of familiar, but how can that be? Then I realize she kind of reminds me of the girl I saw earlier that afternoon over at Pop's. I told you about her, remember? The one who was driving that flatbed truck that said* GRANDPA ZACK'S TREASURES *or some such? The one I figured was maybe an old girlfriend of Will's? Anyhow, like I said, in comes this same girl, and I'm thinking no fuckin' way. Until I look closer and I see it's not her. Can't be. The girl in the flatbed was in her twenties and this* woman's gotta be, like, fortysomething. So, great. I'm not going crazy. But here's what's gonna blow your mind, Little Brother. She's looking around the bar while she waits for her drink, and when she sees me, she's the one who does a double take, and I'm thinking, *Wait. There's two different women who both recognize me as our brother Will? I'm supposed to believe that shit?* But then I see her decide she doesn't know me after all, the same conclusion I came to about her. Which is still weird, right?

Anyhow, she takes her drink and goes over to the cop table and settles in with them. I haven't taken a piss yet, so I make a trip to the head, which is decorated with green hands, all the walls and even the damn ceiling. I'm not talking decals, either. It's like they got all their regulars to dip their hands in buckets of green paint, then print them on the wall. Men's hands, women's hands, little kids' hands, even. So, I'm in there pissing and I notice the little window looks out on the parking lot, so I take a gander. There's the Yellow Sub, sticking out like a sore thumb. I'm half expecting to see the Grandpa Zack's Treasures flatbed, but no. Which settles it. *Different woman.* Doesn't explain her double take when she saw me, though, which makes me jittery, or maybe it's just being in that room with all those green hands.

Back at the bar I settle onto my stool and order another Jack and tell myself that everything's just fine, and there's no reason to be jumpy. Nothing bad's going to happen. When things are about to head south, I can usually tell, even when I'm hammered. I look around the bar to make sure there's nobody I want to punch out, and there isn't. I still can't shake the feeling that something's not right, though, and I wonder again if maybe it's the woman who looked familiar when she came in. She's still over at the cop table, so I watch her for a spell, thinking maybe she'll look over at me, but she doesn't. After a while I realize she's forgotten I exist. Whoever she is, she's nothing to me and I'm nothing to her. I begin to relax a little bit, but then, I don't know why, I start to wonder: *Should I be doing any of this?* I know, I know. It was mostly me that wanted to. You tried to talk me out of it. The way I figure it, though, it's kind of like with the pin. You didn't want to do that, either, but afterward you were proud. This would be like *that. But sitting there in that cop bar I'm thinking maybe that's what this woman I don't know and who doesn't know me is trying to tell me—that I should've stayed in West Virginia. Up here, everything's sort of off. Pop, dressed in clothes that make him look like somebody else. Rub-Not-Rob giving me the evil eye for no good reason. The Grandpa Zack's Treasures girl. Mostly what I feel is defective. Dickweed's word, remember? He'd look at us and say, "What're you, some kind of defective?" Anyhow, that's sort of how I'm feeling. This whole plan of ours. Back when we were talking about how it would go, it seemed like something I could do, but now I'm not so sure.*

*So, I'm thinking about all this and out of nowhere there's this loud* bang! *and everything goes dark except for this little spot of light right between my eyes, like I'm in a tunnel and there's a train in there with me, except it's miles away. Reminds me of that old black-and-white TV we had that year after Pop left? Actually, it was a color one, but the color crapped out and we just kept watching it anyhow. That was what we did with most things, right? Just kept using them till they completely crapped out. But the TV. Remember how when you turned it off or the power went out, the screen would shrink to this little white dot in the center and that dot would just stay there? We used to wonder about that, me and you. Why that didn't go out too? With no electricity, why didn't the whole screen go black? It did, eventually, of course, but for a while it was like there was some magical thing that lived in there behind the screen.*

*Okay, I got sidetracked again, didn't I. The point I was trying to make was that's what it felt like, kind of. That loud bang and then everything going blank except for that little white dot, and then it finally went out, too.*

*Okay, I'll be honest. I wasn't all that surprised to wake up in jail, my shirt all crusty with puke and my head fit to explode. Usually, my hangovers are located right in back of my eyes, but not this time. This one was at the back of my skull, so I felt around back there and sure enough there's this great big knot. It took me a minute, but eventually I put two and two together. Thought to myself, Well, you done it again. You went and fell the fuck off another barstool. There was just the one, low-watt yellow bulb to see by but I could tell I had the cell all to myself, which was kind of surprising. Usually when you black out drunk on a Saturday night you wake up the next morning with company. At least that's how things go down in Boone County. Apparently, it was different up here. Either everybody got their own cell, or I was the only idiot sleeping off a Saturday-night drunk. I didn't hear anybody snoring nearby, so maybe the second one. Anyhow, I laid there for a spell, too sore to move, trying to remember what there was to remember, which wasn't much. The loud cop table. Green hands all over the bathroom wall. But I also had a fuzzy memory of being on my back and staring up at a bunch of faces staring down at me. And voices all running in together, sounding like they were a long way off. And I kind of remembered being in a moving vehicle that for some reason had no windows and the wheels bouncing over potholes and the smell of gasoline making me gag. I figure it must've been then that I puked? The worst part about waking up covered with puke is that it pretty much guarantees there's at least one other person nearby who's disappointed in you. Either you puked on him or he had to clean up your mess. Unless it's a her, which is worse. Anyhow, bottom line? I was in jail and for now there was nothing I could do about it, so I told myself to go back to sleep and then did as I was told. When I woke up again, the cell was all lit up. I was sitting up, or trying to, when a door swung open and a fat old cop waddled in and said, "Look who's awake." And with that he inserted a key in the cell door and pulled it open. His nameplate said:* DAILEY.

*I was pretty stiff from the hard bench I'd been sleeping on, but somehow I got to my feet and grabbed on to the bars to steady myself. I said to this Officer Dailey, "You wouldn't have an aspirin on you?"*

*He shook his head. "If you're concussed, that might not be the best idea. I can probably let you have a Tylenol though. You aren't going to toss your cookies at me, are you?"*

*"I hope not."*

*"You hope."*

*So, I followed him into the station, which was empty except for me and him. He rooted around in the top drawer of his desk until he found a generic acetaminophen. He even tore open the tiny packet for me because my hands were shaking so bad I couldn't manage. Pointing me in the direction of the watercooler, he said, "When you leave here, you should go to the hospital. Get yourself checked out."*

*"I'll sure do that," I told him, though I had no such plans. Hospitals cost money.*

*When I got back from the watercooler, I took a deep breath and said, "Okay, what do I owe you?"*

*"I think Schuyler County can absorb the cost of a Tylenol," he said, unlocking the top drawer of a nearby metal filing cabinet and removing a large envelope with my name on it. Inside was my wallet and keys, which I hadn't even noticed weren't in my pockets. "Your coat's over there on the rack," he said, pointing.*

*"You're saying I'm free to go?"*

*Because in Boone County when you spent the night in jail, you'd have a tab the next morning and that tab has to be cleared before they'd let you out. Your night's stay, plus the cost of transportation and whatever else they could get away with charging you for, cash only, or you stayed put.*

*"I insist, actually," said Officer Dailey.*

*"Mind if I ask how I got here?"*

*"One of the detectives brought you in, is what I heard. I'd be on my way before he shows up. I'm told you threw up in the trunk of his car."*

*"The trunk?" Well, that accounted for the moving vehicle with no windows memory. One of the sick but kind of fun things about the morning after a blackout drunk is fitting the pieces of the puzzle back together until things finally make sense again. Still, even in Boone County the cops don't toss you in the trunk of their car. "Is that, like, legal?"*

*"Most guys prefer a free ride to the cost of an ambulance."*

*I guess I understood that, though it did make me wonder if they treated Schuyler County's women drunks the same way. "Any idea where my car might be?"*

*Officer Dailey snorted at this, like the answer was pretty obvious. "Wherever you left it, would be my guess."*

"*The Green Hand?*"

"*If you say so.*"

"*That's where I was drinking.*"

"*Then that's where it probably is.*"

*I nodded, trying to decide what came next, but not wanting to ask another dumb question. "I'm not sure I could find the place again. Could you maybe draw me a map?"*

*He gave me this you-got-to-be-shitting-me look, but he opened his desk drawer and took out a sheet of scratch paper. In the lower-left-hand corner, he put an* x *and wrote* you are here.

"*Okay, thanks for everything,*" *I said, when he had finished and handed me the map.*

"*Don't mention it.*"

*When I got outside, it occurred to me to check my wallet, which contained about half of what I expected. I admit losing track of how many Jacks I'd drunk, but still. Maybe here wasn't so different from Boone County after all. Maybe instead of telling you how much you owed and demanding payment, they just took the money.*

*Officer Dailey was surprised when he looked up and saw me standing there again. "That must have been one piss-poor map I drew if you ended up back here."*

"*I was just wondering,*" *I said. "There was quite a bit more money in my wallet last night."*

*His face clouded over. "I hope you're not suggesting what I think you're suggesting."*

"*I'm not accusing anybody,*" *I said.*

"*Good.*"

"*But still . . .*"

"*Did you pay your bar tab?*"

*I told him the truth, that I blacked out before I could do that.*

"*Well, there you go.*"

"*There still should be a lot more.*"

"*Maybe you left a generous tip.*"

"*Either that or maybe my ride in the trunk wasn't free after all? Maybe that detective—*"

"*My advice would be to not go there.*"

"*No?*"

"*You threw up in his vehicle. Who should pay to have that cleaned up? Him?*"

"*It's just that I have to drive back home to West Virginia,*" I told him. "*I'm not sure with what's left I've got enough for gas, even.*"

"*Put it on your credit card.*"

"*Maxed out.*"

*Officer Dailey sighed deeply.* "*You want to know what forty-some years of police work has taught me?*"

*I told him I had no clue.*

"*People who have problems never have just one.*"

*That was pretty much my experience, too, but I didn't care much for the way he said it, Little Brother. Like it's our own fault when people like me and you fuck up. Like nobody else had a hand in it. Like it's all on us. Like it's not mostly written in the stars before we're born.*

"*You don't know anybody who can float you a loan?*" *Officer Dailey wanted to know.*

"*Not really.*" *Thinking about Pop. Thinking how there's no way I could take money from him, not and do what we planned.*

"*Well, I'm sorry to hear it, but here's the thing. You maybe should've thought about all this last night. The way I heard it you sat there and downed one shot of whiskey after another until you fell off your fucking stool. Now I'm supposed to feel sorry for you because you drank your gas money? I gave you a Tylenol and drew you a map. I'm not sure what else you want from me.*"

*I remained calm. I did. Didn't raise my voice, even.* "*You didn't give me a Tylenol,*" I told him. "*You gave me a generic acetaminophen. And what I want is for you to tell me what happened to the money in my wallet.*"

*Officer Dailey looked me over real good, then said,* "*Guess what, friend. This right here? This is where I tell you to go fuck yourself.*"

*Anyhow, I wasn't all that surprised there was a patrol car sitting next to the Yellow Sub by the time I got to the Green Hand. The map Officer Dailey had drawn me was a good one, and I went directly there, but it took a while on foot and I was still too late. You know the feeling you get when a cop gets out of his cruiser and looks at you and you know right then it's you he's after? How your first thought is always to run? I thought about booking it, Little Bro. I did. But that acetaminophen hadn't really touched the pain in my head and anyhow what was the point? I couldn't go anywhere without the Sub. If I'd somehow gotten there before this cop, my plan was to just head on home, taking the back roads, get as far as I could. When I ran out of gas money, I'd just stop someplace and sell the Sub and use the money on a bus ticket to get me the rest of the way home. They'd probably corral me before all that could happen, but if I've learned anything in this crazy life, it's that things don't always go like you imagine. Other people fuck up, too, not just guys like me and you, and sometimes you get lucky and life cuts you a break. Not this time, though, Little Brother. Mostly I felt bad for letting you down.*

*So, anyhow, the cop gets out of the patrol car and says he's Officer Miller and is my name Thomas Sullivan. When I tell him it is, he wants to know if I mean to come with him peaceably, so I tell him, yeah, I will. Tell you what, Little Bro. Right then I was feeling mighty low about things not working out, kind of like how you feel when you wake up from one of those dreams where you can fly. So, I just turn around and put my hands behind my back and let this Officer Miller put the cuffs on. He opens the rear door of the cruiser, then, and he's about to put me inside, when a car roars into the lot and a guy gets out who I'm pretty sure is one of the dudes from the cop table last night. He comes over and says, "Hello, asshole. Remember me?"*

*I tell him no, not really, and he says, "No? Well, you puked in my trunk," and before I can say anything to that, he punches me in the face. I go down hard. And then, before I can catch my breath, he's kicking me in the ribs and I'm thinking, I know I fucked up, but I don't deserve this, do I? But then again, maybe I do. Hell, Little Bro. You deserve better than what happened to you, right? It wasn't your fault, none of it.*

# Ruth's List

PETER HAD JUST COME out onto his front porch when a taxi pulled up at the curb. Perhaps because she required the driver's assistance to get out of the vehicle, he didn't immediately recognize Ruth, who was about the last person he expected to pay him an unannounced visit. Face it, their relationship had always been burdened. When he first returned to Bath, full of barely disguised grievance, he'd made no secret of his view that Sully hadn't been much of a father, which was probably why Ruth, in subsequent years, had developed an equally strong conviction that Peter hadn't been much of a son. Since Sully's death, they'd entered into a kind of truce. How long had it been since he'd seen her? Months, surely, during which Ruth seemed to have lost considerable ground. She was using a cane now, and even then seemed unsteady on her feet.

"Have I caught you at a bad time?"

"No, what's up?"

"I was hoping we could talk."

"Sounds ominous," he said. "Want to come inside?"

"Not really," she said, studying the house. "For a second you looked like him standing there on the porch."

"Nope. Sorry."

"Don't be," she told him. "I'm just being silly. It looks like you're having some work done."

"I'm doing most of it myself, actually. Or Rub and I are."

"To what end?"

Which made him smile. Ruth had always been direct. "It's a lot more house than I need, now that it's just me."

She nodded. "And why is it just you?"

He started to explain that Will was gone now, living his own life, but then realized what she meant by the question. "Can't find a woman who'll have me, I guess."

"Maybe you'll have better luck someplace else," she offered, though something about the way she said this suggested she wouldn't be wagering heavily on that possibility. He considered telling her that he'd gotten lucky just last night, but quickly dismissed the idea as boastful, especially given the fact that the woman he'd gotten lucky with was one that his father had apparently had a crush on. Did Ruth know about that? he wondered. Or suspect? It wasn't the sort of thing Sully would have confided.

"You sure you don't want to come in?"

She shook her head. "I was hoping you could give me a lift back home. We can talk on the way."

"Back home," he repeated. "You took a taxi here so I could drive you back where you started from?"

"I tried to call, but the number I had for you was disconnected."

"I just have a cell now."

She chuckled at this. "You think your father would have one of those if he was still alive?"

"I doubt it. They're expensive and he'd probably lose one or two a week."

Ruth, no surprise, frowned at this observation, causing Peter to wonder why. Surely she wasn't denying Sully's carelessness, his defining characteristic. More likely the frown just reflected her view that Peter was, by contrast, far too careful.

"Why don't you take my elbow?" he suggested.

"Because then, when I fall, I'll take you with me," she explained. "These days, I'm mostly on a walker, but if I'd taken that, the driver would've had to put it in the trunk and then take it out again, and I hate being a bother. The older people get, the more stubborn they are. Have you noticed?"

"I have," Peter smiled.

When they made it around to the passenger side of Peter's truck, she said, "If you just hold the door open, I think I can manage." When he did as instructed, she balanced herself against the side of the vehicle and handed him her cane.

"Are you sure you can make it?" Peter said, genuinely worried. "If you fall and hurt yourself, my old man will rise up out of his grave, grab this cane and beat me with it."

"Heck, this is a snap," she said, hauling herself into the cab and taking the cane back. "You've seen that monster my granddaughter drives? I need a crane to get in and out of that." When he climbed in behind the wheel and put the key in the ignition, she said, "Do you remember where I live?"

"I sure do."

"You mind taking the long way?"

He started to ask if she had a particular route in mind, then realized that of course she did.

＝＝

HILLDALE CEMETERY, like Gaul, was divided into three parts: Hill, Dale and, more recently, the Flats. Hill, the oldest and prettiest section, stood on higher ground, its hummocks dotted with shade trees. The treeless Flats was so named because the ground there was level as a tabletop, but also because the gravestones lay horizontally. From a distance it didn't look like part of the cemetery at all, but rather as if the ground had been surveyed, quilt-like, for something to be built later, and that something had fallen through. In between old and new was Dale, a wide, gentle slope where the grass was either urine yellow or fecal brown, depending on the season. Here the ground was soft, its root systems compromised—poisoned, some claimed, by buried toxic waste. Twenty years earlier, when caskets interred in Dale were discovered to be slowly inching their way down the slope, the headline in the Schuyler newspaper had read: "Dead on the Move in Bath." To Peter's way of thinking, Dale was where his father belonged. Sully had lived his whole life on a kind of slant, a creature of constant motion, always headed somewhere close by. Spending eternity on the move would've suited him. Unfortunately, he'd dallied too long among the living, reluctant to surrender his barstool at the Horse, and so he now lay here in the Flats, a nomad no longer.

"There," Ruth pointed, having surmised from Peter's tentativeness that he couldn't remember precisely where his father lay buried. "Follow the car tracks. Five rows, then left."

"Is it okay to—"

"Everybody does," Ruth assured him, and Peter could see that it was true. There were vehicle tracks between the rows of graves.

"Tell me when to—"

"Stop," she said. "We're here."

Turning off the engine, Peter got out and went around the front to help Ruth down from the cab. Seeing that his father's grave was well tended, he said, "You come here regularly?"

She nodded. "My husband is just over there." She pointed to where Zack lay buried. "I don't get to stay as long as I like."

"Why's that?"

"It's usually Janey who brings me, and it still pisses her off to think I carried on with your father all those years."

"I can see where it would."

"Does it piss *you* off?"

"Not really, no. His marriage to my mother was a mistake pretty much from day one."

"I don't think he felt that way."

"No?"

"Well, it resulted in you. And later Will."

"Yeah, Will did win him over. And vice versa."

"He never won *you* over?"

Peter shrugged. "I came to like him quite a lot, actually."

"*Like?*"

He nodded, smiling at her. "As opposed to *dis*like."

"Quite a lot?"

"As opposed to *a little.*"

"But not love."

"The word is overused." When she didn't respond to this, he could feel her trying to decide whether his observation was worth quarreling over or even whether it was him or his father that she'd be quarreling with.

"I don't recall *him* using it all that much either," she said, indicating Sully's stone. "I'm not sure I ever used the word myself, for that matter," she added sadly.

Since the possibility that she hadn't clearly troubled her, he said, "Does it matter? You're standing here."

"I guess."

"And, for the record, so am I."

Which elicited a grudging smile. "Does it count if you're dragged?"

They stood in silence for a time, until Peter finally said, "So, what's this all about?"

"I'm not sure," she admitted. "Maybe nothing."

Peter felt a chill. Had she had a biopsy? Been given a poor prognosis? "Are you not feeling well?"

"Hah!" she said. "That's hilarious. I don't even remember what feeling good is like. Most days I ache from head to toe."

"I'm sorry to hear it."

She waved this away. "More than anything I'm just worn out. Playing out the string, I guess. I belong here at the Hilldale Country Club more than I do among the living." When he didn't respond to this, she nudged him with her elbow. "This is where you're supposed to tell me how wrong I am. Unless you agree?"

"I didn't say that."

"You didn't say anything," she pointed out, and when he didn't say anything to that, either, she said, "If your father was here, he'd at least try to cheer me up."

"He *is* here," Peter reminded her, indicating the stone they stood before.

"I walked right into that one, didn't I," she snorted. Then, just as quickly, she became serious again. "I'm more worried about my daughter and granddaughter than myself."

He waited for her to continue, which she seemed in no hurry to do. Unless he was mistaken, having invoked his father, she was now talking as much to Sully as to him. Maybe more. "I'm listening," he assured her.

"There isn't much I can do for Janey. She's angry and disappointed, and I can't really blame her. I've been where she is. Her situation is worse though."

"How so?"

"The restaurant was never a cash cow, even in the best of times. Which these aren't. She doesn't want to sell the place, but I don't know. Maybe she should."

"Between us," Peter said. "Birdie's wondering how much longer she can hold on in this economy. Whether it's worth the effort."

"With Janey, it's more than just the restaurant. After that shitheel husband of hers, you'd think she would've learned her lesson, but she still gravitates to bad men."

"No shortage of those to choose from," Peter conceded. "Why are you worried about Tina?"

"She's always had her challenges, poor girl," she said. "I doubt she'll ever be right."

"I'm not sure I agree," Peter told her. "You know her better than I do, but she seems to be very good at what she does. She's turned Grandpa Zack's into a thriving business."

"Oh, I know that," Ruth conceded. "I'm proud of her, too. I mostly worry that she's broken inside. Damaged beyond repair. Too much happened to her when she was a child, and now she's trapped in that head of hers."

"Aren't we all trapped in our heads?"

"I suppose," Ruth admitted. "But she's so alone. No friends her own age. There are a lot of simple things that she can't seem to manage . . . like what we're doing right now. Having a simple conversation."

"*This* is a simple conversation?"

She nudged him with her elbow again. "You know what I mean."

"Okay, but Tina's been like she is for a long time, right? What's got you all worked up now?"

She took a deep breath. "She says she drove by your place yesterday."

"Yeah, I saw her," Peter said, remembering how her flatbed truck had slowed in front of the house before proceeding on down the street. Then it had returned again a few minutes later, heading in the other direction. That had struck him as odd, even at the time, but he'd been too flustered by Thomas's unexpected appearance to give the matter much thought.

"Did you know that back in high school she had a crush on your son?" Ruth said.

"Will?" Peter squinted at this. "Wasn't he a couple years ahead of her?"

"Crushes don't have to be realistic to be real," she pointed out. "All that's required is a hole in your heart that you can't fill." Again, Peter sensed that she was speaking as much to his father as to him. "Anyway, when he went off to college, she was just so . . ."

She paused, clearly searching for the right word.

". . . *bereft* that it broke my heart. I mean, the few glimpses she had of him at school were what was keeping her going, and now she didn't even have those. I figured after he left, she'd move on, find some other unattainable boy to fixate on, but if anything, she became even more besotted with his memory. She couldn't wait till the holidays came around, or spring break. When he came home, she'd be able to catch sight of him again."

"I don't think Will had any idea."

"Why would he?"

"But wait. You're saying she still has that same crush?"

"She scours the Internet for news about him."

Peter winced. "Does she know he's engaged?"

"If he posted about it, she knows." Her brow was knit in thought. "Can I ask where he is right now?"

"In England, actually."

Ruth nodded sadly. "She swears she saw him yesterday. On your front porch."

At this, Peter nodded, finally glimpsing what this was all about. "That was actually Thomas, my middle son. They look a lot alike."

"Huh," she said, looking puzzled. "I guess I'd forgotten that Will had siblings."

"That's exactly how Thomas feels, I suspect," Peter admitted. "Forgotten. After his mother and I split up, he and Andy, the youngest, lived with her in West Virginia. Charlotte was clear that I wasn't welcome in their lives. After she remarried . . ." He let the thought trail off. "I haven't seen Thomas or his brother since they were boys."

"Well, at least I know she's not hallucinating. That sets my mind at ease a little. She kept saying she was sure it was him and also sure it wasn't. Kind of like me seeing you on that same porch just now."

When a snowflake landed on the tip of his nose, Peter glanced up into the low, gray sky. Snow, he recalled, was forecast.

"So, what's he like, this son you haven't laid eyes on in so long?"

He decided to answer honestly. "I have no idea," he admitted. And of course now *he* was the one speaking as much to Sully as to the living woman at his elbow. "If I had to guess, I'd say lost."

"Maybe you ought to find out?"

"Too late. He's gone again. He claimed he was on his way up to Montreal for a few days. Then he was heading on back to West Virginia."

"Do you believe him?"

"Nope."

"And now you don't know what to do."

"There's something to do?"

"There's always something to do."

"Yeah, but most of it's wrong. Either wrong or too late."

"Your father used to say, '*Do* some fucking thing. If it doesn't work, do something else.'"

"I don't remember him ever saying that," Peter said, "but it sounds like him. He *was* a bull in a china shop."

"Yeah, but so what?" Ruth said. "A few plates get busted. Who cares?"

Shouldn't *you*? he thought. Wasn't Ruth herself one of those busted plates, thanks, at least in part, to his father's carelessness? Though maybe she didn't see it this way. Maybe she figured a few chips and cracks were worth it, proof she'd lived and loved.

"Well," she said, noticing the snow herself now. "I guess you can take me back home. Three to six inches, they were predicting yesterday. Now they're saying a foot or more."

"Yeah?" He hadn't heard the update. When he held the door for her, Ruth again managed to lever herself up and into the cab, mostly without his help. When she was situated, he closed the door again, went back around front and got in behind the wheel.

"Thanks for indulging an old woman," she told him.

"My pleasure," he said, turning the key in the ignition and starting the windshield wipers. "Tell Tina I said hi."

"I'll do that."

"She was on the list," he said, putting the truck in gear and following the tire tracks between the long row of graves.

"Which?"

"The list of people my father wanted me to check in on after he was gone," he told her. "You didn't get one of those?"

"I did, actually," she told him. "Mine had just the one name on it, though."

"Yeah?" he said, wondering if the name on hers was also on his. "Who was that?"

"You."

# Plumage

---

THE STREET OUTSIDE was rapidly filling up with thick, heavy snow. Inside Hattie's, Raymer and his new roommate were sharing the small booth farthest from the entrance, Raymer smugly basking in the accomplishment of coaxing Jerome out of the apartment. Charice had predicted that wouldn't happen until Monday at the earliest, but here they were, a full day ahead of schedule. In fact, Jerome had gone all in. He'd not only showered, he'd put on—except for Raymer's old cardigan—fresh clothes. Moreover, his two suitcases had been relocated from the entryway to the spare bedroom, an acknowledgment that he would be there for a while. In fact, when Jerome was in the bathroom, Raymer had called Charice to crow.

"Exciting news," he told her. "He's in the shower."

"Really?"

"Also, he defecated."

"Wow," she said, her voice rich with wonder.

"I think I heard him putting his toiletries in the medicine cabinet," he added. The night before, he'd made room and even left a juice glass on the sink for Jerome's toothbrush.

"You're blowing my mind here," Charice admitted.

"He's calling me Dawg." Raymer wasn't certain this qualified as good news, but it seemed worth mentioning.

"Not Doug?"

"Nope. Dawg."

"I can't believe the progress you're making."

"Actually, I have a working hypothesis," he told her.

"Which is?"

"That it was you holding him back this entire time."

"Bye, *Dawg,*" she said, and hung up. Which made him even more smug. He seldom bested Charice in a verbal exchange. Another thought also occurred to him. Was it possible that the best route back into Charice's affections was through her brother?

"So," said Raymer, studying the man sitting across from him. "Why are you dressing like this?"

Jerome continued to stare out the window at the falling snow. "Dressing like what?"

"I don't know," Raymer said. "You always used to look spiffy."

Outside, a nondescript sedan with a county license plate pulled into one of the diagonal parking spaces. Raymer recognized its front-seat passenger as their waitress at the Horse last night. Jane? Janey? Jeannie? Why couldn't he keep women's names straight? Dr. Qadry would have both a theory and a series of leading questions to help him arrive at the intended *aha!* reveal. Janey (he decided) got hurriedly out of the car and made a beeline for the diner's front door. The vehicle's driver, by contrast, was in exactly no hurry. He was a big guy, and something about the way he carried himself, together with the county license plate, suggested he might be a cop. By the time he finished feeding coins into the meter, glancing up and down the street as he did so, Raymer was sure of it.

Once inside, Janey went behind the counter where she located a tub of ibuprofen tablets the size of a football, extracted two with shaking hands and swallowed them dry. "Thanks for opening up," she told the middle-aged man at the grill, who was taking her measure with neither surprise nor visible sympathy.

"I'm gonna go out on a limb and guess tequila," he said and, when she didn't contradict him, added, "Your mother's called already."

"Wonderful," Janey said. "Just wonderful. Back in a minute." She disappeared through the swinging door.

"All in the past," Jerome was saying, still watching it snow. Despite the progress they'd made, he was still having trouble meeting Raymer's eye. "Took all those sharp clothes down to Goodwill, Dawg. Let somebody else look spiffy for a change."

"Why, though?" Raymer asked. "Wearing nice threads. Tooling around in the 'Stang. You always used to cut quite a figure."

At the mention of the 'Stang, Jerome's face clouded over. "That's the other thing I gotta do as soon as I get back home. Sell the Mach."

Not long after returning to North Carolina, he'd traded in his beloved *Goldfinger* 'Stang for the Mach 1 from *Diamonds Are Forever*. According to Charice, the old 'Stang had reminded him of North Bath and Becka and everything else he was anxious to put behind him. Now he was apparently set on selling the new one. It was hard for Raymer to imagine Jerome without a car that was somehow tied to a James Bond movie. How would he deliver his signature line: *The name is Bond* . . . etcetera. "What will you drive now?"

"Don't know," he admitted, "but I'm all done making myself a target."

*Target?* "I don't understand," Raymer confessed.

"Because you aren't Black, is why."

Raymer rubbed his chin. It wasn't just Jerome's unkempt hair and new sartorial choices that he was having trouble adjusting to. His voice was different, as well. Despite his still-elevated diction, he was sounding, well, more Black these days. It used to be Charice who would, upon occasion, allow the lilt of their southern upbringing to creep into her voice—usually when she wanted to make Raymer uncomfortable. By contrast, Jerome had always spoken as if he'd grown up in Iowa with white, Protestant parents. These days, at least to Raymer's ear, he sounded like William F. Buckley would have if he'd been kidnapped and held captive for a month in the front pew of a Southern Baptist church.

"Okay," Raymer said. "Explain it to me."

"Explain being Black?" Jerome said, finally making eye contact.

(Another milestone! Raymer wished he could pause their conversation right there to call Charice and let her know.)

"No," Raymer said, though that didn't sound like a bad idea, either. "Explain why dressing well and driving a Mustang makes you a target."

"Riles some people up, Dawg."

The bell over the diner's front door tinkled now, and the man who Raymer suspected of being a cop entered, took off his parka and hung it up on the coatrack by the door, surveying the sparse crowd as he did. Was it Raymer's imagination, or did his gaze linger for a split second on him and Jerome?

"Consider such accoutrements uppity," Jerome continued. "Got you lynched, if you weren't careful."

"In Schuyler County?"

Jerome snorted. "Anywhere, Dawg. You know they got an interactive map online that marks the precise location of every lynching in these United States, going all the way back to the Reconstruction?"

"I didn't, no." According to Charice, since returning to Schuyler, Jerome, newly insomniac, spent most of the night toggling between websites, muttering and taking notes, to what purpose he refused to reveal.

"You think they didn't hang Black folks up north?" Jerome said. "Set 'em ablaze for good measure?"

"They did?"

Apparently, Jerome considered the answer to this question self-evident, because he went back to staring out the window. Down the counter, Janey's companion was looking not *at* them exactly but in their general direction. Definitely a cop, Raymer thought. The ability to both look at something and *not* look at it was a specialized skill set.

Janey, now wearing a Hattie's uniform, emerged from the back in time to ferry their breakfasts over from the grill. "You again," she said, recognizing them from the night before. "Who gets what?"

"He's the spinach omelet," Raymer told her. "I'm the meat lover's."

"Not the way I had it pegged," Janey said, crossing the platters as she set them down.

"You remember Jerome?" Raymer said.

Jerome continued to stare out the window. If he registered his name, he gave no indication.

"He's very shy," Raymer told her. "Okay if I ask you a question?"

"Shoot."

"Your friend down there. Any chance he's a police officer?"

She nodded. "Detective. How'd you know?"

"How he carries himself, mostly. Also?" he said, nodding at the sedan with the county plates, whose windshield was already completely white with snow. "That's a cop-mobile if there ever was one."

"I'll tell him he was made," she said. "He'll get a kick out of it."

When she was gone, Raymer leaned forward and tapped the edge of Jerome's plate with the tines of his fork. "Our food's here," he said, adding, when Jerome turned his attention to the plate in front of him, "Also, we need to work on your people skills. You were rude to our waitress just now."

"Can't risk it," he said, cocking his head, as if the breakfast before him were a puzzle he needed to solve.

"Risk what?"

"Her falling in love with me."

Picking up both his knife and fork, Jerome began to surgically dissect his omelet, moving each bite-size portion outward from the center of the plate. None of these dissected pieces, Raymer noted, were allowed to touch. Charice had warned him that the farther Jerome went down his OCD rabbit hole the more complicated simple things became. Eating now had a rigid set of rules that must be obeyed. Apparently, he wasn't allowed to actually start eating until those rules had been followed to the letter.

"Falling in love with you," Raymer repeated. He was expecting, at the very least, a sheepish grin, but apparently Jerome was serious.

"It happens, Dawg."

Which made Raymer wonder about his most recent affair, the college professor Charice had told him about. "None of my business, Jerome, but this woman at the college where you worked, the one who was into art therapy? Was she white, too?"

"See that snow?" he said, nodding in the direction of the street. "White as that."

"And she fell in love with you."

Jerome nodded.

"She made the first move?"

"They all do, Dawg."

"Becka, too?" Raymer asked. He was aware that bringing her up might not be a great idea but figured they'd have to talk about her eventually. He'd often wondered how things started between them.

"They *all* do," he repeated. "Laugh all you want."

Raymer hadn't laughed, but he'd wanted to, and Jerome seemed to have intuited that. "You're saying white women all fall in love with you, Jerome?"

"Too many, is what I'm saying. I been damn lucky to avoid getting lynched, is what I'm saying."

Was it possible the man was actually sulking? Had Raymer actually hurt his feelings by suggesting that he might not, in fact, be irresistible to white women? "Okay, so explain your devastating allure," Raymer suggested. "Why are white women irresistibly drawn to you?"

Jerome shrugged. "Probably not just one thing."

"So name five or six things. Explain the magnetism of Jerome Bond."

Jerome nodded agreeably, as if he'd given the matter a lot of thought. "Okay, for one thing? I'm tall. Slender, too. Outstanding fat-to-lean-muscle ratio. Also, you may have noticed that I move through the world with a certain elegance."

"That's three things."

"And like you said. I used to be a spiffy dresser."

"What else?"

"Also, I'm extremely well spoken. I have an excellent vocabulary."

"Right. You defecate."

Jerome nodded in agreement, apparently seeing no humor in this, either.

"I'm also, by nature, gallant. Much more gallant than your average white dude." Like Raymer himself, he seemed to be saying. "Women appreciate that."

"Okay, but those are all very superficial qualities."

Jerome paused the dissection of his omelet to regard Raymer, as if waiting for him to get to his point.

Raymer knew what Dr. Qadry would say if she were here. "You're saying women are superficial?"

"I'm saying plumage has an evolutionary purpose, Dawg."

"So . . . you're irresistible because of your feathers? That's all you have to offer women?"

"Might be a bit more to it," he conceded, reluctantly. "And I'm not saying my feathers magically appeal to *all* white women." Here, he glanced over his shoulder, as if he feared Janey might be close by and listening in. "Just the ones drawn to danger."

"How are you dangerous?"

He shrugged. "Forbidden fruit."

"Time-out," Raymer said. "We're in the Garden of Eden now? Jerome Bond is temptation?"

"Laugh all you want."

"I'm not laughing, Jerome," he said, though maybe he was, a little. "I'm just trying to understand your thinking. On the one hand, you seem to believe that certain white women are magnetically attracted to you . . ."

"Laugh all you want."

". . . but you also believe you can control their attraction by letting your hair grow wild and wearing a cardigan."

"Seems to be working."

"You think so? Okay, let's test your theory. When did you start wearing the sweater?"

"Month ago?"

"Except Charice says you've barely left the house since you got here. During that whole time you probably haven't interacted with a single white woman. Maybe *that's* what's been working."

Down the counter Janey was refilling her cop friend's coffee, and Raymer saw her lean in to whisper something—probably that Raymer had guessed his occupation—because the man rotated on his stool to regard him and Jerome. Grinning, he made a gun out of his thumb and forefinger, pointed it at Raymer and pulled the trigger, as if to say, *I made you, too, pal.*

"I'm also saying," Raymer continued, "there's more to love than plumage." Okay, he was over fifty and he'd only been in love twice, but he still felt like he was on solid ground. "You seem to believe that falling in love is only dangerous for tall, handsome Black men who drive sports cars out of James Bond movies, but it can also mess up overweight white guys who drive cars like Columbo's."

Jerome frowned. "Who's Columbo?"

"Doesn't matter. My point is, loving Becka was damn near the death of me. You saw it yourself, Jerome. How crazy I was there for a while? When I got struck by lightning, I was convinced she was trying to kill me from beyond the grave. You're not the only one love screws things up for."

"See?" Jerome said, shaking his head. "That right there is why Black people can't talk to white people."

"Aren't we talking, Jerome? Isn't that what we're doing right now? Am I not allowed to disagree with you?"

"I'm saying you're drawing a false equivalence," Jerome explained, this time using his knife as a pointer. "You believing your dead wife is trying to kill you with a lightning bolt isn't the same as me believing that messing with white women could get me lynched. One is a white dude losing his mind. The other's a Black dude finally seeing how things really are."

Having finally completed the dissection of his omelet, Jerome set his utensils down and regarded his handiwork. The home fries that had been off to one side of the platter now occupied its center, the perfect wedges of omelet radiating outward from that center in a snail-shell pattern. Seeing this, Raymer sent him an urgent tele-pathic message: *Eat it.*

Only after it became clear that the other man hadn't received it did he continue. "Okay, so, as a Black dude who's finally seen how things really are . . ."

"Laugh all you want."

". . . how would you describe what you just did to your break-fast?"

Jerome thought about it. "I would describe it," he said, "as necessary."

"Huh," Raymer said. "A lot of people would see it as lunatic."

"Okay, but here's what you don't get, Dawg. *Lunatic* and *neces-sary* aren't mutually exclusive." And with this he finally took a bite of omelet.

Raymer watched him chew and swallow. "How is it?"

"Could be hotter," Jerome admitted.

"It *was* hotter. *You*—unnecessarily—let it get cold."

What he was attempting, of course, was precisely what Charice had warned him against—trying to reason with someone whose reason was compromised. She'd also explained that obsessive-compulsives, unlike people who suffered from other mental ill-nesses, were acutely aware that their ritual behaviors were irrational. That they were acting crazy wasn't exactly news to them.

"I'll eat it," Jerome assured him. "Gonna eat every last bite. I'm eating my omelet, see? Masticating? You ate your eggs and now I'm eating mine. Same end result."

"Except I enjoyed mine," Raymer pointed out, "because I didn't let them get cold. My point is that letting your eggs get cold wasn't in your own best interest."

"You always do what's in *your* own best interest? Marrying Becka? Was *that* in your best interest?"

"No," Raymer admitted. "At the time I thought it was, but no. That was a mistake." The same could be said—as he'd feared—of introducing her into the conversation.

"There you go."

"Okay," Raymer said, "but it wasn't the end of the world, either. Things have a way of working out. I found your sister."

Jerome shook his head. "She found *you,* Dawg. You never would've found her. Also? Things have a way of working out for white people."

Give Jerome this much credit. As promised, he was soldiering through his now-cold omelet. Starting at the outer edge of the snail's shell, he worked methodically toward the center. Two bites of omelet, then one of potato. Chew, swallow, repeat. Raymer couldn't tell whether the last bite would be of potato or egg, but he could tell Jerome had it all figured out.

"All I'm trying to say is that things take time—"

"Time," Jerome scoffed. "That's another difference between white folks and Black folks. Y'all operate on white time. Charice and me? We're on Black time."

"Black time."

"Completely different."

Here we go again, Raymer thought. Down another Jerome rabbit hole. *Try to keep him talking,* Charice had advised, as if that would be difficult. "Okay, I'll bite. Tell me how."

No surprise, Jerome was all too happy to explain. "White time goes one, two, three, four," he explained, using his coffee spoon here to tap the side of his water glass. "Ticktock, ticktock. Like that. Quick and easy because all those ticks and tocks are related by sequence and sequence alone. You following this, Dawg?"

Raymer wasn't, not really, but he assured Jerome otherwise.

"Black time is more like jazz, see?" Now he used both the spoon and the tines of his fork to tap out a more syncopated beat on the glass. Several people at the counter swiveled on their stools to watch. "It might go—say—one, seven, three, two, twelve. Ticks and tocks all out of sequence. Why? Because they're related *thematically.*"

"Thematically," Raymer repeated.

"Laugh all you want," Jerome continued. "First tick in Black time is slavery and all the others ticks and tocks return to that."

Raymer massaged his temples.

"See, for Black folks," Jerome went on, "it all comes down to the same thing—to what people see when they look at you. White time's just *you* doing what you do. A, then B, then C, and so on."

*Right,* Raymer thought. First it was numbers, now letters, as if the alphabet would make sense of his cockamamie theory.

"And the best thing about that? You don't have to think about bein' white. You just *are,* Dawg. And do you know what *that's* called?"

"Tell me."

"Freedom."

Raymer started to object, then thought again.

"When you're Black, you keep tryin' to make it work like white time. Make it go in a straight line, but Black time keeps loopin' back. Remindin' you you aren't free. Keepin' you vigilant. Circlin' back to what matters. Like stayin' alive. Like not getting lynched." Jerome paused here, perhaps waiting for Raymer to tell him he was crazy. When Raymer didn't, he continued, "Which is why I'm into white people clothes these days. Cardigans. Khakis. Loafers with tassels. This ugly-ass sweater. Makes it that much harder for white women to fall in love with me. To put that target on my back."

"You've thought this through," Raymer said.

"I have."

"But what you're explaining is why white women fall in love with you. Why do you fall in love with them? Becka, for instance. Why did you fall in love with her?"

Jerome didn't answer right away. Finally, he said, "Long time ago."

"You're saying you don't remember?"

"What I remember?" Jerome said. "What I remember is not wanting to."

"Because Becka was white."

"That," he admitted. "And other things."

"Like what?"

"You and me. Used to be friends."

Raymer swallowed hard. *Had* they been? Yes, their paths used to cross pretty frequently back then. Jerome was not only Charice's brother, but also a Schuyler cop. But had they ever sought out each other's company? Gone out for a beer? Did Jerome have any other friends back then? At the time it hadn't occurred to Raymer to inquire.

Down the counter a cell phone rang and Raymer saw Janey's cop take his cell phone out of its holster and answer it, straightening up as he listened.

"Okay," Raymer said. "I get that you didn't want to. But what I asked was why you did."

Jerome shrugged, as if the question was of little or no interest. "Same reasons as you, probably. Who knows, Dawg?"

"Can I ask you about your sister?" Raymer said. Because the whole time they'd been talking about Becka, it was really Charice he'd been thinking about, Charice that he was desperate to understand. "Growing up, did she have a lot of boyfriends?"

Jerome pushed his plate away. He'd eaten, as promised, every last bite. "A few." He shook his head, clearly ashamed. "Mostly, she was too busy tending to my needs to have much time left over for herself and hers."

"What about your parents?"

"Always working, Dawg."

"Can I ask if any of her boyfriends were white?"

"In rural North Carolina?"

Raymer nodded. "Then . . . why me? I mean . . . I'm not a man with a lot of . . . plumage."

"Dawg," Jerome said sadly. "You got no feathers at all."

The bell above the front door jingled, and Raymer looked up in time to see Janey's cop heading out. Which was just as well. Now, suddenly in a hurry, he wouldn't be coming over to introduce himself, which would've meant Raymer having to introduce Jerome. "Anyhow," he said. "Whatever she used to see in me? I don't think she sees it anymore."

"Don't be too sure," Jerome replied. "I keep trying to get her to leave here and she won't."

"Yeah, but it's her career keeping her here, not me," Raymer assured him. "She needs to see this job through. I'm not sure you understand how much it means to her."

Outside, Janey's cop was fishing in his pants pocket for his car keys. In the time it had taken them to eat their breakfasts several inches of heavy wet snow had accumulated on the sedan's windshield. Raymer expected the guy to pop the trunk, grab a scraper and brush the snow off the vehicle's windows, but instead he just got in behind the wheel and turned on the wipers, which struggled with the snow's weight before finally pushing it aside. The side windows he dealt with by powering them down and allowing the snow to fall inside. Raymer couldn't help wondering what the phone call had been about.

"Can I get you two gentlemen anything else?" said Janey, who had materialized with their check.

"I'm good," Raymer told her.

"How about you, Jerome?" she said, and something about her tone of voice, together with the fact that she'd spoken his name, caused Raymer to pause and reconsider. Earlier, when Jerome had been bragging about his effect on white women, Raymer had written the whole thing off as fantasy. But what if it wasn't?

Without exactly looking up at her, Jerome edged his platter in her direction. "An elegant sufficiency," he said.

"Wow!" Janey said, clearing his plate. "Listen to you!"

Out in the white street her cop was backing out of his angled parking space. "Your friend looked familiar," Raymer ventured. "What's his name?"

"Conrad," she told him, "but everybody calls him Del. Conrad Delgado."

A split second before she said it, Raymer had intuited what the man's name would be, so he was able to not react.

"He made you, too, by the way," Janey informed him. "Soon as he walked in. You cops are strange, strange dudes, you know that?"

When she was gone and Delgado's sedan had slalomed up the street and out of sight, Raymer put a twenty on top of the check and slid out of the booth. "An elegant sufficiency?" he said. "I know how proud of your vocabulary you are, Jerome, but it clashes with your cardigan."

"Just slipped out," Jerome admitted, also sliding out of the booth. "Verbal plumage, kind of. Mind if I wait outside? Need to vacate these premises before that woman falls in love with me completely."

At the register, as Janey rang Raymer out, he found himself wondering how much she might've overheard last night. He and Charice had both kept their voices down, but she'd come by their table several times to see if they needed anything. Had she been nearby when Charice was talking about Delgado? Had he joined her at the Horse when she finished her shift? Had they sat at the bar and discussed what had transpired there with Birdie and her Saturday-night regulars? Or had she gone somewhere else to meet up with him? Judging by her hungover late arrival this morning, they'd tied one on somewhere.

Outside, Jerome was shivering under the diner's overhang. Raymer used his fob to unlock his SUV and started the engine so the vehicle could warm up while he brushed the snow off the windows. When he finished and got in behind the wheel, he just sat for a moment before putting the vehicle in gear, causing Jerome to regard him curiously. "What?"

"Just thinking," Raymer said. Actually, he was playing back the moment when Conrad Delgado had made a gun out of his thumb and forefinger and aimed it at him. Maybe it was Jerome's crazy talk about lynchings, but the more Raymer thought about it, the less sure he was that the imaginary gun had been pointed at him at all.

"You said before that we probably fell in love with Becka for the same reason?" Raymer said. "I think I fell in love with her out of gratitude. She had beautiful plumage, I admit, but it was more than that. I think what I really loved was being loved."

"Like I said, Dawg," Jerome replied. "Same reason as me."

In the end was this what it came down to for all men? Raymer wondered. Or just men like him and Jerome? "You know what I think, Jerome? I think this is going to be okay."

"What is, Dawg?"

"Everything. We're going to figure it out." The identity of the corpse at the Sans Souci. False equivalencies. Black and white time. The evolutionary purpose of plumage. Whether he and Charice had a future. All of it.

They sat silently for a minute. The snow had already covered the windshield again, sealing them in semidarkness.

"Marian," Jerome said. "That was her name. And she was Becka all over again. When we were together, there was nothing wrong with me. Without her . . ." He let the thought drift off. They sat in silence until he said, "So. You still in love with her? My sister?"

Raymer nodded.

"Same deal? Gratitude?"

"Yeah," Raymer admitted. "Same deal."

"Give her time," Jerome advised seriously.

"White time or Black time?" Raymer said.

Jerome continued to stare straight ahead, but he allowed a half smile and tapped out a syncopated rhythm on the dash.

# Benign

T HERE HE IS," said David Proxmire, glancing up from his computer screen when Rub entered, stomping snow off his boots, in the entryway. In the year he'd been working at Harold's Automotive World on the outskirts of North Bath, Rub hadn't missed a single Sunday, nor had he even been late. Yet despite his manifest reliability, his boss always evinced surprise to see him, as if he'd just about given up hope that Rub would appear. Of his four jobs, this one at Harold's was Rub's least favorite, and his least favorite part of his least favorite job was David Proxmire himself, who had inherited the business two years earlier from his older brother Harold. The two brothers could not have been more different. Harold, eight years David's senior, had been tall and lanky and gray from head to toe—hair, eyes, stubble, clothing, even skin color—whereas his younger brother was short, rotund, clean shaven and florid. Had the Proxmires been in a lineup with eight other white men, they would've been the last two you'd have picked as brothers. Temperamentally, they were, if possible, even more dissimilar. Where Harold had been taciturn in the extreme, David was loquacious, a man of numerous, unfettered opinions that appeared linked to nothing in the real world—not personal experience or reading or even television. Where Harold had been soft-spoken, reticent, David was loud and untroubled by self-doubt.

Proof that they were indeed related by blood became evident only when you peered inside their skulls, which everyone who entered the office of Harold's Automotive World was invited to do. Here, along one long wall, David had strung a series of both his brother's and his own CT scans. The first thing you noticed about each was the cloudy white fibroid mass, a benign but inoperable cyst, nestled up against each man's brain. The pictures were chronologically sequenced to illustrate the slow, relentless growth of each man's cyst. Harold's had resulted, two years earlier, in a massive cerebral hemorrhage. The one in David's skull was considerably smaller, but it, too, was clearly growing. If he was on Harold's timetable, he had a half-dozen more years before his brother's destiny became his own.

One would've thought—or at least Rub would have—that such knowledge would occasion in the younger Proxmire a morbid dread, but instead his cyst appeared to inspire only wonder, a dizzying awe that its owner felt compelled to share, at excruciating length, with others. If you didn't know better you'd think he was proud of the damned thing, that it represented proof positive that he was special, rather than genetically befucked. He seemed particularly fixated on and infuriated by the use of the word "benign" to describe something that had killed his brother and would one day, presumably, kill him as well, and more efficiently than many tumors deemed "malignant." "How can it be benign if it's going to kill me?" he asked each new person with whom he shared the ongoing narrative of his head.

Indeed, for someone stalked so inexorably by death, David Proxmire seemed oddly disinterested both in delaying its arrival and figuring out how best to spend the time remaining to him. Another man might've put himself on a strict regimen of exercise and a healthy diet. Indeed, his doctor had urged both. He'd particularly recommended long walks to keep the blood flowing and a diet rich in fiber, vegetables, fruits and legumes. He urged his patient to avoid processed foods, sweets and sugary drinks. Also, alcohol. David listened to this advice carefully, then ignored it completely.

Back when his brother was alive, Harold had kept snack and soda machines in the office for customers who might want something to eat or drink while they waited for their cars to be repaired. David held on to these machines but put masking tape over the coin slots, and jimmied the doors so they would open at will. He then stocked the machines with his own personal favorite snacks—crumb cakes for breakfast, Cheetos for lunch, Diet Cokes for both. They had to be purchased at the supermarket, of course, but he seemed to derive particular satisfaction from being able to access them from the machines without having to insert coins into the slots, as if that made the snacks free. He was also, Rub knew, a drinker. He kept a bottle in the file cabinet drawer of his desk. One week it might be vodka, the next bourbon, the week after that scotch—it didn't seem to matter. He claimed that alcohol had little or no effect on him, and he had a working theory as to why. What if it went straight to the cyst? What if the cyst was acting like a leach field, preventing the alcohol from reaching his brain. What if the alcohol actually slowed the growth of the cyst? That it just might, to David, made sense. His brother had been married to a fundamentalist Christian and was a teetotaler. Consequently, David, who had believed since they were young that everything his brother did was wrong, had become an atheist, and the more he studied his own cyst and compared it with Harold's, the more convinced he became that by not drinking, his brother had hastened his death, which could only mean that pickling David's own cyst in alcohol was the better survival strategy.

He did not, however, believe that alcohol had any such salubrious effects on cystless people. "Don't ever show up plastered," he'd warned Rub that first Sunday, as if inebriation on Sabbath mornings might be a ritual of Rub's that demanded amending. "And no drinking once you're here, either."

Rub had assured the other man that he wouldn't.

"How about drugs?" David continued.

"No thank you," Rub said, misunderstanding the question as an offer.

"I'm asking you if you smoke weed?" David clarified.

Rub said he didn't.

"Well, don't," David clarified further. "Because for this job, you need to be sober."

Rub nodded agreeably.

"Because the one thing that *cannot* happen is this." David Proxmire paused here to let Rub know that the absolutely vital part was coming. *"You can't wreck the wrecker."* Another pause, this one to let the absolutely vital part gain traction. "You wreck the wrecker? It's goodbye to all this." And here David Proxmire made a sweeping gesture to include the entirety of Harold's Automotive World, as if this were a large and growing empire.

It wasn't. In fact, Harold's Automotive World was shrinking. In its heyday, when Harold's wife, who referred to herself as Mrs. Harold, was alive and keeping the books and scheduling appointments, there were always a couple dozen vehicles for sale on the lot, and the garage hummed with activity. Back then, the towing business had been a sideline. After Mrs. Harold's passing, her husband seemed to conclude the gig was up. He hired a girl to do all the things his wife had done, but she could make neither head nor tail of Mrs. Harold's system. The accounting seemed to be done in some sort of code, and her entries in the logbook might as well have been written in Urdu. Invoices? Good luck. There was also an ancient Kaypro computer that hummed as if alive but stubbornly refused to boot up. Had the thing expired when Mrs. Harold herself did? Harold had no idea.

Actually, though he'd loved his wife, Mrs. Harold's death had been clarifying. The automotive business was changing. Cars these days were all about computers and Harold somehow never made that pivot. The cars he sold on the lot went from long in the tooth, mileage-wise, to genuine beaters, half of which wouldn't start without a jump. Customers didn't know what to make of the fact that the man selling them had so little to say in their defense. Could he offer even a limited warranty? He could not. Indeed, he seemed none too sure they would pass inspection when it came time to register them. When a prospective buyer took one of his vehicles out for a test drive, Harold always seemed mildly surprised when he returned that the thing was still running, that the customer hadn't had to call for a tow. Shoppers, of course, were used to a whole different breed of used-car salesman, the kind who would trot out of the office the moment you pulled onto the lot, like a puppy let off its leash, who would greet you like a long-lost relative and assure you that the deal you'd be getting was beyond sweet. Shysters, in other words. Dickheads in loud, plaid sport coats. By contrast, you usually had to hunt for Harold, who always seemed to be hiding in the last place you looked for him. When finally located, he seemed less than thrilled that your search had been successful. Worse, he somehow managed to convey that he had his doubts not just about the vehicles he was selling but also about *you,* that your life had taken a turn that necessitated your coming to him.

Other things about Harold's way of doing business were equally unconventional. In the unlikely event you expressed interest in one of his vehicles, there was no haggling over the price. How much was the vehicle in question? you asked. (You had to. There was no sticker on the window.) "I can let you have it for sixteen hundred," Harold might respond, by which he seemed to mean he'd be happy to take more if you were offering, but he couldn't take a penny less, not and make even a slender profit. The only urgency a buyer ever felt about buying the vehicle now, today, was that Harold's Automotive World might not be around tomorrow. The deal completed, the cash forked over, the handwritten receipt pocketed, the keys transferred, you and Harold would shake hands and he'd wish you good luck like he really meant it and was pretty sure you'd need it. Next week, when the car died, he just hoped you'd remember that he tried to talk you out of buying it. Feeling guilty, he'd send the wrecker.

Anyhow, those days were long gone. The garage now sat empty, and the lot where Harold had sold all those beaters was now a weedy tow yard. These changes allowed Harold's Automotive World to become a one-man operation that focused on towing (hence David Proxmire's injunction against wrecking the wrecker). "You shouldn't have taken that off," he said now, in reference to the parka Rub had just hung up. Rising from behind the desk, he handed Rub the large metal ring that held the key to the wrecker. "You know where the Green Hand is at?"

Rub did and he felt a surge of pride. Back when he first started working for David Proxmire, he'd been mostly lost outside of North Bath. Working with Sully, he hadn't needed to know how to get anywhere because Sully knew and he was the one who always drove. But now, after a year on his own, Rub found that he knew his way around, even in Schuyler Springs. Last week he'd driven the wrecker all the way down the Northway to Clifton Park and returned without incident. Harold's Automotive World might be contracting, but Rub's own, which not that long ago had shrunk to the house he and his wife, Bootsie, had shared, was expanding so rapidly it frightened him. He was now working four different jobs and had his own bank account. Without exactly meaning to, he was of necessity becoming a man capable of making his own decisions and paying his own way, a man able to go places unchaperoned, at least on Sundays when he was at the wheel of the wrecker.

Rub's pride in this newfound autonomy was mitigated, however, by a powerful sense of disloyalty, even betrayal. After all, what would Sully make of the fact that Rub was managing so well without him? Would his feelings be hurt? Would he be pissed off? *What? You don't need me anymore?* Rub imagined his old friend chiding. Much to Rub's surprise, at least when it came to the wrecker, he was getting along on his own just fine. *Yeah,* said Sully's voice in Rub's own head, *but who taught you?* Which was true, Rub had to admit. It *had* been Sully who'd showed him how to safely load vehicles onto a wrecker, securing them there with breakaway chains and wheel straps. Which was why, when David Proxmire offered him the Sunday job, he feared he might not be up to the task without Sully there to supervise, but guess what? Despite his new boss's fear that he would one day wreck the wrecker and put them out of business, Rub hadn't had a single mishap, which was surprising, given how many there'd been when he and Sully were a team. Why? Well, when Sully was in a hurry, he was both impatient and easily distracted, as he'd been the day Carl had sent them in the Tip Top Construction wrecker to retrieve a company pickup truck that had snapped an axle on a jobsite in Schuyler. Because it was late on a Friday afternoon and Sully had been anxious to start the weekend at the Horse where they could wash away another brutal week with cold beer, he told Carl to just leave the truck where it was until Monday morning, but no, Carl wanted it done today. When they got to the jobsite, Sully refused to spend a moment longer than was necessary there. They'd quickly attached the wrecker's chains to the frame of the disabled vehicle and hauled it up onto the wrecker's long bed, then headed back to Bath. In their haste they'd neglected to check that the wheel straps were securely fastened. Even then they might've been okay if they'd stayed in town and gone slow, but Carl, asshole that he was, would refuse to pay them overtime, so Sully had decided to hop onto the Northway instead. Merging, he'd had to apply the brakes hard when some dickhead cut him off, then accelerated so he could get right on the guy's tail and lay on the horn. It was the acceleration more than the earlier application of the brakes that caused the truck to slip its wheel straps and depart the wrecker. Both breakaway chains snapped when the vehicle's rear wheels bounced on the pavement, whereupon the pickup, broken axle and all, became a free agent in the southbound lane, bouncing first off the left guardrail, then off the right, before being plowed into by no fewer than four southbound vehicles. Rush-hour traffic had been tied up for an hour, and it turned out Sully was right. Carl was disinclined to pay an hour's overtime that resulted in a totaled company vehicle.

Perhaps because nothing like that had happened since Rub had been working for David Proxmire, Rub had lately begun to entertain a heretical and shameful notion—that back when he and Sully had been working together and something went wrong, it was Sully, not Rub, who was invariably at fault. Worse, one heretical, prideful thought had a way of leading seamlessly to the next. Just this morning, on the way to Harold's, it had occurred to Rub that *he might buy a car.* Until fairly recently it hadn't occurred to Rub to mind having to walk places, even on cold, snowy winter mornings like this one, even all the way out to Harold's. *So what are you saying?* Sully wanted to know. *That it was me holding you back this whole time?* No. That wasn't what Rub was saying, or at least not what he meant to say. It was just that, having spent so much of his life wishing things were otherwise, he was beginning to wonder if, instead of articulating every single one of these wishes to his best friend like he used to, he might, in Sully's absence, make one or two of those same wishes come true. If he bought a car, he wouldn't have to trudge all the way out to Harold's on cold wintry mornings. With a vehicle of his own, he wouldn't have to take the bus out to the community college on weekdays. What scared him, though, was that if he bought a car, what would he want next? Where would it all end?

"It's a yellow Caddy with West Virginia plates," David Proxmire was saying.

At this, Rub stiffened, because Peter's son had been driving just such a vehicle yesterday. Could this one be that one? Probably not, he decided. By now, *that* yellow Caddy with West Virginia plates had to be in Canada, not the parking lot of a Schuyler Springs tavern.

"Just bring it back here and put it in the impound lot," David Proxmire instructed. "And check the answering machine as soon as you get back. It's supposed to snow hard all day. You might actually earn your pay for once."

In Rub's opinion he earned his pay every single Sunday, especially the slow, off-season ones where he had to sit in the dank office all day waiting for the phone to ring. He much preferred being busy. He'd originally taken the job because there was nothing to do on Sundays but sit around and watch old movies in his tiny apartment above the Rexall and feel guilty about the fact that he didn't miss Bootsie as much as he knew he should. At Harold's he watched those same old movies on David's snowy portable, wishing David would spring for cable, maybe one of the premium movie channels where they showed boobs. He also wished David Proxmire hadn't specifically forbidden him to raid the snack and soda machines. And of course, despite his growing sense of independence, his pride in both his burgeoning bank account and his newfound autonomy, he'd have gladly traded them all to have Sully back, telling him what to do and when and how.

*You sure?* Sully wanted to know.

Yes. Rub was sure.

═══

IT WAS SNOWING harder now, but the streets were empty, so despite traveling at a speed that was unlikely to wreck the wrecker, Rub made it to the Green Hand in under twenty minutes, time he spent trying to convince himself that the Caddy with the West Virginia plates couldn't possibly be Peter's son's. But of course it was. He knew that as soon as he pulled in, though with its windows all smashed, its body covered with dents, its tires flattened, the Caddy was all but unrecognizable. Getting out of the wrecker, Rub went over to where the vehicle sat, battered and forlorn. What in the world had transpired here? he wondered. Yesterday, he himself had taken an instant dislike to Thomas Sullivan. Had someone here at the Green Hand done the same? Had Thomas gotten into some kind of altercation that had spilled out into the parking lot? Or, for reasons Rub couldn't fathom, had Thomas done this to his own vehicle? Had the thing refused to start? Rub had known Sully to become furious at inanimate objects, and Thomas was Sully's grandson, so maybe.

He was on his back under the vehicle, hooking the wrecker's chain to the Caddy's frame, when he heard a nearby door open and boots crunching through the snow and broken glass. A voice said, "They did some job on it, didn't they?"

Rub pulled himself out from under the car. The large man standing over him looked to be in his fifties and he identified himself as Glen, the tavern's owner. When they shook hands, Glen's came away red. "You're bleeding," he told Rub. "Did you know that?"

Rub didn't, though he probably shouldn't have been surprised. The freshly fallen snow glittered with shards of glass from the Caddy's windows, headlights and taillights, mirrors and reflectors. The cut was on the heel of his right hand, and seeing the blood caused the cut to sting. "Darn," Rub said, wishing the man hadn't pointed it out. In his considered opinion there were many things in this world that you were better off not knowing, and whether or not you were bleeding somewhere was one of them. The knowledge of unpleasant things too often led directly to other unpleasant things, and this right here was a case in point. No sooner did he feel the sting of the cut on his hand than he became aware of an identical sting on his left butt cheek, which meant that when he wriggled under the vehicle he'd cut himself there, too. He closed his eyes in an attempt to intuit other nicks, but there didn't seem to be any.

"I wasn't here," Glen said in answer to Rub's unspoken question, "but the way I heard it, the owner of this shit-heap assaulted a police officer. Another officer took exception."

"But how's he going to get back to West Virginia?" Rub said.

"Don't know, don't care," the other man told him, though he was studying Rub curiously now. "What difference does it make to you?"

"None," Rub lied, not wanting to reveal just how invested he was in Peter's son leaving Schuyler County and never, ever returning.

===

CARL ROEBUCK, long one of Rub's least favorite people in the whole world, was just emerging from Peter's Upper Main Street house when Rub pulled up at the curb, hoping to catch Peter at home. Taking in the spectacularly ruined Caddy sitting on the long bed of the wrecker, Carl sauntered down the sidewalk for a closer look. "You know what this looks like?" he said, when Rub got out and joined him on the sidewalk. "It looks like the sort of vehicle our old friend Sully might've owned. One he meant to trade in on something even worse."

Rub ignored this and nodded at the house. "Is he in there?" Meaning Peter, of course.

"No, Rub, I'm sorry to report that Sully died."

"I know that," Rub told him, adding, to his own astonishment, "I dug his grave." Immediately ashamed for having given voice to something he didn't want to remember, much less talk about, and feeling his eyes start to fill up, he had to look away. When he finally looked back, Carl was regarding him curiously. "Who exactly *are* you?" he wanted to know. "And what have you done with Rub Squeers?"

It was not unusual for Rub to find himself lost in simple-seeming conversations. Somehow, though, when talking to Carl Roebuck, he was never *not* lost. It was why—or one of many reasons why—Carl was one of his least favorite people. "What do you mean?" he said.

"You said you dug Sully's grave," Carl explained. "The real Rub Squeers would've *duh-duh-dug* it. What happened to your *stuh-stuh-stutter*?"

"I don't know," Rub said, even more ashamed now. Was he being accused of carelessness? Of misplacing something valuable? "It just . . . went away." Suddenly wanting his stutter back to prove who he was, he would've liked to say *wuh-wuh-went*. Anxious for this grueling conversation to be over, he asked again if Peter was inside.

"Left about an hour ago," Carl informed him.

Given that Peter's truck was nowhere in evidence, Rub was inclined to believe Carl was telling him the truth, though it did beg an obvious question. "Then . . . how come . . ."

"How come I was inside?" Carl smiled, pausing to light a cigarette. One of the things that baffled Rub was why Carl always seemed to enjoy the very conversations that Rub himself was so anxious to conclude. "Because I live there," he finally explained.

Rub started to contradict him, then thought better of it, even though he knew for a fact that Carl *didn't* live there. The problem was that a fair amount of what Rub knew for absolute certain turned out in the final analysis not to be true at all, and this made him cautious. Was this one of those times? If it turned out that Carl *did* live there, it would mean that history was repeating itself, because once upon a time, when Sully was alive and living out back in a trailer, he had indeed rented the upstairs flat to Carl. To Rub it made a kind of sense that with Sully gone Carl would return there now. If Rub didn't want him to—and he didn't—then of course he would. Just as he'd once had to share Sully, he would now have to share Peter. Rub could feel the stars aligning to make this happen. "Since when?" Rub asked.

"I moved in last night," Carl said, inhaling deeply, triumphantly, it seemed to Rub.

"It's all torn up in there," Rub objected.

Carl spit a fleck of tobacco into the snow. "Not the part I'm living in," Carl said. "Look, you wouldn't happen to have a spare grand or two on you?"

"No," Rub said quickly, worried now. He hadn't let on to any-body about his checking account. Was it possible that someone like Carl could tell just by looking at him that he did have that kind of money. Had somebody at the bank blabbed?

"Don't worry, Rubberhead," Carl said, dropping the half-smoked cigarette into the snow and grinding it out under his boot. "I'm just pulling your leg. What would *you* be doing with two grand, right?"

To Rub's surprise, instead of being relieved to know that his secret was safe, he felt a strong urge to set Carl Roebuck straight, to let him know just how wrong he was, that by dint of working seven days a week and never going anywhere or buying anything, he *could,* in fact, loan Carl Roebuck the sum he had in mind.

"Anyhow," Carl was saying. "I'm glad you're here. If you can't loan me two grand, you can at least give me a lift."

"Where?" Rub said, realizing, even as he did so, that it was a mistake. He *should*'ve just said no. David Proxmire had told him explicitly to fetch the Caddy, bring it directly back to the yard. He'd already disobeyed orders by making this unauthorized detour, which for all he knew might be a firing offense. And he had more than once reminded Rub that the wrecker was not to be used for anything not work-related, which giving Carl Roebuck a lift would be.

"Spa City Realty," Carl Roebuck informed him.

"That's in Schuyler."

Carl waved this off. "Fifteen minutes," he said, opening the wrecker's passenger-side door and climbing in. Once situated, he rolled down the window. "It's right on the main drag. Practically on your way."

"It's in the other direction," Rub corrected him.

"That's why I said practically," Carl told him, rolling the window back up and effectively ending the discussion.

Somehow, Rub realized, the wrong man was now inside the wrecker, the right one outside of it. This didn't seem like a problem with no solution, but if there was an obvious one, Rub couldn't see it. He supposed he might remain standing there in the snow and wait for the man inside to get back out, but Carl's relaxed posture in the cab suggested that wouldn't happen anytime soon. Alternatively, he could join Carl in the warm, dry wrecker and drive him back to Schuyler like he wanted. How would David Proxmire ever learn that he'd done this? A third option would be to get back into the wrecker, ignore both Carl's presence and his pleas and just return to the yard with the Caddy like he was supposed to, after which Carl would be farther from his hoped-for destination than he was now. Which would serve him right. Of the three options, this one was the most satisfying to contemplate, and another man might actually make it work. Rub had spent pretty much his entire life wishing he *was* another man, *any* other man but, unfortunately, he never was and, he felt certain, never would be.

"I could get in trouble," he told Carl petulantly, climbing back into the wrecker. "I'm not supposed to give people rides."

"Aah," Carl said, lighting another cigarette. "You worry too much."

"And nobody's supposed to smoke in the truck," he added.

"Silly rule."

"Also?" Rub said, allowing a frightening impulse to roll over him. "I don't even . . . *like* you."

Carl tapped his cigarette into the pristine ashtray. Rub made a mental note to empty it when he got back to the yard. "That's okay, booby," Carl assured him. "I like you. Whoever you are."

Rub pulled away from the curb, still trapped in a conversation he couldn't seem to escape.

"*I don't even luh-luh-like you,*" Carl said, taking another deep drag on his cigarette. "That's what you would've said if you were really Rub Squeers."

# Dithering

DESPITE PETER'S DOGGED EFFORTS to ignore them, Ruth's words—*Maybe you ought to find out*—kept on repeating on an unwelcome loop in his brain. After the cemetery he'd driven her home, then headed to Schuyler. Cuppa, his regular Sunday-morning coffee shop, was located a convenient block from Edison College, where, later in the morning, he played in a regular Sunday racquetball league. In the meantime, he ordered a latte, found a small table along the back wall where he connected his laptop to the shop's Wi-Fi. Tomorrow he would meet with his staff to discuss which new books, movies, art and music deserved their attention and match those with their growing list of regular contributors. Against his better judgment he'd also promised Jack Julowitz to add to their agenda his proposal to expand the paper's focus to include some hard news. In J.J.'s view, the *Schuyler Springs Democrat*, despite its left-leaning opinion page, had become too timid and conservative in its news division, too unwilling to cover tough local stories. What *Schuyler Arts* needed to become, in J.J.'s view, was a genuine alternative newspaper, one willing to do deep dives into local politics and government. Peter didn't object to the idea in principle. He just wasn't anxious to undertake such a significant change, one that would almost certainly require additional funding to implement, especially given that he hoped his own days in Schuyler County were numbered. Also, J.J., the paper's principal photographer, was a gadfly and pot stirrer, always anxious to rile people up. His "deep dive" stories, Peter feared, would be more muckraking than news, perhaps even an invitation to lawsuits.

After staring at the blinking cursor of his laptop long enough for his coffee to get cold, he gave up and clicked out of his *Schuyler Arts* folder. Part of him, he realized, was still back at Hilldale. When Ruth, blunt as usual, had suggested it might be a good idea to find out what kind of man the son he'd abandoned so long ago had become, he'd voiced his reluctance to embark upon what would likely be a pointless exercise. No surprise, she'd responded by quoting his father: *Do some fucking thing. If that doesn't work, do something else.* Which, Peter had to admit, was pure Sully. Your only options were bad? Choose the least awful one and get to work. If the result was unintended consequences that made matters worse, well, you could at least say you tried. What it all came down to, Peter supposed, was life experience. During the war his father had learned that indecision was as likely to get you killed as resolute action. Sure, you'd make mistakes, and a really bad one might cost you your life, but waiting around for the situation to clarify could prove deadly as well. In wartime, data often arrived in the form of live ammunition. Dithering led to further dithering and, in the end, to paralysis. Peacetime had only reinforced his father's conviction that trial and error—or, as he put it, *Do something, even if it's wrong*—were preferable to armchair theorizing. The latter involved sitting down, which told you a lot right there. In Sully's view, life demanded being on your feet and—speaking of feet— putting one in front of the other. You sat down only when you were done doing.

What kept Peter from fully embracing his father's philosophy, at least as it manifested in Sully himself, was that it was too often born of impulse or impatience. Human beings had a lot of moving parts, and what ailed them wasn't easily diagnosed. His father's pragmatic approach also ignored the very real possibility that there *was* no remedy for the problem you were trying to fix. Hadn't Ruth herself acknowledged as much when she worried that her grand-daughter might be broken beyond repair? If this was also true of Thomas, if the injury Peter and Charlotte had inflicted on him as a boy was both grave and permanent, what good would knowing all about it do? Was it even possible to *do* after decades of *not* doing? The best reason for risking dire unintended consequences was that things couldn't get any worse. In Peter's own experience, however, this was seldom true. Almost every situation could be made worse, even when it wasn't immediately clear how.

Feeling a sudden urge to talk to the son he *hadn't* neglected, Peter shot Will a quick email. *Got a few minutes to chat?*

A minute later his cell rang. "Dad," Will said, the sound of his voice causing Peter to smile. His son was, Peter realized, a kind of genetic resolution to the philosophical dispute between his father and grandfather—a calm, patient, hardworking, resolute problem solver. "What's up?"

"I was just wondering," Peter said, suddenly reluctant to launch right in. "Do you remember your grandfather ever saying, 'Do something. If it doesn't work, do something else'?"

"Sure. All the time."

"Not 'Do something, even if it's wrong'?"

"That, too," Will chuckled, then grew serious. "Is anything wrong? You sound weird."

Peter took a deep breath. "You'll never guess who showed up here yesterday."

"Ummm . . . Mom?"

"No, but you're not far off."

"Don't tell me Wacker!"

"Yep."

"Whoa. No advance warning?"

"Nope. He was sitting there on the porch when I pulled up. He claimed he was on his way to Montreal and decided to stop and say hello."

"You don't sound like you believed him."

"Would you have?"

"Well, I wasn't there to hear him say it, but it doesn't make a lot of sense, I admit. You don't decide on the spur of the moment to stop by and 'say hello' to someone you're estranged from."

*Estranged.* The word landed like a gut punch. He was pretty sure he used it with Thomas.

"How long did he stay?"

"An hour?"

"Huh," Will said. "That part kind of makes sense if he really was just passing through. If the whole purpose of the trip was to see you, he would've stayed longer, right? How did he look?"

"A lot like you. Or how you'd look if you'd been in a bunch of bar fights."

"That sounds kind of harsh."

"You're right," Peter admitted. "Put it this way. He looks like life hasn't done him many favors." That black tooth, revealed when Thomas smiled, was what he was recalling. How glimpsing it had caused his heart to sink.

"You think he blames you?"

"Weirdly, no."

"Why weirdly?"

"Well, in a similar situation, I did blame your grandfather."

"Similar, but not identical. You at least tried. It was Mom who refused to let us be part of their lives."

To his shame, Peter realized that this was why he'd called—so that Will could confirm what had happened—that Charlotte, not he, was to blame. Why, then, did the words, once spoken, produce so little comfort? "Yeah, but I should've fought harder. Another man wouldn't have just given in."

"What do you think you could've done differently?"

"I don't know," Peter confessed. "A bunch of things, probably. The truth is, I wasn't all that unhappy with how everything worked out. You were the one who needed me most. Back then, splitting you and Wacker up for a while didn't seem like the worst idea in the world."

"I remember being really glad," Will said, and Peter could hear the sadness in his voice. "Relieved it would be just the two of us. And Grandpa Sully, of course."

Peter had to chuckle at this. Sully might've been no great shakes as a father, but he'd somehow come into his own as a grandfather. "You began to thrive right away. I figured down the road there'd be an opportunity to get you and your brothers back together again, but there never was. Either that or I just didn't look hard enough. Maybe your mother was right. She said at the time that you were the one I wanted. She made it sound as if I saw her and your brothers as dispensable."

"For what it's worth, I don't believe you ever thought that."

Here again, Peter would have liked to embrace his son's good opinion, but he had his doubts. "I did try to call her at one point. You were in junior high, I think. But the number I had was disconnected and I remember thinking, *Good*. Like maybe it was a sign that things were as they should be. Or, even if they weren't, it was too late to do anything."

"You never told me about that."

"It was your grandfather's idea, actually. He offered to look after you if I wanted to drive to West Virginia to see if I could find them."

"Right," Will said. "Do something. If it doesn't work, do something else."

"But I argued it would probably be a waste of time. For all we knew they weren't even living there anymore. They could be in Texas or Montana. I also told myself that if things were ever really bad, your mother would swallow her pride and call."

Now it was Will's turn to chuckle. "Mom? Swallow her pride?"

"Like I said, it's what I told myself. Anyhow, when I saw your brother sitting there on the porch yesterday, I figured he'd come to tell me what I told your grandfather. That I'd abandoned him and his brother to a crazy woman."

"But he didn't?"

"Not really. He did kind of needle me a couple times. Told me he'd gotten a girl pregnant but not to worry, they'd taken care of it. Then he just grinned and said he was only joking."

"Some joke."

"He also said your brother Andy had come out as gay, then said that wasn't true, either."

"Huh."

"The point seemed to be that he could tell me anything and how would I know?"

They were quiet then, until Will said, "I actually Googled him a couple years ago."

"Yeah?"

"Turns out there are quite a few Thomas Sullivans in West Virginia, but only one the same age as Wacker, and he was living in the southern part of the state, a long way from Morgantown. I was offered the opportunity to purchase information concerning his various arrests for disorderly conduct and aggravated assault."

"So, not our Wacker."

"Probably not, but the reason I didn't pay to find out was that I was afraid it might be."

Which of course was the same reason Peter hadn't taken Sully up on his offer to look after Will while he searched for the rest of his family. With Will flourishing, he hadn't wanted to risk it. The possibility that the two sons he'd left behind might be living with ongoing trauma was something he tried not to think about, and mostly he succeeded. "Look, I probably shouldn't have called. There's no point in your fretting over the mess your mother and I made of things."

But apparently Will wasn't quite ready to put the matter to rest. "You say he looks a lot like me?"

"Tina thought he *was* you. Ruth's granddaughter?"

"God, I'd forgotten all about her," Will confessed.

"Well, she hasn't forgotten you. According to Ruth she had a pretty bad crush on you in high school. Still does, apparently."

"I remember feeling sorry for her. That wandering eye. Kids made fun of her."

"I guess seeing Wacker on the porch kind of threw her for a loop. She knew it wasn't you, but somehow it was."

"Ha! Genetics in a nutshell."

"My exact reaction."

"So, did he ask about me? Wacker?"

"He did. I told him you were in London on a fellowship." Recalling Thomas's eye twitch at this revelation.

"You say he only stayed an hour?"

"I invited him to hang out for a few days, but he said he needed to get back on the road."

"And he left no contact information?"

"I didn't think to ask." Though, was that true? Had he really not thought to? Or had not wanting to be in touch with the sons he'd deserted become his default mode?

"It sounds like the whole thing really threw you."

"I guess it did," Peter admitted, ashamed that he'd let it. "Anyhow, I should let you go."

"How are the renovations going?"

"Slow," he said, "but we're getting there."

"When will you be putting the place on the market?"

"Fall, maybe? Why?"

"I don't suppose you'd consider selling the place to me."

Peter started to chuckle, then realized his son was serious. "Why would you want it?"

"I don't know," he said. "Maybe to live in?"

"Have you run this by Clare?" Who, now that Peter thought about it, he hadn't even inquired about. He'd met his son's fiancée just once, last summer in New York, right before the two of them headed off to London, but he'd liked her a lot. For some reason the fact that they were clearly in the midst of a whirlwind romance had cheered him, perhaps because he himself had never had one of those. Women had always been attracted to Peter and he to them, but he hadn't ever really lost his head over one. Sadly, that included Charlotte, who'd gotten pregnant with Will before Peter could decide whether he had any deep feelings for her. That his son should have a more romantic temperament Peter took as a good sign. It meant that later in life he was unlikely to have a woman like

Toby Roebuck touch his chest with a painted fingernail and wonder out loud if he had a heart in there.

"Yeah, about Clare," Will said. "I've been meaning to call. We're kind of taking a break."

It took Peter a moment to locate meaning in this bland phrase.

"In fact, she's back in the States."

"Sounds serious."

"We might be finished," Will admitted. "And just so you know, I'm the one who messed things up, not her."

"How? Not that it's any of my business."

His son didn't answer immediately. Finally, he said, "How do we all?"

History repeating itself, then. Speaking of genetics. "Okay, but buying your grandfather's house doesn't fix that."

"I know. Actually, there's something else I've been meaning to tell you. Not long after I got over here I was at a party where I met this American editor. She was in town for the book fair. When I mentioned I was writing something that I hoped might turn into a book, she offered to read a few pages. Long story short, she thinks she might want to publish it." When Peter didn't say anything to that, Will said, "You're kind of quiet."

"I was just thinking about your grandmother," Peter said. "If she's hearing this, she has to be smiling ear to ear. First a Fulbright, now a book publication? Vindicated at last."

"How about you, Dad? Are you smiling?"

"I'm still processing," he said. Wondering if this editor's entrance and Clare's exit might be causally linked. *I was at a party,* he'd said, not *we were at a party.* But again, none of his business. "Last I knew, you were researching racism in the London theater. Is this a different project?"

"Completely. I haven't said anything because I didn't want to have to walk it back later if things didn't work out. But if they do, I'm thinking that when I get back to the States I might take a year off and finish writing it. Grandpa's house might be just the place."

"You don't have to buy a house to write a book."

"I know that. But I wouldn't mind owning it for other reasons. I grew up there. It's a place I like returning to. That should make you feel good, right? Evidence of a happy childhood?"

This was true but also, somehow, not.

"And Grandpa would approve, right?"

No doubt. Though Sully had never wanted Miss Beryl's house for himself, Peter was pretty sure his feelings had been hurt when he himself had shown no interest in the property beyond its market value. "So, what's this book about?"

"I'm not sure I want to say much about it right now," Will confessed. "It doesn't feel entirely real yet, I guess."

"Does it have a title?"

"A working one."

"I won't hold you to it."

"Okay," Will said, but Peter could hear his son's reluctance to share even this much. "For now, I'm calling it *Stopwatch*."

=====

"WOW!" said a voice at Peter's elbow, and when he turned to see who it belonged to, there, looming over him, stood Jack Julowitz, a folded copy of the *Schuyler Springs Democrat* under one arm, his laptop bag slung over his shoulder. "Do you have any idea how long you've been staring at that brick wall?"

"I was thinking," Peter explained.

Snagging a chair from a nearby table, J.J. drew it up next to Peter's, then cleared a space on the table for his coffee and the newspaper. Planting himself in the chair, he unzipped his shoulder bag and took out his laptop. All of this without invitation. Most of what J.J. did was, of necessity, without invitation. In the face of much evidence to the contrary, he appeared to operate on the assumption that people would, or maybe should, be glad to see him. His myriad, strident opinions on a wide range of subjects he viewed as proof of enviable intellectual acuity, whereas, in reality, they rendered him tiresome in the extreme, at times a genuine pain in the ass, though for some reason Peter couldn't bring himself to truly dislike the man. What he appeared to want most out of life was to be at the center of things, and life wasn't cooperating. For most people, in Peter's view, life never did.

"Fifteen minutes, at least," J.J. informed him, his tone borderline belligerent, as if remaining deep in thought for so long required justification.

Peter doubted it had been anything like fifteen minutes, as J.J. was prone to exaggeration. Strange that it never seemed to occur to him that this was not an ideal quality in a journalist, which he was angling to become, if he could just convince Peter to expand the focus of *Schuyler Arts* to include hard news.

"So, what profound question were you pondering?" J.J. said as he waited for his laptop to boot up. "Man's inhumanity to man? The origins of the universe? Why the Yankees suck?"

In truth, what he'd been mulling was destiny. What Thomas's sudden appearance yesterday had brought home to him so force- fully was that the figure in the carpet that was his life was becoming discernible, and it wasn't one Peter had intended to weave. Would Will come to a similar realization one day? Because he, too, was busy at the loom, though for him it would be years before the inev- itable mix of intended and unintended consequences, of fate and free will, of errors in judgment and dumb luck, would yield a rec- ognizable pattern. Peter wanted Will to succeed, of course. What father didn't? But until now it hadn't occurred to him that his son's success might shine a bright light on his own failures. Unable to rec- oncile his parents' very different hopes for him, Peter had somehow managed to let them both down. Had he charted his own course and succeeded on his own terms, his disappointing them wouldn't have mattered so much, but he hadn't. No, he'd dithered. Clearly, the book Will wasn't anxious to talk about was a memoir, and if its working title was any indication, it was his grandfather who would emerge the hero of the tale. Oh, sure, the portrait Will would paint of Peter himself would be loving and kind. But the facts were the facts, and they would be damning. Peter had dutifully looked after the welfare of one son, even as he'd neglected two others. And face it, the time to take action, even if he could figure out what action to take, was fast running out.

Peter had no intention of sharing any part of this reverie with J.J. "Right now, I'm pondering what you're doing here," he replied. After all, J.J.'s regular morning spot was a blue-collar diner on the other side of town, where "real people" with "real jobs" drank "honest coffee." "I thought you hated this place."

"I do, but you need to see these photos," he said, nudging Peter's laptop aside to make room for his own. "What's the Wi-Fi password in this elitist dump?"

Peter told him.

The newspaper J.J. had brought with him, Peter noticed, had been folded so that a photograph—credited to J.J.—was faceup. Peter picked it up for a better look. It took him a moment to recognize the man in it as a startled Doug Raymer, until recently North Bath's chief of police. The foreground of the photo was dark, but through an open doorway a great expanse of green was brightly visible, the vast lawn in front of the old Sans Souci.

"Have a look," J.J. said, angling the laptop so Peter could view the screen.

"Jesus," Peter said, when it became clear what he was looking at.

J.J. forwarded to the next photograph, then the one after that, each more ghastly than the last. "The *Dumb-o-crat* didn't want them, of course."

"Didn't want photos of a rotting corpse?" Peter said. "Imagine that."

"Check out the composition on this one," said J.J., who recognized no clear boundary between aesthetics and epistemology.

"Very arty," Peter said, "I can't believe you were allowed to take these."

"I got there before the cops."

"How is that possible?"

"I was in the neighborhood when the call came in," he explained, cycling through the photos a second time. "I keep telling you. Get yourself a police scanner and learn the codes. You wouldn't believe the stuff that goes on in this town."

"What's the code for a hanging corpse?"

"Ten-fifty-six. All suicides are fifty-sixes."

"And you *wanted* to see this one?"

"Actually, it was the urgency in the dispatcher's voice that caught my attention. That and the location. I mean, come on. The Sans Souci? A corpse hanging in a boarded-up hotel? There had to be a story, right? Anyhow, by the time I got kicked out, I already had what I needed."

Peter returned to the photo of Raymer. "So," he said, "were you *trying* to make the poor sap look like a fool."

J.J. grinned, clearly pleased with himself. "You gotta admit, the beach towel accessory is pretty great."

"Is it me, or does the picture also imply that he might be involved somehow?"

J.J. shrugged. "Who knows? Maybe he was. I mean, what was he *doing* there? I checked and he's not even a Schuyler cop. Anyhow, photographs don't imply. They just record what the lens sees."

"You might feel differently about a photo of you and Jeffrey Dahmer at the car wash."

"Could never happen."

"No?"

"I never wash my car. That's what rain's for."

"Okay," Peter said, pushing the laptop away. "Why did you want me to see these?"

"Because they illustrate what I keep telling you—in this town the real news goes unreported. If I hadn't been on the scene, this whole thing would've been swept under the rug."

Peter shook his head. "Come on. The whole town was talking about it yesterday."

"Okay, maybe it would've made the paper," J.J. conceded, "but now it's a front-page story instead of getting buried beneath the fold in local news."

"Yeah, but isn't that where it belonged? Some poor guy comes to the end of the road and kills himself. Isn't that a story of private despair? Why should it be on the front page?"

"How do we know it's private until we look into it? Maybe it's connected to other stuff that's front-page news. I mean, this fucked-up country of ours? Opioid addiction? Corrupt cops and politicians? Lobbyists writing rules that benefit the wealthy and undermine workers? Maybe the guy at the Sans Souci got one of those subprime mortgages, and the bank foreclosed on him. Or he lost his job to the recession and now he's got no place to live. You think shit like that doesn't happen here?"

"No, I'm questioning whether it's *our* job to report it."

"If not us, who?"

Peter sighed. "I don't know, J.J. Maybe people who went to journalism school? Who can boast actual credentials?"

"I've got credentials."

"As a sports reporter."

Before moving upstate J.J. had covered local sports for a paper on Staten Island, where he'd been fired, or so he claimed, for doing his job too well. As he'd seen it, his mission was to expose the dark underbelly of athletics at every level, including high school. (Everything, in J.J.'s view, had a dark underbelly.)

"Yeah, okay, I covered sports," J.J. conceded, "but the point is I've worked in a newsroom and know the ropes. Also, I know of at least two reporters at the *Dumb-o-crat* who'd join us in a heartbeat."

"Sure, if we matched their salaries and provided health insurance. Have you thought how doing that would make our other writers feel?" Because, like Peter and J.J., just about everybody who contributed to *Schuyler Arts* was paid either poorly or not at all. Most were faculty at Edison or SCCC who regarded the paper as a side hustle, an opportunity to pad their academic résumés and reach audiences outside of academic journals nobody read.

"Okay, so we start small," J.J. suggested. "Maybe one investigative piece a month. Gradually work our way up to one a week. Can we at least discuss it?"

"It will be on tomorrow's agenda, I promise," Peter assured him.

"Yeah, but will you support it? The timing is right. We won that award last year. Our circulation is bigger than the *Dumb-o-crat*'s."

"We're free."

"If we expand into news, we could put them out of their misery. The town could be ours." Which of course was always J.J.'s true endgame: to be a mover and a shaker.

"From what I'm hearing," Peter said, "they may go out of business regardless."

"So?" J.J. countered. "Like I said. An opportunity."

"Yeah, to lose our shirts. You say the timing is right, but actually it couldn't be worse. The whole newspaper industry is on life support. Ad revenue is migrating online."

"Then we go digital ourselves."

"I don't really know that model. Do you?"

"We could learn."

"I'm pushing sixty," Peter reminded him. "And you're no spring chick yourself."

"We bring experience," J.J. insisted. "Wisdom."

"Really? You feel wise?"

He started to reply, but before he could, Peter's cell rang. *Good,* he thought, until he saw that the caller was Will. Had something else occurred to him about Thomas's visit? Or was there more troubling personal news he'd decided to come clean about? "Umm . . . I need to take this," he told J.J., hoping the other man would take the hint, pack up his laptop and leave. Fat chance. Pressing ANSWER to prevent the call from going to voice mail, Peter said, "Hang on, okay? I'll call you back in two seconds."

Outside, thanks to the thick blanket of wet snow, the street was preternaturally still. To Peter it felt almost like a living thing that had taken a deep breath a moment earlier and was waiting to exhale, though of course it was Peter himself who was holding his breath. Waiting for the call to go through, he was visited by the same sense of foreboding he'd felt yesterday when he'd pulled up in front of the house and saw Thomas sitting on the porch, looking like retribution personified. "Sorry about that," he said when Will answered. "I was in a meeting."

"It's him," Will said simply. "I did another Google search."

Peter swallowed hard. "You're sure?"

"There's a photo. You're right. We do look a lot alike." When Peter didn't know how to respond to that, his son continued, "I think you need to take this seriously. His showing up, I mean. He's been in all kinds of trouble. Drunk and disorderly. Assault. Resisting arrest."

"Okay, I appreciate the heads-up, but I doubt there's anything to worry about," Peter said. "By now he's probably halfway back to West Virginia."

"What if he's not?"

"If he's still around, it's because he plans to come by again. If he does, I'll get to the bottom of it."

"Be careful."

"Are you saying I should be afraid of him?" As he'd actually *been,* just last night?

"I'm saying you don't know who he is." *Or what he's become.* No need to actually put that into words.

"Okay, but whose fault is that?"

Suddenly there was a loud thud, concussion-like, that seemed to originate in downtown Schuyler. Was it Peter's imagination, or had the ground actually vibrated? He looked around to see if anybody else had noticed, but he was the only one in the street.

"Dad?" Will was saying. "Are you there?"

"I'm here," he said.

"Should I come home? We could look for him together."

"Absolutely not. Like I said earlier, your mother and I made this mess a long time ago. If it needs cleaning up, that's on us, not you."

"Okay, but Dad? What *I* said before? It wasn't the whole truth. I really *hated* him. If you never went looking for him, it was probably because you knew I would've begged you not to."

"You were just a kid," Peter reminded him. "Look, I'm going to say it again. None of this is your fault."

What his son said next wrong-footed him completely. "I cheated on her, Dad. That's why Clare left me."

He didn't respond immediately. "Okay, but how is that related to your brother?"

"Maybe it isn't," Will admitted. "But when she left? I remember telling myself that this was the first time I'd ever done something really bad, something that couldn't be undone. Trying to make myself feel better, I guess. Except that wasn't true. Hating Wacker, wanting to be free of him forever, my own little brother? That was worse. A lot worse."

"Is it too late to fix things with Clare?"

"I don't know? Do you think I should try?"

"Do you want to?"

"Yeah? I guess?"

"Will," Peter said. "Are you going to make me quote your grandfather?"

Though he was on the other side of the world, Peter, in his mind's eye, could visualize son's sad smile. "Do some fucking thing, even if it's wrong?"

"Right," Peter said. "If it doesn't work, do something else."

"Okay," Will replied. "I'll let you know how that works out. And if my brother shows up again, you'll let me know."

This latter was phrased as a demand, not a question. "Deal."

Hanging up, Peter glanced up the street, half expecting Thomas's yellow Caddy to roll into view, his son, made criminal by Peter's neglect, grinning at him from behind the wheel. But it also occurred to Peter that he and Will might be worried about the wrong thing. Yes, it was possible that Thomas had come for retribution. But couldn't retribution also manifest as absence? What if Thomas had come by to see if he still had any feelings for his father, or, equally important, if his father had any lingering feelings for him? What if he'd come to offer Peter one last opportunity to *be* his father? What if, instead of retribution, he'd been hoping for a heartfelt embrace, an expression of brokenhearted regret for how things had worked out? And received instead a tour of the house he hadn't had a chance to grow up in, an offer to "hang out" there for a couple days? What if, when Thomas left this time, he was gone for good?

The door to the coffee shop opened then, and J.J. emerged, his laptop bag slung over his shoulder. "Sorry," he said. "My scanner just went off. There's been some sort of explosion downtown."

"I heard it, actually," Peter told him.

"You want to tag along?"

"Not really."

"I'm telling you," he said, already heading across the street to where his car was parked. "Hard news is where it's at."

Back inside, Peter gathered his things. What he needed, he decided, was some spirited racquetball, something to not just exhaust his body but also take his mind off Thomas and, yes, Will, too. He was on his way out the door when his phone rang in his pocket. *Dear God, what now?* Thankfully, it wasn't Will again, but rather Birdie at the Horse.

"Can you come by?"

"I guess?" he sighed. "I was just on my way to play racquetball."

"Okay," she said, but her voice didn't sound right. Outside, a fire truck raced by, siren blaring.

"Is something wrong?"

"You remember David Proxmire?"

"Harold's brother?"

"He just died."

"I'm sorry to hear it."

"No, I mean here. Just now."

"At the Horse?"

"I'm looking at him. He's sitting in your father's stool."

Though it didn't seem to be, he had to ask, "Is this a joke?"

"He was showing me the latest CT scan of that thing in his skull.

He kind of stopped midsentence and this little trickle of blood came out of one nostril."

"Jesus, Birdie. Did you call 911?"

"I just hung up with them."

"So, the ambulance hasn't arrived yet?"

"No."

Outside, right on cue, an ambulance raced by, though if it was headed to the Horse it was going in the wrong direction.

"All right, I'm on my way."

"Peter?"

"Yeah?"

"Do you think maybe this is a sign?"

"Of what?"

"I don't know. Maybe we should close?"

"Look," he said. "Just sit tight, okay?"

"Yeah, well, that's the thing, isn't it," she replied. "Where would I go?"

# Mission Creep

WHAT DO YOU MEAN, you lost him?" Charice wanted to know. "How do you lose a six-foot-five-inch Black man in lily-white North Bath during a snowstorm?"

Well, it was embarrassing, Raymer had to admit. "We stopped at Play It Again Electronics, thinking they might have a charger for the BlackBerry," he explained. "Jerome wasn't wearing boots, so he decided to stay in the car. When I came back out, he was gone."

"Gone," she repeated.

"Well, not from the planet. I doubt he was abducted by aliens. He's just no longer in the car."

"How long were you in there?"

"Ten minutes, max," he told her, though it was hard to say exactly how long he and Larry, the shop's owner, had spent going bin to bin in the labyrinth of rickety shelves, pulling out nests of cords and chargers. Part repair shop, part outdated technology museum, Play It Again had doubled in size since Raymer's last visit, taking over the vacant space next door. The shop next to that was also vacant, and Larry said he had his eye on it as well. Who knew? Maybe he'd end up with the whole mall.

"And this place is where, exactly?"

"You know the little strip mall on the way to Performing Arts?

There used to be a travel agency and a Chinese restaurant? The Happy something? Lucky something?"

"Is there a coffee shop there? Jerome likes his espresso."

"There's no coffee shop," he assured her. "Except for Play It Again, there isn't much of anything. Most of the storefronts are vacant." Except for one other vehicle at the far end of the mall, the entire parking lot was empty.

"So, this Larry person?" she said. "Did he have a charger for the BlackBerry?"

"He found a couple that might work. Apparently there are several different models. I'll check them out later."

"Did you have some sort of argument?"

"Why would I argue with Larry?"

"No, with Jerome. Did you argue with my brother?"

Raymer allowed himself an audible sigh. "I told you before. We were getting along fine."

"Well, something must've set him off. What were you talking about?"

"Lots of stuff. Why white women find him irresistible. His excellent vocabulary. His sartorial choices. The evolutionary purpose of plumage. Also slavery and lynching and the difference between white time and Black time."

"There's a difference?"

"Apparently. He explained the whole thing to me with spoons and a water glass. Everybody in the restaurant turned to watch."

"I bet."

"We also talked about you."

"What about me?" Was it Raymer's imagination or did she suddenly sound anxious?

"How, when you were young, you spent more time worrying about him than about your own happiness."

"Jerome said that?" Her voice had become thick with emotion, and when he let her question sit in silence, she changed the subject. "Have you tried his cell?"

"Straight to voice mail. Do you think maybe he called a cab?"

"To go where?"

"The airport? Maybe he changed his mind again and decided to leave."

"Did you say anything that would make him feel unwelcome?"

Right. Here it was again, right on schedule, what loathsome Dougie had warned him about from the beginning, that when push came to shove, Charice would always side with her brother. "You know what? Here's an idea. Let's have him fitted with an ankle bracelet. That way you'll always know his precise location."

A long, apologetic beat of silence followed. "I'm sorry," she said finally. "I didn't mean to blame you."

"Actually," he told her, "the last thing I said to him was not to worry, that everything was going to work out. I guess I was trying to cheer him up." Except that wasn't really true, was it? What had led to that momentary surge of optimism was the fact that Jerome had unexpectedly confided in him that when Becka was alive, he'd thought of Raymer as a friend, which implied that they weren't anymore.

"Cheer him up about what?"

"He seemed to want me to understand what being Black felt like. As if I might wake up Black one day myself and be grateful to know how to proceed. He seems to think he's got a target on his back."

"That's not entirely crazy."

Raymer would have liked to disagree but decided to hold his tongue. In truth, his and Jerome's conversation at Hattie's unsettled him more than he cared to admit. The old Jerome (*The name is Bond . . . Jerome Bond*) had been determined to be seen and acknowledged. In his own way he'd been as cool and composed as the secret agent he riffed on. It was an act, of course. Raymer had always understood that. But it had been a good one, entertaining to observe precisely because it was difficult to take seriously, though it was entirely possible that Jerome did. Becka's death had shattered that pose, sending the man into a psychotic spiral from which he'd been lucky to emerge. Still, with Charice's and, yes, Dr. Qadry's help, he *had* emerged, his lost mojo gradually returning until he'd felt confident enough to go back to North Carolina and begin a new life there. What happened between him and the art therapy woman, so far as Raymer knew, had been nothing more than a breakup, but for some reason it had affected Jerome even more profoundly than Becka's death. Had he arrived at some sort of snapping point? Was he peering into the abyss? Though Charice hadn't said so in so many words, she clearly feared that her brother's steroidal anxieties had morphed into full-blown clinical depression, that this time, as she put it, he'd simply given up. And maybe she was right. This morning Jerome had explained why he found it necessary to attract less notice as he navigated the world, but Raymer couldn't help wondering if what the man really had in mind was to *dis*appear completely. If so, at least for the moment, he seemed to have succeeded.

They were both quiet until Charice said, in a voice he wasn't sure he'd ever heard before, "You promised."

"Promised what?"

"You've only had him one morning. You can't give him back."

Raymer looked out across the unnecessarily large parking lot of the failing strip mall, as if Jerome might magically appear in the middle of it. "I'm not giving him back," he assured her. "I've just . . . temporarily misplaced him."

What did worry him, though, was that he might become a victim of what the military called "mission creep." The job he'd signed on for was looking after Jerome while Charice took care of things at the station. And sure, having lost his charge, it was Raymer's job to find him again. That much was fair enough. More disconcerting was his sense that the Jerome Charice wanted him to find wasn't the one who'd gone missing fifteen minutes ago, but rather the brother she remembered before his breakdown. Earlier, listening to the man explain how he saw the world and his place in it, Raymer had wondered if his own best (perhaps only) chance of finding his way back into Charice's affections was through her brother. But what if she was really asking Raymer to get to the bottom of what ailed Jerome and fix him, something she herself had been trying and failing to do since his return from North Carolina? What if when Raymer assured Jerome that things would work out, it was really himself he'd been attempting to cheer up?

"I don't know. Maybe you should just go home," Charice suggested. "If he's headed there on foot, you'll beat him."

"And then do what?"

"You'll think of something. Look, I'm in the middle of a shit-storm here."

"More Delgado?"

"Call it Delgado-adjacent."

"He was at Hattie's this morning, actually. He aimed an imaginary gun at me and pulled the trigger."

"Like . . . in a menacing way?"

"No. At least that's not how I took it. More like a brothers-in-arms thing. I made him as a cop as soon as he walked in. He apparently did the same when he saw me."

"I doubt that. Nobody ever makes you as a cop."

"Thanks."

"I meant it as a compliment."

"So, what's going on now?"

"There was a problem at the station this morning. Some asshole from the drunk tank went ballistic on the desk sergeant. Punched him in the face. Broke his nose and knocked out a couple teeth. Just what the poor guy needed, two months from retirement."

"Is the assailant back in custody, at least?"

"He will be when he gets out of the hospital. I'm told it was not a gentle arrest."

So that's where Delgado had been headed when he left Hattie's in such a hurry.

"Apparently, the whole thing started last night. The guy was pounding shots at the Green Hand until he blacked out and fell off his barstool. Delgado was the one who brought him into the station and tossed him in the drunk tank to sleep it off. Now he's claiming the guy's injuries came from falling off the stool, not from his arrest this morning." Raymer heard a knock on the door, then, and

Charice's voice became muffled, her hand over the phone. "Look, I gotta go," she said. "Apparently, some car exploded in the middle of Main Street."

"Anything I can do?"

"Just find my brother?"

Right. Find Jerome.

Hanging up, Raymer put the SUV in reverse, started to back out, then stopped, trying to make sense of what he was seeing. Where the SUV had been parked, there was now a car-shaped rectangle where the snow wasn't as deep as elsewhere. Also in evidence were his own footprints in the snow, leading from the driver's-side door all the way to the entrance of Play It Again Electronics and then back again. Where were Jerome's footprints? When he exited the vehicle, what had he done? Flown? *Had* he been abducted by aliens? Raymer adjusted the rearview mirror so he could see into the back of the SUV, where he half expected to find Jerome grinning at him, not because this was the kind of prank Jerome—even the old Jerome—was likely to play, but because if he wasn't in the vehicle, *Where on earth was he?*

*Think,* Raymer thought. When this produced no results, he gave in and asked himself a truly humiliating question: *What would Dougie do?* Because, though Dougie might have been an asshole, he was usually a step or two ahead, and Raymer was pretty sure he'd have Jerome's disappearance figured out by now and, worse, would be taunting Raymer mercilessly for being slow-witted:

DOUGIE: True or false. Men cannot fly.

RAYMER: True.

DOUGIE: Jerome is a man. Therefore:

RAYMER: Jerome cannot fly.

DOUGIE: True or false. All men leave footprints in the snow.

RAYMER: True.

DOUGIE: Jerome is a man. Therefore:

RAYMER: Jerome would leave footprints in the snow.

DOUGIE: Except if he . . .

Raymer smiled. He knew—of course he did—that Dr. Qadry was right. Dougie wasn't smarter than Raymer. He was exactly as smart as Raymer for the simple reason that he *was* Raymer and apart from Raymer *didn't fucking exist.* Still, granting him temporary reality status, as a kind of thought experiment, had yielded results, so why not?

Pulling back into the space that the SUV had recently occupied, Raymer opened the door and stepped into the footprint he'd made earlier, just as Jerome must've done after sliding across the passenger seat to the driver's side. Then, just as Jerome would have done to keep from ruining his shoes, Raymer stepped in his own footprints all the way to the front door of Play It Again Electronics. Along the wall, thanks to the overhang of the roof, there was a narrow strip of concrete where only a thin skin of snow had collected, and sure enough, there were Jerome's footprints. Raymer tracked them to the far end of the strip mall, where there was a used bookstore with an OPEN sign in the window

Inside the store, Jerome was at the register, paying for what appeared to be a large art book. "You're not going to believe what I just found, Dawg," Jerome said excitedly when he turned and saw who'd just entered the shop.

"Sorry," said the man at the register, who was running Jerome's credit card. "Everything's slow today. Probably the storm."

Raymer took out his phone and texted Charice: *Got him. All's well.*

Returning the device to his pocket, he found himself staring at a faded hardbound book sitting face out on the nearest shelf. *Great Expectations,* the edition identical to the one old Beryl Peoples had given him as a present back in eighth grade. The book fell open to the first of its many illustrations, and there was the boy, Pip, with whom Raymer had immediately identified, and, off in the darker distance, the menacing figure of the escaped convict hiding in the marsh. Why, why, why had the old woman wanted him to read this book? He was about to set it back on the shelf when he noticed that something had been scrawled on the inside cover. The ink had faded, but you could still make out the words, and when Raymer read them, time—white time? Black time?—collapsed, and he felt the world wobble. *For Douglas Raymer,* the inscription read. *Not all books speak to all people, but I feel certain this one will speak to you.* She'd underlined the *you.*

Jerome, finished at the register now, his purchase under his arm, was waiting impatiently. "Let's go," he said.

"Go where?" said a still-weak-kneed Raymer.

"Here," Jerome said, showing Raymer the coffee-table book he'd just purchased. "The Sans Souci."

# The Score

THOUGH THE HOSPITAL CAFETERIA was empty except for a couple workers in hairnets, Lieutenant Delgado had steered Miller to a table along the far wall where they wouldn't be overheard. Between them sat the arrest report that the lieutenant, back at the station, had insisted upon writing up. It fit neatly on one page, and it already bore the lieutenant's signature. Below it was a space for Miller's. The lieutenant tapped the spot. "Right there," he said, adding, when he noted Miller's hesitation, "Just sign. There's nothing to fucking *think* about." The way he said the word made it sound as if thinking inevitably led to bad outcomes. As if, of all the despicable things a man might do, thought was the most indefensible.

"Chief Bond—" Miller began.

"Chief Bond," Delgado sneered. "You mean Char-Easy? What about her?"

"Chief Bond is the chief," Miller replied, all too aware of just how weak and pitiful this remark would sound to a man like the lieutenant, something a Boy Scout in pursuit of a merit badge might say. "We're not supposed to lie to the chief."

Miller didn't need to read the report to know that it would be neither accurate nor true. Lieutenant Delgado had punched a defenseless suspect in the face, then repeatedly kicked him in the ribs as he lay on the ground, ignoring Miller's protests, until the man passed out. Then he'd calmly popped the trunk of his vehicle and taken out a tire iron. At first Miller thought he meant to beat the suspect to death right there, but instead he'd gone over to the subject's yellow Caddy and commenced smashing whatever could be smashed—the windshield, headlamps, reflectors, side windows. When he noticed that Miller was still kneeling over the unconscious man, he said, "Hey, look at me having all the fun," offering Miller the tire iron. "No?" he said, when Miller shook his head. "Well, suit yourself." And he went back to smashing windows. When he paused to catch his breath, Miller rose to his feet and said, "We should take this man to the hospital."

The lieutenant clearly considered this a lunatic suggestion. "Why?"

"He's hurt pretty bad," Miller offered, not unreasonably.

"Good," said the lieutenant. "From what I hear, he hurt Sarge pretty bad."

At this point an older man who looked like he might be the Green Hand's owner emerged to watch the lieutenant finish demolishing the Caddy.

"I don't suppose your phone is one of those newfangled jobs that has a camera?" the lieutenant said.

"Sure is," the man confirmed, taking the device from his pocket and showing him.

"Good," said the lieutenant. "We should document this."

The other man looked surprised by this suggestion. The lieutenant, taking no notice, turned his attention to Miller. "I forget your name," he admitted.

Miller reminded him.

"Come over here," the lieutenant ordered.

"We should—" Miller began.

"Miller," said the lieutenant. "You need to chill. Come over here. This'll only take a minute."

Feeling he had little choice. Miller did as instructed, and together they posed in front of the ruined Caddy. "Put your hand right there," the lieutenant instructed, so that they both had a hand on the tire iron. "No need for me to hog all the glory. Big smile now."

Had Miller actually smiled? He couldn't remember. Probably. He'd done every single thing he was told to do, even though he'd known it was all wrong. It was the lieutenant's calm confidence, as much as his rank, that had numbed him, short-circuiting his ability to resist. He wore that same calm, confident expression now.

"Not supposed to lie to the chief?" Delgado repeated. Though there was no one near enough to eavesdrop on their conversation, the lieutenant kept his voice low. "Okay, back up. Rule number one? What cops are *supposed* to do is stick together. I've got your back and you've got mine. That's how it works. What kind of sorry-ass cop doesn't get that?"

Miller's kind, apparently, and it was more than a little unnerving for the lieutenant to go, as if by instinct, right to the heart of the matter. *Sorry-ass cop.* That Miller would never get the hang of police work was something he'd worried about for as long as he'd worn a badge. Chief Raymer had been good to him, patiently waiting for the job to make sense, even confiding to Miller that he, too, had been slow to fully grasp what he called its nuances. He'd even shared some funny stories about dumb things he'd done when he was a young officer. Miller had appreciated the chief's faith in him and tried to convince himself that one day he'd wake up and understand his job and be able to perform it.

Having Lieutenant Delgado size him up as a "sorry-ass cop," however, suggested that maybe the time had come to admit that wasn't ever going to happen. More than anything, Miller wished Raymer was still chief, so he could go to him for advice. He wasn't, though, and just yesterday he'd reminded Miller that work-related questions should now be addressed to Chief Bond. He wanted to believe his old boss was just reminding him that the chain of command had changed and not just passing the buck, but what if the chief was really trying to tell him that by now he was supposed to know what he was doing? If so, then Lieutenant Delgado was right to hold him in low esteem, perhaps even contempt. Yesterday, when Miller saw that decomposing body hanging in the ballroom of the Sans Souci, he'd spent the next two hours puking his guts out. Lieutenant Delgado wouldn't have done that. Chief Raymer hadn't. Hell, even Chief Bond hadn't, and she was a girl. How much more evidence did he need that law enforcement wasn't for him?

"But Chief Bond——" Miller tried again, stopping short when the lieutenant leaned forward across the table so that his forehead was mere inches away from Miller's own, as if he meant to whisper a secret.

"Did you *see* what that asshole did to Francis? Crushed his fucking nose? Knocked out four of his front teeth? He fucking *swallowed* two of them."

Miller had seen and did know. He'd just been upstairs in Sarge's room and seen the poor man's ruined face. Nobody in the Schuyler PD had welcomed Miller more warmly or treated him with more deference than Sarge.

"How'd you like for something like that to happen to you?" the lieutenant wanted to know. "How'd you like to swallow your own fucking teeth?"

To Miller, neither of these questions seemed entirely rhetorical. Indeed, his impression was that if he answered them wrong he might find out, right there in the cafeteria, what swallowing your own teeth felt like. Leaning back, the lieutenant again tapped the spot on the report where Miller was supposed to sign, this time handing him a ballpoint pen from the inside pocket of his sport coat.

Taking it, Miller sighed, thinking, Why not just sign and be done with it? The lieutenant was his superior officer, and also wasn't he right about the need for cops to stick together? Hadn't that been stressed over and over at the academy? If there was one thing that all the instructors there seemed to agree on, it was that cops were engaged in a war against the bad guys, who wouldn't be fighting fair. The only people you could count on were other cops. At the end of your shift you had every right to go home to your wife and kids. In fact, it was your solemn duty to make that happen. Miller didn't have any kids yet, but he'd married earlier that year and he knew that Judy, who worked in a clothing store, worried about him, that some bad guy would shoot him and leave her a widow. So, yeah, he understood that his fellow cops were, literally, brothers-in-arms.

What Miller would've liked the lieutenant—or anybody, really—to explain was what in the world was wrong with him. Why, after a decade on the job, was he still unable to reconcile or, failing that, make peace with its many contradictions. For instance, it was the public that cops were supposed to serve and protect. However, this same public—and this, too, had been stressed at the academy—was notoriously fickle and couldn't be counted on to see things like cops did, to understand that you were putting your life on the line for them every single time you put on the uniform. If cops didn't always do things strictly by the book, if they didn't always play by the rules, it was because that was the only way the public could effectively be served. Take this present case. As much as Miller disliked the lieutenant, didn't he sort of have a point? Didn't the guy the lieutenant roughed up that morning have it coming? That was what you were told at the academy about bad guys. If a cop showed up in your life, it was because you'd done something bad to bring him there. If you didn't want to encounter somebody like Lieutenant Delgado in the parking lot of the Green Hand, then don't knock the Sarge's teeth out. It was the shit that bad guys did that caused cops to magically appear.

How, though, was Miller supposed to square all that with the undeniable fact that the man sitting across from him—despite playing for the good guys' team, despite being Miller's brother-in-arms—was *not* a good guy? Shouldn't his being a bad guy himself have disqualified him from wearing the badge? Apparently not. Quite the opposite, in fact. As lawless as the men he arrested, Lieutenant Delgado had risen through the ranks and had become—at least according to the precepts of the academy—a good cop, one who served and protected a mostly unappreciative public, had the backs of his fellow officers and made sure both he and they went home to their families at the end of their shifts. All the lieutenant wanted from Miller, who by his own admission wasn't nearly as good a cop, was to sign off on an inaccurate arrest report. Had Chief Raymer—or Chief Bond, for that matter—asked him to do the same thing, he would have, wouldn't he?

So . . . in the end, what exactly *was* a good cop? What did it mean that cops themselves couldn't seem to agree? Though he and Chief Raymer had never discussed any of this in so many words, he was pretty sure the chief would've listed a whole different set of qualities from the lieutenant, and honesty would've been somewhere in the mix. Clearly, the man sitting across the table from him, and impatiently tapping the spot on the arrest report where Miller was supposed to sign, shared no such conviction. He was not only lying about what he'd done, but also about his motives, and to Miller that was even more troubling than the lies themselves. The lieutenant wanted everyone to believe that he was acting on principle—cops needed to stick together—whereas it seemed to Miller that he'd done it for the simple reason that he wanted to. And the reason he believed he could get away with it was . . . well . . . Miller himself. The lieutenant had sized him up, probably when they first met, and concluded that here was somebody who not only could be bullied but afterward would pose for an incriminating photo. Someone who was not just a coward but a fool to boot.

Given these undeniable facts, Miller was surprised to hear himself say, "None of this happened like it says here." After which he braced for the impact of the lieutenant's fist and the entirely new sensation of swallowing his own teeth. Instead, all the lieutenant did was smile, though behind that smile was something Miller feared even more than the fist. "Sure it did," he said softly. "Trust me. It all happened just like that."

"But . . . the suspect *didn't* resist arrest," Miller said, pointing to the sentence where the lieutenant claimed he did. "Or even try to flee. When I asked him to turn around so I could cuff him, he complied."

"Aww," Delgado said. "That's so sweet! You *asked* him to turn around? Did you say, *Pretty please?*"

For some reason, Miller continued, "It says here that you assisted in the arrest, but the suspect was already cuffed by the time you arrived. His hands were secured behind his back when you punched him in the face. He never had a chance."

The lieutenant's expression darkened now. "How about Francis?" he said. "An old man sitting behind a desk. Did *he* have a chance?"

"You kicked the suspect when he was on the ground. Even after he was unconscious."

"You're goddamn right I kicked him. What did you expect? You thought I'd just stand there with my dick in my hand, like you? Whining like a little girl." Here he mimicked Miller to cruel effect. *"Stop . . . stop . . . stop."*

As Miller, to his shame, had done. "You say here the suspect grabbed for my gun, which he couldn't have done with his hands cuffed behind his back."

This time the lieutenant said nothing in the way of contradiction, just tapped the signature line on the report.

"This is all lies."

Delgado lowered his voice even further now. "And you need to fucking memorize them. You need to be able to recite them like the pope recites the Lord's Prayer."

Miller shook his head. "Nobody will believe us," he said. Again, he couldn't believe how weak and pitiful this came out sounding.

Delgado leaned back in his chair and locked his fingers behind his head, studying Miller as if he were some sort of exotic exhibit, a mermaid preserved in formaldehyde. "Wow," he said, his voice rich with wonder. "And all this time I've been thinking you were just *pretending* to be stupid. You really don't get it, do you."

Miller had to look away.

"Okay, then allow me to explain what you're missing. It's three or four things, actually. The report makes sense? Doesn't make sense? It's all a lie? It's God's own truth? None of that matters. Not even a little. They're gonna believe us because we're both saying the same thing. They're gonna accept the report as true because every time they ask us what happened in that parking lot, we're gonna say the same fucking thing. We don't change a syllable. We repeat what the report says, no more, no less. They're gonna believe us because we're cops and so are they, and this cracker from Bumfuck, West Virginia, put one of our guys in the hospital. Because the cracker is nobody. Less than nobody. A violent drunk who was actually crazy enough to assault a police officer *in a police station.* They're gonna believe us because they *want* to. Even if they think we're fucking lying, they're going to believe us. Why? Because we're a tribe. Because the one thing cops understand that civilians don't is that this is how the world works. Not *part* of the world. The whole fucking world. The difference between us and them is that we admit it." Again, he leaned forward, all four legs of the chair back on the floor now. "You think the assholes at that forty-grand-a-year private college across town aren't a tribe? You think trust funders aren't a tribe? Rich Jews? You think the people who come up here from the city in August to watch the races and eat sushi aren't a tribe? You can pretend they aren't all you want, but that's what it comes down to." He paused here to let this sink in. "You say we're all Americans? Bullshit. We all *live* in America. Not the same thing. You're either a member of a tribe, or bad things happen to you. If we all had eyes in the back of our fucking heads, it might be differ-ent, but we don't. You watch my back, I watch yours." Yet again he tapped the report with his index finger. "You know what hap-pens if you don't sign off on this? Don't bother to answer. I already know what you're thinking. Frankly, I'm embarrassed to put it into words. You're thinking it'll be your word against mine, and Char-Easy will believe you, because you and her worked together in Bath. Because she's decided I'm an asshole. You probably think she'll shit-can me over this and then, who knows? Maybe you'll get promoted. For all I know you've got the hots for her and you think if you're a good boy she'll let you have a taste." When Miller opened his mouth to say he wasn't thinking any of this, the lieutenant held up his hand. "And, hey, you know what? To each his own. Not my cup of tea, but maybe you're different. Anyhow, here's where your thinking is fucked up. It won't *be* your word against mine. Because you know what I just this fucking minute remembered? It wasn't just you and me there in the parking lot this morning. My partner Bobby was there, too. How did I forget that?" Again, when Miller started to object, the other man stopped him. "Bobby *wasn't* there, you say?" Which, yes, *was* what Miller had been about to point out. "Doesn't matter. If I ask him to, he'll back me up and say he was there, because unlike you he's a real fucking cop. It won't be your word against mine. It'll be your word against *ours*. Two against one. But, hey, I can tell by the look on your face, you don't believe me. So, let's find out."

Taking out his phone, Delgado flipped it open and commenced tapping, then put it to his ear. "Bobby," he said a moment later, his voice louder now. "It's me. I need a favor." A brief pause, then, "That's great. I appreciate it. Don't you want to know what the favor is?" Glancing over at Miller, he covered the phone with his hand. "He doesn't give a shit. Says just tell him what it is." Then he went back to the phone. "Nah, it's just that I'm writing up this arrest report. Yeah, the parking lot one. What I just remembered is, you were there, right? I ask because Miller and I are remembering things a little differently. We might need a third memory, and you got a good one." He glanced at Miller again, gave him a grinning thumbs-up. "Yeah, I'll do that. Later, then. First round's on me."

Flipping the phone shut, he set it on top of the report. "Jeez," he said, studying Miller again. "All of a sudden you look kind of bummed. Reality bites, does it not? But you know what? The good news is you'll get over it. Quicker than you think, because actually it's like Santa Claus. The only reason kids believe in Santa is because their parents say it's true, and they wouldn't lie to you, right? Until one day you ask the question, and guess what? They admit it. They fuckin' lied. But about two seconds after that, you think, Hey, this isn't so terrible. No Santa Claus? You can live with that. It's not like you have to give back all the toys. You get to keep those, so really, who gives a shit where they came from? Also, you get to feel smart, because now at least you know the score. An hour later, tops, you're completely over it. Santa Claus, you think. What a fucking joke."

"Chief Bond—" Miller began again.

Delgado threw up his hands in mock surrender. "No, you're right," he admitted. "You're right. This whole deal *could* go down like you're hoping. Maybe Char-Easy will side with you. It's possible, because that twat's no more a real cop than you are. But whether she believes you or she believes me and Bobby doesn't matter, because *she* doesn't matter. You think she's your boss, but guess what? She's only your boss as long as she's your boss, and here's the problem. She's got a boss, too, and *her* boss—the mayor? I have it on excellent authority that his patience is wearing pretty fucking thin. Trust me, he's thinking to himself, What the ever-loving *fuck* was I thinking when I gave that job to a *mulignan*? The timing's tricky, I admit. It's possible she lasts long enough to shit-can me, or maybe me and Bobby both. But you know what happens next? We just get hired in some other department, and our rank and pension follow us there. Know why? Because we're real cops and there aren't enough of us to go around. We're like priests, except we don't diddle altar boys. For us, it's not a job, is what I'm saying. It's a calling. You either hear the call, or you don't. And speaking of hearing the call? You want proof of just how pathetic you are?"

Miller didn't. It was the one thing he didn't require proof of.

"You actually believed it, didn't you?" the lieutenant chuckled.

Miller knew better than to ask, but he couldn't help himself. "Believed what?"

"That phone call I made just now? Nothing about that seemed weird to you?"

Miller thought back on it, and yes, now that the lieutenant mentioned it, something *had* been odd about it. "Your partner," Miller said. "He picked up right away."

"Go on," Delgado encouraged him. "And?"

"He was waiting for the call. The two of you planned the whole conversation in advance."

Delgado continued to study him expectantly, like you would a toaster when the bread's about to pop up any second. "Jesus," he said finally when the bread stayed in the toaster. "I don't even know what to say, except that if anybody ever needed to belong to a fucking tribe it's you. No, Miller, you shit-for-brains, we didn't plan the phone call in advance. *There was no call*."

Miller blinked, opened his mouth to say that of course there was. He'd sat right there and listened to it.

Lieutenant Delgado picked up the phone again, flipped it open and started tapping, but this time each tap was followed by a tiny, barely audible beep. After the seventh beep came the distant ring of the call going through. A moment later a tinny female voice said, "Hattie's."

"Hey," said the lieutenant, who hadn't taken his eyes off Miller. "It's me. I'm demonstrating what a real phone call sounds like to the dumbest cop I ever met. You wanna do something later?"

"How about I call you after I close up?"

He winked at Miller now. "I may have another date by then."

"Who else would go out with you?"

A shadow crossed his features. "Be careful that mouth of yours isn't the death of you," he said, flipping the phone shut again. "Another one who thinks she doesn't need a tribe," he remarked before turning his attention back to Miller. "I was wrong about Santa Claus, wasn't I," he said, again tapping the signature line of the report. "You were one of those kids who didn't want to know the score. You cried your little eyes out, didn't you."

=

LATER, after the lieutenant left, Miller wouldn't be able to say exactly how long he remained in the cafeteria, staring at the Formica tabletop and listening to the sound of distant sirens. What he couldn't get over was how cannily the other man had read his innermost secrets. He'd not only peered deeply into Miller's soul but held up what he found there for Miller's inspection, forcing him to recognize the ridiculous reflection in the mirror as himself. He'd even intuited his long crush on Chief Bond, the one that even marriage hadn't cured him of, as Miller had hoped it might. How silly he'd sounded invoking her name over and over. How shameful that he hadn't defended her when the lieutenant had referred to her as "Char-Easy." No wonder his imagination failed him whenever he attempted to dream up a scenario where a woman like her would look twice at a man like him. For that to happen, he would have to be a different man altogether, and this, he realized bitterly, was the reason he'd wanted to become a police officer to begin with, in the hopes of becoming that other man. Yesterday, in the ballroom of the Sans Souci, staring up at the decomposing corpse, he'd asked himself what would bring a man to do such a terrible thing to himself. Despite being tormented by self-doubt his entire life, Miller still couldn't imagine any event ever bringing him to such a place. What he understood now, sitting alone in the cafeteria, listening to those distant sirens, was that it wasn't doubt that leads a man to give up on life and tie a rope around his neck. It was certainty.

# Businesses and Hobbies

I T WAS STILL SNOWING when Janey finally shooed the last of her
Sunday breakfast crowd out the door and closed up the restaurant. By then the plow had been by and according to the radio the
storm was supposed to taper off later that afternoon, which meant
she could do something or go somewhere, if only she could think of
what to do or where to go. She'd told Del she would call him after
she closed up, but he'd been kind of a dick on the phone, warning her that her big mouth might just be the death of her, which
she didn't want to hear because, well, it was true, but also because
coming from him it also sounded vaguely threatening. Though he'd
never raised his hand to her, she couldn't entirely banish from her
mind the possibility that he might. Her mother was right. What she
needed in her life was a different sort of man altogether, someone
more like . . . but no. No, no, no. She was emphatically *not* looking
for a man like Sully.

And yet. What if the terrible thing she'd said to her mother
last night—that she was jealous because Janey was still young and
had a man in her life, while Ruth was old and alone—was not just
cruel but due south of the truth? What if she, Janey, was the jealous one? Jealous because by the time she was Janey's age Ruth had
already been in a decade-long relationship with a man who might
at times have been his own worst enemy but didn't have it in him to

be hers. Growing up, Janey had done her level best to hate the man for wrecking her parents' marriage and making them into a family that other people gossiped about, but she had to admit that Sully had been better for her mother than any of the men in Janey's life had been for her, including the present one.

What particularly troubled her about Del was that she didn't like waking up next to him, as she'd done this morning. Her entire life she'd enjoyed waking up with a man in her bed, even if it was one she didn't particularly like, even if it was Roy Purdy, the worst of the lot. Asleep, Roy looked downright innocent, as if whatever possessed him when he was awake vacated his body when he slept. In the first few drowsy moments of wakefulness, he could be gentle, even playful, causing Janey to wonder if maybe the demon that made him ball up his fist could be exorcised. Fat chance. Before long, she'd either do or say the wrong thing, or Roy would recall something she did or said yesterday or last week, and then his fist would ball up and she'd feel like a fool for imagining it would ever be different, because, basically, Roy *was* a balled-up fist.

Not Del. At least not yet. Awake, he was usually relaxed and in control, even easygoing. Nor was he jealous, like Roy. Asleep, though, his features would clench into something like a grimace, and he ground his teeth audibly, which made Janey wonder if he might be beating her in his dreams. Which was ridiculous, really. He was probably dreaming of something else entirely, some situation he couldn't control, like arriving at the scene of an armed robbery, only to discover that his holster was empty. His teeth grinding probably had nothing to do with women. And even if he *was* dreaming of beating up a woman, it was probably one of his ex-wives, or Charice Bond, who was making his life miserable. Still, Del's first few moments of wakefulness, like Roy's, were clearly transitional. You could see him regaining control over whatever had caused his facial muscles to clench. Rolling over and seeing her in bed with him, he'd smile, or try to. It was disconcerting, though, how that smile arrived in stages. To Janey, it looked like he was putting on a mask, which in turn made her wonder if he might one day take it off.

The other thing she found puzzling was why, after a night out with Del and his cop friends, she so often woke up feeling ashamed. Because, really, why should she? All she'd done was kick up her heels and have a few laughs. Okay, she'd probably drunk too much, but so what? She was entitled to a little fun, wasn't she? Hard as she worked the rest of the week? Why, then, when she recollected the previous night's high spirits and raucous laughter, did she struggle to remember what had been so funny? Part of it was that while Del liked to have fun, that fun always seemed to come at somebody else's expense, like the guy from the drunk tank in the lie detector story. Del had dozens of yarns like that one—war stories, he called them—every cop had them. How could you not, in that line of work? He seemed not just to enjoy the stories for their own sake but also for his ability to get his listeners to see the world his way, which they invariably did. Still, did she even like these people? There were certain things about them that she admired, in particular their confidence. No matter how bizarre the circumstance, they always seemed to know what to do. Del especially.

Take last night. After leaving the Hand with the drunk who'd fallen off his barstool in the trunk of Del's car, they'd driven straight to the police station, where Del had hauled the guy out, sat him up against the rear bumper and kicked his boot in the hopes of waking him up. Unfortunately, the guy was out cold, his shirt glistening with vomit. "Okay, wait here," Del instructed, handing her a tire iron. "If he wakes up and causes trouble, hit him with it. I'll be right back."

Janey assumed he'd gone in search of someone to help, but instead he returned wheeling a platform trolley, the sort used in self-storage facilities. "Here," he said, handing Janey a long bungee cord. Then, hoisting the comatose man onto the trolley, Del had folded him into a sitting position so that his forehead was resting against his upraised knees. Running the bungee cord under the man's knees and armpits, he then attached the hooked ends between the guy's shoulder blades and gave the cord a good loud snap to make sure it was secure.

Okay, it *was* kind of a comical sight—Del wheeling the guy into the police station, his knuckles dragging along the pavement. But was it really all that funny? Was *any* of it funny? Maybe not, but that's what it was destined to become. Like that long-ago night in Philly when the old Black man failed the lie detector test, last night's festivities at the Hand would live on in story form: how that bumpkin from West Virginia had leaned back on his barstool and just kept going; how, when he landed, everyone had ducked for cover, thinking they'd heard a gunshot; how they'd agreed not to call an ambulance but instead to just toss the guy into the trunk of Del's car and drop him off at the police station; how she and Del had been warned not to forget the asshole was in there, lest they open the trunk in the morning and discover him frozen to death. No doubt about it, last night at the Hand was destined to become another of Del's war stories, their point always the same—that in addition to constant danger and endless sacrifice, a cop's life was also a never-ending parade of fools who were seemingly put on earth for the sole purpose of entertaining them. It wasn't their job to worry about whether tonight's lunatic might be concussed after falling off his barstool or that he might choke to death on his vomit while locked in an airless trunk, any more than it was their job to imagine the humiliation of the man who'd failed the lie detector test, because, well, how would *that* be funny?

What also occurred to Janey through the haze of her still-not-completely-vanquished hangover, was that despite the fact that Del and his cop friends were never troubled by self-doubt, maybe they weren't as clever and competent as both she and they imagined. Didn't she, in fact, recognize them from eighth grade? Hadn't their junior-high-school iterations been placed in the same vocational classes she'd been relegated to, their relentless B-minus/C-plus grades evidence that they were not college material? Law enforcement suited them because it provided a perch from which to look down on those even less fortunate and tell stories at their expense in bars like the Green Hand, where the booze was cheap and the music loud.

Did Janey belong with these people? If not, then where on earth *did* she belong?

=

NOT AT GRANDPA ZACK'S TREASURES, that was for sure, though that was where she was headed. What made the idea of going there palatable, Janey suspected, was the likelihood that the trip would be in vain. If the long, steep driveway wasn't plowed, there was no way her Jetta would make the climb. But so much the better if this should be the case, because then she could give herself credit for trying to do the right thing—to look in on her daughter and make sure she was okay—without actually having to do it. Who knew if Tina would even be there? Janey could've phoned ahead to find out, of course, but then she would've known and she preferred the satisfaction of driving all the way out there for nothing. "What do you mean she's not home?" she would demand of her mother, propelled by a full, righteous head of steam. "We're in the middle of a fucking blizzard."

To which Ruth would reply, "What do you want from me? I'm not her keeper. She's a grown woman."

"You know what?" Janey would say then. "Why the fuck do I even try?"

"I don't know, Janey. *Are* you trying? Is that what you call this?"

To Janey, such imaginary conversations always felt as real and disheartening as actual ones. That she could never best her mother in an argument, even when she herself controlled both sides of the dialogue, seemed particularly unfair.

Anyway, it didn't matter, because when she arrived, the driveway was freshly plowed, and though the Jetta's wheels spun a couple times, it managed the steep ascent just fine. At the summit she briefly considered parking next to the house, maybe stopping in to see Ruth first, but she decided that would be stalling, so she instead pulled into the Grandpa Zack's lot and parked next to her daughter's flatbed truck. Instead of getting out, though, she just sat there with the engine running, as if that weren't stalling, too. Staring at the massive structure that housed Grandpa Zack's Treasures, Janey could feel her blood begin to boil at the unfairness of it all, though she had to admit she herself was partly to blame. If she'd just pretended a bit more interest in her father's scavenging, she might've come in for a share of the business. But, come on. Who could have predicted that that first prefab shed her father purchased to store all the worthless crap he liberated from the dump and people's front terraces would over time morph into this? The venture hadn't even had a name back then, and why should it? *Businesses* had names, and this, Ruth maintained, wasn't that. *Hattie's* was a business. It was located in the *business district. This* was a hobby.

And now, dear God, just *look* at the fucker. Was it five times bigger than the original shed? Ten times? You could actually see it from the highway, a scar on the landscape. The dirt parking lot had recently been expanded and paved, room now for a couple dozen vehicles. Weekdays that was sufficient but not on Saturdays when, once the lot filled to capacity, people parked along both sides of the steep drive, two wheels on the pavement, the other two in the ditch, or on the shoulder of the road below. Twenty years ago, the whole property had been heavily wooded, but over time the trees had all been felled so that the business—because, yes, that's what it was and always had been, though her mother refused to admit it—could expand. No doubt the house itself would be the next to go. When Ruth died, Tina would have it razed and expand Grandpa Zack's even farther. The point of all this, or so it seemed to Janey, wasn't so much to make a lot of money—though her daughter was clearly doing that—as to declare victory. They'd started out as a family, but at some point they'd cleaved and chosen up sides: Ruth and Janey on Team Hattie's, Grandpa Zack and Tina on Team Junkheap. And face it. Team Junkheap had the sturdier bond. Though Tina had never said it in so many words (or, being Tina, any words at all), Janey couldn't help feeling that her daughter's intention wasn't just to venerate her grandfather but to rub Janey's nose in their success, to make her feel like shit. Which she did, every single time she visited. Which was why she seldom did. And why she shouldn't have now.

In fact, she was about to shift into reverse and head back home when there came a sharp rap on the Jetta's window, causing Janey to jump nearly out of her skin. In the space between her car and Tina's flatbed truck, Roger Thorne, her daughter's foreman and all-around handyman, had materialized and was peering in at her. Next to him, still as a statue, stood her daughter's ancient black lab Jacks, its muzzle gray, its eyes red and draining. "Christ, Roger," she said, rolling down the window. "Sneak up on a person, why don't you."

"Hah! I've been trying to sneak up on somebody for over a decade," said Roger, who had a prosthesis that severely altered his gait. It was his cane that he'd used to rap on the window. "For some reason people usually see me coming."

"Well, I didn't," Janey assured him. "Lord, but that is one ugly-assed dog."

"Don't listen to her, Jacks," Roger said, as if the dog might be doing just that.

"Why are his eyes all red?" Janey wondered out loud, and maybe Jacks *was* listening because the animal's heavy eyelids lowered just then and remained closed for a beat before rising again.

"Conjunctivitis," Roger said. "We put pills in his food, but when he's done eating, the only thing left in his bowl is the pill." The dog's eyelids lowered again, as if in confirmation. "Mind if I ask what you're doing sitting out here in the cold parking lot?"

"Wishing I'd stayed home," Janey admitted, nodding at Grandpa Zack's. "She inside?"

"Which she?"

"My daughter."

"I'm guessing so," he shrugged. "Wasn't my turn to watch her, though."

Janey had to smile at that. For some time she'd suspected Roger, who was old enough to be Tina's father, of having feelings for her. In fact, she'd caught him watching her more than once when she was pretty sure it wasn't his turn. "How's she doing?"

"How do you mean?"

"My mother said she seemed out of sorts yesterday."

"About what?" Roger wanted to know. Clearly this was news to him.

"I was hoping you could tell me, Roger. That's why my damn window is still down, letting all the cold air in."

Roger gave her another shrug. "No clue. I suppose you could go inside and ask her. Then you'd know."

"I agree with the first part," Janey told him. "I *could* go in. Whether I'd learn anything is the part I'm not so sure about."

"She does keep a fair amount to herself," he agreed, as if he, too, wished this were otherwise.

"Not a fair amount," Janey corrected him. "Everything."

Which elicited a noncommittal nod. "Well," Roger grinned. "I suppose you could stay out here in the parking lot, if that's working for you."

The cell phone in his holster buzzed then. "Hey?" he said, putting the device to his ear and then, after a second or two, to his chest. "It's her. She wants to know if it's you sitting out here."

Janey raised her voice then in the direction of Roger's phone. "Who else does she know that drives a ten-year-old Jetta with a hundred and seventy thousand miles on it?"

"You get all that?" Roger said into the phone. Then, again, to Janey, "She says why don't you come inside?"

"Tell her for the same reason she never comes into Hattie's."

Roger started to obey, but just then the front door opened and Tina emerged, flipping her own phone shut.

"Now you done it," Roger said, also hanging up. "Good luck."

Watching the man limp off, using his cane to help him stay upright on the already snowy surface of the recently plowed lot, Janey felt an unexpected tug at her heart. Two years earlier, when

Roger started working for her daughter, Janey had asked him where he was from, to which he'd replied, "Right here in Bath." That had surprised her because she figured they were roughly the same age. How had their paths not crossed? "We were in the same graduating class," he informed her. "I must not've made much of an impression."

That night, not wanting to believe he was telling the truth, she'd gotten out her old North Bath yearbook, and sure enough, there he was: Roger Thorne, a goofy-looking kid with a cowlick, but nevertheless instantly recognizable. "Okay, so where have you been hiding this whole time," she asked, the next time she saw him. "Oh, all over," he said, explaining that he'd left town right after graduation. At some point he'd joined the army and been sent to the Gulf, where an IED had taken his leg off at the knee. Though a lot of her classmates had left North Bath at their first opportunity, Roger, so far as Janey knew, was the only one to return. Why had he? she wondered.

Rolling up her window, she saw that instead of following Roger, Jacks had ambled arthritically over to meet her daughter, who'd gone into a crouch so she'd be at eye level with the animal, their noses actually touching. When Jacks licked the tip of Tina's nose, Janey cringed. Her daughter didn't flinch, though, and for a second Janey half expected her to lick the animal's wet nose in return. How was it possible, she wondered, for your own adult child to remain such a complete mystery to you? God knew, Janey and her own mother had had their problems over the years, but those seemed to result from knowing each other too well. This with Tina was different. Even when her daughter was little, Janey'd had no idea what she was thinking. Lately, though, Janey was even more mystified by what, if anything, was going on in her daughter's heart. Janey had always assumed that Tina must have feelings but, just as it wasn't clear whether she was intellectually slow or somehow smarter than other children her age, it was also unclear, at least to Janey, whether her daughter was emotionally stunted or just exceptionally skilled at keeping her emotions in check. And if the latter, was this yet another repudiation of Janey herself, whose emotions, as Ruth liked to say, had always played through a bullhorn? Which they were doing now as she watched her daughter have what looked to be an interspecies meeting of minds with a blind dog. Somewhere off in the direction of Schuyler Springs, sirens wailed. Janey closed her eyes and listened until the Jetta's door opened and her daughter climbed in. No *Hi, Mom,* of course. No hug. No peck on the cheek. Instead Tina just leaned across the seat for a better view of the dashboard. Straightening up again, she said, "Not quite."

"Not quite what?"

"Not quite one hundred and seventy thousand miles."

"Thanks for pointing that out," Janey told her. "Here I was feeling shitty about things. Now I see there was no need."

Unsurprisingly, Tina didn't register this remark. Sarcasm had always eluded her, which was one reason that Janey often wondered how, despite their obvious physical similarities, Tina could possibly be her child. Had there been some mix-up with the bassinets in the hospital? If so, then somewhere in the world there was a young woman Tina's age spewing sarcasm at some poor, literalminded woman who could not for the life of her figure out where her daughter got that mouth of hers.

Staring straight ahead, Tina scratched the tip of her nose where the dog had licked it. "So," she said, "how come you're here?"

Janey was pretty sure this wasn't intended as an accusation, but it was hard not to take it as one. "What?" she said. "I can't visit my own daughter?"

No immediate response to this, either. Rhetorical questions, Janey knew all too well, baffled her daughter as completely as sarcasm. "How come you're here?" she repeated.

"I'm worried about you," she said. "Is that okay? If I worry about you sometimes?"

At last her daughter turned to face her, though her bad eye wandered off, as if it knew better, even if its owner didn't, than to look for enlightenment in her mother's visage. "It's okay," she said finally, causing Janey's own eyes to fill with tears. As a child, Tina was forever saying this same, exact sort of heartbreaking shit. It was enough to make you want to break right down and sob. Back then Janey had imagined it was the innocence of childhood she was hearing. Now, of course, she knew better.

"Ah, shit," she said, wiping the tears away on her sleeve, and thinking, *Yes. This is my daughter and not somebody's else's.*

"You don't have to, though," Tina continued. "Worry about me. I'm okay."

"Are you?" Janey said. "Your grandmother wondered if you might be having your spells again."

"I'm not."

"You wouldn't lie to me, would you?"

Tina shook her head.

"Okay," Janey said. "I believe you, I guess." She'd never known her daughter to lie and wasn't even certain she was capable of doing so. "You look kind of down, though. Is there anything you want to talk about?" *Like still having a crush on a boy you haven't seen in a decade? Any other thoughts you might like to share? Maybe level an accusation or two? Like how I messed up your life by taking your asshole father back over and over. How I chose him over you because I was more scared of being alone than I was of his fists?*

Her daughter seemed to seriously consider the question of whether there was something she wanted to discuss, causing the wandering eye to return. "Would you like me to buy you a new car?" she said finally.

"What?"

"Would you like me to buy you a new car?" Same words. Identical inflection. Like she'd recorded her initial response and just hit the playback button.

"No," Janey told her. "I can buy my own damn car when the time comes."

Had Ruth been there she'd have howled at that, but all Tina did was shrug and say, "Okay," the way a person would who'd regretted making such an impulsive offer and was relieved that it had been turned down.

"You'd do that? Buy me a car if I asked you to?"

Tina nodded seriously. "I have the money."

Janey gestured at the huge structure before them. "No shit." More sarcasm, same result. Same blank stare. "I just wish—" she began, but that was all she could get out before her throat closed up.

"Wish what?" said Tina after a long silence.

"Hell, I don't know," Janey admitted. There were so many things to wish for. A new car didn't even crack the top ten. "I wish I wasn't always so pissed off. I don't know why, but I have this nutty idea that I used to be a nice person. Weird, huh? I can't remember the last time I was nice to anybody that mattered. I mean, I'm nice to people at the restaurant because I have to be, but that uses up every last ounce of nice I've got in me. And the people I'm maddest at are the ones I care about most."

"Are you mad at *me*?"

"No, not really," Janey told her, surprised when the words were out that they felt true. "Maybe a little hacked off that you ended up with everything and I got squat, but whatever."

"What do you want?"

Janey snorted. "You mean, if not a car, what?"

Her daughter just shrugged.

"Right this minute I'd like it a lot if I thought all this"—here she made a sweeping gesture that encompassed all of Grandpa Zack's Treasures—"made you happy." Her daughter blinked, slow, like Jacks had earlier. "And I guess I wish we were more a part of each other's lives. That my whole life wasn't at Hattie's and your whole life wasn't up here on this damned hill. I wish you'd let me know you better."

"What do you want to know?"

Janey studied her daughter. "Search me. Your plans, maybe? What kind of music you listen to or what you like to watch on TV. Hell, I don't even know what size clothes you wear."

"Twelve."

Right. Of course. Her own size.

"I mean . . . if you fell in love, would you even tell me?"

"Maybe?"

"Maybe," Janey repeated. "Depending on what?"

"I wouldn't if I thought you'd get angry."

"And I'm angry most of the time, right?" Janey said. When Tina didn't deny this, she continued, "Your grandmother thinks you might still have a crush on Will Sullivan."

Again, her daughter turned to regard her, but said nothing.

"Can you tell me what you liked about him?"

"He was like Grandpa."

"Whoa," Janey said, not expecting this. "Grandpa Zack? How?"

"It didn't bother him that I'm like I am."

"Do you mean your eye?"

She shook her head.

"What, then?"

"That I'm not like other people."

"What do you mean?" she said, though she was suddenly afraid of what her daughter might tell her.

"There are lots of things everybody but me understands, which makes me dumb. But I can multiply large numbers in my head, which makes me smart. He was okay with that."

"But that was a long time ago, right? When you liked him? I mean, there are lots of nice boys in the world." (Did she really say that? That there were lots of nice boys?)

If Tina had an opinion about whether there were or weren't, she kept it to herself.

"Anyway, I gather it wasn't him that you saw earlier?"

Tina shook her head. "I'm glad, I think."

"Why?"

"Because he wasn't a nice person," she said. "The man on the porch."

"How could you tell that?"

"I just can sometimes." Another of those ways she wasn't like other people, apparently.

"Yeah?" Janey said, smiling bitterly at the idea. "I should introduce you to this guy I've been seeing. I can't make up my mind about him." When her daughter had no response to this, she said, "They must've looked a lot alike, though, huh?"

Tina nodded. "Grandma says they're brothers. He grew up with his mother, though. Somewhere else."

The chill Janey felt then preceded its cause, but only by a split second. "Where?" she asked, but she already knew the answer.

"I don't know," Tina admitted. "But the license plate on his car said West Virginia."

Janey didn't want to ask but couldn't help herself. "What kind of car was it?"

"Big," her daughter replied. "Yellow."

# What, Exactly?

WHEN PETER ARRIVED at the Horse, the parking lot was blanketed with close to a foot of undisturbed snow, which meant, despite the slow going, that he'd somehow managed to arrive before the ambulance. Heading around back, he parked behind Birdie and let himself in the rear entrance. Though he'd been prepared for a bizarre scene, what he saw when he opened the door at the top of the stairs still surprised him. Across the room David Proxmire was seated on Sully's barstool, leaning forward, his elbows on the bar, just as Birdie had reported over the phone. She herself was standing next to him, one hand on his shoulder, looking as if she'd just that second asked him if he was still feeling poorly. Peter actually paused in the doorway to hear how he would respond, because clearly there'd been a mistake. After phoning him, Birdie must have realized the man wasn't dead after all, only . . . what? Narcoleptic? Why else would she have her hand on his shoulder, if not to offer comfort?

Spying him in the doorway, she said, "Finally. You're here. Do you mind?"

Did he mind what? That David Proxmire was alive after all? Of course not. True, Peter had always found the man to be a crashing bore, but he'd never wished him dead. As he made his way toward them, Proxmire remained preternaturally still, showing not the slightest interest in Peter's arrival. That was because the man was, in fact, dead, just as Birdie had reported.

"Do you mind?" Birdie repeated. "Put your hand right there?" She indicated the spot on David Proxmire's shoulder where her own hand rested.

"Why?" Peter asked. Having concluded earlier that she'd been attempting to comfort the man when Peter entered, he found the inference difficult to surrender. He himself felt no need to comfort a dead man.

"Because," Birdie explained with some irritation, "I need to pee." When this only deepened Peter's confusion, she grabbed his wrist with her free hand and placed his where she wanted it to go. "You got him?"

Only when she removed her own hand and Peter felt the man's weight did he understand what she was asking of him. At some point after she'd hung up with Peter, the deceased must have begun to list on his stool. For the last twenty minutes, then, she'd been preventing him from toppling onto the floor.

When the kitchen door swung shut behind her, Peter was left alone with what had been a living human being, and was now . . . what, exactly? He was no longer alive, but perhaps because of his circumstance—the fact that he was seated on a barstool, his elbows resting comfortably on the bar, as if he might at any moment strike up a conversation—he didn't seem to quite qualify as a corpse. He wouldn't become that until the ambulance arrived and he was loaded into it. Until then, for as long as he required someone to keep him upright on his barstool, David Proxmire was somehow neither here nor there.

What struck Peter—and not for the first time—was that his present situation, ludicrous in the extreme, was the fault of one Donald Sullivan. That the dead man should be perched on Sully's barstool felt entirely appropriate. Somehow his old man was still calling the shots. Peter hadn't objected when he was given that list of people to check in on after Sully was gone, the one that included Rub and Ruth and Carl Roebuck and Tina and Birdie. The problem was that the list kept expanding. All these people had lists of their own, lists that overlapped. Take Birdie. Peter was fond of her and didn't mind keeping an eye on her. Nor had he minded investing in the Horse (okay, it was Sully's money, but still) to keep both it and her afloat. The problem was that keeping his promise to his father inevitably trailed unforeseen and unforeseeable consequences. Who could've predicted, for instance, that Sully's fondness for Birdie meant that it would one day fall to him to keep David Proxmire upright on a barstool until the ambulance—*Where the hell was it?*—arrived? When Peter thought about it, how much of what had befallen him since his return to North Bath had he actually signed up for?

When his cell phone vibrated in the back-left pocket of his jeans, Peter, whose left hand was on David Proxmire's shoulder, tried his best to fish it out with his right, but that proved impossible. When he switched hands, David Proxmire let out a soft moan, and the air was suddenly redolent of fresh feces. Was it Peter's imagination, or did the man now look both dismayed and apologetic? Finally managing to extract the phone from his pocket, Peter pressed ANSWER and put the device to his ear without bothering to see who was calling. "Have I caught you at a bad time?" said Carl Roebuck.

"You could say that," Peter told him.

"Where are you?"

"At the Horse. Where are *you*?" Because there was street noise in the background—men shouting, metal grating and another sound he couldn't quite place, though it seemed oddly familiar.

"Schuyler. I'm with your buddy Rub. He needs a lift back to Bath." Peter started to ask why Rub would be in Schuyler Springs, but then he remembered that on Sundays Rub worked for the very man Peter was keeping upright on his father's barstool. "He's been in an accident," Carl was saying. "That's him blubbering. Can you hear?"

Apparently Carl was holding his phone up closer to Rub now, because the sound Peter hadn't been able to identify earlier was now clear. Rub had a very distinctive blubber. "Is he okay?"

"Define *okay*."

"Is he injured?"

"No, just upset. He's convinced his boss is going to blame him for the accident."

Peter glanced over his shoulder at David Proxmire. "Tell him not to worry," he said, though the dead man's expression did seem to have changed subtly, his earlier dismay having morphed into something darker. He now had the look of a man who had foreseen this eventuality, just not how to prevent it. "So . . . ," Peter said, again turning away from the dead man. "What happened, exactly?"

"The vehicle he was towing burst into flames."

"How is that possible?"

"Who knows?" Carl said. "Shit happens. Anyhow, the flames somehow ignited the wrecker's gas tank."

Was that the boom that Peter had heard when he was standing outside the coffee shop?

"The fireball was fucking impressive," Carl said. "We're damn lucky we weren't both killed."

"Time-out," Peter said. "The two of you were together?"

"I ran into him at our place," Carl explained.

Momentarily forgetting that Carl now lived with him on Upper Main, he started to say, *Our place?* but caught himself in time. "What was he doing there?"

"Looking for you. My impression was that he wanted to tell you something."

"What?"

"How would I know? Anyhow, I told him you weren't home and he offered me a lift, didn't you, Rubberhead? He'd just dropped me off, when . . . boom!"

None of this made any sense. If Rub had come looking for Peter after putting a vehicle onto the wrecker, he would've immediately returned that vehicle to the yard. There's no way he would've offered Carl a lift in the opposite direction. Which probably meant that Carl had bullied him into taking him there. Had Carl's presence somehow factored into the accident? Because yes, shit did happen, but in Peter's experience it was much more likely to happen when Carl was nearby. "You say the vehicle just burst into flame."

"Boom!" said Carl. "Whoooosh!"

The blubbering stopped now, and Peter heard Rub wail, "It was *your fault!*"

"Hey, now!" Peter heard Carl say. "How about a little gratitude? Who pulled you out of that cab just in the nick of time?"

Rub howled something else now, but Peter couldn't make it out.

"Don't pay him any attention," Carl advised. "He's just in a tizzy. But explain something to me. What the hell happened to his stutter? Why isn't he claiming that it was all my fuh-fuh-fault."

Peter was fast losing patience. "Carl. Whose fuh-fuh-fault was it?"

"I guess I'd say whoever owns the vehicle that caught fire was mostly to blame," Carl stated, as if he were giving the matter serious thought. "I mean, come on. Who drives around with five full gas cans in the trunk? It also could be partly the city's fault. We hit a couple potholes on the way here and maybe one of those popped the trunk open. Hard to say for sure. Call it the convergence of several factors."

"Were you one of those factors?"

"Me?" Carl said, indignant now, which made Peter more suspicious, not less.

"Carl."

"Okay, fine," Carl sighed, "it kind of was my cigarette. I was going to just drop it on the pavement, you know, but then I thought, Why litter?"

Peter closed his eyes tightly. "That would be an unselfish thought, and we both know you don't have those."

Carl ignored this. "I noticed the trunk of the Caddy was wide open and—"

"Hold on," Peter said. Suddenly, he had a sick feeling in the pit of his stomach. "Caddy?"

"Right. The car on the wrecker."

"What color was it?"

"Yellow, though I don't see the relevance—"

"Did it by any chance have out-of-state plates?" Because that would explain why Rub had come by to see him.

"For some reason I want to say West Virginia," Carl replied. "I noticed because—"

This time it wasn't Peter who interrupted Carl Roebuck but rather the thunderous crash. "Jesus," Carl said. "What the hell was that?"

Birdie, returning through the swinging door a split second later, was clearly about to ask the same thing, but then she saw that the barstool David Proxmire had been sitting on was now empty.

# Art

---

THE SUICIDE'S BODY had been removed the day before, so the Sans Souci was again locked up tight, which meant a stop at the town manager's office for a key. Bert Franklin, no surprise, was reluctant to hand one over to someone who had no official standing in Schuyler Springs. Raymer explained that he was assisting Charice in trying to identify the dead man, but this only made Franklin more skeptical. "Okay, but what exactly are you hoping to find out there, Doug? Everything's been bagged and tagged, right?"

Which, of course, was precisely the objection Raymer had been hoping Franklin wouldn't raise. "It's possible we missed something," he said weakly.

"Charice authorized this?"

"Call her, if you don't believe me," Raymer suggested, hoping that Franklin wouldn't. He hadn't wanted to bother Charice, who had no idea he and Jerome meant to go out there. She'd back him up, of course. She was counting on him to keep her brother occupied and out of her hair, and returning to the Sans Souci would fall under this general rubric. Actually, Raymer had a reason of his own to return to that eerie ballroom. Something he'd seen there—he couldn't say exactly what—had been nagging at him all morning. A second visit might drag whatever was lurking in his subconscious to the front of his brain where he could examine it.

Franklin, a puzzled expression on his face, was peering out his office window at Raymer's vehicle at the curb. "Is that Jerome out there?" he wanted to know.

"It is."

"Huh. How long has he been back?"

"A while," Raymer said.

Franklin cocked his head. "He doesn't look right. What is going on with his hair? He looks like that guy in *Pulp Fiction*."

"He's going through a rough patch," Raymer admitted.

"I'm sorry to hear it," Franklin said, returning his attention to Raymer. "I always liked Jerome. Not easy being a Black man in these parts."

"So he's been telling me."

Reluctantly, Franklin went over to the key cabinet, where he located the right one. "I'm glad you're giving Charice a hand," he said, handing it to Raymer. "She's surrounded by men who aren't nearly as smart as she is. It's hard to do your job right when you're constantly putting out fires."

"I keep hearing about this Conrad Delgado?" Raymer said, hoping the other man might tell him something he didn't already know.

"He's one of the arsonists, no question," Franklin said, then made a zipping motion over his lips to indicate he wasn't at liberty to say more. "You need me to come out there with you?"

"No, we're good," Raymer said, immediately regretting the use of the plural pronoun, which revealed that Jerome, who had even less standing in Schuyler than Raymer, would be accompanying him.

Clearly, Franklin picked up on it. "You both used to be cops," he said when they reached the door, "so I don't need to remind you not to remove anything from the premises, right?"

"Gotcha," Raymer said as the two men shook hands. After all, it was unlikely that either he or Jerome would find what they were looking for.

Only when Raymer was outside did what Franklin had just said sink in: he *used to be* a cop. Which meant he wasn't one anymore.

═══

TWENTY MINUTES LATER he and Jerome were standing in the dark lobby of the old hotel. Raymer had flicked the light switch, to no avail. The electricity had been turned on late yesterday afternoon to help with the investigation, but now it was off again. Jerome, who had the book he'd purchased at the strip mall under one arm, had the look of a man who understands what he needs to do but not where to begin. "What exactly are we looking for?" Raymer asked him.

"Not what," Jerome replied. "Who."

"Okay, who?"

"Her name is Posey Gold," Jerome informed him unhelpfully. "She's an artist from the Harlem Renaissance."

"Harlem had a renaissance?"

Jerome just stared at him.

"What?" Raymer said. Unless he was mistaken, another lecture was quivering on the horizon. He just hoped it would make more sense than the one about Black time and white time.

"Dawg," Jerome said. "Langston Hughes. Paul Robeson. Josephine Baker. Zora Neale Hurston."

A couple of these names rang faint bells, but Raymer made a circular motion in the air for Jerome to keep going.

"Louis Armstrong?"

"Him I've heard of."

"Count Basie? Duke Ellington?"

"Those too."

"Billie Holiday."

"Hmmm. Second baseman?"

"Singer. *She* was a singer."

"Oh."

"Fats Waller," Jerome continued. "Jelly Roll Morton."

Whatever this game was about, Raymer was already weary of it. "Right. Both hockey players."

Jerome sighed mightily. "Damn," he said. "I can't tell."

"Can't tell what?"

"If you really think they were hockey players."

"I know they weren't hockey players," Raymer assured him. "Do hockey players even come in black?"

Jerome ignored this. "How about Billie Holiday? Did you really think she was a baseball player?"

Raymer decided to tell the truth. "I'm sorry," he said. "But doesn't that sound like a baseball player's name to you?"

"No!" shouted Jerome, unable to contain his outrage. "It sounds like the name of the greatest jazz and blues singer of all time."

"Jerome," Raymer said, not really caring if his own exasperation showed through. "I'm white, okay? I'm sorry, but that's what I am. How am I supposed to know who all these people are?"

Jerome massaged his temples. "The same way I know who Charles Dickens was."

This, Raymer gathered, was in reference to the copy of *Great Expectations* he'd purchased back at the bookstore. He'd started to put it back on the shelf but then thought again and brought it up to the register.

"The same way I know who James Bond is," Jerome continued.

"What do you want from me?" Raymer said. "I'm sorry I don't know the same things you know."

"That's not the point, Dawg. The *point* is that it's part of your privilege to *not* know who these Black folks are. I, on the other hand, am *supposed* to know who Dickens is. *You* get to skate on Langston Hughes and nobody busts your balls."

"Isn't that what you're doing?" Raymer said. "Aren't you *in fact* busting my balls for not knowing what you know?"

Jerome paused to consider this possibility. "It's true I'm busting your balls," he admitted, "but it's the *why* that's important. What I'm saying is that you're incurious."

This might, Raymer had to admit, be a valid criticism. Miss Beryl had accused him of much the same thing back in eighth grade, concerned that he never read anything that wasn't assigned and not all of what was. His world, she'd insisted, needed to grow. At the time, since none of his other teachers had offered the same complaint, he decided not to worry about it. Did his purchasing *Great Expectations* earlier mean that he was finally coming around to her (and Jerome's) point of view?

"It's okay that you don't know who these people are," Jerome was explaining. "What's not okay is that you see no need to."

Raymer had to laugh. "Do you know what your sister told me this morning?" he said. "That it would be a challenge getting you to talk."

"And here's the sad part," Jerome continued, as if Raymer hadn't spoken. "Deep down, you really want to hear about Posey Gold."

Raymer shook his head. "You just finished accusing me of being incurious. Now you claim to know that deep down I want you to enlighten me. Which is it?"

"What I'm saying is that lack of curiosity is a habit of mind, Dawg, and habits can be broken. Broke a few myself, lately. You see the result before you. A whole new man."

"Okay, but do you mind my saying I kind of miss the old one?"

"Long gone," Jerome said sadly, as if he missed the old Jerome, too.

"Are you sure?" Raymer said. "I bet he's still in there somewhere."

"Nope," Jerome insisted. "He's vacated the premises. Vanished without a trace. No forwarding address."

"Let's find out," Raymer suggested. "Repeat after me. The name is Bond."

Jerome just stared at him.

"*Jerome* Bond," employing the emphasis the old Jerome had favored.

"Gone," Jerome insisted.

Raymer sighed. "Okay, you win. Tell me about Posey Golden. I'm all ears."

"Posey *Gold*," Jerome corrected. "Her parents were working

class, but they believed in education. Made sure she went to college. She would've majored in art, but back then if you were a woman, you couldn't. You had to major in art history so you could become a teacher. She got around these restrictions by cozying up to male artists who saw she was talented and agreed to work with her. She started out as a painter, but as a child her mother had taught her to sew. She decided that sewing could be art, too. She also made what she called soft sculptures, using foam and rubber and fabric. What really changed her life, though, was visiting West Africa, where her ancestors were enslaved."

"What happened there?"

"This," Jerome said, opening the book he'd purchased back at the bookstore and tapping his index finger on the page in question. At its center was a painting of a rowboat tied to a rotting dock. "I thought you said she gave up painting," Raymer said.

Jerome shook his head. "You're looking at the wrong piece of art. Come over to the window."

There, where the light was better, Raymer saw what he'd missed earlier. The boat painting wasn't hung on the wall but rather sat on an easel. Behind it, in the shadows, seemingly hanging in midair, was a gruesome-looking mask, below which an elaborate costume was draped.

"The painting," Jerome explained, pointing at the artist's signature, "is a John Marin. That's what the folks who published the book wanted you to see." He closed the book again so Raymer could take in its title: *The Art of the Sans Souci.* "Art *by* white folks *for* white folks. Whereas this thing?" Again, he opened the book and pointed at the ghostly figure in the shadows. "*This* they didn't even recognize as art. They probably thought it was a Halloween costume somebody left behind."

"What's it supposed to be?"

"Don't know, Dawg. I'm not even sure it's a Posey Gold. A lot of Black artists back then were into discovering their history. Could be the work of an imitator. Maybe one of her students. To make ends meet, she became what they wanted her to be. A teacher."

"The mask is kind of scary," Raymer said. In fact, the way it and the attached costume appeared to float in the air reminded Raymer of the hanged man in the ballroom.

"Supposed to be scary, Dawg. Probably some sort of witch doctor."

"Are you sure it's not just a costume?"

"No, it *is* a costume," Jerome told him. "That was the deal. To her, costumes were works of art, except they were meant to be worn at certain ceremonies, not hung on some museum wall. Which was just as well. No museum back then would have wanted them."

"Would they now?"

"You kidding me? A Posey Gold? If that's what it is, it might be worth more than the Marin."

"What's it doing here in the Sans Souci?"

Sighing deeply, Jerome shook his head. "Been cogitating on that. Could be she had a relative up here. Black folks who lived in the city used to come up in the summer to clean hotel rooms. A few stayed, bought houses on the North Side and rented out rooms during the season. If we don't find anything here, we can make a trip to the library and look at some old Schuyler phone books. See if there's anybody around here named Gold. Or, could be she got some sort of summer teaching gig at the college or the writers' colony. Toward the end of her life, people began to know who she was. I think she even wrote a memoir. Maybe go online and see if we can find a copy."

To Raymer, all of those seemed like more logical starting points than the Sans Souci, but Jerome was determined and Raymer had to admit that he was right about one thing. Deep down he *had* wanted to know about Posey Gold. "Assume the costume in that book really is a Posey Gold," he suggested. "Why would it still be here all these years later? You said yourself it's not likely anybody here would've thought it was worth money. Why hold on to something of little value? Wouldn't you be more likely to come upon it in a flea market or a yard sale? Also, what happens if only part of it survived? The mask is pretty cool-looking. What if somebody kept that and tossed the gown part."

Jerome shrugged. "Half a Posey Gold is better than no Posey Gold."

And just maybe, Raymer thought but did not say, this new, unfamiliar, diminished Jerome was better than no Jerome. "Okay," he said. "How about this Langston guy. Who was he?"

"Charice's favorite poet. You didn't know that?"

"His name's never come up," Raymer told him, pleased with himself, feeling like maybe he'd scored a point.

"Think about that," Jerome suggested.

=

PROMISING TO RETURN SOON, Raymer left Jerome to begin his search for the Gold woman in the hotel's numerous first-floor public rooms. In the unlikely event that her "sculpture" was still somewhere on the premises, it probably wouldn't be in the upstairs guest rooms, where lodgers expected to see horse-racing-themed prints, not a terrifying West African witch-doctor mask. The search would probably take most of the day, and though Raymer couldn't help thinking it was a fool's errand, Charice was probably right—it was best for her brother to have something to occupy his mind. He might not be the Jerome of old, but talking about Posey Gold he'd become animated, alive with purpose, which was something. According to Charice, when he'd arrived in Schuyler a month ago, he'd been not just depressed but borderline catatonic, so hats off to Posey, wherever the hell she was.

What also occurred to Raymer as he entered the hotel's vast ballroom was that his own emotional landscape differed only in degree from Jerome's. How many times over the last month had he wondered if he himself was becoming despondent? If he was truthful, closing up the North Bath police station had left him feeling diminished. He refused to feel jealous about Charice landing the Schuyler job, but hadn't her good fortune, coupled with Raymer's own loss of employment, left him, at the very least, feeling pretty sorry for himself? He appreciated Charice assigning him the task of identifying the suicide, but he also had to wonder if maybe she was handling him the same way she was handling her brother—keeping him occupied and out of her hair while she attended to more important matters. The fact that Dr. Qadry wasn't around to ask it didn't prevent Raymer from hearing one of her leading questions—*And how does that make you feel?*—in his head. Odious Dougie's assessment would've been more provocative: *Dude! Are you blind? She's paying you back for all those years you kept her behind that desk! Did I or did I not warn you this would happen?*

Just as it had the day before, weak light streamed through the old ballroom's filthy upper windows, partially illuminating its vast, empty interior. Bert Franklin had been right, of course. Talk about a fool's errand. Raymer stood about as much chance of finding overlooked evidence here as Jerome had of finding his witch doctor. Climbing the stairs to the balcony, he positioned himself where he'd stood yesterday, hoping that doing so might bring into focus whatever had been eating at him all morning. The dead man didn't add up. That much had been evident from the start. He should've had an ID on him and, given that it was probably winter when he took his life, he should've been wearing a winter coat. His Timberland boots and Lands' End chinos suggested neither poverty nor vagrancy, but if he wasn't poor or homeless, then what was he doing in an old boarded-up hotel? He and Charice had been all over this yesterday, of course, and he was pretty sure that it was something else that was troubling him. Though it made no sense, what he kept coming back to was the lunatic notion that the hanged man reminded him of someone. But given the body's advanced state of decomposition, its teeth scattered on the floor, the skull hollowed out by some hungry, sharp-toothed thing, how was that even possible?

Fearing that a cautious Bert Franklin might've had second thoughts and called Charice to make sure she really had deputized him, Raymer decided to call her himself. If she had a minute, maybe they could together puzzle through whatever was nagging at him. No sooner did this possibility occur to him than his phone rang in his pocket and his heart leaped at the thrilling possibility that

Charice might be thinking about him at the precise moment he was thinking about her. Because if they were on the same wavelength, wouldn't that mean . . .

But no. The caller was Miller, a man whose wavelength Raymer had no desire to share. He considered just letting the call go to voice mail, but then he remembered how talking to the man sometimes, inexplicably, cheered him up. "Miller," he said. "What's going on?"

The line was silent. A pocket call?

"Miller?"

"I'm sorry, Chief." It was Miller's voice all right, but it was strangely listless. "I know I'm not supposed to call you anymore."

"That's okay," Raymer assured him. "You don't sound so good, though."

Another long silence. Finally: "I'm resigning. I just wanted you to know."

Lord, Raymer thought. This was like having a child. Always a crucible of self-recrimination, Miller was no doubt mortified by how poorly he'd performed the day before. Actually barfing in the bushes. In front of his old boss, no less. "If this is about yesterday—"

"I know you tried . . . ," the other man continued, as if Raymer hadn't spoken, ". . . tried really hard to make me a good cop . . ."

"You *are* a good cop," Raymer told him, trying his best to sound convincing.

"I did a bad thing."

What Charice had told Raymer earlier came back to him now. "I hear you had a tough arrest this morning." How had she described it? Not gentle? After yesterday's humiliation at the Sans Souci had Miller decided to be a tough guy? "Did the suspect resist?"

"No. I had him cuffed by the time the lieutenant arrived."

*The lieutenant.* Raymer could hear in the man's voice his veneration of rank. "So . . . what happened?"

"He was angry because of what the suspect did to Sarge. He just walked up and punched the suspect in the face."

"Sounds like it's the lieutenant who did a bad thing, not you."

"Then, when the guy was all curled up on the ground, he started kicking him. I should've done something. Made him stop."

"Miller, listen to me," Raymer said. "Maybe you showed poor judgment, but he was your superior officer."

"I just stood there," Miller repeated. "Watching."

"Okay," Raymer said. "Not your finest hour, but—"

"And I signed the arrest report."

Which made sense. There was no way Delgado would permit any of what Miller was describing to appear in an official document. "Let me guess," he said. "He's claiming the suspect became violent and had to be restrained. That's when his injuries occurred." Silence on the line, so yes. "How badly was the suspect injured?"

"He was coughing up blood."

"Where is he now?"

"In the hospital," Miller said, adding, after a long pause. "What if he dies?"

*What would that make me?* was what he seemed to want Raymer to tell him. "Where are you now?"

"At the station."

"Have you met with Chief Bond?"

"She's with the lieutenant."

"You need to tell her the truth."

More silence. In his mind's eye Raymer could see the other man shaking his head. "I already signed the lie."

"Look—"

"The lieutenant's right," Miller continued miserably. "I'm a joke. All these years on the job and I still didn't know what to do."

"Okay," Raymer said. "But you knew what *not* to do. You knew not to assault an unarmed suspect who was under your control. You knew not to kick a man who was lying helpless on the ground."

Another long beat of disconsolate silence, until finally, "I just . . . I just wish I was . . . different, you know? Better?"

Before he could assure Miller that he knew that feeling all too well, there was a click and the line was dead. Raymer started to call him back but thought better of it. In truth he couldn't think of anything else to say. The poor guy would either find his way through his misery or he wouldn't.

Even though he knew that Charice was at this very moment dealing with Delgado, he decided to call her anyway. When her cell went directly to voice mail, he said, "Look, I know you're in the middle of a shitstorm, but I just talked to Miller. He said he plans to resign over the arrest he and Delgado made this morning. I feel sorry for the guy, but who knows? Maybe it's for the best. Anyway, give me a call when you can? Jerome and I are out at the Sans Souci. He's got this idea in his head that there's a famous work of art stashed somewhere in the hotel. Done by some lady from the Harlem Renaissance? Is that even a real thing? This Renaissance? I'd never heard of it." He paused here as if Charice were actually on the line and he was giving her an opportunity to chide him for his ignorance. "It kind of made me wonder, you know? If maybe that's what's been going on with us? We don't know the same things? Haven't had the same experiences?" *Hang up,* he told himself, but he didn't. "You know what Miller said to me just now? That he wished he was a whole different man. A better one. Your brother claims that's what he's become. According to him, the old Jerome is gone." Here he paused again. "Okay, I'm rambling and you're busy. We'll probably be out here all afternoon . . . if you feel like dropping by."

Only after hanging up did he remember the reason he'd wanted to call her in the first place—to ask if anything else had occurred to her about the man they'd found in the ballroom yesterday, though that was pretty unlikely. If anything had struck her as odd, she probably would have mentioned it when they were brainstorming at the Horse last night. Besides, he was pretty sure that whatever was troubling him was specific to himself, that whatever he'd seen yesterday would have meaning to him and him alone. What, though? And why was he unable to shake the bizarre notion that there'd been something familiar about the hanged man? Was it possible that the familiarity wasn't physical? What if what he'd recognized in the dead man was the state of his psyche, what the poor devil had been feeling when he climbed those stairs, tied one end of the rope he'd brought with him to the iron railing and the other around his neck? What if it was the utter desolation of the man's soul that had felt familiar?

But how could that be? Wouldn't such familiarity imply that his *own* soul was similarly desolate? Granted, he'd been in a funk since he and Charice had agreed to their time-out and, yes, he'd suffered his own bouts of Milleresque self-doubt going all the way back to childhood, but the man who'd climbed over that banister and leaped to a violent, punishing death hadn't been tormented by doubt. He'd been in the throes of despair, and Raymer's own problem had always been the exact opposite: his seemingly congenital inability to surrender hope. However untethered from reality hope might be, he'd always clung tenaciously to the possibility that somehow, some way, things just might work out. He'd felt that way about Becka, and it was how he continued to feel about Charice.

This time with Charice *did* feel different, though, didn't it? Raymer found himself thinking back to what Jerome said earlier. Why *hadn't* Charice ever mentioned this Langston Hughes? If he was her favorite poet, why hadn't she ever given Raymer one of his poems and demanded he read the damned thing? That's what Miss Beryl would've done. Okay, getting him to read things he didn't want to read had been her job, but still. Didn't her constant badgering imply a kind of faith in him? Was Charice as frustrated—no, exasperated—as Jerome seemed to be about the many things Raymer was ignorant of? Had she over time decided there was no point in sharing certain things with him for the simple reason that he wouldn't understand? He'd never seen any need to question his conviction that if they loved each other everything else would fall into place, but what if Charice didn't share that conviction? What if she'd known for a long time that things weren't going to work out and was just trying to spare his feelings?

Was he really such a lost cause? Other people didn't seem to think so. Dr. Qadry's litany of leading questions suggested that *she* hadn't given up on him. No doubt she'd drawn any number of conclusions about him, some probably unflattering and, yes, she was forever trying to get him to own things. But unless he was mistaken, what she really wanted him to own was, well, himself. Why would she lead him toward a destination she'd already concluded he had no chance of arriving at? And other people clearly didn't consider him a lost cause. Most people, as Charice herself was fond of reminding him, liked him. Wasn't that what they were saying by reelecting him over and over as North Bath's chief of police? Why should it trouble him that they liked him *anyway . . . despite the fact that . . . even though . . . regardless.* Wasn't that how most people were liked?

As Raymer saw it, his problem was that being liked was different from being loved, and transitioning from one to the other, at least for him, had always been fraught. According to Dr. Qadry, many people who had problems with relationships followed fairly predictable patterns. They'd go along fine for a while, but then, three or six months in, right on schedule, they'd mess up, and from there it would be all downhill. For them it was like trying to quit smoking. You'd tell yourself that this time would be different, but it never was because you were still you. He thought again, as he had so often this past month, about that magical week they'd spent on Cape Cod in the days after they finally admitted to their feelings for each other. They had been on the same page back then about everything, hadn't they? What happened? It wasn't long after they'd returned to North Bath that they'd had their first real difference of opinion, the one about old Mr. Hynes, who most days could be found sitting in his folding lawn chair outside the Morrison Arms, waving his tiny American flag at passersby. Raymer had believed—indeed still believed—that the old man was simply patriotic. Charice had argued that what Mr. Hynes was actually doing was demanding that people really see him, see the injustice of his circumstance, that the country he loved did not love him back. At the time they'd agreed to disagree and it hadn't seemed like such a big deal, but what if that had been Charice's first inkling that their mutual affection would not be enough to sustain them? What if everything thereafter had merely confirmed this fear?

"Dawg?" said a voice so loud and close that it seemed to originate inside Raymer's skull. Was Jerome in his head now, like odious Dougie had been before? But no, the man had somehow materialized at his elbow and was regarding him with a look of profound concern, and for the second time that day Raymer suspected Jerome of being able to levitate. Otherwise, how had he managed to climb the creaky stairs without Raymer hearing his approach? Was it even possible to be *that* deep in thought?

"Jerome," he said, embarrassed. "What's up?"

"We need to go," he said. "Right now."

"Why?"

"*Now,*" Jerome repeated.

# Too Late

"HOLD ON," Ruth said. "You're asking my advice?"

Janey sighed. Nothing was ever easy with her mother. Why did she think this would be? "That's right, Ma. That's why I'm here. To ask you for your wisdom. Is that okay with you?"

They were seated in her mother's kitchen, which, except for appliances that had crapped out and been replaced over the years, hadn't changed much since Janey was a child, probably because Ruth never really thought of it—or the rest of the house for that matter—as truly hers. It had originally belonged to Zack's mother, a horrid old woman. For years, patiently waiting for her to die, Ruth had imagined all the changes she'd make, but by the time the old woman finally kicked the bucket Ruth had realized that her mother-in-law wouldn't truly be gone until her mama's boy son was gone as well. After Zack's passing, Janey had expected her mother to gut the house back to studs, but she didn't, because, Ruth explained, there was such a thing as being too late. At the time Janey hadn't known what to make of this uncharacteristic pronouncement. Her mother wasn't usually a defeatist. But who knew? Maybe she just realized that what she thought she wanted for so long no longer mattered. A depressing thought. As was the idea that there was such a thing as being too late, which, despite being obviously true, had never really occurred to Janey. Or if it had, she'd imagined it applied only to people her mother's age, not her own. Once you accepted the possibility that it might also apply to you, it was hard not to begin a mental list of all the other things in your own life that it might be too late for.

"Of course, it's okay to ask for advice," Ruth assured her. "I just can't remember the last time you did, is all."

"That's because you're always giving it before you're asked," Janey explained.

"In any event, you never take it."

"Ma," Janey said. "Could you not, please, just this once—"

"You're right," Ruth said. "I'm sorry. What's going on?"

"I'm not sure," she admitted. "Remember yesterday when you were telling me Tina thought she saw Sully's grandson Will at the Upper Main Street house?"

"Yes, but it wasn't," Ruth told her, then explained how she'd talked to Peter earlier that morning. "Turns out it was Will's younger brother. I guess they look a lot alike."

"Here's the thing, though," Janey said. "I'm pretty sure he was out at the Hand last night."

Ruth looked dubious. "According to Peter, he was on his way to Canada. He'd just stopped by for a quick visit. That was late morning. By the time you got out to the Green Hand he would've been long gone."

Janey shook her head. "He must've changed his mind. There was a bright yellow car with West Virginia plates in the parking lot when we left."

Ruth clearly found this possibility unsettling.

"I noticed him at the bar when I walked in," Janey continued, "though it didn't dawn on me why until this morning. It's not just his brother he looks like. He also looks like his grandfather."

Ruth still appeared unconvinced. "Why would he have gone there, of all places?"

"I don't know, but he got really hammered and ended up blacking out and falling off his barstool."

"Was he hurt?"

Janey shrugged. "They tried to wake him up, but he was out cold. Del and I ended up dropping him off at the station so he could sleep it off in the drunk tank." Knowing how her mother would react, she left out how they'd tossed him in the trunk of Del's vehicle and later bungeed him onto a trolley.

"Seriously? What if he had a concussion and needed to go to the hospital?"

"Don't start, Ma, okay? I wasn't the one in charge, and at the time it kind of made sense. Everybody was pretty shit-faced."

Ruth shook her head. "The more you tell me about this Del character the more I think you need to lose him."

"See what I mean about you not waiting for me to ask advice?"

They were both quiet then, until Janey said, "It gets even weirder. At one point I glanced in his direction and he was watching me. It was almost like he'd recognized me, too. He pretended it wasn't me he was watching but it definitely was."

"Maybe he was trying to figure out why you were looking at him earlier. Or wondering if you were easy."

"Thanks, Ma. Thanks for that."

"I'm kidding, Janey. Jesus."

Janey ran her fingers through her hair. "You *say* you're kidding, but sometimes it's like you think I'm this horrible person."

"No," Ruth said, suddenly serious. "I never think that."

"What *do* you think?" Janey said, and hearing the words, she realized she actually wanted to know. "Of me, I mean."

Her mother didn't answer immediately. "When I look at you, I mostly see myself," Ruth said finally, as if she wished it were otherwise. "I see someone who's good and trapped who keeps on doing the same things over and over hoping for different results."

Janey would've liked to take issue with this blunt assessment but found she couldn't. More than anything she disliked the idea that she was living her mother's life, not her own. "Okay," she said, "how about this? If you could do things over, what would you do differently?"

"I think about that a lot," Ruth admitted. "I know you wish I hadn't carried on with Sully all those years, and I admit that was selfish of me. But I can't imagine what my life would've been like without him. He was the only thing that made me even close to happy."

"Thanks again, Ma."

"Come on. You know what I mean. I'm just talking men. Can I ask *you* a question?"

"Okay?" Janey said, wishing now that she hadn't started them down this road.

"Do you have any women friends?"

"Fuck, no."

"Have you ever?"

"Fuck, no."

"You never wanted one?"

"Fuck. No."

Ruth nodded. "Me either. My question is, how did we get that way? How did we learn to put such a high value on male companionship?"

"I have no idea where *you* got the idea from, but I know where I did, and I'm looking at her."

Ruth nodded sadly. "Sorry."

"Speaking of sorry," Janey said, taking a deep breath. "That was a terrible thing I said to you last night."

"What?" Ruth wanted to know.

*"What,"* Janey repeated, incredulous.

"Oh. You mean about me being old and ugly and not having a man in my life anymore and being jealous of you because you do?" Ruth said, with a wave of her hand. "Heck, I forgot all about that."

"Yeah, right," Janey said, adding, "And I never said you were ugly."

Ruth smiled. "Maybe not, but that's what I heard."

"So, I'm forgiven?"

"Of course you're forgiven."

"I don't know why I get like that," she said. "I'll try not to be so mean."

"Mean is fine," Ruth assured her. "Just try not to be so truthful."

That didn't seem like a bad way to end things, so Janey got to her feet. Her mother, much more stiffly, followed suit. At the door, Janey paused, staring out the window at the façade of Grandpa Zack's Treasures. "Do you think Tina takes after us?"

"I don't think she has any girlfriends, if that's what you mean."

"Does she have any men friends?"

"None that I'm aware of. She does have Jacks."

"Don't get me started on that fucking dog," Janey said, remembering with horror how her daughter had gotten down on her knees and gazed into the animal's runny eyes, the way she seemed to peer into its very soul. "If only I knew what was going on in that head of hers. What she's feeling. Hell, I can't even tell if she *has* feelings."

"Maybe she isn't as isolated as you think," Ruth said. "And of course she has feelings."

"You think?" Janey said, suddenly not wanting to leave. This was the longest conversation she and her mother had had in years that didn't involve shouting and recrimination. "If only she could find somebody. He's old enough to be her father, but I'm pretty sure Roger dotes on her. I think she's the reason he hangs around."

Her mother was regarding her strangely now.

"What?" Janey said.

Ruth shrugged. "Nothing."

"No, what?"

"The reason Roger stays around isn't Tina. It's you."

Stunned, Janey just stared at her. "You're crazy."

Another maddening shrug.

"No, I mean it. You're fucking crazy. I've seen how he looks at her."

"Yeah," Ruth said, "but what you *haven't* noticed is how he looks at you."

And just that quickly Janey was furious again. "That is such a crock, Ma," she said. "I mean where do you come *up* with this shit?"

"Fine," Ruth said, throwing up her hands. "Have it your way."

"No, seriously. Why would you *say* something like that?"

Though now that she thought about it, the idea wasn't so much lunatic as completely unexpected. "Has he ever said anything to you about me?"

"Of course not."

"So you . . . what? Just pulled him being in love with me out of your ass?"

"Whatever," Ruth told her. "If you think that's what I did, then that's what I did."

As usual, Janey wanted to scream. Only the fact that she'd just a minute earlier promised not to be so mean kept her from doing so. Instead, trying her best to control her voice, she said, "Ma. Explain something to me. Why, why, *why* is it always like this between us?"

Instead of answering, Ruth pulled her in close and gave her a hug. Janey didn't hug back, but neither did she pull away. She allowed the embrace to linger and then linger some more. "For what it's worth," her mother said, "I think you're probably right about who you saw at the Hand last night."

"Yeah?" Janey said, still not stepping away from her mother's embrace. *Huh,* she thought. She hadn't screamed something hateful like she wanted to and her mother had responded by conceding that she might be right about something. She was still in her mother's arms. Was this how things were supposed to work? Could it be so simple?

# Tag Team

TRAFFIC IN FRONT of the courthouse in downtown Schuyler was still being rerouted when Peter arrived there. The crowd that had gathered earlier to witness the fiery spectacle Carl Roebuck described on the phone had mostly dispersed, but the scene—which featured a wrecker towing away another wrecker that had in its bed a third, incinerated vehicle—still struck Peter as impressively surreal.

Even before he got there, his mind had been reeling thanks to a call from Ruth, who wanted to know if he'd heard from his son since yesterday. When he said no and wondered why she was asking, she told him she was pretty sure Thomas hadn't headed up the Northway to Montreal like he said he was going to. Instead, he'd apparently gone to a local bar called the Green Hand where he'd gotten so blind drunk that he passed out and fell off his barstool. Her daughter, Janey, had been there and witnessed the whole thing. In fact, she and the guy she was seeing these days, who happened to be a cop, had gathered Thomas up and taken him to the police station so he could sleep it off in the drunk tank.

Where was Thomas now? Ruth couldn't say, but given how much he'd had to drink, he might still be sleeping it off at the police station. The other possibility—and to Peter, this one seemed more

likely—was that he was being detained there. Ruth hadn't said anything about Thomas being arrested, but maybe he had been, and
if he couldn't make bail, he'd likely remain where he was until he
could be brought before a magistrate on Monday. Having never
spent a night in a drunk tank himself, Peter wasn't that clear on the
protocols. What troubled him most was the likelihood that neither
he nor Ruth had a full understanding of what had transpired at the
Green Hand. For instance, why had the Caddy been towed to begin
with? Was it parked somewhere it shouldn't have been? Blocking
a delivery door, for instance? Maybe. But given Thomas's various
run-ins with the law in West Virginia, wasn't it also possible that
he'd done something to piss somebody off? Had he become belligerent? Run up a tab he couldn't pay? Peter also wondered why,
if Carl Roebuck was to be believed, there'd been several containers
of gas in the trunk of the car. Somewhat bizarrely, the explanation
that occurred to him first was genetic. Sully, who all his life had
driven beaters whose engines ran hot, always kept a half-dozen cans
of motor oil in his toolbox for when smoke began to billow from
beneath their hoods. Maybe his grandson's ancient Caddy had a
broken fuel gauge and Thomas kept enough gas on hand to get him
to the nearest service station when the vehicle sputtered to a halt in
the middle of nowhere.

Eventually, Peter figured, these minor mysteries would get
cleared up, and a more coherent picture would emerge. In the
meantime, though, the gaps in the narrative begged obvious questions. What had possessed his son to go out and get so purposefully
drunk? Desperation? Despair? Was it possible he'd driven all the
way from West Virginia because he needed money? Had he meant
to ask Peter for a loan, then at the last minute found that his pride
wouldn't allow it? Peter hoped this wasn't the case, but if it was,
might it not be the very opportunity Peter had been hoping for?
The chance to offer Thomas the same much-needed helping hand
that Sully had once extended to Peter himself? Earlier this morning
he'd been worried that it might be too late to make things right, but

what if it wasn't? With his Caddy reduced to charred scrap metal, Thomas was going to need his help getting back home whether he wanted it or not.

But first things first: Rub. Peter spied him on a park bench halfway down the block with his head in his hands, a study in dejection. Next to him sat Carl Roebuck, who'd promised to hang around until Peter arrived and apparently kept his word. Unlike Rub, he seemed to be in excellent spirits, perhaps because there was a third person on the bench, his ex-wife, whose expression suggested that the last half hour of her life would not be the one she'd tell people about if asked to explain why life was worth living. She and Carl both clocked Peter's approach at the same moment and rose from the bench. "Hey, Rubberhead," Carl said. "Look who's here."

If Rub heard this, he gave no indication.

"You've met my wife, right?" Carl said, nodding at Toby.

"I have, yes," Peter assured him.

"Poor Carlos," Toby sighed, giving him a chaste peck on the cheek. "Can I go back to work now?"

"Why not?" Carl told her. "The cavalry has arrived."

At this Toby raised a dubious eyebrow. "Some cavalry."

"Sorry," Peter said. "My horse is back at the stable."

"Too bad," she said, flirty now, apparently for her ex-husband's benefit. "We could've gone for a ride."

Carl ignored the flirtation as if it was not happening. "Look at that ass, would you?" he marveled as they watched her go. "Forty-eight years old. I mean, seriously. How old would you guess that ass is?"

"Forty-eight," Peter said, though Carl was right, it did look like a thirty-something-year-old tuchus.

"That," Carl said, returning his attention to Peter now, "is exactly the sort of snide remark that will deliver her back into my arms one of these days. Which, as we both know, is where she belongs. Because, be honest. What've you ever done to deserve a woman like that?"

"Not a thing," Peter admitted, though he couldn't help smiling to himself. It was vintage Carl Roebuck to ask others the very question that might better have been directed at himself.

"And how about this?" Carl said, reaching into his pocket and pulling out a wad of cash. "The lady with the great ass generously offered to float me a loan for operating expenses."

"Knowing the kind of operator you are, that surprises me," Peter said.

"Go ahead and scoff, but all those years we were man and wife? Two hearts beating as one? Deep down, she still has deep feelings for me."

"Either that," Peter said, "or she's paying you to go away and leave her alone."

Seeing that Rub's head was still in his hands, Peter sat down next to him. He was no longer blubbering, but his cheeks were tearstained and his nose crusted, as was the sleeve of his parka. "Hey, Sancho," Peter said, nudging him. "What's up?"

Rub refused to look at him. "What do you want?" he asked darkly.

Despite having been given unambiguous permission to leave, Carl sat back down on the bench so that Rub was sandwiched tightly between them, having apparently concluded that cheering Rub up was a two-man job.

"I got a question for you," Peter said, nudging Rub again. "If you could wish somebody dead, who would it be?"

Rub, who spent a large part of his life wishing things were other than they were, answered without hesitation, "Carl."

This time it was Carl who nudged him. "You don't really muh-muh-mean that." And give the man credit: he was a natural mimic. It had been months since Rub had stuttered, but Carl still had it down. It was as if he'd spent the whole time practicing. Peter's only grounds for objection would've been cruelty, but he knew from experience that being made fun of sometimes had the counterintuitive effect of lifting Rub's spirits, perhaps because it reminded him of Sully, who'd always ribbed him mercilessly.

"Who else?" Peter prodded.

"Me?" Rub suggested pitifully.

Peter shook his head. "Nah. I need you to help me finish work on the Main Street house. Try again."

Rub sighed deeply. "Why? Wishes don't come true."

"Wuh-wuh-wishes don't come true," Carl translated, as if for Peter's benefit.

"Except sometimes they do," Peter said. "Who else do you wish would just disappear."

A trace of a smile formed on Rub's lips. "Mr. Proxmire?"

Peter nodded encouragement. "Yeah? How come?"

"Every Sunday morning he says the same thing."

"Wuh-wuh-what's that?" Carl wanted to know.

Rub's expression darkened again. "Don't wreck the wrecker." Clearly, he was still chafing at what he considered unnecessary instruction. "Like I'm always getting in accidents, even though I never had a single one."

"Until today," Carl added, for the record. Rub shot him a look of pure hatred.

"Okay, but guess what?" Peter said, nudging Rub again. "Your wish is granted. He died an hour ago."

Rub's brow furrowed. Clearly, this was too good to be true. "Did not."

"Did too."

"Really?" Rub said, won over just that easily, no evidence required, his face brightening.

Carl, by contrast, appeared stricken. "Don't tell me," he said. "That fucking thing in his head?"

Peter nodded. "Birdie said he was talking to her and stopped midsentence."

Carl cocked his head, like a dog. "And this happened where?"

"At the Horse."

"Huh," Carl said, puzzled. "You don't suppose they were . . . ?"

"I wouldn't know," Peter told him. It would've pleased him to learn that Birdie had a sex life, but he didn't care to contemplate the particulars. "Anyhow," he said, turning his attention back to Rub, "cheer up. He's all done ragging you about the wrecker."

But Rub's shoulders had slumped again. "Except now I'm out of a job," he pointed out. The look on his face suggested that he was coming to terms—and not for the first time—with a sad, eternal truth: that nothing in this life ever comes to you clean.

"True," Carl said, nudging Rub again, harder this time, so that he leaned into Peter. "But what do you care? You're rich, right?" When Peter raised an eyebrow at this, Carl said, "You didn't know our friend here was loaded?"

"I have no idea what you're talking about," Peter admitted, shouldering Rub up straight again. Another man might've objected to being buffeted about like this, but Rub seemed to consider it his due, or, if not his due, then yet another life circumstance over which he had no control.

"Forty grand in the bank is what he told me," Carl explained. "Personally, I found that difficult to credit."

So did Peter until he thought about it. "Hey, he works seven days a week and lets other people buy his donuts."

At this, Rub again sighed deeply.

"What interests me," Peter said, eyeing Carl suspiciously now, "is how the subject came up."

Carl gave Rub another nudge. "He brought it up himself, didn't you, Rub."

Rub apparently saw no need to deny this.

"Admit it," Carl continued. "You wanted your old buddy Carl to know that even though you had all this money in the bank and he was going through a rough patch, you weren't going to help him out."

Rub didn't deny this, either. You only had to look at him to know how utterly devoted he was to Carl's financial ruin.

Peter decided it might be time to shift rhetorical gears. He wasn't sure they'd lifted Rub's spirits, but his former dejection seemed to have been replaced by red-hot, glowing animosity toward Carl, which struck Peter as an excellent trade-off. "So, Carl," Peter said. "Don't you have someplace to be?"

"Not really," Carl told him cheerfully, as if Peter would be relieved to hear this.

"But hey, I know when I'm not wanted." Rising from the bench, he said, as if the thought had just occurred to him, "Hey, Rubber-head, do you know what I miss? Those poker games we used to have at the Horse. We should start those up again. What do you think?"

"You just want to take my money," Rub told him.

Carl winked at Peter. "The thing about our good friend Rub?" he told Peter. "He's a lot smarter than people give him credit for. He's a handsome devil, too."

"Am not," Rub said, in answer, perhaps, to both of Carl's observations.

"Well, not handsome like me." Carl conceded. "But not bad looking for a man of your height and weight and overall appearance. And women like guys with money. They hate it when you run out, though, so if I were you I'd keep saving."

"Goodbye, Carl," Peter said.

Together he and Rub watched the other man head up the street. When he disappeared around the corner, Peter nudged Rub again.

"What?" said Rub, though he was reluctantly smiling now.

"You've really got that much money in the bank?"

Rub shrugged.

"Hey, I'm glad," Peter assured him, feeling an unexpected surge of emotion. Could it be pride in how far Rub had come since Peter found him living all alone in the ramshackle house he'd shared with Bootsie, hollow eyed and half starved, completely disinterested in life? "Look, I'm sorry about the wrecker. It wasn't your fault."

Rub shook his head. "If I'd done like Mr. Proxmire said and gone straight back to the yard—"

"He'd still be dead," Peter told him. "And you'd still be out of a job."

"I just wish . . . ," he began.

"What?" Peter said, figuring Rub would say he was sorry for wishing his boss dead.

"How come Carl gets to live with you?"

"It's just until he gets back on his feet and finds a place of his own," Peter assured him.

"What if he doesn't?"

At this, Peter snorted. "Guys like Carl always land on their feet," he said, though in truth he was far from certain. Beneath his bravado, Carl did seem genuinely untethered lately. Did he really think Toby would ever come back to him? That they'd be husband and wife again? Two hearts beating as one?

Rub nodded, but there was clearly something else on his mind. "When we're done working on the house, you're really going to move away?"

Peter nodded. "That's the plan."

"How come?"

"You'd rather I didn't?"

Again, Rub's brow knit. You didn't need to be a mind reader to know the question he was trying to formulate: *What about me?*

"Carl was right about one thing, though," Peter told him. "You are smarter than people give you credit for."

Rub turned to regard him now, as if he might be waiting to see if Peter would say he was good-looking, too, because then he would know that Peter was ribbing him. When Peter didn't, his eyes filled with tears.

"Hey," Peter said, nudging him one last time. "No crying on the street."

Rub swallowed hard and wiped his runny eyes on the crusty sleeve of his parka. "That's not a rule."

"You know what? You're right," Peter admitted. "In fact, you're free to think and behave however you want. You don't have to check with me or anybody."

"Okay," Rub said, though he didn't look all that thrilled by his freedom.

"By the way," Peter said. "Why *didn't* you go straight back to the yard after you picked up the Caddy this morning?"

"I figured you'd want to know your son never went up to Canada like he said. And you'd want to see what they did to his car. How they smashed all the windows and everything."

"Who did?"

"The cops."

So, Peter thought. He'd been right. He and Ruth knew only part of the story. Thomas had done a lot more than get drunk and fall off his barstool.

*Little Bro—*

*This time when I come to, I'm in the hospital, not jail, so my first thought is, Hey, things are looking up, right? Except not really. I'm hooked up to an IV and surrounded by beeping machines and the first real deep breath I take tells me I'm pretty busted up. I remember the parking lot, that second cop showing up, feeling his fist on my chin, the toe of his boot in my ribs, over and over, and me laying there on the ground, my hands cuffed behind me, unable to fight back, even. No wonder everything hurts. I try telling myself to cheer the fuck up, I've been here before. But have I? Have things ever been this bad? So far from home, racking up a hospital bill I can't pay, no chance anymore of carrying out the plan I swore I wouldn't fuck up and then did? In fact, I can kind of feel myself giving up, so I close my eyes and make a mental list of things that could be worse. Like, I'm not dead. That's good, right? Also, I might be busted up, but it doesn't look like I'm dying. If I was, there'd be doctors running around yelling* Stat! *like they do on TV. And let's not forget, this isn't the first time I've gotten my ass kicked by cops. It's never been a big deal before. No reason it should be now. Hey, it's one of the ways me and you are different, right? How much pain I can suck up? Okay, that sounds like bragging and saying you're a wimp, and I don't mean it to. You've been through your share, too. More than your share. It's just somewhere along the* line I learned to put hurt in a different room from the one I'm in. I know it's there, but it's like there's a door between me and it. You could never do that.

This time does feel different, though. Before, it was always parts of me that got broke. A hand. My nose. A knee. This time? This time it feels like maybe it's me they broke, Little Bro. I wouldn't admit that to anybody but you. Could be I'll feel different later on—tomorrow, maybe—but right now? I'm thinking maybe this is it. Maybe I've taken my last beating. Remember the poker game I got into that time? How I caught that guy dealing off the bottom of the deck and me and him got into it? I always told that story like I was the hero, you know? Like I was the smart one, because I caught him cheating. Anymore, I don't know. Could be that I was the dumb one for being in the game to begin with. For thinking I could win. Is that what you've been trying to tell me all these years? You figured that out? Hell, maybe you've known that all along, even back when we were kids and living with Mom and Dickweed. Maybe that's why me and you turned out so different. Why I always have such a hard time convincing you to do things my way. Like our plan this time. Could you see from the start that it wasn't going to work? That I'd find a way to screw things up? That it would just be more of the same? Me pretending to be a hero? Me thinking we can win? You knowing better?

Anyhow, I'm laying here feeling sorry for myself when the door opens and in comes a doc and a nurse, except the doc is a girl and the nurse is a guy. "Somebody's awake," one of them says, I can't tell which, what with them both wearing masks. I hear someone moan and realize it's me. "Don't try to talk," the doc tells me. "Your jaw's broken." She leans over and shines a light in one eye and then the other. She tells me that as soon as the surgeon gets here, they'll take me down to surgery, but in the meantime here's something for pain. Good, I think, because if the pain went away maybe I wouldn't feel so low? I see the nurse inject something into my drip. The doc does a countdown on her fingers and says, "It should be kicking in right about . . . now." And sure enough, when she says "now" I feel whatever they put in the IV crash over me like a big, beautiful wave. Just before it carries me *off, I wonder who I'll see when I wake up again and I think how nice it would be if it was you, but that's not going to happen, is it. Pop maybe? But, hey, that's almost as crazy. How would he even know where I am? Nah, I'm on my own, like always, but before I can stop myself, I think, Hey, it wouldn't be so bad, would it? If Pop was there when I woke up? Crazy, right? I guess what they say is true. Drugs do fuck you up.*

*How long am I out? An hour? A day? No idea, Little Bro. I'd probably still be asleep, except I feel this sudden sharp pain in my side and whoa! I'm wide awake. And you'll never guess who's sitting there next to the bed, looking at me like I'm some kind of puzzle with no solution. Hah! I know what you're thinking. Pop, right? Even though he's got no idea I'm here? And I said you'd never guess? But no, it's even weirder than that. It's the cop from the parking lot. The one that broke my jaw and kicked me when I was on the ground, not the other one. Can you believe it? And the pain that woke me up? I'm pretty sure that was him poking me in the ribs where he kicked me. And, hey, get this! What do you suppose he's got on his lap? A fucking pillow. I shit you not. So, I'm thinking, What's he going to do? Smother me? Finish what he started out there in the parking lot? When he sees me staring at the pillow, he gives me this big, shit-eating grin, like he knows what I'm thinking. But no, instead of getting up and putting it over my face, he just tosses it onto a nearby bed.*

*Leaning forward and shaking his head, he says, "Look at you, Thomas." And I'm thinking, He knows my name? "Concussion, multiple contusions and abrasions, a fractured jaw, three cracked ribs. Amazing, really, how bad you can hurt yourself falling off a barstool."*

*I just lay there, because I can't decide if he's real, if he's actually there in the room with me, or if I'm dreaming him because of the drugs they gave me before. Or maybe from the anesthesia. Because I just had surgery, right? Wasn't that where they were taking me when that big, beautiful painkiller carried me off? And I've got that drugged feel. You know the one I mean? Where everything's kind of blurry around the edges? Am I still in the hospital even? Where did all the doctors and nurses go?*

When he sees me looking around, all confused, he says, "You're in recovery. The good news is, the operation was a success."

I'm thinking, *The good news? Nobody ever says "good news" like that unless there's bad news coming.*

"Best not to talk," he says, when he sees me trying to. "Your mouth's wired shut."

Now that he's told me this, I can feel it.

"Never mind," he says, waving this off like it doesn't matter. "I'll do all the talking. There's a fair amount of ground to cover and not much time. Nod, if you understand."

It hurts to nod but I do because I'm still thinking about that pillow, wondering why it was in his lap.

"Like I said, the surgery was successful. You lucked out, actually. There was just the one clean break, right here."

He lifts and angles his chin and points to the spot on his own lower jaw where mine's broke.

"That's some kind of strong jaw you got there," he continues, flexing the fingers of his right hand, which I can see are swollen. "Usually when I land that kind of uppercut, the result is multiple fractures. All you needed was one small plate and a couple screws." He pauses, so I can appreciate my good fortune. "Interesting procedure, actually. I watched." He scoots his chair up closer. "They do an incision on the inside of the gum," he explains, opening his mouth so he can demonstrate with his index finger, which makes him hard to understand. "Then they realign the upper and lower jaw and screw everything in place so it heals right." When I don't say anything, he says, "Stop me if I'm telling you something you already know." I just stare at him, his face inches from mine. He could still grab that pillow and finish me. "I only bring it up, because you seem like the sort of guy who naturally invites a fair amount of blunt force trauma. I mean, assaulting a police officer at the station? You thought that would lead to a good outcome?" He pauses here, as if he's forgotten my jaw is wired shut and thinks I might explain why I would do such a thing. "Nah," he continues, "I know. You weren't thinking at all. And, hey, I get it. Sometimes you just see red, right? Nod, if you agree."

*I nod. You bet I do.*

*"Well," he says. "We have that much in common."* I must look skeptical because he says, *"No, I mean it. Roughing you up like I did back there in the parking lot? If I'm thinking? I just help Officer Miller secure you in the back seat of his cruiser. Trust the system to fuck you up. After all, that's what it's designed to do. But in the end it all comes down to hubris."* I expect him to say, Nod if you agree, but he doesn't. *"I wanted to be the one to fuck you up. Me. And now, as a result, I've got some problems I shouldn't have."* He gives me this look that says we're brothers under the skin, me and him, cut from the same bolt of cloth, unable to govern our impulses. *"Okay, my problems aren't like yours. I don't mean that. My problems have solutions. My problems are an annoyance. Yours?"* He pauses here to let me reflect on the difference between his problems and mine. *"The way I see it, you got two options, bad and worse, and I have this feeling you're going to choose worse. Why? Because you always do. I ran a quick check on you, Thomas, and you fall neatly into several well-established categories that most people try to avoid, like knucklehead, slow learner and ungifted thinker. You keep doing things the same way, thinking this time things'll break in your favor, but somehow they never do, right? Nod, if you agree."*

*I don't want to nod, Little Bro, but what he's saying is kind of true, right? I mean, you've never said that in so many words, but I can tell that's what you think. You just love me too much to say it. Anyhow, I nod.*

*"Now, in your present circumstance—if you were a gifted thinker?—you might just see a path forward. It's narrow but it's there. I'm not saying it's a great hand you're holding, but you do have a card or two that might be worth playing, and even if you don't take the trick, what've you lost? Because who knows? If you were to help me solve my problem, I might just return the favor, right?"* He puts his hands on his knees, hunches his shoulders. *"Except that's not how you're seeing it. I can tell that just by looking at you. You're thinking, This fucker who broke my jaw and kicked me in the ribs wants me to help him? Fuck that. And I'll tell you what else you're thinking. You're*

*thinking, If I do what he wants, what guarantee do I have that he won't turn right around and fuck me?" He pauses here, smiling at me. "Answer? None. All I can guarantee is what happens if you don't." Is it my imagination or does he glance over at the pillow?*

*When I take a slightly deeper breath than usual, I feel a sharp pain between my ribs and close my eyes until it passes. When I open them again, he's studying me with that same odd expression he wore earlier, like I'm some kind of riddle he can't quite solve. Like who the hell am I and how did I show up in his world? Like until he figures that out he can't be sure what his next move should be. This whole time he's been trying to convince me his problems are small compared to mine and there's no way out for me unless I do like he says, but I can tell he's tense. "Sullivan," he says finally, his brow knit. "Why is that name so familiar, Thomas? You here visiting relatives?"*

*I consider nodding, because maybe it would be good if he thought there was somebody around here who gave a shit if I lived or died, but I decide against it and shake my head no, which results in another shooting pain. When he sees me grimace, he scoots his chair forward and actually reaches to touch my face, like he's some kind of healer. I try to lean back, away from him, but there's no place for me to go. "Oh, don't be a baby," he chides me when I flinch, as if the pain I'm in's got nothing to do with him. "I'm not going to hurt you." Inserting the tip of his index finger between my upper and lower lips, he tugs the lower one down. "You lost a tooth," he tells me. "Did you know that?" Like I've looked in the mirror lately. "Fell right out when they were setting your jaw. You know the tooth I mean? The black one?" When he touches the spot where it used to be, I can feel its absence. He peers at me critically. "Don't you ever brush your teeth?" he says, sliding his chair back. "Go to the dentist?" When I don't respond, he just shrugs, like okay, fine, it's none of his business. "Anyhow, doesn't matter," he tells me. "You won't be chewing for a while. You're going to be sucking your meals through a straw for the foreseeable future. You like smoothies? Pureed vegetables?"*

*There's noise out in the hall. Voices. A squeaky gurney going by.*

"Okay, it sounds like we're going to have company soon. Time to wrap this up. Later today you're going to get a visit from the chief of police." He kind of makes a face when he says "chief of police." "Black chick. She'll show a police report that says you were arrested in the parking lot of the Green Hand without incident, that your injuries—all of them—were the result of blacking out and falling off your barstool the night before. The report will bear the signatures of Officer Miller and Lieutenant Delgado. That's me, in case you were wondering. She'll ask you if the report is accurate. She'll say there's no way you sustained all those injuries falling off a barstool. She'll tell you your broken jaw and cracked ribs are more likely to have occurred when you were arrested. She'll want you to say you were roughed up. But you? You'll assure her you were treated with courtesy and that the report is true, every word. She'll know you're lying and she won't be happy. Just try to remember that my happiness is more important to you than hers. Nod, if you understand."

I nod. He puzzles over this, like there are twenty or thirty different kinds of nods and he's trying to figure out whether the one I just gave him was the you-can-count-on-me nod or the fuck-you one. Eventually, he gives up.

"You're probably wondering when you get to go home, right?"

He doesn't ask me to nod if I agree, but I do, anyway.

"That depends on whether Sergeant Dailey presses charges or not. But when he learns the shape you're in? The full extent of the injuries you sustained falling off that barstool? I'm guessing he'll feel that justice has been served. If so, you'll be free to head back as soon as you're well enough to leave the hospital. In fact, I'll put you on the bus myself."

I think, Bus? I know it's not important, but I want to correct him, so I make a motion, like I'm gripping the steering wheel of the Yellow Sub and driving home.

"Oh, right, I forgot," he says, though I know that's not true. The one thing I know for sure about this guy is that he doesn't forget stuff. "Your vehicle?" His cheeks billow and from deep in his throat comes *the sound of a violent explosion, played through a muffler. So. No more Yellow Sub. It's gone, Little Bro. I'm sorry. I am. I try not to let him see that to me and you the Sub isn't just some old wreck.*

*Clearly, something is still bothering him. "West Virginia," he says, as if where we live is part of whatever's on his mind. "People do that down there? Drive around with full gas cans in the trunk? Is that, like, a local custom?"*

*I shake my head.*

*"So, what, then?" he says. "Explain why you'd be doing that."*

*I motion to my jaw.*

*He nods. "Right, you can't talk." And for the first time he actually seems to wish I could.*

*When his cell phone vibrates, he pulls it out, glances to see who's calling and flips it open. "Bobby," he says, heading for the door, his voice low. "Can you hear me?" I figure he's going to take the call out into the hall, but instead he just peers through the tiny rectangular window in the door. For the first time it occurs to me that he's not supposed to be in here with me. I see his face light up, and even with his voice low, I hear him say, "You're shitting me. Really? When?" For some reason he glances over at me and gives me a thumbs-up, like we're on the same team and we both just got good news. "How can that be?" he says. "I was just with her." He checks his watch. "I don't know. Forty-five minutes, maybe? No, she looked fine. All high and mighty. You hear she suspended me again?" He glances over at me. "Okay, do me a favor? See what you can find out? I can't be anywhere near this, or I'd do it myself. Right. Okay, great. Thanks for letting me know."*

*When he hangs up, he stands there, staring at the phone, like he can't believe what he was just told. Finally, he remembers me and comes back over. Noticing the pillow where he tossed it on the bed, he picks it up and plumps it, like maybe he plans to put it behind my head, and if that's what he means to do I'd almost rather he smothered me.*

*"You know who does that?" he says, studying me closely, like he did before. "You know who drives around with full cans of gasoline in the trunk of his car?"*

*And now I'm glad—really glad—that when he mentioned our last name before, I didn't say anything about Pop.*

*"Somebody who's planning to start a fire," he says. "Is that what you were planning, Thomas Sullivan? Were you planning to burn something down?"*

# Mojo

J EROME WAS BACK. "She's starting to wake up," he reported. When Raymer, holding his head in his hands, didn't respond, he said, "Dawg? You okay?"

No, he was not. For the last twenty minutes he'd been sitting alone on the floor of the brightly lit hospital corridor, adrift on a sea of turbulent thoughts, the darkest of which was the memory of the day he'd returned home unexpectedly and found Becka dead at the foot of the stairs. Nobody had blamed him, at least not that he was aware of. She'd fallen because she was in a hurry. If she hadn't been fleeing her marriage, running off with another man, she'd still be alive. Everyone agreed: she had only herself to blame.

Everyone except Raymer, who had *himself* to blame. He'd been promising to put a mat under the slippy rug at the top of the stairs but hadn't gotten around to it, and now here was the result. Dead wife. And if Charice were to die now, *her* death would be his fault as well. Okay, he hadn't worked out exactly how just yet, but he had the rest of his miserable life to figure it out. If you were dumb enough to fall in love with Douglas Raymer, however briefly, dead was how you ended up.

Despite being awash in self-pity, Raymer was surprised to discover there was also plenty of room in his unruly heart for a shitload of seething resentment. As Charice's brother, Jerome had been allowed into the recovery room, while Raymer, her significant other (though his significance seemed to be waning), had to remain in the corridor. Being ostracized like this only confirmed his sense of how things stood, how they'd stood, in fact, for a very long time. After all, it was Jerome—batshit, nutcase, bizarro Jerome—that Charice had taken into her confidence about being pregnant, and Raymer who'd been kept in the dark. Who had she texted from the ambulance on her way to the hospital? Again, her brother. Would Jerome even have told Raymer where he was going if he'd had any other way to get there?

They'd bickered the entire way, Raymer driving at unsafe speed. "How could she be pregnant?" he said, glaring at Jerome in the passenger seat.

"The usual way, Dawg," Jerome said, one hand gripping the door's armrest, the other bracing against the dashboard.

Raymer shook his head. "She's forty, Jerome. She's on the pill." Though having declared this, he now wondered if the latter was true. Back when they were still living together (before his significance as her other had begun to wane), Charice had told him that her periods were becoming more irregular of late, leading her to speculate that she might be premenopausal. Had she stopped taking the pill?

"Watch the road, Dawg," Jerome said, noting that Raymer had crossed the centerline.

"No, I mean it. How can she be pregnant?"

"It happens."

Since there was no arguing this, Raymer shifted gears to a different resentment. "How long have you known?"

At this, Jerome let out an audible sigh. "What difference does it make?"

To Raymer, it made a difference. "How long, Jerome?"

"A while."

"She told you and not me."

"I'm her brother," Jerome pointed out unnecessarily. "Her twin. Also, she didn't tell me. I guessed."

"Oh, come on. Why would you think she'd be pregnant?"

"We live in the same apartment."

"I'm aware of that," Raymer said. "*I* used to live there."

"The walls are thin. Mornings, I could hear her . . . regurgitating."

The word sent Raymer over the edge. "You mean she's throwing up, right? Vomiting. Puking her guts out."

Each word caused Jerome to wince, as if from a series of stiff left jabs.

"Barfing," Raymer continued. "Hurling. Tossing her cookies."

Jerome took a deep breath, as if he might toss his own. "It wasn't just the morning sickness. There were other signs as well."

*Right,* Raymer thought, understanding the implication here. Other signs that he, being an idiot, had missed.

"Look," Jerome said. "She was going to tell you, okay?"

"When?"

"As soon as she made up her mind about what to do."

*About what?* Just in time Raymer had saved himself the humiliation of asking yet another dumb-ass question out loud.

"Dawg?" Jerome repeated now, taking a seat beside Raymer on the cold linoleum floor. "She's going to be okay."

At this, Raymer sat up straight, allowing the back of his head to bang against the wall. "She was hemorrhaging blood, Jerome. If someone hadn't come into the bathroom and found her when they did, she could've died."

"But they *did* find her," Jerome pointed out, not unreasonably, "and she didn't die." Painful though it was to admit, Jerome was dealing with the present moment better than Raymer was. Charice had explained more than once how things worked with obsessive-compulsives. When there was nothing real to worry about, they would invent things to stress over, as Jerome had been doing all morning, imagining that he had a target on his back, that some white woman would get him lynched if he wasn't careful. But now that the world had unexpectedly conformed to his perception of it, Jerome became a different man—calm, rational, collected. "The D and C fixed things," he assured Raymer. "She's no longer bleeding. She's no longer pregnant."

"What about the infection?" Her doctor *had* mentioned an infection, right? The possibility of sepsis?

"The antibiotics will clear it up," Jerome said. "A week of bed rest and she'll be good as new."

They were both quiet then, Raymer feeling his various resentments finally begin to leak away despite his grim determination to hold on to them. "I don't understand why she didn't tell me, Jerome. I would've supported whatever she wanted to do. If she didn't want . . ." He let his voice trail off, unable to say the word *baby*. Her baby. His. Theirs.

"She knows that. It's just . . ."

"Just what?"

But the recovery room door swung open just then, and the same nurse who had earlier allowed Jerome inside and made Raymer wait in the corridor appeared, saying, "She's asking for you," causing Jerome to stir. "Not you," she said. "Him." Raymer quickly rose to his feet, then balked, surprised to discover he would have preferred that Jerome accompany him.

"Go," said Jerome, who had noticed his hesitation.

Inside, Charice lay on a gurney, its metal railings halfway up, her eyes closed. Had she fallen back to sleep? Apparently not, because when the nurse touched her shoulder, her eyes opened. "Your friend is here."

*Friend,* Raymer thought, feeling yet again the sting of diminished significance. Was this how Charice had described their relationship, or did he have Jerome to thank? A chair had been placed next to the gurney, so Raymer sank into it gratefully, his knees suddenly weak.

"Five minutes," the nurse warned them, before leaving him and the woman he couldn't stop loving alone together. Raymer swallowed hard, unsure what came next.

"You're here," Charice said, trying and failing to smile.

He took her hand carefully, so as to not disturb the IV. "Where else would I be?"

"You don't hate me?"

"Hate you," he repeated.

"I would, if I were you."

He wanted desperately to tell her that nothing could be further from the truth, but of course that might be the exact wrong thing. What if she was planning to tell him that it was time for her to stop pretending things were ever going to work out between them?

"It was wrong of me," she continued. "Keeping it a secret from you. Jerome begged me to tell you."

*Really?* he thought. *Jerome had?* "I should've figured it out on my own." Which was true. Last night at the Horse when she ordered that diet soda? Why hadn't he put two and two together? And again this morning on the phone, when she'd admitted to having an upset stomach? He hadn't questioned that, either. Why, he wondered—and not for the first, or even the twentieth, time—did he always accept what people told him? Why had he believed Charice's story about having a butterfly tattooed on her buttock? Because he was stupid, that's why. Because he didn't think she would lie to him. Even after Becka, who'd done nothing but lie. He was, in a word, gullible, and was there anything in the world more pitiful than a gullible cop? No wonder even odious Dougie had given up on him and fled the headspace they'd for a time shared, no doubt sick and tired of Raymer's refusal to accept—admit it—his often sage advice, especially where women were concerned. "I guess I wasn't paying attention."

Charice shook her head and this time did manage something akin to a smile. "People who love you are the easiest to lie to. I took unfair advantage of that." She looked away now, no longer able to meet his eye. "I wanted this job so bad. Or, I used to."

"You will again," he assured her. "You just need a break."

She sighed. "Nah, they'll fire me now. This gives them the excuse they've been looking for. Oh, they'll be nice about it. They'll say it's my health they're worried about. But what they'll really mean is that they need somebody who can bear up under pressure. I don't blame them, really. Five minutes after interviewing Delgado, I'm bleeding all over the bathroom floor."

"It was that sudden?" Raymer said, wanting to understand. "There was no warning?"

The smile she offered him this time was real but wan. "Actually, there were all kinds of warnings. Dizziness. Lower back pain. Spotting. Even some mild cramps. Not constant. Just off and on this last week. I told myself it was stress. The job. Worrying about Jerome." She paused here to meet his eye. "Us."

"And I made things worse?" he said, prepared to accept responsibility for yet another slippy rug. Prepared, yes, to own it.

She made a face. "Why do you do that?"

"Do what?"

"Blame yourself for other people's mistakes? You gave me everything I asked for. I just asked for the wrong things. I lied to you when I should've taken you into my confidence. Yesterday? When you called? There wasn't any conference of police chiefs. I was in Albany to get some tests run. Ultrasound. Pelvic exam. When I spoke to you, I actually had my feet in the stirrups."

Yet another story he'd bought hook, line and sinker. "Why not do the tests here?"

"I guess I was afraid word would get out."

"Yesterday?" Raymer said. "At the Sans Souci? How did you manage? Feeling like you did?"

"It was the best I'd felt in days. It gave me something to focus on. You were there. That made me feel good. And last night. At the restaurant. That was good, too." When she saw that he was shaking his head, she said, "What?"

"I'm lost," he admitted miserably. "What happens next?"

"You mean after I'm fired?"

"I don't know what I mean. You said just now that me being around yesterday made you feel good."

"It did."

"I'd like to believe we have a future, but all day it's been like

Jerome's trying to prepare me for the day when you won't be in my life anymore. Like maybe you've already made a decision about us and just haven't gotten around to telling me."

Her eyes were full now. "I haven't made any decisions," she said. "But . . ."

He waited. "But what?"

"I listened to your voice mail."

In truth, Raymer had forgotten all about the rambling message he'd left when she was interviewing Delgado.

"You were worried that what was wrong between us was that we knew different things. You didn't know what the Harlem Renaissance was. You were afraid maybe you might have to become a whole different man for me to love you."

"I don't?"

"Of course, you don't. You're already a good man. A very good man."

"But?" Because he could feel that *but* coming.

She gave his fingers a squeeze. "Do you know what worried me most about being pregnant? I wasn't sure you understood—really understood—that a child of ours wouldn't be white. Do you get what I'm saying?"

Raymer nodded, feeling he should, but did he?

"Also, I think you're reading Jerome all wrong. I don't think he's trying to prepare you for the day I won't be in your life anymore. I think . . . in his own loopy way . . . he was trying to help you understand that if you had a son, he'd be Black."

"A son," Raymer repeated, trying for the first time to picture what a hypothetical child of theirs would look like, and why what he looked like should matter if it didn't matter to him.

"Well, that's the conclusion *he* leaped to. Being Jerome."

"It sounds like what you're saying is that I haven't been looking after Jerome. He's been looking after me."

"You've been looking after each other. And doing a pretty decent job." She paused here. "You're his only friend. You know that, right?"

Raymer nodded, though that hadn't occurred to him—at least not in such stark terms—until she said it. Over the last twenty-four hours the list of painfully obvious things that he'd somehow managed not to fully comprehend had grown exponentially. Nor, he sensed, was his education complete. Which was probably why, when the door opened and the nurse announced that their five minutes were up, he felt the shame of relief.

He was both surprised and thankful that when he rose Charice seemed reluctant to let go of his hand. "What about you?" she said. "Have you made any decisions?"

"Only that I'm not going anywhere until you tell me to."

"Good," she whispered, finally letting go of his hand and closing her eyes.

"You," said the nurse when he lingered. "Out."

—

WHEN RAYMER RETURNED to the narrow corridor outside the recovery room, Jerome was sitting on the floor with his back against the wall, his long legs stretched out, his big shoes forming a V. Anyone passing by would have to step over them. Raymer slid down the wall beside him, pulling his knees up and interlocking his fingers around his ankles. Both men were silent until Jerome said, "They're keeping her overnight for observation. If the antibiotics work and her temperature comes down, she can go home tomorrow."

Raymer nodded, though he couldn't help wondering what the other man meant by *home*. Her apartment? The one that until fairly recently had also been Raymer's home? His own second-floor flat on Upper Main Street? Which, for the time being at least, was also Jerome's home? Neither space would be large enough to accommodate all three of them comfortably. As recently as yesterday, Raymer would've blamed Jerome for the skewed geography of their lives. Wasn't he forever inserting himself between them, as he'd done last night at the Horse by claiming the middle seat in the horseshoe booth, leaving Raymer and Charice with little choice but to flank him? Now, though, he was beginning to see things differently. If what Charice just told him in the recovery room was true ("You're his only friend. You know that, right?"), then maybe he'd been wrong about Jerome's long game. For Raymer had too readily accepted at face value vile Dougie's dire warnings that he and Jerome would be locked in an eternal struggle for Charice's attention and affection, a competition Raymer stood no chance of winning. But what if he and Jerome weren't competing after all? If Jerome had accepted his and Charice's affection for each other as real and unalterable, then maybe he was preparing for the day when his sister would no longer be in his *own* life. Raymer had assumed that his lectures on Posey Gold and the Harlem Renaissance were designed to mock him for his ignorance about Black history and culture, but maybe not. Maybe the problem Jerome was highlighting was Raymer's naïveté. Because Charice was right. It never *had* occurred to him that in the eyes of the world a child of theirs would be Black. Or that the world would immediately start going about its business of erecting obstacles to that child's happiness and well-being. Ensuring that the world wouldn't succeed would be a major undertaking for both parents, an impossible task if one of them didn't recognize the challenge.

"Also," Jerome was saying. "When you were in there? Bert Franklin came by. He claimed he was here to check up on 'our girl,' but when I mentioned you were with her, he said he was hoping to run into you."

"Did he say why?"

Jerome shook his head. "His cell phone rang right then and my impression was that he didn't want to talk to whoever it was in front of me."

Raymer didn't like the sound of this. "Your sister thinks she's going to be fired."

Jerome seemed unsurprised by this possibility. "What do you think?"

"I think Bert Franklin's the last person I want to talk to right now, but maybe I should."

"Well," said Jerome, nodding in the direction of the nurses' station, "in that case you're in luck."

Sure enough, Franklin, slipping his phone into an outside pocket of his shoulder bag, was striding down the corridor toward them. When Raymer got to his feet, Jerome remained seated. "Doug," Franklin said, stepping over Jerome's long legs and extending his hand. "How's our girl?"

Out of the corner of his eye, Raymer saw Jerome arch an eyebrow. "Pretty wiped out."

"Well, we'll make sure she gets all the time she needs to rest. How about you and I take a walk?" He regarded Jerome now, clearly puzzled by the fact that he hadn't gotten to his feet or even gathered up his long legs. "Jerome, would you excuse us?"

"Depends," said Jerome, "on what you're up to."

"What was that supposed to mean?" Franklin wanted to know when they were out of earshot.

"Maybe he suspects you're here to tell his sister she's going to be fired?"

"Why would he think that?"

Raymer shrugged.

"That's not why I'm here, Doug," Franklin assured him, but when Raymer offered no reaction, the other man relented a little. "Okay, sure, there's some concern on the council about the trajectory of recent events, but nobody's talking about firing anybody."

"What *are* they talking about?"

"Right now? You."

Raymer regarded the other man warily. "Me."

Franklin put a hand on his shoulder. "That was good work you did at the Sans Souci yesterday."

"It was Charice's show. I was just tagging along."

"Okay," he conceded, "but you played a part, too."

Raymer massaged his temples. "Can we just cut to the chase? What are you getting at?"

The other man took his hand off Raymer's shoulder. "You're between gigs, right?"

Raymer nodded, though he wasn't sure this was the most apt description. *Gig-less* was closer to the truth. *Gig-free. Sans gig.*

"I was hoping you might be willing to fill in for a few days until our girl's back on her feet. Given some internal politics in the police department right now, we could use somebody from the outside. I thought you'd want to help out. Was I wrong about that?"

"No, but . . ."

"But you're afraid Charice might not be crazy about the idea? Okay, I get it. You used to be her boss and all that. But could we at least ask her? If she doesn't like the idea, we'll go in a different direction. I just figured there was no point pitching it to her if you were opposed."

Which he wasn't. After the last few months of transitioning the business of North Bath's police department to Schuyler Springs, it would be good to be busy again, to have a purpose. He'd tried hard to convince himself that he didn't miss real police work, but after yesterday, working with Charice, he knew better.

"Not everyone will be happy," Franklin admitted.

"Delgado?"

Franklin rolled his eyes. "You know him?"

Raymer shook his head. "Until this morning I'd never laid eyes on the man." He again pictured the guy making a gun of his thumb and forefinger at Hattie's that morning. A gesture of acknowledgment—even camaraderie—was how he'd taken it at the time. Now he wasn't so sure. "I gather he's a loose cannon?"

"You could say that. But he's got a lot of seniority and quite a following among the rank and file, not to mention some support among the old guard on the council."

Raymer nodded. "I hear there was a problem at the station this morning?"

Franklin nodded. "Some asshole assaulted the desk sergeant. Hurt him pretty bad, I hear."

"And Delgado was involved in the guy's arrest?"

Franklin unzipped his shoulder bag. "Here's a copy of the report."

Raymer quickly scanned the document, which claimed that the man taken into custody—one Thomas Sullivan—resisted and had to be forcibly subdued, resulting in further injury. The report was signed by both Delgado and Miller. "I know Miller from Bath," Raymer said. "He called me this morning to say he was turning in his resignation. He claims Delgado insisted on writing the report himself and made Miller sign it, even though it's a pack of lies."

"Charice suspected as much, not that it probably matters. The guy assaulted a police officer. The union will have Delgado's back. Meanwhile, he's been suspended pending an investigation."

"Which would fall to me?"

Franklin shrugged. "That's for you and Charice to decide. Slow walk the whole thing until she can resume her duties, if you want. The main thing is that we have a temporary fire wall."

"What do we know about this Thomas Sullivan?"

"Not much," Franklin admitted. "Apparently he's not from around here."

"No relation to our old friend Sully, then?"

"Jesus," Franklin chortled. "Sully. I'd forgotten all about him. But no, I can't imagine he would be. Sullivan's a pretty common name."

"His son Peter lives about a block from me in Bath," Raymer said. "I'll check it out."

Franklin was grinning now. "Bath? I have it on excellent authority there's no such place. Look, I know this is a lot to put on you, but if you think you're up to it and Charice agrees, I'll make sure you get the support you need. I don't suppose you still have your old badge?"

"Turned it in last week."

"Your firearm?"

"Also."

"I'll see you're issued new ones. Will you need a vehicle?"

"Not really."

"How about you give me your cell number and I'll call when I have things set up."

Raymer reluctantly gave it to him. "Like I said, Charice may not like the idea. She's asked me to look after her brother and she may not want me to take on additional duties."

Franklin shook his head. "What the hell happened to Jerome, anyway? He looks demented. The crazy hair. That ratty sweater. He used to be a dapper guy."

"That's my sweater, actually," Raymer told him. "And he's not as crazy as he looks. He's just lost his . . ." Raymer shook his head, trying to find the right word for what Jerome had lost.

Franklin clearly commiserated. "Back there in the hallway?" he said. "I kept waiting for him to rise up tall and say, 'The name is Bond. *Jerome* Bond.'"

"His mojo," Raymer said, finally locating the word he'd been in search of. What Jerome had lost was his Jerome-ness.

"Actually," Franklin said. "That gives me an idea."

*Fuck me,* Raymer thought, the same idea having just occurred to him.

===

DESPITE BERT FRANKLIN'S CONVICTION that no such place existed, Raymer headed home to North Bath where—assuming the charger he'd acquired earlier that morning was the correct one—he would juice the suicide's BlackBerry. It would be nice to be able to report at least that much progress when he returned to the hospital later in the evening. For the time being, Jerome would stay behind with Charice.

By the time Raymer turned onto Upper Main, the snow had finally begun to taper off and the streetlamps had come on. A pretty street in all seasons, Upper Main was especially beautiful in winter when the snow on the branches of its giant elms provided such a stark contrast against the darkening sky. Instead of pulling into his own driveway, Raymer continued on up the block to Peter Sullivan's place, thinking he might knock on the door and make sure the Thomas Sullivan taken into custody at the Green Hand was no relation. Though the windows were all dark and there was no sign of Peter's pickup, Raymer pulled over to the curb anyway and just sat. At the far end of the street was the entrance to the Sans Souci and, seeing it, Raymer was again visited by the gnawing feeling that he'd seen something important there yesterday, something that wanted to be remembered.

On the SUV's dashboard sat the copy of *Great Expectations* he'd been miraculously reunited with when he followed Jerome into the bookshop that morning. Now, sitting outside the house that had once belonged to his eighth-grade teacher, Raymer was struck by just how complex and multilayered even the simplest of lives were, how they intersected in strange, unpredictable ways, people magically appearing at just the right moment, others turning up at the exact wrong one, often giving the impression that fate must be at work, though in all probability it was little more than chance, like Raymer entering that used bookshop and noticing *Great Expectations.* Finding meaning in such happenstance often seemed impossible in the moment, but over time patterns did emerge, or seemed to. Like everyone, Raymer had been mystified by Beryl Peoples's leaving her house to Sully, her upstairs tenant. Now, decades later, the gift made a kind of sense. Her own son had earlier fled North Bath in disgrace, never to return, and in his own desultory fashion, Sully had looked after the woman in her old age. According to Peter, she'd found his clomping about overhead like Captain Ahab reassuring. Because of him she'd been able to stay in her own home instead of going to some nursing facility. And though at first Sully hadn't wanted her house any more than Raymer had wanted her gift of *Great Expectations,* in the end he'd been grateful to her for giving him something he could pass to his son.

Picking the book up off the dashboard, Raymer studied the faded dust jacket by the light of the streetlamp. He remembered that cover, the boy, Pip, staring out across the marsh to where the dark figure of the escaped convict lurked. Interspersed throughout the book were a dozen or more dark illustrations, including a particularly terrifying one on the first chapter's facing page. Here the convict was not at a distance across the marsh, but rather hiding behind a gravestone in a churchyard cemetery. Turning on the SUV's dome light, Raymer read the book's long opening paragraph. What had frightened him as a boy, he now suspected, wasn't so much the convict leaping out from behind the gravestone and threatening to slit his throat. It was the fact that the poor kid was there to mourn the loss of his parents and five brothers, all of whom lay interred there. Why, Raymer had wondered at the time, did Miss Beryl want him to dwell, even briefly, in a world so cruelly determined to punish this poor, innocent boy? The answer, of course, was obvious now. Despite how the story began, it would have a happy ending, or if not a happy one, at least one that did not utterly destroy its protagonist. Nor, by extension, would the world destroy Raymer, either. What the old woman had wanted him to understand was that scary beginnings needn't always lead to dismal outcomes. He'd quit reading because he'd been afraid the convict would return to menace Pip anew. That Pip would not remain a terrified boy forever hadn't occurred to him, probably because Raymer couldn't imagine himself as anything other than what he was right then. Couldn't imagine that one day he would be a man. If he'd just kept reading, he would have learned this valuable lesson and been comforted by it, but he'd been too frightened.

Well, he thought, he would read the book now. There was a job that needed doing first, but after that, after Charice resumed her duties, Raymer would return to this churchyard, to this marsh, to this frightened boy. He owed that much to the old woman who'd had a higher opinion of him than he had of himself. Prove to her that he was no longer a frightened child.

======

AT HOME, Raymer plugged in the charger and set the BlackBerry on the kitchen counter, then stood there staring at it. Expecting . . . what? That it would vibrate or ping or give some other dramatic sign of returning to life? No such luck, though a tiny red light did appear in the middle of the device, which Raymer decided was probably a good omen. The thing was charging. Unless of course the charger was meant for another BlackBerry model entirely and was now quietly frying this one's innards. He'd check back later and find out.

He'd just sunk heavily onto the sofa when his own cell phone vibrated, and for a brief, irrational moment he thought that it must be the BlackBerry calling him, its owner anxious to explain things. But no, it was Charice. "Are you sure you want to do this?" she said when he picked up.

So. Bert Franklin hadn't wasted any time pitching his plan to make Raymer acting chief of police. "Do you want me to?"

"No?" she said. "Yes?"

"My feelings exactly," Raymer admitted. "What if I mess things up?"

"You won't."

"How about Jerome?" Because that had been Bert Franklin's great idea—to have Jerome come on board in a purely administrative role as Raymer's assistant, which would allow Raymer to keep an eye on him as he'd promised Charice he would do.

"He's gone out shopping," she informed him. "He says he needs some decent clothes to look the part. I just hope he stops there and doesn't buy a car."

"Wait. He left you alone?"

"I told him to go. Gave him the keys to my vehicle, in fact. He's pretending that he's doing this for me, but I can tell how excited he is. You've been good for him."

"He's been good for me, actually. But I'll come back to the hospital."

"No, they just gave me a sedative," she said, yawning convincingly. "I'm told I'll probably sleep until morning. Just promise me one thing?"

"What's that?"

"You won't do *too* good a job?" she said. "When I return to work, I want everybody but Delgado to be glad to see me."

"Hey, no worries," he assured her. "I'm not happy till you're not happy, right?"

She chuckled at this. "The problem is that the man who ran on that slogan doesn't really exist anymore."

# Atypical Behavior

INSTEAD OF TAKING Rub home to his studio apartment above the Rexall, Peter dropped him off at Harold's Automotive World so he could close the place up, and by the time Peter returned to Schuyler Springs it was late afternoon. At the police station a uniformed policewoman whose nameplate read D. HARRIS looked up from her desktop computer screen and smiled when Peter entered. "Please tell me the snow's stopped," she said, a friendly fellow sufferer.

"Just about," Peter told her.

"The streets bad?"

"They're not great."

"Lovely," she said, consulting her watch. "And me with a forty-minute drive over back roads to get home."

A common story, this. Increasingly, people who worked in the service sector—cops, firefighters, city employees—especially those with families, couldn't afford to live in Schuyler, the community they served. If *Schuyler Arts* were ever to expand its focus and mission to include deep-dive local news, as J.J. Julowitz was advocating, this would be a tale worth telling. "Go slow," he advised Officer Harris.

"Oh, I will," she smiled. "How can I help you?"

"I'm not sure. I was told my son spent the night here at the station."

"His name?" Her fingers were poised above the keyboard, her eyes on the screen.

"Thomas," he said. "Sullivan."

Her smile vanished. "Thomas Sullivan," she repeated, her eyes on him now, not the computer screen.

"That's right. Is he still here?"

She didn't answer right away. He could see her mind whirring, though why it should be, given his straightforward question, he couldn't imagine. "Are you aware that your son assaulted a police officer here at the station this morning?"

"No," Peter said. "Why would he do that?"

"You'd have to ask him."

"I will. Can I see him?"

"He's no longer at the station."

"Where is he?"

"First," she said, stone-faced, "I'll need to see some identification?"

"You need an ID to answer a simple question?"

"I'll need to be certain I know who I'm talking to," she informed him.

Peter gave her his driver's license. She studied it, compared its photo with the man who stood before her. "And you say you're his father?"

"Is that so hard to believe?"

"My understanding was that he's not from around here," she said, handing him his license back.

"You don't have relatives who live in other places?" he said.

She offered no response to this. Her mind was still buffering, he could tell.

"Okay, if he's not here, where is he?"

She seemed to arrive at a decision. "In the hospital, last I heard," she told him. "He was injured while resisting arrest."

*Ah,* Peter thought. *That* was the information she'd been so reluctant to reveal. "Injured how?"

"I just told you. He was resisting arrest."

"Right, but that's not what I was asking. Were his injuries serious? How many injuries are we talking about?"

"I wouldn't know. I do know it took two officers to subdue him, so . . ."

What another father would probably have said at this point was something along the lines of *That doesn't sound like my Tommy,* but what Will had said earlier was true. Peter really had no idea who Thomas was. "Would it be possible for me to speak to the arresting officers?"

More buffering now, until finally, as if under protest, she picked up the phone and punched two numbers. Elsewhere in the building a phone rang, but just once. "Bobby?" said Officer Harris. "Deb. Where's Del?" Peter could hear a male voice on the other end of the line, but not what the man said. "There's a guy here who claims to be Sullivan's father." Again that other muffled male voice. "I'm aware of that," Deb said. "That, too. Okay." She hung up.

"You can have a seat over there," she told him, indicating a small, adjacent waiting room. "Lieutenant Delgado's on his way to the station now."

"There's nothing else you can tell me, Deb?" Peter said, hoping that using her given name might restore their earlier friendly footing, but no dice.

"The lieutenant will speak to you when he arrives," she said, still stony-faced. When he was slow to obey her command, she again pointed to the waiting room.

What he ought to do, of course, was just leave. His most urgent questions about his son would be answered at the hospital, not here. Why continue to spin his wheels at the police station? Well, there were two reasons that he could think of. First, something definitely felt off about the way he was being received. If Thomas had in fact assaulted a police officer, it made sense that he himself wouldn't be warmly welcomed. But in addition to exhibiting anger, Officer Harris also seemed wary, as if she saw Peter as some sort of threat. Why? Had she and the other cops at the precinct been counting on Thomas being a friendless out-of-towner, someone without recourse or remedy? But admit it. There was another reason Peter wasn't eager to go to the hospital. A long-overdue reckoning awaited him there. Of course he'd be seen as complicit in whatever trouble his son had gotten himself into. How could he not? He could tell himself that he wasn't to blame if Thomas got so drunk he injured himself falling off a barstool. Nor would Peter be the proximate cause of any injuries inflicted on him by pissed-off cops. But still, if his son was a bad man, Peter had had a hand in making him one. Will would argue the point, but only out of loyalty. The facts were the facts, and when Peter went to the hospital, those facts, like so many chickens, would come home to roost.

There was a TV in the waiting room. A college basketball game was on with the sound turned down. There weren't any signs prohibiting cell phone use, so he used the remote to turn the TV up a notch and called J.J. Julowitz, who answered on the first ring. "What's up?"

"I'm at the police station. My son's been arrested."

"I thought he was in England."

"Different son. I'm being told that he assaulted a police officer, but, beyond that, nothing. I thought you might've picked up something on that scanner of yours."

"Nope, but I've got a contact or two down there. I'll rattle the cage."

"Okay, thanks."

"If I find out something juicy, it could be our first hard-news story."

"J.J.—"

"I'll call you back."

They hung up and a moment later the phone rang in the next room. Deb answered. "J.J.," she said. "What's going on?" As she listened, her face clouded over. "Sorry, J.J.," she said, peering around her computer screen at Peter. "I'm not at liberty to discuss that." And she abruptly hung up.

A moment later Peter's phone vibrated with a text from J.J.: *WOW! Tight lid on this.*

Peter texted back: *Heard that Schuyler cops smashed all the windows in my son's car last night. Why?*

J.J. came back immediately: *On it.* As Peter knew he would be. J.J. had yet to meet a pot he didn't want to stir. There were many groups of people he disapproved of, but cops were at or near the top of the list.

Outside, a horn tooted and tires sounded on gravel. Peter rose and parted the blinds, expecting to see a police cruiser pulling in. Instead, it was a nondescript sedan with a county license plate. At the wheel was a man wearing a plaid sport coat, no tie and dark glasses despite the low gray sky. His companion in the passenger seat was older, a uniformed policeman whose face was bruised and swollen. Three other uniformed cops and a fourth in plain clothes emerged from a side door to greet them. Peter saw that Deb Harris had left her desk to join them. When the cop with the swollen face was helped out of the vehicle a cheer went up. The man smiled in response, and Peter could see that he was missing several front teeth. *Thomas* did this? Peter thought, his heart sinking. A son of his had assaulted a police officer?

The plainclothes cop—Peter assumed he must be the Bobby that Deb just spoke to on the phone—now huddled with the sedan's driver, who still hadn't removed his sunglasses. Delgado, surely, and to Peter he had the look of a man who was receiving very unwelcome news. Deb joined them, nodding in the direction of the waiting room, and when all three turned in his direction, Peter let the blinds close and resumed his seat. He would wait here another five minutes, he decided, after which, though his stomach roiled at the thought, he would head to the hospital. Delgado arrived in two. He'd taken off his dark glasses and Peter thought he saw why the man chose to wear them even when they weren't needed. If those small, dark, too-close-together eyes were his, he'd have worn sunglasses, too. "Are you Mr. Sullivan?" the man said, extending his hand in greeting. Surprised by the gesture, Peter shook it. "I'm Lieutenant Delgado. How about we go somewhere we can talk privately."

Peter, wondering whose privacy the other man was concerned

for, nevertheless followed him down the long corridor at the end of which was an office with Delgado's name on it. Inside, the plain-clothes policeman from the parking lot leaned against a file cabinet.

"Have a seat," Delgado said, not bothering to introduce his colleague. He seemed intent on sizing Peter up—his chinos and V-neck sweater peeking out from his open parka, his clean-shaven face and clipped fingernails and white teeth—probably trying to square Peter's smooth appearance with Thomas's rougher one. "So, I understand you're the father of the man we arrested for assaulting our desk sergeant this morning?"

"Thomas, yes. If that's what happened, I apologize on his behalf."

"Oh, there's no *if* about it," said the man leaning against the file cabinet. "That's what happened."

"And now I understand Thomas is in the hospital?" Peter said.

"He resisted arrest," said the lieutenant. "Vigorously."

"Were you the arresting officers?" Peter asked.

"I was," Delgado said.

Peter regarded the other policeman.

"I'm just here to observe," he said. "In case assaulting police officers runs in the family."

Delgado held up a hand. "Now, now, Bobby. Let's not get off on the wrong foot here." Then, to Peter. "We're all a bit on edge today."

Peter nodded. "Again, I'm sorry about what happened to your sergeant."

"Thank you. We appreciate that, don't we, Bobby?"

Bobby looked like he appreciated it right up there with classical ballet, or maybe the foreign-language requirement back in high school.

"About your son," Delgado continued. "Last night, at a local establishment, he got so drunk he blacked out and fell off his barstool. Landed on his head. He's lucky he didn't kill himself."

"So I heard," Peter said, clearly startling the lieutenant. "I'm surprised no one thought to have him checked out before he was taken to jail."

Clearly wrong-footed, Delgado glanced over at the man called

Bobby. "I'm curious," he said. "How did *you* hear about the incident?"

It was tempting to say, *From your girlfriend,* but instead Peter said, "From someone who was there."

Delgado nodded thoughtfully. Bobby looked down at the floor. "Does this person have a name?"

Peter shrugged. "I wouldn't want to get anybody in trouble. I understand the establishment in question was open and serving alcohol long past closing time?"

The lieutenant studied Peter carefully, drumming the desktop with his fingertips. "Okay," he said finally, "let's return to your son. Would you describe his getting blackout drunk last night as typical or atypical?"

"I can't really say."

"Why not? You're his father."

"Because I really don't know him that well. His mother and I divorced when our kids were small. Thomas grew up with her and her second husband in West Virginia."

Bobby broke in now. "How about assaulting police officers? Would you describe that behavior as typical or atypical?"

"Again," Peter said.

"Right," Bobby snorted. "He's your son, but you don't know him."

"So, just to be clear," Delgado interrupted, "all those years? You never spent holidays together? Never went on vacations? Nothing like that?"

"No, nothing like that."

Now Bobby again. "And that doesn't strike you as fucked up? I only ask, because that's how it strikes me. As pretty fucked up."

"Thanks for weighing in," Peter said, though yeah, stated this baldly, it *did* seem pretty fucked up. "I was wondering how you felt about it."

Bobby stiffened at this, but Delgado held up his hand. "So," he continued, "you're saying all those years and no contact at all? Until yesterday?"

"That's correct."

Here Delgado paused, giving Peter the opportunity to volunteer more. When Peter just smiled, he continued, "What? He just dropped by? No warning?"

"Again, correct."

"You must've been pretty surprised."

Peter said nothing. When Delgado continued to stare at him expectantly, he said, "I'm sorry. Was that a question?"

"It was, but never mind," Delgado said. "So. You quarreled?"

"Not at all."

"Not at all," the other man repeated. "Really. So . . . a pleasant conversation?"

"Very."

"What did you talk about?"

"He brought me up to date on him and his brother. My house is being renovated. I showed him how the work was going."

"Would you say you parted on good terms?"

"Good enough. He said he was on his way to Montreal and needed to get back on the road. I invited him to stop by on his way back."

"And how did he respond to that invitation?"

"He said there wouldn't be time. He had to get back to work."

"Doing what?"

"He didn't say."

"And you didn't ask."

"Correct."

Bobby snorted. Delgado just sat there, smiling and drumming his fingers. He seemed to be under the mistaken impression that silence would be more uncomfortable to Peter than to him and his colleague. Having stood in front of a great many classrooms full of disinterested, resentful students who hadn't read the assignment, Peter felt no such discomfort. To this point both men had exuded confidence in their ability to make Peter feel complicit in his son's criminal behavior. They were clearly used to bullying and would continue to bully him if he let them. What they didn't suspect—why would they?—was that Peter understood a bit about bullying himself. In the end it all came down to authority, both real and imagined. His maternal grandfather, an imperious scholar, had possessed both types in spades, and he taught Vera, Peter's mother, a keen student, that education could serve many often-conflicting purposes. On the one hand, it could lead to a comfortable, if not extravagant, life. It could also make you a better person, a more dutiful and thoughtful citizen. On the other hand, it could be weaponized. The language spoken by highly educated people—its vocabulary and syntax, even its cadence—could be used as a cudgel, to demonstrate status and the power that came with it. Unlike his mother and grandfather, Peter didn't enjoy using language for such purposes, but he knew how.

"So," Delgado was saying, a smug smile on his face, "he lied to you about being headed to Montreal."

"Or," Peter said, smiling back, just as smugly, "he changed his mind."

"Which? If you had to guess."

"But I don't have to. I can just ask him when I see him. In the meantime, though, how about I ask *you* a question?"

Again, Delgado glanced over at his colleague. *Do you believe this guy?*

"Why am I being interviewed? Am I suspected of something besides negligent parenting?"

Delgado shrugged. "Just trying to understand why your son behaved like he did. He visits dear old dad after all these years and later that same night drinks himself into a coma. But you *say* you didn't quarrel."

"Because we didn't."

"I understand he was asked at some point if he had relatives here and he said no. Why would he do that if the two of you were getting along?"

"I have no idea," Peter said. "When exactly did this interview take place?"

Neither man seemed inclined to answer. When Peter's phone pinged with a text, both men heard it. In another situation he would have apologized for interrupting a conversation to look at his phone, but not now. The text, no surprise, was from J.J.: *RE: DELGADO. Of all the dirty Schuyler cops, this guy's the dirtiest. Long history of violence particularly in the North Side. He's the one who broke the car windows.*

Returning the phone to his pocket, Peter continued, "So, Mr. Delgado—"

"Lieutenant Delgado," the man corrected.

Peter waved this away. "Whatever. Am I to understand that you were involved in both last night's incident at the tavern *and* my son's arrest this morning?"

"Yes."

"Would you describe that as unusual? Being at the tavern where Thomas was drinking last night, and then being the arresting officer this morning? I only ask," he said, glancing over at Bobby now, "because it strikes *me* as unusual. Possibly even fucked up."

Both men stiffened, but Delgado remained calm. "I wouldn't say it was that unusual," he said. "How about you, Bobby? Would you say it was unusual?"

"Fuck, no," Bobby said. "Not at all."

"I understand you broke all the windows in my son's car this morning," Peter continued, pausing to see if Delgado would deny this. He didn't. "Would you describe such behavior as typical or atypical of the police here in Schuyler Springs?"

"You know what?" Bobby said. "Fuck you."

Delgado just smiled and leaned back in his chair, locking his fingers behind his head. He studied Peter for a long beat. "You're one cool customer, Mr. Sullivan. Most people are nervous when questioned by the police. But you? You feel free to mock us. Do you mind if I ask what you do for a living?"

"Not at all," Peter told him. "I'm a professor at SCCC. I also edit *Schuyler Arts,* a local magazine."

Bobby snorted at this. "Never heard of it."

Peter smiled at him. "The magazine or the college?"

"See what I mean, Bobby?" Delgado said. His small eyes had

gotten even darker, a place where light went to die. "More mockery. I think what Mr. Sullivan is *really* saying here is that he makes more money than we do. That's why he's not scared of us."

"Or that I'm smarter," Peter offered. "I might be saying that."

Bobby, who this whole time had been leaning against the filing cabinet, now stood up straight.

"Or," Peter continued, really channeling his mother and grandfather now, "I might just be saying that I have an excellent lawyer. I *might* be saying all of those things." He paused here for a long beat. "But then again, you could just be imagining it."

"What do you think, Bobby?" Delgado said, swiveling now in his chair. "Are we imagining Mr. Sullivan's mockery?"

"Seems pretty real to me."

Was it Peter's imagination, or had some of the wind gone from both men's sails?

"Anyway," Peter said, rising to his feet. "It's time I went to the hospital to see what sort of injury you've done to my son. Before I go, though, would you mind giving me the name of the other arresting officer?"

"He's no longer a member of the department, actually."

"He was this morning but not now?"

"That's correct."

Peter nodded. "This whole thing might make an interesting article. That magazine I mentioned earlier? We're thinking about expanding our focus to include in-depth local news. You know. Race relations, corrupt politicians, sadistic cops. That sort of thing." Opening the office door, he paused in the entryway. "Open or shut?"

"Close it, please," Delgado said. "Gently." As if he suspected Peter intended to slam it. Peter did as instructed, but once outside, instead of heading back up the corridor, he lingered by the door. It was Bobby who finally broke the silence inside the office. "You know what, Del?" he said. "The way I see it, this can now officially be classified as a shitshow."

# More

W HEN HER CELL PHONE rang and she saw that it was Del calling again, Janey happened to be staring at Roger Thorne's tenth-grade photo in her high-school yearbook and thinking about what her mother said earlier—that there was such a thing as being too late. Was it possible, she wondered, that these two seemingly unrelated activities were somehow linked? She decided not. *Was it too late to sell Hattie's?* Probably. The time to do that was before the recession took hold, back when there was still a place called North Bath. Now she'd basically be giving it away. Her mother was right, though. She was exhausted all the time, and bad decisions were often born of exhaustion. The problem was that if she sold, like Del wanted her to, she would likely descend even further into what she'd come to think of as Del World. She'd have to find a cheap apartment in Schuyler and pick up waitressing shifts at the Green Hand until something better came along, which might never happen. She was pretty sure she and Del weren't going to last much longer. Still, even if her mother was right about her need to start making changes while she still could, there didn't seem to be a way to do so incrementally. Once the dominoes started falling, there'd be no stopping them. She'd lose her work, her home and the only man in her life, with no clear plan for replacing any of these, at least not in the near future.

She thought about letting Del's call just go to voice mail, but he'd just call back a few minutes later, and if she still didn't answer, he'd probably come looking for her, and she wanted to see him even less than she wanted to talk to him. "Del," she said, finally picking up on the eighth ring, and not bothering to sound happy that he was calling.

Nor did he bother to sound anything but miffed. "Where are you?" This question, she knew all too well, was not born of curiosity. His point was that she was not with him, not where she was supposed to be, which rendered where she actually was irrelevant.

"Home," she told him.

"I thought we were going to meet up tonight."

Immediately, her hackles went up. "Why?"

He didn't answer right away, which probably meant that he was segueing from miffed to aggravated. From there he'd slow burn his way through his narrow, all-too-predictable range of negative emotions, from upset to riled up, to incensed, all the way to infuriated. Hacked off would also be in there somewhere.

"We discussed this when I called you earlier," he reminded her.

"I had a restaurant full of customers," she told him, though this wasn't true. By then the morning rush was over, just a few stragglers at the counter chatting over the dregs of their third free coffee refill. "I said I'd think about it. *You* said by then you might have another date."

"That was a fucking joke and you know it."

"It sounded like a fucking threat."

"Look," he said, "can we stop with the bullshit?"

And *whoa!* Just like that, she'd made her decision. Here again, though she hated to admit it, her mother was right. It was time to quit doing the same things over and over and expecting different results. "I don't want to see you tonight, Del," she told him. "In fact, I don't think we should see each other at all anymore."

"And just where the *fuck* is this coming from all of a sudden?"

*Okay,* she thought. Forget the slow burn. In a matter of seconds the never completely cold embers of his anger had flared into a blaze. She wondered yet again if it was only a matter of time before he hit her. "It's not all of a sudden," she told him.

"Bullshit. We fucked each other's brains loose last night."

This was kind of true, but also not. Their sex—what she remembered of it—had been energetic but otherwise unexceptional. Okay, he'd scratched an itch, give him that much. But fucking *Roy* had scratched that same itch, which suggested there wasn't a whole lot of skill involved. Maybe the time had come to take a page from her own daughter's playbook. Learn to live without a man in her life, at least for a while. Maybe get a dog. They were a lot less trouble. Surely she'd be able to find one that wasn't as pitiful as Jacks. "Look, Del," she said. "No hard feelings, okay? We had a few laughs. But I'm not in love with you and I know you're not in love with me. Half the time I don't think you even like me."

"I like you fine except when you're being a cunt."

"Which you think is pretty much all the time, right?"

"You said that, I didn't."

"So why would you even give a shit if we stopped seeing each other?"

"Tell me why. Last night everything was fine. Now it isn't. Who have you been talking to?"

"Myself."

That seemed to bring him up short, but only for a second. "And that's supposed to mean what, exactly?"

"It means when I wake up in the morning after being out with you, I don't like myself." No need to mention how much she hated the way he ground his teeth when he was asleep, especially after they had sex, as if dreaming about it pissed him off. "I mean, really. Last night? We tossed a guy who might've been seriously hurt into the fucking trunk of your car. And then later? Bungeeing the poor guy to that trolley and wheeling him inside?"

"I don't recall you objecting."

"That's my point, Del. Doing crazy shit like that always seems kind of funny at the time, but the next day I think, What the fuck? I'm sorry, but I don't like who I am when I'm with you."

"Sounds like your problem is you."

She ignored this. "And I don't like the stories you tell. They're all about humiliating people."

"They're about being a cop."

She ignored this. "And what I *really* don't like," she explained, "is that I laugh at them because I don't want to be the only one who doesn't think they're funny."

He was quiet then for a long beat. Finally, he said, "It was you, wasn't it."

"I'm sorry, what?"

"What did you tell him?"

"Tell who?"

"Do *not* fucking bullshit me, Janey. It wasn't one of my crew, so it had to be you."

"Del," she said. "What the fuck are you talking about?" Though she had a pretty good idea.

"That 'poor guy' we bungeed to the trolley? His name was Sullivan. Thomas Sullivan. His father was just in here. He knew all about last night at the Hand."

"That's because he and my mother are friends."

"And how did *she* know?"

"Because I told her."

"And why would you do that?"

"Why *wouldn't* I? She asked me if I had a good time at the Hand last night and I gave her a recap. What was I supposed to say? Mind your own business?"

"So what exactly did you tell her?"

"I told her what happened, okay? That there was a guy at the bar who got so shit-faced, he fell off his stool and we ended up dropping him off at the police station on our way home."

"And from this she figured out who the guy was?"

"No, she recognized his car. She knew Peter Sullivan's son was in town and he was driving an old yellow Caddy with West Virginia plates."

"Great. So now, as if I didn't have enough problems, I have to deal with *this*."

"The reason you have problems is because you do stupid shit, Del. You and your dumb-ass cop friends."

"Okay, fuck this. You've got thirty minutes."

"To do what?"

"To get your ass out to the Hand. You're going to tell me every single thing you said to your mother, and I'm going to tell you every single thing you're going to say to the cops if they want to talk to you."

"I'm not fucking lying for you, Del. I'm not."

"Thirty minutes."

"Or what, Del? What happens then?"

"Thirty minutes," he repeated, and then the line was dead.

Probably just as well, or he would've heard her tell him to go fuck himself.

═══

TINA PICKED UP on the first ring. "Wow," she said. "We're talking twice in one day."

"Yeah, I know," Janey said. "I don't know what to make of it myself."

"You sound kind of . . ."

"Kind of what?" she said, because whatever she was sounding like, she was trying not to, and here was her daughter, emotional tuning fork that she was, picking up on it.

"Not like you," Tina explained.

"I'm fine," Janey lied, she hoped, convincingly. "Have I caught you at a bad time?"

"No."

"Okay," Janey said, then stalled. Where to begin? "I'm thinking about selling the restaurant."

"Wow," Tina said again. Her daughter was the only person Janey knew who could say that word without conveying a lick of excitement or surprise.

"I guess I'm wondering if you have any thoughts on the subject."

"Do you want to?"

"I don't know," she said. "I'm exhausted all the time. It's barely breaking even. I guess the real question is who'd want to buy it."

"Do you want me to?"

*Jesus,* Janey thought. Earlier she'd offered to buy her a new car. Now the restaurant. "You could really do that?" she said, dumbfounded, though she shouldn't have been. "Just decide to buy a restaurant without having to think about it?"

"If you want me to."

"Well, I don't."

"Okay."

Janey could almost hear her daughter thinking the obvious question she wouldn't give voice to: *Then what do you want?* "It's just that your grandmother thinks I should make some changes in my life while there's still time. She's right, I guess. I'm definitely in a rut. I just don't know how to go about getting out of it, you know?"

Silence. She *didn't* know. How would she?

"Actually," Janey continued, "since talking to you this morning, I've been wondering how *you* do it."

"Do what?"

*Live,* she seemed to mean. *Face the unending days. Put one foot in front of the other.* "You just seem so . . . together. So self-contained. Like you have everything you need."

"What do *you* need?"

God, Janey thought, the conversation wasn't going anywhere. What had possessed her to think it would? "Actually, I called to get Roger Thorne's phone number. Do you think he'd mind me having it?"

Tina recited the number, and Janey tapped it into her phone. Though her daughter hadn't asked for an explanation, Janey decided to offer one anyway. "Your grandmother told me this completely ridiculous thing about him earlier and I want to ask him about it."

"Okay."

*Okay?* Janey wanted to scream. Who could hear the phrase *completely ridiculous thing* and not want to know what that thing was? "All right," she sighed. "I'll let you go." Though she didn't want to. There were all sorts of other things she wanted to say, a whole litany of questions she wanted to ask, but even if she could remember what they were, they'd all get one-word responses, and they'd make her want to cry. In fact, she was on the verge of tears right now. "One last quick question, okay?"

"Okay."

Again, she stalled. How to ask it? If she sold Hattie's and moved to Schuyler and found a job there, they'd be that much farther apart. Would Tina care? Would she even notice? Finally, she said, "Would you like more of me in your life or less?"

Her daughter didn't hesitate. "More," she said.

"Okay," Janey said, the tears coming fast now. "Okay."

═

THE OLD HIGH-SCHOOL yearbook still lay open on her lap, and though she still didn't see what fifteen-year-old Roger Thorne had to do with the dilemma of whether or not to sell the restaurant and otherwise extricate herself from the rut she was in, she decided they must be connected somehow or she wouldn't have asked Tina for his number.

"Hey," Roger said, when Janey identified herself. "Are you crying?"

"No," Janey said, then thought, *What the hell.* "Maybe a little."

"Something wrong?"

"Not really," she told him. "I just got off the phone with Tina, is all. She makes me cry, sometimes."

"Yeah," he said. "I guess I can understand that."

Really? He could? "I was wondering if maybe you might want to go out for a beer sometime."

"Like when?"

"How about now? Your job would be to cheer me up. Do you think you're up to that?"

"I could try," he said. "Where?"

"Someplace close, given the weather," she said, then immediately felt like an idiot because she had no idea where Roger lived. If he lived in the boonies, where the roads probably weren't plowed yet, getting into town might be a chore. "The Horse maybe?" On a Sunday night the place would be slow and quiet. Birdie would be pleased to see them.

"Sounds good," Roger said. "How about I pick you up? You still living out back of Hattie's?"

So, she thought. She had no idea where he lived and he knew right where she did. Was it possible that what Ruth had told her was true? Had her mother been right, as Tina had just put it, "twice in one day"? "If it's not too much trouble," she said.

"I'll be there in ten."

"Great," she said, wiping away the last of her tears. "Thank you." But he'd already hung up.

# Ad Infinitum

$R$AYMER AWOKE in his recliner when a cat jumped into his lap. Except that when he opened his eyes, there was no cat. There wouldn't be, of course, since Raymer didn't have one. What had somehow dropped into his lap was his own threadbare sweater, the one Jerome had been wearing to ward off attractive white women. Looking up, Raymer saw that a tall, slender, clean-shaven, elegantly dressed Black man was standing over him. "Who you are you?" Raymer said.

Jerome looked pleased to be asked. "The name is Bond," he said, in a vaguely British accent. "Jerome Bond."

"Ah," Raymer said, sitting up straight. "Welcome back, double-oh-seven. I didn't hear you come in."

"You were really out, Dawg. Thanks for the loan," he added, indicating the cat/cardigan. "I won't be needing it anymore."

"So I see," Raymer said, rubbing the sleep out of his eyes. Charice hadn't been kidding. Her brother had indeed gone shopping. His new ensemble—gray dress slacks over shiny new ankle-high boots, charcoal crew-neck sweater, leather sport coat—looked costly. His hair, Raymer noted, was different, too, shorter and more symmetrical. "Where'd you find a barber open on a Sunday afternoon in the middle of a snowstorm?"

"Did the deed myself," Jerome informed him proudly, holding up an electric razor that had a comblike attachment. When he turned it on, the thing buzzed angrily, and Raymer realized he'd actually been hearing that same buzzing in his sleep. With the bathroom door closed, it hadn't been loud enough to wake him up.

"Do I want to look in the sink?" Raymer asked.

"Cleaned up after myself," Jerome assured him. "I'm not a slob, like some people. I'd give it another minute or two before going in there, though."

Raymer nodded. "You defecated?"

Jerome looked embarrassed to admit that a man like himself, who cut such a fine sartorial figure, would be subject to the same disagreeable bodily functions as slobs like Raymer.

"Okay, I'm curious," Raymer said. "What happened to your fear of white women falling in love with you and getting you lynched?"

"Gonna be wearing a badge again," said Jerome. "Need to look the part. Already paying dividends, too. Got myself invited out for drinks at that wine bar in Schuyler."

"Infinitum?"

Jerome sighed. "Infinity, Dawg. The place is called Infinity. The Latin phrase you're thinking of is 'ad infinitum,' not 'infinitum.'"

Raymer ignored this. "So where did you meet this woman?" He wondered if it might be a grateful saleswoman at the mall where he'd purchase all these pricey new clothes.

"The hospital," Jerome informed him.

"Seriously?"

"I stopped by to show Charice my new threads, but she was fast asleep."

"And a white woman you never met before took one look at you and asked you out?"

Jerome shook his head. "I knew her from when I lived here before, Dawg. Pam Qadry. She—"

"Whoa! Time-out," Raymer said, making a referee's T with his hands. "Are we talking about *Doctor* Qadry?"

Jerome nodded. "Used to see her, back when I was crazy." After Becka's death, he meant. Fascinating, really, that Jerome considered himself sane now. In Raymer's opinion the jury was still out.

"I still do," Raymer informed him.

Jerome made a face. "This whole time?"

"What can I say, Jerome. I'm seriously messed up." Also confused. "So, she was visiting Charice?" He'd long suspected the two women of being in cahoots, of waging some sort of covert psychological warfare designed to improve him. Working against this theory was its extreme unlikelihood. Maybe, it occurred to Raymer, Jerome wasn't the only one whose sanity was in question.

Now it was Jerome who looked confused. "Why would Pam be visiting Charice?"

"I don't know," Raymer admitted. "Why else would she be at the hospital?"

Jerome shrugged. "I assumed she was visiting some crazy person in the psych ward. That's where *I* met her."

"Also?" Raymer said. "How do you know her name is Pam?"

"She told me."

"Why?"

"I don't know, Dawg. Isn't that what people do?"

It certainly wasn't what she'd done with Raymer, despite having a good decade's worth of opportunity. "So, she just walked up to you and said, *Hey, there, Jerome. Remember me? Pam Qadry? How about you and I go out for a drink?*"

Jerome studied him now. "You know what I think?" he said. "I think you're jealous because it's me she liked the look of and not you."

"Here we go again," Raymer said. "We're back to plumage."

"Admit it," Jerome said, heading for the bedroom he'd so recently refused to occupy. "When you go see her, you wear that sweater."

Did he? It was possible. *Was* he jealous? Also possible.

Raymer had put his cell on silent mode before drifting off, and there were now two new messages. Needing to pee, he took the phone with him into the bathroom, closing the door behind him. Jerome was right. He should've given it another minute or two, but the sink, as promised, was pristine. Here was the upside of having an obsessive-compulsive for a roommate.

The first message was from Bert Franklin, who'd called to let him know that he and Jerome were all set up. An email had gone out to the whole department informing its members that Raymer would be in charge of operations for a few days until Chief Bond was ready to resume her duties. To which, Franklin admitted, the response had so far been mixed. The union rep would be filing a complaint, but no worries on that score, since Charice would be back on the job before it could be formally considered. Raymer and Jerome could pick up their badges and radios first thing in the morning. Raymer would be issued a weapon. Unfortunately, since Jerome's duties would be primarily administrative and because it had been a decade since he'd been a police officer in the state of New York, he did not qualify for a firearm, though Franklin promised to check on whether he might be issued a taser. In any event, probably best to avoid shoot-out-type situations. Raymer couldn't tell how much of this was said in jest.

The second message came from a local number Raymer didn't recognize. Flushing the toilet and lowering the lid, he sat down and pressed RETURN. A young woman answered on the first ring. "Oh, God," she said, "thank you so much for calling me back. I'm at my wit's end. I've never seen him like this before."

"I'm sorry," Raymer replied, since the woman's voice wasn't familiar. "Who am I speaking to?"

"Fawn Miller," she said. "Jimmy's wife."

"What's going on?"

"A creepy reporter came by earlier wanting to talk to him. I think his name was Julowitz."

Which was the name of the photographer who'd taken his picture at the Sans Souci yesterday.

"Now Jimmy says we have to leave Schuyler. He's packing his things right now."

"Really?"

"I'm happy here. I love my job. But he won't listen."

"Okay, let me talk to him."

Though he couldn't imagine why, Fawn Miller put her hand over the phone then, so that both her and her husband's voices were muffled. After a brief exchange she came back on the line. "He says you're not his boss anymore. He says, 'Chief Bond is the chief.'" Here she imitated Miller's voice, causing Raymer to wonder what it would be like to be married to a woman so skilled at mimicry. Charice made fun of him all the time, but always in her own voice, not his. It hadn't occurred to him to be grateful for that until now.

"Tell him I actually am his boss again," he instructed Miller's wife. "Tell him I've just been named acting chief of police while Chief Bond is in the hospital. Until his resignation letter is officially accepted, he's still a member of the department and has to do what I say." This was utter bullshit, of course, but he knew Miller and knew that he was one of those people who actually enjoyed being ordered around, who wanted nothing more in life than a detailed behavioral blueprint.

More muffled voices, then, "He says okay."

"Good," Raymer said. "Has he stopped packing?"

"Yes," she told him. "He's just sitting on the edge of the bed and staring off into space. He looks so pitiful."

Raymer didn't know what to say to this, but he could picture the man, and *pitiful* was the right word.

"He told me . . ."

"What?" Raymer said.

"He said he was in love with Chief Bond and that she was in the hospital because of him."

"Tell him that's not true."

"He says he failed her and he failed me and he failed you and he failed his profession and that I deserved better and so do you and Chief Bond and he can't live here anymore because he would be a laughingstock."

"Tell him none of that is true."

"I already did."

"Okay, but tell him *I* said it's not." Because for Miller it was always about authority, which at the moment Raymer possessed and his wife didn't.

This time she didn't put her hand over the phone. "Chief Raymer says you're not a laughingstock."

"Tell him he's the only officer I know personally who actually saved somebody's life."

Raymer waited while she relayed this to Miller.

"He wants to know who."

"Put him on the phone."

Raymer heard heavy footsteps approach, then Miller taking the phone from his wife. "Chief," he said, nearly choking on the word.

"Miller."

"Whose life did I save?"

"Sully's, remember? The night he had the heart attack in his driveway and you rushed him straight to the hospital?"

"You said I should've called an ambulance."

"I was wrong," Raymer told him, though that *was* what he should've done.

"You're really the chief again?" Miller wanted to know.

"Just for a couple days, but here's what I want you to do. First, tell your wife you love her."

"Okay, I will."

"Not later. Now," Raymer clarified. There was a pause, but Raymer heard him say it. "Now tell her you were infatuated with Chief Bond a long time ago, before you met Fawn, but that's over now."

"Except it isn't."

"Yes, it is." Raymer insisted, as if he and not Miller was the final arbiter of the other man's emotions. "Tell her."

Reluctantly, Miller did as instructed. To Raymer, it didn't sound entirely convincing, but it wasn't completely unconvincing, either.

It would have to do, regardless. "Okay, good," Raymer said. "Now unpack everything you packed and put it back where it was. You and I will meet first thing in the morning and figure all this out."

"I can't go back to the station," Miller said, and *this* did sound convincing.

"Okay, how about Hattie's in Bath?" Raymer suggested, since at some point he would probably want to interview Janey. He didn't know how long she'd been seeing Delgado or how committed she might be to their relationship, but it was possible she had information that would be useful if she could be persuaded to part with it.

"What time?" Miller wanted to know.

"Seven-thirty."

"Seven-thirty," Miller repeated.

"Okay, good," Raymer said. "Now give the phone back to your wife."

When Fawn Miller was back on the line, he said, "He'll be okay now." Which, for all Raymer knew, might even be true. "After I hang up, tell him you're proud of him. Tell him he's a good policeman. Tell him he's doing the right thing. Tell him Chief Bond is on his side and so am I."

"Okay," she said, but he could hear in her voice that she was a much-tougher sell than her husband. "What's going to happen?" was what she wanted him to tell her. To her husband's job, she seemed to mean. To their marriage and future.

Raymer started to tell her he didn't know, but then thought, Why start telling the truth now? "It's all going to work out," he said.

"Promise?"

"I promise," Raymer said, then quickly hung up, because if he stayed on the line, his next sentence would likely begin with the word *maybe,* or a phrase like *with a little luck,* and what this poor, suffering woman wanted from him was certainty.

When he opened the bathroom door, Jerome, who'd donned a handsome topcoat and a dark, tweed flatcap, was standing on the other side of it. "That was good work," he said. If he was embarrassed to have been caught eavesdropping, he gave no sign.

"Yeah?" Raymer said. "I think I just told her what she wanted to hear."

"*Needed* to hear, Dawg."

Which sounded to Raymer like the sort of thing Dr. Qadry (Pam!) would say. She, too, seemed to believe the truth was overrated, or if not overrated at least inadequate in many real-world situations. "She really asked you out? Dr. Qadry?"

Jerome nodded somberly, as if suddenly assailed by doubt. "You think I should've said no?"

"It's none of my business, Jerome."

"I don't have to go if you need me," he said, following Raymer into the front room.

"Go," Raymer told him. "I won't need you until tomorrow morning. If anything unexpected comes up, I'll call your cell and leave a message." And since the cat/cardigan was his again, he pulled it on, causing Jerome to wince.

"I've been wearing that, Dawg. Like every day. Don't you don't want to have it dry-cleaned first?"

Raymer ignored this. "Go," he repeated. "And if you order food, eat it while it's hot. Don't chop it into little pieces first. Pretend you're not crazy."

"Is that what you do?"

"Exactly. That's exactly what I do."

And off Jerome went, tripping down the three flights of stairs like a teenager who'd just been given the keys to the family station wagon. Raymer went over to the window and watched him emerge onto the unshoveled walkway below. Only when Jerome had gotten into Charice's SUV, backed out of his parking space, made the turn onto Upper Main Street and disappeared from view, did Raymer realize he was apprehensive. This morning at Hattie's he'd found Jerome's crippling anxieties, especially his fear some white woman would fall in love with him and get him lynched, beyond ludicrous. Now here he was worried those anxieties might be rooted in something akin to reality. Moreover, he was pretty sure that if Charice were here, she'd be worried as well, though for a different reason.

She'd be worried about Jerome being Jerome. For her brother the act of falling in love was dangerous in itself. It happened quickly and irrevocably, his reason subverted, all of his defenses collapsing at once, as they had done with Becka and later, apparently, with the art therapy woman down south. As Charice had explained to Raymer more than once, Jerome believed that women possessed the power to free him from himself, from the toxic mix of obsessions and pathologies and rituals that otherwise governed his life. They could, he believed, cure him. Under love's spell he became a different kind of crazy, a borderline ecstatic, or so Charice believed. When love didn't last—and according to Charice, it never did—the old Jerome would return, even more incapacitated than before.

But who knew? Maybe this time it would be different. Maybe Dr. Qadry (Pam!) would be the one. Raymer hoped so. In fact, he couldn't quite believe how much he hoped so. Was it only twenty-four hours ago that his spirits had plummeted at the sight of this same man standing there with his two suitcases, looking like a Black Willy Loman, in the middle of the Horse's dining room, wanting to be driven to the airport so he could fly back home? Right then, Raymer would have cheerfully offered his services. Whereas now he was worried that Jerome's going out for drinks with a registered therapist at Infinitum, an upscale wine bar, might be dangerous. Thank God odious Dougie had been banished. What a field day he would've had with this.

Below, the street was quiet, blanketed with snow. The plow had covered all but the very top of the FOR SALE sign on the terrace. He told himself the same thing he'd told Fawn Miller a few minutes earlier—that it would work out. All of it. Every last thing.

# Gasoline

A T THE HOSPITAL, Peter told the woman at the welcome desk that he was there to see his son. When he gave her Thomas's name, she peered at her computer screen and said, "Huh. According to this, he's been transferred."

"To another hospital?"

"No, to the ICU. An hour ago."

"I don't understand," Peter told her, though she clearly didn't, either.

"They should be able to tell you more upstairs," she said, then gave him directions to intensive care.

When he stepped off the elevator, an attractive woman at the nurses' station appeared to recognize him. She looked to be in her early thirties. "Professor Sullivan," she smiled, extending her hand. Her ID read R. DECKER, but that didn't ring any bells. "You don't remember me. Rebecca. I took your intro to lit class at Edison. My name was Clooney back then."

That she remembered him after so long—it had been well over a decade since he'd taught at Edison—was flattering, but then an alarming thought slithered into his brain. Had he slept with her? Which was absurd. Of course he hadn't. In his years as an adjunct professor, both at Edison and later in the New York City area, he'd had his share of hookups, but never with students, though there'd been opportunities for those as well. Why, then, should he be visited by such an outlandish fictional scenario? Was it possible that his encounter with Delgado and his partner back at the police station had rattled him more than he cared to admit? After successfully parrying their thinly veiled accusations and taunts—*And that doesn't strike you as fucked up?*—and actually turning the rhetorical tables on them, he'd left the station feeling borderline jubilant. Now, though, he wondered if their innuendos had done more damage than he realized. Arriving here at the ICU, had he been subconsciously expecting more suspicion and mistrust? Was that why Rebecca Decker's remembering him fondly wrong-footed him? If so, it made a kind of sense. Had he been asked yesterday if he was a good father, he would have thought of Will, a model son, and replied in the affirmative. But Thomas's reappearance had provided powerful evidence to the contrary, casting into doubt some fundamental assumptions about himself.

"I enjoy reading *Schuyler Arts,*" Rebecca Decker was saying. "Your reviews in particular."

He thanked her for that, then explained why he'd come.

"Oh, of course!" she said. "Thomas Sullivan is your son. I just this minute came from his room. I didn't make the connection."

Peter thought about saying, *Neither did I,* but the joke would've been both lame and too heavily freighted with truth. "I'm surprised he's in intensive care. I was told his injuries weren't life-threatening."

She nodded. "I understand. He seemed to be recovering just fine from surgery on his jaw, but then he began vomiting. That's not unusual for someone who has a concussion, but his jaw was wired shut." Here, she winced. "He could've choked to death."

"This is the first I've heard about any concussion," he told her, though the news wasn't terribly surprising, given the hard fall he'd taken off his barstool the night before.

"One of the doctors noticed a large knot on the back of his head, so he was taken for a CT scan and, sure enough, he's suffered a severe concussion."

"Will he be okay?"

"Dr. Malik is with him now. He's our traumatic brain injury specialist. I'll let him know you're here."

There was a waiting area nearby where three other people were all talking on cell phones despite a sign on the wall prohibiting their use. Since the rule wasn't being enforced, Peter decided to call Ruth, who had surprised him at the cemetery that morning by revealing that his father had asked her to check on him. Why, Peter wondered, had Sully thought that would be necessary? Had he somehow foreseen Thomas's return, or did he harbor some other misgiving? When she picked up, he said, "You were right. That was Thomas at the Green Hand last night."

"Where is he now?"

"In the hospital. The ICU actually."

"That doesn't sound good."

"I don't know the whole story, but he apparently assaulted a police officer at the station this morning. Knocked a couple of his teeth out."

"Why would he do that?"

"I don't know, but he resisted arrest and got roughed up pretty bad. Broken jaw, among other injuries."

"That's terrible."

"There's more. The cops took a tire iron to his car. Broke all the windows and mirrors. Basically totaled the thing. Guess who the arresting officer was?"

Ruth was quiet then. "Should I come down to the hospital? It sounds like you could use some moral support."

"There's no need for that," he assured her, though he was moved that she would offer, since she'd either have to beg a ride or take a taxi. "There's something else," he continued. The real reason he'd called her, actually, though now that he had the opportunity, he wasn't sure he wanted to give voice to a suspicion that over the course of the day had morphed into a conviction. "Thomas had several containers of gasoline in the trunk of his car."

Again Ruth was silent. Finally she said, "What are you thinking,

Peter?" When he didn't immediately answer, she said, "You might as well tell me."

"He claimed he was on his way to Montreal, that he just stopped by Bath on a whim, but I don't believe that."

"I don't either," she said. "He came to see his father."

"Turns out he's been in trouble in West Virginia. Multiple arrests for drunk and disorderly. A bunch of dustups with the cops there. He's spent a fair amount of time in the county lockup. For all I know this might be just the tip of the iceberg."

"What are you saying?"

"I think he blames me. For both his shitty life and Will's good one. And I think he came here to burn down the house that he and his younger brother never got to live in."

"Aren't you getting a little ahead of yourself?" she said. "There could be a perfectly innocent explanation, you know. For the gas."

"Not really, Ruth. One gas can, maybe. But not a trunkful of them. I didn't want to admit it yesterday, but everything about his visit rang false."

"Still," Ruth said, clearly dubious. "Were you ever that angry at your own father?"

"No," Peter admitted, "but he didn't completely disappear from my life. And when I was older, as you know, he threw me a rope when I needed one. If Thomas really is angry enough to burn down the house that Will got to live in and he and his brother didn't . . ." He let the thought trail off.

"Have you considered the possibility that he *didn't* want to?"

"I don't follow."

"Well, say you're right. Say he came here intending to burn your house down. But in the end, he didn't, right? He drove to the Green Hand and drank until he passed out. Sounds to me like maybe he turned his anger at you against himself."

That possibility hadn't occurred to him. "Do *you* think that's what happened?"

"I have no idea," she told him. "And neither do you."

*And if he dies,* Peter thought, *I never will.*

═══

"IT'S NOT A COMA, exactly," Dr. Malik explained. "It's called a minimally conscious state."

They were standing at the foot of Thomas's bed, where he lay hooked up to an IV and several beeping monitors. His eyes were almost, but not quite, shut, giving him the appearance of someone pretending to be asleep but all the while slyly observing.

"The good news," Malik continued, "is that the scan showed no fracturing of the skull, and there's no evidence of hematoma or swelling of the brain."

"Was it the fall off his barstool that caused the concussion?" Peter said. "Or having his jaw broken?" Better if it was the latter, of course, because that would mean the arresting officers were at fault. Otherwise, even if Ruth was right and his son drank until he blacked out to avoid doing what he came all this way to do, then his son's "minimally conscious state" was on Peter.

"It's impossible to know for sure," Malik told him, "but most likely it was the fall. The broken jaw was what's called a secondary insult. That's not to say it wasn't a contributing factor."

"And his prognosis?"

Malik massaged his chin. "For the time being, he's stable, and the objective is to keep him that way. Let new axons form in the cortex. Basically, his brain will try its best to repair itself, and will succeed or fail depending on the amount of damage done to it. Some patients with MCS simply wake up. Others can slip into a coma or even a vegetative state."

Peter studied his son, whose face was grotesquely swollen. He'd been cleaned up, but whoever did it had missed a spot of vomit on his neck. "Is he in pain?"

"Unlikely. It's a bit like being under anesthesia during an operation. You're mostly unaware, but even though other parts of the brain are offline, auditory stimuli in particular can and often do penetrate. That's why we encourage talking to MCS patients, even if they're unresponsive. The voices of loved ones are often helpful."

"Unfortunately, my son and I are estranged," Peter told him. Somehow that admission was even more painful now than it had been at the police station. "He might not even recognize my voice."

"Then tell him who you are."

Peter inhaled deeply. "The thing is, I'm pretty sure he's angry at me. What if hearing my voice causes him further distress?" What if it was causing him distress right now? Was it Peter's imagination or had Thomas's eyes just flickered?

Dr. Malik shook his head. "The problem is that you're imagining him *thinking,* and that's not really what he's doing. He's just responding to external stimuli. Light. Sound. Touch. If someone were to take his hand, he might register the fact and know he's not alone. If you talk to him, he probably won't have much understanding of what you're saying beyond noting your presence. It won't remind him that he's angry or why. Your presence will simply be noted. Later, if he wakes up, it's unlikely he'll remember any specifics, only that you were here, talking to him."

Peter noted that the man had said *if,* not *when.* "So, it doesn't matter what I say?"

"I wouldn't go quite that far, but I wouldn't worry too much about saying the wrong thing. Tell him a funny story. Tell him what you had for breakfast. The plot of a movie, even." Peter must have looked discouraged or uncertain, because the other man said, "Can I ask you something?"

Peter nodded.

"You say you and your son are estranged?"

"For a long time, yes. He's had a difficult life."

"Do you think he wants to live?"

Peter remembered what Ruth had said on the phone about Thomas possibly turning his anger at Peter inward. "I don't know," he admitted.

Dr. Malik nodded. "Then I suggest you give him a reason to."

# Hairball

---

B ACK AT Harold's Automotive World, there were a dozen or so
messages on the answering machine, all left by people needing
tows. Several of these unfortunates had called a second time wanting to know why "Harold" hadn't gotten back to them. They meant
David, of course, Harold being long dead. But now David was dead
as well and the wrecker was wrecked and all that remained of Harold's Automotive World was its cluttered office, the vacant yard
and Rub himself, whose lone remaining duty was to close the place
up. Unsure where to begin, Rub tried a thought experiment. *What,*
he asked himself, *would Sully do?* He'd posed this question before,
though not lately, mostly because the results were always so dispiriting. To ask what Sully would do was to admit that he was no longer
there to do it. For some reason, though, this time was different. He
immediately sensed that his old friend was near at hand and anxious to help. Untroubled by self-doubt, unafraid to be wrong and
immune to after-the-fact criticism, Sully was Rub's polar opposite
and exactly what his present circumstance called for. Where should
he begin?

*Doesn't matter, knucklehead.* Sully advised. *Just start.*

The phone, then. The good news was that most of those who
had left messages would by now have made other arrangements.
The bad news was that though the snow was tapering off, the roads

remained treacherous, which meant there would likely be other callers. The message on the answering machine should probably be changed to let people know that nobody from Harold's Automotive World would be coming to their rescue, now or ever. Unfortunately, that would involve erasing the old message (which Rub wasn't sure how to do) and recording a new one. That new message would entail figuring out exactly what to say and then recording it. Couldn't the same basic effect be achieved by unplugging the phone from the wall, flipping the OPEN sign on the office door to CLOSED, turning off the lights, making sure the place was locked up and going home?

Before Rub was able to put this sensible plan in motion, however, the phone rang. There was no reason to answer it except that doing so would allow Rub to say what he'd been wanting to say since he started working for David Proxmire, which was simply, "Harold's." Alas, this simple, effective greeting had not been allowed. Instead, Rub had been instructed to say: "Harold's Automotive World. This is Rub Squeers speaking. How may I help you?" Not a word of this script was to be left out, not even the completely unnecessary ones like *this is.* Nor were substitutions, like *can I* for *may I,* permitted. Rub had been made to practice this greeting, over and over, with the phone to his ear, its dial tone buzzing, until David Proxmire was satisfied he had it down. The whole experience had been profoundly demoralizing. As a parting farewell he would do it his way. Picking up the receiver, he said, "Harold's," and felt a wave of pure satisfaction wash over him. Only then did the obvious downside to answering the phone at all occur to him—he would now have to speak to the caller.

"Hey," said a man's voice. "I'm out on the Northway. I need a tow."

"Sorry," Rub told him. "We're out of business."

"Since when?" the caller wanted to know, as if the very concept of going out of business was purely theoretical and had never been tested in the real world. As if half the small businesses in Schuyler County hadn't failed since 2008.

"Since today," Rub informed him.

There was a pause. "But . . . if you're out of business, why are you answering the phone?" Rub had to admit this was a fair question, one he had no ready answer for. "I mean, are you *sure* you're out of business?" The man seemed to be encouraging Rub to entertain the possibility that he was mistaken.

"I'm sure," he informed the man.

"Because the cops just told me you were the guys to call," the man persisted, unwilling to let the matter drop.

"We're out of business," Rub said again.

Now the man let out a loud sigh. "Okay, so, who *should* I call?"

Rub tried to remember the name on the door of the wrecker that had towed the Proxmire wrecker off but couldn't. "I don't know," he confessed.

"Jesus H. Christ," the man said. "You know what I hope? I hope your own car breaks down on the way home."

Rub considered telling the man that he didn't own a car but decided not to.

"I hope you have to stand by the side of the road and freeze your nuts off," the man continued. "I hope—"

Rub was pretty sure that what Sully would do now, or would already have done, was hang up, so he placed the receiver gently back onto its cradle in the hopes that the man wouldn't notice he'd been hung up on, but a moment later the phone rang again. This time Rub let the answering machine pick up. "How would you like it if I came out there and kicked your ass?" the same man wanted to know, apparently confident that Rub was listening, so Rub did what he should've done in the beginning and unplugged the phone from the wall. In the resulting silence he was able to conjure Sully's sardonic congratulations: *There you go, Dummy. Was that so difficult?*

Okay, Rub thought. What next?

In his mind's eye he saw Sully shrug. *You tell me.*

Glancing around the office, Rub couldn't think of anything. All that remained was to turn down the thermostat, switch off the lights and close up. The thermostat, however, was located on the wall next to the snack machine, and staring at its contents made Rub's stomach growl audibly. Having missed lunch, he wished there was someplace to stop between Harold's and downtown Bath, but there wasn't. David Proxmire had warned Rub that the snack machine, which contained his boss's private stash of goodies, including Cheetos, Rub's personal favorite, was off-limits. He'd deeply resented the man for being so stingy but had nevertheless obeyed the injunction. Now, though, standing before the machine, his stomach rumbling, Rub thought, *Would it be so wrong?* Nor was the question entirely rhetorical. Earlier, when he'd answered the phone like he'd always wanted to, there'd been an unforeseen penalty for his insubordination and Rub now wondered if there might be another for eating a dead man's treats. Sully, of course, scoffed at the notion. *He's all done eating Cheetos. You know that, right?* And since Rub did, in fact, know that, he opened the machine and took out a bag of Cheetos, then quickly shut the door again. *Also,* Sully reminded him, *he's the one who'd died owing you money, not the other way around.* This was also true. Today was Sunday and Rub had come to work, on time, and done his job. And now, with David Proxmire dead, he'd never be able to collect his pay. Rub tore open the bag of Cheetos, then paused. *Had* he done his job? He'd told Peter that Carl Roebuck was to blame for what happened to the wrecker, but was this true? If he'd taken the yellow Caddy directly back to the yard like he was supposed to, things would've been different. Well, not everything. As Peter had pointed out, David Proxmire would still be dead, but he'd be a dead man with a wrecker, not a dead man without one. The fact that the man now had no more use for a wrecker than he did for the bag of Cheetos Rub was holding didn't mean that Rub bore no responsibility for the wrecker's destruction. Seen in this light, eating the man's Cheetos added insult to injury. Sully, of course, was having none of this. *Eat the damn things,* he advised, and when Rub's stomach growled again, he popped a Cheeto in his mouth. A minute later the entire bag was empty and Rub now found himself standing in front of the soda machine, which was also off-limits. *He's all done drinking soda, too,* Sully assured him. Rub grabbed a Diet Coke, and soon it also was gone. Wadding up the empty Cheetos bag, he dropped both it and the empty Coke can into the wastepaper basket. David Proxmire didn't recycle.

Go home, Rub thought, but now he stalled in front of the long wall where David Proxmire had hung the ghostly images of his and his brother's cysts. These had always given Rub the willies. To him, they looked like shadowy hairballs. Each individual filament was sort of like a thought, thousands of them all tangled up, impossible to follow. Rub's own thoughts were often like this. How strange that you could peer inside a man's skull and still have no idea what was going on in there. Not so different, really, from peering inside your own confused head, your brain a vast hairball of thoughts and memories and wishes. You yourself were in there, but so were other people, some of them dead but acting as if they weren't. You could carry on conversations with them, as he'd just been doing with Sully. Ask them questions even, and they would answer, just like when they were alive. You could also tell them things. Bring them up to date on what's happened in their absence. There were probably all sorts of things they were wondering about.

"Peter still calls me Sancho," Rub said now, as if this was something Sully might be interested to know.

*I wouldn't worry about it,* came Sully's reply.

Rub didn't. There'd been a time when he'd hated the nickname, but not anymore.

"Sometimes?" Rub continued, trying to figure out where this hairball thought might be headed and not wanting it to get so tangled with other thoughts he couldn't follow it to conclusion. "When we're working together? He asks my opinion."

*About what?*

"Like, what's the best way to do something?"

Sully seemed to know what he was getting at. *And I never did that, right?*

"How come?" Rub said, afraid now that his old friend might not like being interrogated.

*Maybe I should've,* Sully admitted. *Remind me next time and I will.*

Except there would be no next time. Rub knew that. Had known it for a long time. Now, though, he seemed to be entering some new reality where it was possible for him to remember Sully without feeling gutted by his loss. His fear had been that one day he'd forget Sully altogether, but what if dead wasn't the same as gone? Maybe in Sully's absence he was belatedly learning how to fend for himself. Maybe that's what eating David Proxmire's Cheetos and drinking his Diet Coke meant. Maybe the time had come to wean himself from his lifelong habit of obeying instructions. It wasn't so much that he'd grown weary of doing as he was told. He was just running out of people to give him his marching orders. Back when his wife was alive, Bootsie had been a regular drill sergeant. Her voluminous instructions had been both clear and thorough, and they'd covered all imaginable contingencies. But then she died and her many directives perished with her. Same with Sully, whose death had left Rub even further adrift. Now it was Peter giving the orders, but apparently that arrangement was also coming to an end. When they finished work on the Upper Main Street house and Peter moved on, Rub would be left entirely to his own devices, which meant he'd better come up with some and quick. A year ago the idea of self-reliance had so frightened him that he'd sequestered himself in his and Bootsie's house and refused to come out until Peter showed up and tugged him back into the world of the living, a world he doubted he'd ever learn to navigate solo. Even now he would've preferred that Peter not move away like he was planning, but he had to admit that the prospect of deciding for himself what to do and how to do it was no longer as intimidating as it had once been. In fact, he felt . . . what? Rub couldn't really say. The feeling was too new, so new, in fact, that he wasn't even sure it had a name.

====

BY THE TIME Rub finished up at Harold's the snow had stopped completely. Before long the city plows would be out, and with a good foot of snow on the ground they'd create three-foot-high snowbanks everywhere, including here at the entrance to Harold's. He was about to lock the door and slip the key through the metal slot when a vehicle pulled into the snowy yard. His first thought was that it must be the caller who'd threatened to come out there and kick his ass, but no, there was a woman at the wheel. When she brought the vehicle to a stop and rolled down her window, Rub saw there was a child, a little girl in a puffy snowsuit, buckled into a kid seat in back. The driver, presumably the child's mother, had dirty-blond hair tied into a careless ponytail. She appeared to be in her twenties, though Rub was no judge of women's ages. Her eyes looked red and puffy, like maybe she'd been crying, and the smile she offered him seemed forced. "Don't tell me y'all are closed after I came all this way," she said, like that would be the absolute last straw.

Rub pointed at the CLOSED sign in the window. "Sorry," he said.

"What time do you open tomorrow?"

"We're out of business," he informed her.

"No, really?"

Rub hoped she wasn't going to start crying again. The child in the back seat began to kick her legs and squeal.

"We're not getting out, Abigail, so you can just quit kicking the back of my seat, okay?" The child seemed to understand and stopped. "Durn," her mother said, like she'd been considering using a swear word but changed her mind at the last second, probably because of her daughter. "I was hoping Harold would tell me what my car's worth."

Rub wondered if she meant David, since most people did, but decided not to ask. "You're looking to sell it?" The car looked pretty nice, no rust that he could see. It was a stripped-down model, though, the kind of car you'd buy if you weren't sure you could afford a car. In this respect it reminded him of his and Bootsie's, though theirs had been bigger, because of Bootsie herself being bigger and needing the extra room. This woman was about half her size, maybe less.

"I wish I didn't have to, but I lost my job."

"When?" Rub asked.

"Yesterday."

Rub nodded at Harold's. "I just lost mine. Today."

The woman's brow furrowed. "What're you gonna do?" Like, if he had a good plan, maybe she'd copy it.

"I got three others," he admitted, feeling guilty now for implying that they were in the same boat. "This was just my Sunday one."

The woman sighed. "My durn husband warned me this would happen," she said. "That I'd end up having to sell it. He tried to talk me into buying used, but I'd never had a new car before, and I liked how they smell. Serves me right, I guess."

"Where's he?"

"Who?"

"Your husband."

"Gone," she said. "He found a job in Texas. There's work there apparently. Lucky the car was in my name. Knowing him, he would've taken it and left me and Abigail with no way to git around."

Though if Rub understood her circumstance correctly, this was exactly where she'd be when she sold the vehicle. "Maybe you could join him there?" he suggested.

"I don't want to."

"How come?"

"Well, for one thing, then I'd be in Texas," she said, surprising Rub, because she sounded like she might be from someplace like Texas. "And for another *he's* there. And after I sell this car, I won't have a way to git there, even if I wanted to move to Texas, which I don't."

Rub nodded. Despite being half Bootsie's size, the woman kind of reminded him of her, the way she used to dispense with his objections and suggestions, effortlessly listing all her reasons. To Rub, a man who'd always had trouble explaining himself, it was a mysterious skill that he'd envied in others his whole life. It seemed like some people were be born with it, like the ability to see colors, while others, like him, couldn't learn the trick no matter how hard they tried.

For some reason another "hairball" type idea occurred to him at this point—that if he and Bootsie had had a daughter, she would be about this young woman's age, which would make the little girl in the child seat their granddaughter. Odd, now that he thought about it, that he'd spent so much of his life wishing things were other than how they were and yet never once wished he and Bootsie had had kids. This in turn led him to wonder what kind of parent he would've been. Would fatherhood be yet another skill he was unable to master, like the ability to explain himself? Would it have fallen to him to explain to the child what they should do and how and why? Or would Bootsie have taken care of all that? Among the many things you were supposed to be able to teach children was right from wrong, and Rub feared he wouldn't be much good at that. Not an hour ago he'd learned he was not above eating a dead man's Cheetos, which struck him as a moral failing, though perhaps not serious enough to be disqualifying, parent-wise. It was possible he had other, more important qualities. This woman's husband had left her and their child and gone off to Texas, and Rub couldn't imagine ever doing such a thing himself. He'd never even considered leaving Bootsie, who could be a holy terror when she wanted to.

"I don't suppose *you* could tell me what it's worth?" said the young woman. "You look like you know all about cars."

"I don't, though," he admitted. "Maybe take it to a used-car lot?"

The woman shook her head. "I don't trust those people. I wouldn't have come here except my dad used to go to the same church as Harold and he said Harold was a good, honest Christian."

"Where's *he* now?" Rub asked, wondering if her father might've also gone to Texas.

"Oh, he died," she said, and just like that her eyes were full again. "Not a durn thing's gone right since he passed, either."

"I'm sorry," Rub said again.

"He tried to warn me that my husband was a poop, but I wouldn't listen. He told me not to drop out of school, too, but I did anyway. Some people are just stupid, I guess." She was clearly referring to herself, but the way she was looking at Rub made him wonder if she was trying to decide whether he was another. "Never mind," she said, getting ready to roll the window back up. "We'll figure it out, won't we, Abigail?"

"I'll buy your car," Rub said, surprising himself, though he'd been thinking just this morning how nice it would be not to have to walk everywhere.

"You will?" she said.

Rub shrugged. It was possible he'd only made the offer to keep her from rolling up the window, but he now felt obligated. He'd only just met this young woman, but for some reason he didn't want to disappoint her.

"You hear that, Abby? This nice man's gonna buy our car. Which means we'll be able to pay the rent and not have to live out on the street."

There was a rumbling sound, then, and Rub saw a snowplow heading their way. The young woman saw it, too, and said, "Durn," as the plow thundered by, creating the very three-foot-high snowbank Rub had foreseen earlier, sealing them in. "Double durn," said the woman. "Now what do we do, Abigail?"

The child squealed again and kicked her feet, just like she did every time her mother said her name.

The good news was that Rub was still holding the key to the office door that he'd been about to drop through the slot when the woman pulled in. He used it now to unlock the door and fetch the shovel from inside. He then suggested that she and her daughter stay in the car while he shoveled them out, but instead she unstrapped the child from her seat and they all three tramped down the long driveway through the snow. Rub noticed that the child was now pointing at his face.

"I know," said her mother. "He looks funny, doesn't he?" Then to Rub, "Did you know your lips are all orange?"

And here it was, Rub thought, the hidden penalty for swiping David Proxmire's Cheetos. This time the price was being laughed at by a child.

"He's a nice man, though," Abigail's mother explained, "even if he does look funny. Look how he's helping us out when he doesn't even have to? Isn't he about the nicest man we ever met?"

The child jumped up and down in agreement, and Rub commenced shoveling as mother and daughter looked on.

"Wouldn't it be nice if we knew more nice men," the woman continued, picking her daughter up so she'd have a better view, "instead of ones like your daddy?"

Which made Rub wish there was something else he could do for them. "I wouldn't need it all the time," he told her.

"Need what?" she said, confused.

"The car," he explained. "You could borrow it if you needed to go someplace important. Like to the store or to take Abigail to the doctor."

Hearing him say her name, the little girl squealed and kicked just like she did when her mother said it, and Rub found himself smiling as he shoveled.

"Look at him go, Abigail!" the young woman said. "Look at him shovel that snow!"

And here, right here, Rub thought, was another strange, new feeling that he had no name for. Because even though this woman was the right age to be his daughter, she wasn't that. In fact, having just met her she wasn't anything to him at all. There was no reason he could think of that he should feel responsible for her and her child. Even stranger was life itself, how when you least expected it, things could change. In his experience they mostly changed for the worse, but sometimes they could improve, too, and that's how it felt now, like things had just gotten better. Imagine. Such a thing happening on the same day he'd wrecked the wrecker.

"Look at him go, Abby!" the young woman said, bouncing the child on her hip. "Just look at the nice man shovel that snow!"

The child squealed and kicked her legs, as Rub tossed the snow higher and higher.

# Prophecy

No!" JANEY SAID, shocked by what she'd just been told. Earlier in the day, one of Birdie's regular customers had dropped dead right here in the Horse. "That must've been awful. Was he a friend?"

"Sort of," Birdie replied. "Actually, he was kind of a bore. Always banging on about this thing he had growing in his head. Some sort of a cyst. You'd change the subject and he'd change it right back."

Janey took a long swig of cold beer and felt the last remnants of her tequila hangover dissipate. She made a mental note not to switch to hard stuff if she started feeling really good, and another mental note not to forget the first one, which she had a habit of doing. "Was that what killed him?"

Birdie shrugged, as if the precise cause of the man's death was a mystery she had no urgent need to get to the bottom of. Something else seemed to be on her mind, though. "This is going to sound kind of crazy," she said, "but I'm wondering if maybe it was a sign."

"Of what?"

"I don't know," Birdie admitted. "This damned recession doesn't seem to want to end. Maybe it's time to negotiate my surrender. Sell this place before *I* keel over?"

"I've been wondering the same thing about Hattie's," Janey confessed. "My daughter offered to buy it this morning."

At this Birdie raised an eyebrow. "You think you'll take her up on it?"

"It's tempting."

"What would you do then?"

"That's just it. I'd have to find something. Also, someplace to live?"

"I'm in the same boat," said Birdie, who lived above the tavern. "The difference is that you're still young."

"Not that young."

"Young compared to me."

"You'd really sell this place?" Janey knew the Horse always struggled in the off-season, but it bustled all summer long.

"If I owned it free and clear, I might. The problem is, a couple years ago I borrowed some money to stay afloat. If I sell in a depressed market the people who loaned it to me would probably lose their investment, and that's not fair."

"You mind me asking who it was?"

Birdie regarded her strangely now. "Peter Sullivan, mostly, but your Tina pitched in as well."

"Seriously?"

"I thought you knew."

Janey shook her head. "She doesn't share a lot. I wish she did. I have no idea what goes on in that head of hers." Though having said this, Janey realized it wasn't entirely true. Earlier, when she'd asked her daughter if she wanted more or less of Janey in her life, she'd answered more, no hesitation at all. Of course, she'd said it in that odd, unemotional way of hers, but Janey believed her, or wanted to, because it would mean that maybe her daughter had forgiven her for the trauma her father had inflicted on both of them. It was possible, of course, that Tina had never blamed her. Maybe it was just Janey blaming herself.

"I see her around town sometimes," Birdie said thoughtfully. "I'm not sure she even knows who I am. That I'm the person she helped save from going under."

"I wouldn't worry about it," Janey said. "She seems to have more money than she knows what to do with." Which came out sounding more bitter than she meant it to.

Both women fell silent then, the only sound coming from outside, Roger plowing the Horse's parking lot. Birdie's regular guy had called that afternoon to say his truck had broken down and he wouldn't be able to take care of her until tomorrow at the earliest. Roger, who'd picked Janey up in the same truck he'd used to plow Grandpa Zack's that afternoon, had volunteered to take care of it. "The man you're with seems nice," Birdie offered.

To Janey, this observation sounded like a question, the kind women seldom put to each other directly. Earlier, when she'd asked Birdie if the guy who dropped dead that morning had been a friend, what she'd really been wondering was whether he might've been more than that. The tavern didn't open until midafternoon on Sundays, so what was he even doing there? Now here was her own curiosity coming right back at her. *Was* she with Roger? She'd invited the man out for a beer, so yeah, technically, she supposed, she was, though the purpose of her invitation had been to signal, if only to herself, that she was no longer with Del. Roger Thorne was probably just a placeholder until she ran across some other man who truly interested her. Which, now that she thought about it, was pretty shitty. "He works for Tina, actually," she said, which made her feel even worse. Why was it so important for Roger to belong to somebody else? Was it because he had a prosthetic limb? Was she really so shallow?

"That's a big-ass parking lot he's plowing," Birdie said. "Is he going to let me pay him?"

"If I had to guess, I'd say no, but I don't know him that well. He *is* a nice guy, though."

Birdie, no fool, clearly registered her ambivalence. "Faint praise is what I'm hearing."

"I know," Janey sighed, "but here's the thing. I don't usually do nice men."

Birdie chuckled at this. "No?"

"I'm serious. My husband was a complete asshole. A mean, ignorant shit-heel."

"I remember him," Birdie said, offering no objection to Janey's characterization.

"And this guy I've been seeing lately isn't much better."

Birdie gave her a wry grin. "Cheer up," she said. "Maybe this Roger will turn out to be a dick, too. Most men don't improve upon further acquaintance."

"True," Janey conceded, "but that's not what I'm afraid of. What if he's even nicer than he seems. *Then* what do I do?"

Birdie shrugged. "Marry him? Let him be nice to you? That's what I'd do."

"I don't know. He's awfully quiet."

Birdie snorted at this. "You like guys who yap all the time?"

Did she? Del was certainly a talker. Roy had been a font of bullshit, too. "What if I have to talk for both of us?" Janey said. "My mother says I talk too damn much as it is."

"She isn't exactly the shy, retiring type herself," Birdie pointed out. "How is Ruth, by the way? God, I haven't seen her in forever."

"I don't know," she said. "Her doctor says she's healthy enough, but lately it seems like she's just going through the motions."

"You're worried about her."

To Janey's surprise, she realized this was true. It also occurred to her that if Ruth were to ask her the same question Janey had asked Tina earlier—did she want more or less of her mother in her life—her own answer would be the same. Which was a new thing. Ever since Janey was a teenager and figured out that her mother was carrying on with Sully, she'd been determined to punish her. Today, for the first time really, she'd felt inclined to cut Ruth some slack. After all, how long could you stay pissed off at somebody for trying to be happy? Wasn't happiness what Janey herself had been pursuing so doggedly for as long as she could remember? Granted, the happiness afforded by the men in her life didn't last much longer than an orgasm, and to the casual observer it probably looked more like she was pursuing misery than happiness, but still.

"Here's a thought," Birdie said. "Sell Hattie's and partner with me in this place."

Janey blinked. "Are you serious?"

Birdie shrugged. "I've got more than I can handle here. If you've got more than you can handle there, wouldn't it make sense?"

"I'd be getting a way better deal," she pointed out. "How would it even work?"

"I don't know," Birdie admitted. "Anyway, think about it."

Outside, the plowing had ceased, and from the tavern's entryway came the sound of stomping feet. Or, rather, foot. Closing her eyes, Janey reluctantly pictured what was taking place between the tavern's outer and inner doors—Roger, first stomping the snow off the boot on his good foot, then using his cane to whack it off the one on his prosthesis. For some reason she thought again about Roger's tenth-grade yearbook photo. You could tell from that goofy grin of his that the kid had no clue what life had in store for him. Janey herself had been far better prepared, and why not? There was her mother, front and center, every day of her young life, a genetic prophecy in the flesh if there ever was one. Who the hell else would she become?

Birdie, too, was listening to the sounds emanating from the entryway, Janey could tell. Why all that clomping about should cause her to smile so fondly, Janey couldn't imagine, and before she could inquire the inner door opened and Roger entered. Hanging his parka on the coatrack next to Janey's, he leaned his cane up against the wall and joined them at the bar.

"I guess you're all set till the next one," he said, sliding onto the stool next to Janey.

"You're a lifesaver," Birdie said. "What do I owe you?"

"I'd take a Coke, I guess."

Janey swiveled on her stool to regard him. "Hold on. I invite you out for a beer and you accept, and now you're saying you don't drink?"

"Oh, I drink just fine," he told her, thanking Birdie for the soda she set in front of him. "Stopping is what I'm not real great at. Why? Is it a deal breaker?"

"I don't know," Janey admitted. "I've never dated a man who didn't drink before."

"Is this a date we're on?" He was grinning at her now, clearly enjoying himself, delighted at having wrong-footed her. *Wrong-footed,* she thought. Here was an expression she'd have to find a substitute for if they started seeing each other for real. No doubt there would be others. Would she have to examine every damn thing she said before she said it?

She ignored his question. "Is it because of Iraq?" His not drinking, she meant.

"No," he assured her, rapping his prosthetic shin with his knuckles. "*That's* because of Iraq. Not drinking is because I'm an alcoholic, like my father and his father."

"Well, shit. I'm sorry," she said, though she wasn't sure what for, exactly. The prosthesis? The fact that he was an alcoholic? Her own stupidity for calling attention to both?

"Don't be. You can drink all you want. It won't bother me."

And there it was, the same goofy grin from his tenth-grade photograph. Seeing it, Janey felt the same unexpected tug at her heart that she'd felt earlier in the day at Grandpa Zack's when Roger tromped off through the snow, using his cane to keep his footing. "Okay," she said, "you got any other surprises for me?"

He shrugged. "I might have one or two."

"Just don't tell me you're a vegan. Because that *would* be a deal breaker."

"Remind me what a vegan is."

"Like a vegetarian, only worse."

"No, I eat meat."

"He could be lying," Birdie pointed out. "How about I throw a couple steaks on the grill? See what he does." Having concluded that Roger wasn't going to let her pay him for plowing the lot, she'd apparently decided that the least she could do was feed the man.

"What do you think?" Janey said.

"Why not?" Roger replied. "If this is a date, let's do it up right."

Birdie grabbed an order pad. "How do you like your steak?"

"Like a good vet could still save it."

Janey ordered hers medium. "You need help in the kitchen?"

"If I do, I'll holler," Birdie said, disappearing through the swinging door and leaving her and Roger alone.

When Janey rotated back to face him, she noticed the stool Roger was seated on was the one engraved with Sully's name. And Sully, she realized, was probably the reason Birdie had been smiling so fondly as they listened to Roger clomping about in the entryway. Sully hadn't had a prosthetic limb, of course, but he'd limped painfully through the last two decades of his life after falling off a ladder and shattering his knee. The sounds Roger made out there in the entryway had no doubt reminded Birdie of him, maybe even made her wonder if, when the door finally opened, it would be Sully who entered. Ruth had told Janey once that when the bell tinkled above the door at Hattie's, it was always Sully she expected to see limping in. At the time that had pissed Janey off, but now, for some reason, it didn't. *Good Lord,* she thought. Did deciding to cut her mother some slack mean she'd have to cut Sully some as well? Where would it all end?

"What?" Roger said, breaking into her reverie.

"Sorry?"

"You were looking at me funny."

She had little doubt this was true, because seeing Roger Thorne so comfortably ensconced on Sully's barstool made her wonder if maybe the world was trying to tell her something. Could it be that the man occupying the stool marked SULLY might serve the same function in Janey's life that Sully had served in her mother's? That maybe—just maybe—he would make life worth the living?

# Handset

---

RAYMER READ and read and read some more, putting *Great Expectations* aside only when he could no longer keep his eyes open. By then it was midnight and Jerome had still not returned from his date with Dr. Qadry at Infinitum. Had they gone back to her place? *Was* Jerome really irresistible to white women? Would this new development mean the end of his own therapy sessions, or would those continue unabated? More likely the latter, Raymer decided. He could easily imagine Dr. Qadry introducing the subject as if it were hypothetical. *If* she and Jerome were to enter into a relationship, how would that make him feel? He could picture her, notebook in hand, pen poised to dutifully record whatever lie he chose to tell her. How many such notebooks had she filled over the years and to what possible end? He had no doubt there were people who benefited from therapy. Miss Havisham in *Great Expectations,* for instance, definitely could have used a shrink. On the other hand, what possible good would Freud himself have done Joe Gargery?

In bed, both physically and mentally exhausted, Raymer fell into a deep sleep, his subconscious mind summoning a series of vivid dreams, only the last of which was memorable. Perhaps not surprisingly, Dr. Qadry was in it and so was Miss Havisham. Wait, no. Dr. Qadry *was* Miss Havisham. This was apparent from the white wedding dress she was wearing. It had a plunging neckline (a detail conjured by Raymer's imagination, not Dickens's) that exposed most of one pale breast (Pam!). Interestingly, instead of asking Raymer her usual leading questions, she was talking on a landline phone in a foreign language, possibly German, and though he couldn't understand a word, Raymer gathered from the fact that she kept glancing at him that he himself was the conversation's subject, which he took to mean that Charice was on the other end of the line. *So,* he thought. *This* was how they'd been sharing information about him! Though he told himself to quit looking at his therapist's bare breast, he found he couldn't stop. Catching him in the act, Miss Havisham, man-hater that she was, smiled knowingly. Only when she placed the receiver back in its cradle did he notice something strange. The handset had no cord.

And just that quickly he was wide awake, his heart thudding in his chest, transported back to the empty ballroom of the Sans Souci, ghostly light streaming in from the second-story windows, revealing the eerie emptiness of that cavernous space, devoid as it was of furniture, its walls stripped of their decorations and fixtures, the dusty floor empty except for a few broken-down cardboard boxes, a discarded roll of packing tape and . . .

And there it was, the elusive detail he'd been trying to remember: *the handset of a telephone.* Dear God, Raymer thought. Sleep forgotten now, he switched on his bedroom lamp and located his cell phone. A moment later, standing before the kitchen counter where the suicide's BlackBerry lay, still attached to its charger, Raymer clicked on his own phone's contacts list, found the entry he was looking for, and pressed CALL. Immediately, though he prayed it wouldn't, the device on the counter began to vibrate.

Ten minutes later, that's where Jerome found him, watching the BlackBerry inch its way along the kitchen countertop. When it reached the end of its tether, Jerome touched Raymer's elbow. "Dawg?" he said. "Dawg?"

# Men in General

I T WAS NEARLY MIDNIGHT when Peter finally left his son's bedside. On the way home from the hospital, he'd stopped at the
Horse, thinking he might commiserate with Birdie, whose day had
been equally punishing and who could probably use some company.
The place was dark, though, its recently plowed parking lot empty.
On Upper Main Street, the second story of Miss Beryl's house was
ablaze with lights, which maybe meant that Carl Roebuck was in
residence. Either that or he'd forgotten to turn off the lights when
he left that morning, also possible. If he *was* upstairs, he, too, might
appreciate some company. But no, Peter thought, he was procrasti-
nating. So instead of climbing the stairs and knocking on the door,
he let himself into his own downstairs flat, which was dark and
quiet.

Except, not completely dark and not completely quiet. The TV
in the den, which had been off when he left that morning, was now
on, its volume low. Carl lay stretched out on the sofa when Peter
pushed the door open. *Saving Private Ryan* was playing on the TV.
With the sound down, he'd apparently heard Peter pull into the
drive, then enter the flat, because he spoke without taking his eyes
off the screen, "Can we talk about your DVD collection?"

Peter moved Carl's feet aside so he could perch on the arm of the sofa. "Can we talk about the fact that you're down here and not upstairs?"

"There isn't much to do up there," Carl explained. "No Xbox. No TV even."

"There's a TV."

"It's not hooked up."

"Hook it up."

"Too much trouble," Carl said. "Besides, your door was unlocked, so . . ."

That Peter had neglected to lock his inner door this morning was further evidence, were any needed, of just how thoroughly recent events had untethered him.

From the TV came a burst of muted machine-gun fire, and a German tank, filling the screen, crested a mound of rubble, sending GIs scurrying out of its way. Peter found the remote and turned it off. He and Carl continued to stare at the dark screen.

"Those were men," Carl said sadly. "Your old man? Mine?"

"They had their moments," Peter agreed. An understatement if ever there was one. Back at the hospital, doing what Thomas's doctor suggested, Peter had talked quietly to his son, telling him, among other things, that what he most regretted about losing touch with him and his brother was that they'd never gotten to know their grandfather. Sully had been no great shakes as a father, but to everyone's surprise he'd been a gifted grandfather. Will's numerous successes in life were probably as attributable to Sully as to Peter himself. Had Thomas also been exposed to the man, things might've turned out differently.

"And look at us," said Carl, still staring darkly at the TV.

"Must we?" Peter replied.

Carl shook his head miserably. "My *wife* is more of a man than I am."

"Your ex-wife," Peter corrected. Unless he was mistaken, Carl's earlier conviction that Toby would soon return to him had eroded significantly over the course of the day. His presence in Peter's downstairs flat wasn't about how little there was to do upstairs. The poor bastard just wanted to see if Toby was with him when Peter returned home, as she had been the night before.

"She's also more of a man than you are," Carl said thoughtfully.

"Yeah," Peter said. "I'm fond of her, too."

"I know you are," said Carl, finally looking at him. "Here. Join me."

On the floor next to the sofa was an open bottle of red wine, which Carl handed to him. "Do you have any idea how long it took me to locate your corkscrew?"

Peter thought about going to the kitchen for a glass, but he could tell by feel that the bottle was basically empty. "It was right on top of the wine rack you took this bottle from."

Carl ignored this, too. "I searched every single drawer in that kitchen," he complained.

Finishing the dregs of the bottle in one swallow, Peter turned it upside down so Carl could see. "Thanks for sharing."

Carl sighed deeply. "So, I guess my question is, what are we even for?"

"Men in general or you and me? I should probably warn you I have no idea what you're for." Getting to his feet, he said, "Should I open another bottle?"

"Please. I would myself, but I'm too drunk."

In the kitchen Peter grabbed another red from the rack, only to discover that thanks to Carl the corkscrew was now missing. Rather than hunt for it, he put the bottle back and selected one with a screw cap. There were several of these, which begged the question of why Carl had spent so long looking for a wine key to begin with.

Outside, a vehicle pulled up at the curb and Peter arrived at the front window in time to see J.J. Julowitz get out, climb over the snowbank and head up the unshoveled walk.

"Good idea," he said, spying the wine, when Peter met him at the door.

In the kitchen Peter poured them each a glass.

"Guess where I've been?" J.J. said, taking a seat at the kitchen island.

"Hold on a sec," Peter told him, returning to the den, where Carl had turned the TV back on and then promptly fallen asleep in the midst of its mayhem. In the front pocket of his chinos, Peter noted, was something shaped like a corkscrew. He gently closed the door on the way out.

"What?" J.J. said when Peter returned and joined him at the kitchen island. "You got a woman in there?"

"If only," Peter said, though tonight, in truth, he was glad he didn't.

They clinked glasses. "You look like shit," J.J. observed.

"Thanks."

"I stopped by the hospital. They told me you'd been there most of the evening."

Peter filled him in on Thomas's situation, his injuries, the concussion that led to his current semiconscious state. "The doctors are afraid he might slip into a coma."

"Like I told you earlier," J.J. said, "this Delgado's one bad dude. The other guy I don't know about. Miller? I tried to interview him, but his wife wouldn't let me in the door. I'm hearing he's resigned."

"But not Delgado?"

J.J. shook his head. "Nope. All indications are he's doubling down."

"You know this how?"

"That's what I started to tell you. Before I went to the hospital, I paid a visit to this dive bar called the Green Hand. The cops all hang out there."

"That's where this whole thing started," Peter told him. "God only knows why, but Thomas went there last night and got so drunk he blacked out and fell off his barstool. That's probably where he got his concussion."

"Well, the same crew was back there tonight," J.J. said, "having what I would describe as a spirited conversation. Deb Harris was there and she knows me, so I had to sit at the bar with my back to them. From what I could gather they were all trying to convince our Mr. Delgado that the situation was serious. I heard somebody say, 'What if he dies?'"

"So they know Thomas is in the ICU."

"I also heard your name a couple times. Like you were going to be trouble, but Delgado was having none of it. He called them all a bunch of pussies and stormed off. When he was gone, they all sat around shaking their heads, like, Now *what the fuck do we do?* Tomorrow, I'll go see Deb. She looked pretty worried. She might talk to me."

"You might also have a word with Janey at Hattie's Lunch here in Bath," Peter told him. "According to her mother, she and Delgado were the ones who dropped Thomas off at the police station instead of taking him to the hospital. I get the impression their relationship has soured."

J.J. took a small, spiral-ring pad out of his shirt pocket and made a note. "So, you're telling me to follow up. I mean, this is a real story, right?"

"It is," Peter reluctantly agreed. "You see the problem, though. I'm right in the center of it. Whatever we write, it can't come across as a personal vendetta."

J.J. tucked the notepad back in his shirt pocket. "So," he said, nodding in the direction of the den. "If it's not a woman, who do you have in there?"

Peter couldn't help smiling. How to explain Carl Roebuck? "An old friend of my father's, actually," he said. "He's going through a rough patch."

J.J. was looking around now, taking the place in, clearly impressed. "You're doing all this work yourself?"

"Me and one other guy."

"It should be worth a fortune when you're done. Bath is going to explode."

"Your lips to God's ear."

"Well, I should get going," J.J. said, pushing back from the island. "Thanks for the vino. Tomorrow, we nail these bastards."

They shook on it.

When J.J. was gone, Peter poked his head into the den where the movie's credits were scrolling and Carl was still snoring peacefully. What he'd told J.J. was true, Peter thought, but not the whole truth. Yes, Carl Roebuck had been a friend of his father's, but he was also, it appeared, now a friend of Peter's. Had he been on Sully's original list of people he was supposed to check up on? Peter couldn't remember, but it didn't matter. He was apparently on it now. Grabbing a blanket from the closet, Peter draped it over him.

Back in the kitchen he poured himself another glass of wine, then set up his laptop on the island and waited for it to boot up. J.J. was right. The house probably was worth a fortune, or would be once the recession ended. His long-awaited ticket out. During the course of the day, though, something had shifted. When he awoke this morning, the place had been his to do with as he pleased. Now things felt more complicated. Maybe he was only part owner? Didn't the fact that the house had been Will's home and he loved it mean he, too, had a say in what happened to it? And if that was true, perhaps the converse was as well. Maybe the fact that Thomas and Andy had been unfairly denied that home meant they, too, had a claim. Even if, as Peter suspected, Thomas came all this way to burn the place to the ground, it was still part his inheritance. That was the other thing he'd given voice to at the hospital on the off chance Thomas was still in there somewhere, trying to decide if he wanted to live. Maybe, he told his son, it wasn't too late. If he wanted to, they could start over. Right here in this very house.

One last thing, then, before bed. He thought again about putting it off until morning. After all, what possible difference would a few hours make? But no, he'd do it now. In Google's search rectangle he typed: *SULLIVAN. ANDREW JAMES. WEST VIRGINIA.*

And hit search.

*Me, Again—*

*The weirdest thing, Little Bro!*

*I know, I know. It's all been pretty weird, right? Everything I've been telling you since I got here? Pop taking me on a grand tour of the house we planned to torch? Rub-Not-Rob giving me the stink eye, like somehow he took* just one look *and he* knew, knew, KNEW *why I was there? Then that Grandpa Zack's Treasures chick in the flatbed who maybe thinks I'm Brother Will? Then me going out and getting hammered and waking up in jail? That crazy cop damn near killing me before I could hightail it back home? And me almost choking to death on my own puke after they wired my jaw shut?*

*Except, wait! I haven't even told you about that part yet, have I? Doesn't matter. All that can wait. And you know what, Little Bro? Even if I never get to tell you about it, so what? You can guess, right? It's not like you don't know what a fuckup I am when things head south, like they always do, eventually. Which is why I really can't blame you for taking off like you did. After all these years, you've had about enough of me, am I right? All I can say is move over. You want to know the truth? I've had about enough of myself. You ever feel that way, Little Bro? Like you've had just about enough of yourself?*

*Anyhow, before I tell you about this totally weird new thing, I should probably let you in on a secret. It might not even be real. Could be I dreamed it. Could be I'm still dreaming. You can be the judge, okay?*

*So, here goes: I think I might be dead.*

*Hah! Bet you weren't expecting that!*

*Dead but also . . . not dead. Because, you can't think you're dead and be right. It's impossible, because dead people don't think. But here's the thing. If I'm not dead, then where did all that pain go? Answer me that. Before—after that cop busted me up—there wasn't a single part of me that didn't ache. Now? Nothing. Instead of pain it's like I'm floating. Almost like before you're born, you know? You're just an embryo, all dark and warm, not a care in the world, because, like, there is no world, not yet anyhow, not for you. So, all you do is just float there, happy, no idea what you're in for. That's kind of what this feels like, except I'm not alone in here. Wherever here is. Pop's with me, or anyway his voice is. Inside my head, kind of. Like he means to guide me through it, this whole being dead thing. So there won't be any surprises and I can hit the ground (ha!) running. Mostly he wants me to know everything's okay. Death, I guess he means. Why? Basically because I can quit worrying about stuff. Like money, which you'd have to be either rich or dead not to worry about, right? Also, transportation. Don't ask me how, but Pop's figured out the Yellow Sub's gone, which means there's no way for me to get back home. Don't worry about it. That's what I keep hearing him tell me, but come on. How am I ever going to find you again with no wheels and no idea where you went?*

*There's more. Pop wants me to know there's no reason to feel guilty about what we were planning. Like, that whole time him and Rub-Not-Rob spent fixing up the place, only to have me show up and burn it down? Nothing to get all worked up about, he says. That's kind of the gist of everything he's telling me. No worries. It's all good. Turns out there's nothing to be scared of, either. Why? You're gonna love this, Little Bro. Because he brought the stopwatch. Remember? The one me and Will fought over? It's mine now, Pop says. I can time myself being brave if I want to. Lucky me, right? Oh, and here's the kicker. Even if I'm dead? Turns out it's not too late to start over, me and him. All I gotta do is want to. That's what he keeps coming back to, like it's super important, even more important than me being dead:* IT'S NOT TOO LATE!

*Hah! You thinking what I'm thinking? Because that was the other song Mom was always playing on that cassette tape of hers, remember? In the Yellow Sub? Before Dickweed?* Oh, it's too late baby, now it's too late, though we really did try to make it. *Remember that? And also* something has died. *That was part of it, too. Something has died, but damned if I can remember what. Can you? In the song, I mean?*

*Me, is what it feels like. Just floating like I am, the pain all gone, Pop trying to get me to believe it's not too late when it is. It feels like maybe it's me that died.*

*Wait, though. I just remembered another line.* There'll be good times again for both me and you. *Remember? And hey, that would be cool, right? If that was true? I'd like that. I definitely would. Because they weren't all bad, right? Those times? Me and you? Despite me always being so messed up? I mean, hey, I did get you away from Mom and Dickweed. I get that much credit, don't I? When I heard about what they did? Making you go to that place? I came back for you, right? Okay, I never should've left in the first place. I know that now. I know what you must've thought. That I was gone for good. But, hey, I did come back. And you did better for a while, right? I mean, things were still pretty fucked up, but you did better? Or were you just pretending so I wouldn't feel bad? Was it already* just *too late?*

*I guess what I'm trying to say is, I get it. About why you had to split like you did, not even saying goodbye. Because of me and my plans to get even, right? Me bullying you into agreeing about what had to happen. Same as with that blood oath when we were kids. Me wanting actual blood. You wanting to just say the words. You'd always go along, pretend my idea was a good one. Figuring it was just talk, that I'd either change my mind or forget and that would be the end of it. Except not this time, right? I think when it dawned on you that I meant business, that's when you decided to take off. Go someplace far away.*

*I'm sorry, Little Bro. I am. I should've been more on your side all along. Remember that time when you asked me if I was ashamed of you, and I said I wasn't? The look on your face? You could tell I was lying. That I'd broken that blood oath of ours—never to lie to each other. You* knew, knew, KNEW *that I was ashamed. Of you being what you are, even though it's not your fault. I wish it wasn't too late to take that back. That shame. Like I said before, you deserved better. Better parents. A better big brother, too.*

*Crazy, all of it, right? And now here I am floating somewhere that isn't even a real place, no company except for Pop's voice saying how it's not too late, even though I know it is. That's what dead means, right, Little Bro? That it's too late?*

*But we really did try to make it, didn't we? Me and you?*

# Superpower

"YOU SURE you don't want to come in?" Janey said.

She and Roger were sitting in his truck in the alley behind Hattie's, his cane balanced on the seat between them, as if to suggest that both the thing itself and what it represented would always be there, not just a barrier but a challenge to overcome. Nor, apparently, was it the only one. If they continued to see each other, she'd be dating a man who both limped through life (like Sully) and drove a vehicle with a snowplow blade attached (also like Sully), which meant she'd be that much closer to living her mother's life, the very thing she'd always been determined to avoid, even if it meant settling for something worse.

But apparently she was getting ahead of herself, because if Roger was in love with her, as Ruth claimed, he was doing a pretty good job of disguising the fact. Oh, they'd had a good time tonight, better than good, really. He'd cheered her up like she hoped he would, but now here they were, half an hour later, sitting awkwardly in the cab of his truck with the heat blasting and he hadn't even tried to kiss her. Back at the Horse she hadn't been sure she wanted him to, but it was now clear that she hadn't wanted him *not* to, either.

"No," Roger said in response to her second invitation. "I should be moseying along. Tina will be expecting me at Grandpa Zack's bright and early."

"Fine," she said. "Whatever."

"I had fun tonight, though," he said when she reached for the door handle.

"Really?"

He nodded. "We should do it again sometime."

She took her hand off the door handle and turned back to him. "Okay if I ask you a question?" she said.

"Shoot."

She exhaled deeply. "My mother . . . who's generally full of shit . . . has this crazy idea that you're in love with me."

At this he grinned. "Does she?"

She waited for him to elaborate. When it became clear that he had no such intention, she continued, "But, obviously, you're not."

He appeared to give this statement more careful deliberation—at least to Janey's thinking—than should have been necessary. "Could be I just want to go slow?" he said, as if this were one possibility among many and he really had no more idea than she did as to its validity.

She had to chuckle at this. "If so, you'd be the first," she said. "Every man who's ever been interested in me was determined to break the speed limit."

"Could be I'd rather not be one of those." Great. More hypothesizing.

"Okay, but what sort of pace did you have in mind?" she asked, pleased that he hadn't categorically denied having feelings for her but disappointed by the ease with which he appeared to keep them in check. "Neither of us is getting any younger. How long have we known each other?"

"I've known you longer than you've known me."

She blinked at him. "That makes exactly no sense, Roger."

"Put it this way. I've been paying attention to you longer. Your attention has been elsewhere. I'm just giving you a chance to catch up. Also, you're seeing somebody, right?"

"Not anymore."

"Since when?"

"Since tonight. That's what me asking you out means, in case you were wondering."

"Does he know he's history? This other guy?"

"I told him, but I'm not sure he was listening."

"Well, once you're shut of him, we can start a headlong romance of our own." He was enjoying himself now, she could tell. "Maybe try holding hands or something."

"You really don't want to come in?"

"I never said I didn't want to. I said I wasn't going to."

"Well, crap, Roger. There's no changing your mind?"

"Not tonight."

She shook her head. "You could be missing your one chance. Did you ever think of that?"

"I sure hope not."

"All right then," she said, opening the door and climbing out, thereby upsetting the balance of his cane, which tumbled out of the cab and onto the snowy pavement.

"Don't worry," he said, when she picked it up and wiped it off. "You can't hurt that thing."

"What's it made of?" she said, surprised by its weight, when she handed it back into the cab.

"Some alloy or other," he said. "Titanium? Who knows?" And there it was again, that goofy grin from the tenth-grade photo, the one that tugged at her heart.

"Just so you know," she said. "Tonight won't be your last chance."

"Good."

"Call me?"

"I will," he promised, and somehow she knew he would. Men had lied to her her whole life, but she knew this one was telling the truth. Only after watching him back out of the alley and head up the deserted street and out of sight did she insert her key in the lock. Something immediately felt wrong, but it took a moment for her to understand what—the door was already unlocked. So, when she pushed it open and flipped on the light switch, she wasn't entirely surprised to see Del sitting there on the sofa.

He looked calm, but then he always did, even when she knew he was roiling inside. She thought about making a run for it, but he'd likely catch her before she got very far, and at this hour there'd be no one around to hear if she called for help. So instead she put the keys back in her purse and set it on the end table. "This door was locked when I left," she told him.

"My professional advice would be to install a dead bolt," Del smiled. "I picked that lock in about ten seconds."

She shut the door behind her and leaned against it. "So how long have you been sitting here in the dark?"

"A while. Where've you been?"

"Out."

He nodded. "I already knew that. Where?"

"None of your business, Del."

"I waited for you at the Hand."

"That was dumb. I told you I wasn't coming."

"I waited for you," he repeated.

"That was your mistake."

"No," he said, getting to his feet. "It was yours."

"*My* mistake?" she said, amazed by how she always went from zero to sixty, anger-wise, with men like Roy and Del. Once the die was cast and there was no hope of de-escalating things, why not hasten the inevitable along? At least that way she felt some agency. "My mistake was wasting the last four months of my life with you and your dumb-ass cop friends."

He took a step closer now. "I explained the situation to you. That I needed your help. Was I unclear?"

"No, you were clear. You were asking me to lie for you."

"Which you *are* going to do."

She let out a barking laugh at this, knowing full well that it was the exact wrong thing to do. Somewhere in the world there might be a man who didn't mind being laughed at, but she hadn't met him yet. She glanced at Del's hands to see if they were balled into fists yet, but they weren't. That didn't mean he wasn't going to punch her, just that he had a longer fuse than Roy, her late unlamented husband, who would've dispensed with all these preliminaries and put her on the floor two seconds after she walked in the door.

"Did I say something funny?" Del wanted to know.

"Yeah, you did. I'd just about given up but, yep, you finally said something funny."

He cocked his head at this, his face a thundercloud, and she sensed that she'd struck the nerve she was looking for. So . . . more like this, then.

"What do you mean, *finally*?"

"See, that's the thing, Del. It's what I was trying to tell you before. *You* think the stories you tell out at the Hand are funny. *You* think you're a funny guy."

He was watching her intently now, his brow furrowed, his eyes dark and unblinking. She glanced down at his hands again. Still no fists. "People laugh," he said. "*You* laugh."

"Because everybody's scared of you, Del. People laugh because they know underneath it all you're cruel and completely batshit and they don't want to be on your bad side."

"And you think what? That being on my bad side is a *good* idea?"

"No, Del, I'm sure it's a shitty idea, but guess what? I'm through pretending. Your stories aren't funny and how you treat people isn't funny and I'm pretty sure what goes on in that twisted brain of yours isn't funny. In fact, you could be summed up in two little words: *not funny.* I'm going to go out on a limb here and bet both your ex-wives would agree."

And just that quickly she was down. She didn't see the blow coming, but then she never did. Or rather, she'd seen it coming for months, just hadn't taken evasive action. Why it never seemed important to do so until it was too late was a mystery. Was it curiosity? To see if she was right? That this new man would be like all the others? Or was it sheer defiance, a stubborn refusal to accept how things were—that men could talk shit till the cows came home, mostly without consequence, but let a woman speak her mind and *wham!* Hubris probably played a role as well. She'd believed that if she could survive Roy, she could survive anything. But clearly she'd miscalculated. She saw that now. Roy had enjoyed punching her almost as much as he enjoyed fucking her, but the two were connected in his feeble brain. As soon as he put her on the floor and saw blood flow from her nose or her busted lip, he would begin to soften, to feel . . . what? Not remorse exactly—to his mind Janey definitely needed punching—but something like remembered tenderness. Oh, sure, he might hit her again if she continued to mouth off, but the second punch would lack the fury of the first. And the one after that would feel obligatory, the law of diminishing returns having already kicked in. Either that or he'd already begun to think about fucking her again.

This, though, was different. The man standing silently over her now, his fist still clenched, might have a longer fuse, but now that the device had finally detonated, he was more dangerous than Roy. He would never remember feeling tenderness toward Janey because he'd never felt any to begin with. In fact, now that she thought about it, she wasn't even sure he'd enjoyed fucking her. Which meant that the next blow would be delivered with the same conviction as the first, as would the one after that. It wouldn't occur to Del that at some point he might want to fuck her again. For all its ferocity, their sex served pretty much the same purpose as the stories he told at the Hand. Both provided periodic release from the pressure that seemed to build inside him so relentlessly. Equally frightening was the possibility that Del might now be in uncharted territory. He'd been at war with women his whole life, but this might be the first time he'd ever struck one. It was entirely possible she'd just now pushed a button no other woman had pushed, thereby piercing his defenses and untethering the inner demon that made him grind his teeth in his sleep. Was *this* her superpower, Janey wondered: an untutored, innate ability to know the exact wrong thing to say to violent men? Even Ruth, who'd warned Janey repeatedly that her big mouth would be the death of her one day, never would've predicted this—that telling a humorless man that he wasn't funny would be the thing that set him off. Strange that this belated gift of self-knowledge should arrive at the precise moment that it would be useless to her. But maybe that was just how things went. Maybe the ringing in her ears was the sound of God's laughter. Tonight, at the Horse, she'd glimpsed a path forward that might just lead to a better outcome. Roger was part of it. He was the better man she'd been in search of for so long. She saw that clearly now. And Birdie's offer to make her a partner in the Horse wasn't just about saving both their businesses. Unless Janey was mistaken, she was also offering the possibility of friendship, the kind of female companionship that Ruth had been lamenting the lack of earlier that very day. And now, just that quickly, both possibilities erased, and no one to blame but herself. So, when Del grabbed her by the hair and cocked his fist, she closed her eyes, resigned herself to the next vicious blow, for her destiny—because that's what this whole thing felt like—to be fulfilled at last.

But for some reason that blow didn't come. In fact, she felt Del let go of her hair, and when she opened her eyes to see why and blinked him into focus, she discovered that he'd turned away from her entirely and was now facing the door as if he meant to leave. Was it her imagination, or had she heard that door open and close over the ringing in her ears? "Who the fuck are you?" she heard Del ask.

"A friend of the woman you're beating on," said a voice that she didn't immediately recognize as Roger's. When it dawned on her that that's who it was, she heard herself scream, "No!"—because now Del would kill them both, and poor Roger had done nothing to merit the destiny she herself so richly deserved. Unable to watch what happened next, she looked away and sure enough there came the sound of a vicious blow being struck, followed by a howl and a body crumpling to the floor. She assumed that body would be Roger's, but when she turned to look, it was Del writhing in pain on the floor and Roger standing over him, wielding his cane like a baseball bat. "You broke my fucking knee!" Del howled.

"Good," Roger said calmly. "Stay down or I'll break the other one." Then he turned his attention to Janey, who began to sob with relief and gratitude. "Stay still a minute," he told her, getting down, with difficulty, to one knee as she attempted to sit up. "Let me look at your face." Where she'd been struck was already swelling, she could tell, but he took her gently by the chin and rotated it for a better look. "You might have a broken cheekbone," he reported, "but you'll be okay."

Out of the corner of her eye she saw Del rolling away from them and reaching as he did for something inside his coat. "He's got a gun," Janey whispered to Roger, as if this were a secret she didn't want Del to overhear.

"What?" Roger said.

"A gun!" she whispered louder.

This time he understood, but when he attempted to lever himself into a standing position, he found he couldn't, at least not quickly enough. "Looks like you're going to have to do the honors," he said, handing Janey his cane.

By the time she was able to get to her feet Del was upright, too, though only one foot was planted on the floor. His other leg was bent at the knee. His revolver was out of its holster, but when he tried to raise it, he lost his balance and had to hop on his good leg, elbows akimbo, to regain it. This gave Janey the beat she needed, so that when he raised the weapon a second time—at her? at still-kneeling Roger?—she was close enough to swing Roger's cane, which she did, hard as she could. When it connected, she could feel the delicate bones in Del's wrist snap like twigs. The gun sailed across the room, exploding on impact against the wall, the report loud enough to drown out Janey's shriek. In the quiet that ensued, Del examined his shattered wrist. He appeared surprised that his hand was still attached. It dangled there as if held in place by skin alone. He looked at Janey, as if for explanation, then collapsed, ass first, onto the glass coffee table, which shattered and folded in on him like an accordion.

Janey went over to where he lay and gave serious thought to bringing Roger's lethal cane down on his skull. Blinking up at her, Del said, "Go ahead. You might as well."

Instead, she lowered the weapon and said, "You know what I

can't wait for, Del? I can't *wait* to hear how you're going to tell this story at the Hand. How you're going to explain to all your asshole friends how you got your butt kicked by a girl and a cripple."

She had more to say, a lot more, but from behind her came Roger's plaintive voice. "Umm. Little help?"

He was still down on one knee, unable, without his cane, to lever himself upright. "My position back in Little League was catcher," Roger said when, with Janey's help, he was back on his feet and leaning heavily on his cane. "I used to have to spring out of my crouch. You should've seen it."

She rested her forehead against his. "You came back," she said.

"I made it about a block," he told her sheepishly, "before changing my mind."

"I'm glad you did."

"You want to hand me that?" he said, indicating the revolver on the floor.

Janey went over to where it lay and picked it up as you would something not just dead but decomposing. Roger took it from her, expertly unloaded it and put the shells in his pocket. The gun itself he tucked in his waistband. Across the room Del was attempting to extricate himself from the ruined coffee table, no easy task, given his injuries.

Remembering what she'd just said, Janey began to cry again.

"What?" Roger said.

"I'm so sorry," she blubbered. "I called you a cripple."

"It's what I am," he said cheerfully. "Just don't call me worthless, because that *would* hurt my feelings."

"I won't," she said. "I promise."

It took a while, but despite having only one working hand, Del was finally able to regain his feet, though the knee Roger had clobbered with his cane still couldn't bear much weight.

"Now what?" Janey said, to both men really.

"I guess I'll be on my way, then," Del said, limping painfully toward the door. There, he held out his hand to Roger. "I'll take my piece," he said.

"Don't give it to him," Janey said. She knew the gun was unloaded but still.

"I won't be back," he assured Roger, ignoring Janey completely. "You have my word."

She watched in disbelief as Roger handed him the gun, which Del holstered. "Where'd you lose it?" he said, indicating Roger's prosthesis.

"Iraq," Roger told him.

Del nodded. "Do you understand this fucking world?"

Roger shook his head. "Not really, no."

How effortlessly men recognized each other, Janey thought. The simple fact that they were men and not women. She was comforted, however, by the fact that the recognition only went so far and probably didn't mean much. What Del didn't understand about the world and never would was completely different from what baffled Roger. And Janey herself? Oh, there was a lot that baffled her as well, but something had shifted, hadn't it? It seemed, in fact, that thanks to Roger, she'd finally turned a corner she'd been trying to turn her whole damn life. Who knew? Maybe turning it would only lead to more disappointment, but she'd give it a try, even if it meant going at Roger's pace, not her own, even if Roger *was* too damn much like the man her mother had loved so defiantly and at such great cost, even if it meant Ruth got to say *I told you so.*

"What a mess," Roger said, looking around. It wasn't clear to Janey whether he was referring to her destroyed apartment or life in general. Hard to argue with, either way.

# MONDAY

# Knowing

"WHAT'S THE DIFFERENCE between knowing something and knowing *about* something?" Peter said, dropping the stack of essays his students had handed in last Friday onto the table beside him. Seeing this and knowing what it portended, several students groaned. It was his practice to select a page or paragraph to read aloud in the hopes of spurring discussion. He never identified the writer, but his students still universally loathed the practice. Bad enough they had to write for him. His sharing what they'd written with a wider audience struck them as out-of-bounds, a violation of their privacy. He'd skimmed this particular batch of essays last night before turning out the light, and not one had grabbed his attention. This morning, distracted and unprepared to teach, he'd thought about canceling class, but he decided not to. If Thomas's condition deteriorated, as the neurologist hinted it might, he would need to cancel other classes in the coming days.

"Imani," he said, calling on a Black woman in her midtwenties, who often yawned in class and once or twice had actually fallen fast asleep. She looked half asleep now, in fact. "What's the difference between knowing and knowing about?"

"I have no idea," she admitted. The pained expression on her face said, *Why are you picking on me?*

Peter sent her a telepathic message. *Because you're the one most likely to know the answer.* "Okay," he said. "Until now I've let you guys choose your own essay topics. The idea was to give you the opportunity to write about things that were important to you, that you were passionate about. Not many of you have, though. The topics you've chosen have mostly been safe—things you know some facts about, like sports, popular music, TV. The problem is that what we know *about* often doesn't matter that much. It's what the culture tells us is important. Again, sports, popular music, TV."

"Isn't that what *you* write about in *Schuyler Arts*?" somebody wondered.

"Fair point," Peter conceded. "Each week I ask myself what our audience wants and I try to give it to them. But my question is: What's wrong with letting your audience call the shots?"

"Nothing?"

Imani, he was pleased to note, actually seemed engaged by the question. "Imani. What's wrong with that?"

She shrugged. "Well, what if there's something worth saying and you don't say it because you don't think anybody would care."

"Like what?"

"I don't know. Like, something personal? A secret?"

"Like what?" he repeated, and she again gave him that why-are-you-picking-on-me look. "Okay," he said. "How about I go first. I have three sons, all adults now. My wife and I divorced when they were little. I raised my oldest son here. His brothers grew up with their mother in West Virginia. One of them—I haven't seen him since he was a boy—showed up unexpectedly over the weekend. That same night he got so drunk he blacked out and fell on his head. Gave himself a concussion. He's now in the hospital in what doctors call a minimally conscious state. Sort of like a coma. He may not wake up."

Now, he saw, it wasn't just Imani who was engaged. Even the bros in the back row who complained that required courses like composition were irrelevant to the jobs they were training for, the lives they hoped to lead, were sitting up straight. One of them, clearly shocked that Peter would share something so personal, said, "Is that true?"

"Unfortunately, yes. Who wants to know more?" The bros all shared nervous glances. Were they supposed to?

"Why did you get divorced?" somebody said.

"Right. What else do you want to know?"

"Why didn't you see more of your son?"

"What else?"

"Why did he come to see you after so long?"

"All good questions," he said. "Imani. Your turn. Tell me something you think is worth saying. Something you're reluctant to share because you think people won't care."

"Do I have to?"

"No, of course not."

The whole class was shifting nervously in their seats.

"Okay, here's the thing," she began, immediately tearing up. "I'm just . . ." Her voice trailed off.

"Come on, man," said one of the bros. "Leave her alone."

And maybe he was right. Imani looked like she was considering whether to gather her things and leave. Finally, having composed herself, she continued, "I'm just . . . so tired all the time. And so fucking angry."

"Whoa!" somebody said. In this setting the word was shocking.

Though her voice had fallen, Peter could see she had more to say. "Go on?" he suggested.

"I've got two little girls and a sick mother, you know? There's never enough time to do everything I need to do. It feels like I fail at everything. There's never enough money, either, so on weekends I clean houses. End of the month is the worst. Usually, I have to take a couple shifts at the House of Pancakes to make next month's rent. My teachers here are mostly okay. They cut me some slack on deadlines."

As Peter had done, more than once.

"But it's like they know what's coming."

"What's that?"

She shook her head. "The day when it all gets to be too much, I guess. When I throw in the towel? When I quit wishing things were different and get it through my thick head that they never will be? Accept my lot in life?"

Peter paused to let this statement register with the rest of the class. "See the difference?" he said. "Exhaustion isn't something Imani knows *about*. It's something she knows."

"I wasn't finished, actually," she said, surprising him.

"Please," he said. "Continue."

"The being tired part I can kind of handle. It's the anger that wipes me out. I mean, why is there even such a thing as a lot in life? Back in high school? Junior high, even? I'd see the special ones, you know? The ones in the gifted and talented classes? They had a lot in life, too, and theirs was sweet. After high school they all went off to places like Edison College, then to law school or maybe med school. I guess things went pretty much as expected for them, too. I'm not saying it was all smooth sailing. They probably had problems, too, but their problems came one at a time, and they had family and friends to help them. In the end things worked out. I know they did because people like me clean their houses for them."

This time, when her voice fell you could hear a pin drop.

"Okay," she said. "That's it. I'll shut the fuck up now."

Another *Whoa!*

"Interesting word, *gifted*," Peter said, addressing the whole class now. "Think back. What did it mean to you, back when you first heard it?"

"Smart?" somebody suggested.

"Anything else?"

"Superior?"

"What else?"

"White?" said the only other Black student in the class.

"White people have problems, too," one of the bros said.

"Okay," Peter said, "but let's not overlook the obvious. What if gifted just means you're somebody who's been given gifts. Piano lessons. Tennis camp. A home full of books. Spring break with the family at Disney. Summer vacations abroad. Have you ever noticed how people who get gifts tend to get a lot of them?"

Pretty much universal agreement on this.

"How about the expectation of success? Isn't that the gift that underlies so many of the others? Take my sons. All three were smart, but only one was gifted. By that I mean he grew up in a nice big house in a safe neighborhood and went to a good school and his father was a college professor. He got into all those gifted and talented classes Imani was talking about. He excelled in school because he was smart and hardworking, but also because that environment was familiar to him. He's now a college professor himself, in a postdoctoral program in England. I don't think he has anyone to clean his house yet, but the day will probably come. I'm pretty sure the son who came to visit me this weekend was given very few of the gifts my gifted son was given and as a result he was not seen as gifted. I suspect he spent much of his young life like Imani, wishing things were different, and I wouldn't be surprised to learn that he'd recently come to the same conclusion she did—that they weren't likely to change, not ever. One of you asked earlier why he came to visit me after so long. One possible answer is that he came all this way to throw in the towel and he wanted his father to see him do it."

One young woman who Peter was pretty sure was a fundamentalist Christian was shaking her head. "I'm sorry about your son and I'm sorry Imani's so tired all the time, but I don't understand what's going on here. I thought the whole idea of going to college was to know *about* things. Isn't that the whole point of taking classes? To learn *about* things? You're making it sound like none of that matters. I don't know why you want us to tell you our secrets. So you can read them out loud and embarrass us?" Now *her* eyes were full. This was either a good class or a very bad one.

"I don't want you to tell me anything you'd rather keep private," he assured her.

"Then I don't know what you want. I don't know what you expect of us."

"I expect you, all of you," he said, "to succeed. If someone's told you you're not smart or talented, I expect you to prove them wrong. I expect you to beat the odds. That's my gift to you, in fact, that gift of expectation." He checked his watch. "That and the remaining twenty minutes of this class."

"You're not going to read from our essays?"

"Not today."

"We can go?"

"Yep. In fact, I insist."

As the other students filed out of the class and Peter stuffed their essays back into his shoulder bag, Imani remained seated, a puzzled look on her face. "What happened to your other son?" she said. "The third one."

"Don't you dare give up," he told her.

"Why not?"

"Because you're *way* too smart."

Out in the corridor, J.J. Julowitz was seated on the floor with his back against the wall. Peter slid down next to him.

"Wow," said J.J. "That was some class. Did you plan all that or just wing it?"

"I wung it," Peter admitted.

J.J. nodded. "Knowing and knowing about," he said. "Cool distinction. I might steal that."

"Feel free."

"And on the subject of gifted, did you know that nobody from SCCC has ever been admitted to Edison for their junior year?"

"Seriously?"

"I shit you not. You still know people there, right?"

Peter admitted that he did.

"Ask them about it some time."

"I will," he promised. "So . . . what's up?" Because if J.J. had been sitting out here in the hall for the last thirty minutes, something must be.

"Well, the lede is that our friend Delgado is gone."

"Gone as in . . ."

"As in, yesterday he was here and today he isn't. At least that's what I'm hearing."

"Huh," Peter said, not sure he believed this. "He didn't impress me as the kind of guy who cuts and runs."

"There are two competing theories on that. The first is that the writing was on the wall. Everything was unraveling. When Delgado lost it and roughed up your son, nobody worried much because cops all stick together and they assumed your son was nobody. Then you show up and all that changes. Also, the second arresting officer, who isn't one of Delgado's crew, is reneging. Claims he was pressured into signing a false arrest report. So, maybe, game over?"

It was possible, Peter supposed. What was it that he'd overheard Delgado's partner say as he was leaving the station? That the whole thing was now officially a shitshow?

"Also, I stopped by Hattie's, like you suggested. The woman you wanted me to talk to refused, but guess what? One whole side of her face is bruised and swollen."

"What's the competing theory?" Peter said, making a mental note to call Ruth later about her daughter.

"Delgado may have an enemy we don't know about. He was seen this morning limping badly. One arm in a sling. Like somebody beat the shit out of him. I'm thinking maybe there's a vigilante out there. Your Imani, except a dude. Maybe a North Sider. Like everybody, he's been hoping that one day things would be different, but that hasn't happened, even with a Black chief of police, and now he's decided it never will. He snaps. Finds out where Delgado lives and waits for him to come home."

Peter shook his head. "Occam's razor, J.J. The simplest explanation is probably right. Like you said before, everything's unraveling. Even his girlfriend won't back up his story. He goes out to the Green Hand and gets gloriously shit-faced, falls down in the parking lot and breaks his arm. If he assaulted Janey last night, he probably took off to avoid being arrested."

J.J. shrugged. "Pretty good story either way, though, right?"

"It has the makings," Peter admitted.

"Actually?" J.J. said. "It's half a story. The other half is your student. What do you say I write the Delgado part and you write the Imani part? We use both stories to transition the magazine from *Schuyler Arts* to the *Schuyler Review.*"

Peter couldn't help smiling. What J.J. wanted, of course, was what just about everybody he knew—Rub, Birdie, Ruth, Carl—seemed to want: for Peter to remain in the very place he was determined to escape. Was that what his father had in mind as well? Why else would he have given Peter that list of people to check on? His mother, of course, would be crushed if he stayed. She'd taken advantage of Sully's absence to convince Peter that he was made for finer things and better places. The way she saw it, his escape—from Bath, from his father and his father's friends—was his rightful destiny. What she *wouldn't* be, however, was surprised. In all likelihood Vera had known the battle was lost that first time he'd showed up in her house wearing a tool belt. To her it was probably a foregone conclusion that he would one day slide onto the stool at the Horse that had his father's name on it.

What was less clear to Peter was what his doing so would mean. Was this, to borrow Imani's term, his "lot in life"? Would it mean he was "throwing in the towel"? Probably not, he decided. Maybe the choice wasn't even his. Free will was not the Get Out of Jail Free card people wanted it to be. You begin to understand that when you start inheriting things—money and houses, yes, but also obligations. What would be difficult to give up, Peter thought, was not the idea of finding a finer place to live out what remained of his life, so much as his fond hope that when he at last arrived there, he would find a finer version of himself, as if that other Peter Sullivan already existed and had been patiently awaiting his arrival, wondering what the hell was taking him so long to show up, so their real life could begin.

There was a word for this, of course, and Peter knew what it was: *folly.*

# Cahoots

"HEY, it's your own damn fault," Charice told him, apparently attempting to tease Raymer out of his dismay over her sudden and, to his mind, inexplicable decision to resign as Schuyler's chief of police. By the time he arrived at the hospital she'd already called Bert Franklin to give her notice. Had Jerome been involved in the decision in some way? Raymer had run into him in the parking lot on his way in. He'd looked excited about something but refused to say what or where he was off to in such a hurry. When he asked Charice what was up, she claimed not to know, but he wasn't sure he believed her. Odious Dougie, he still feared, had been right about their being in cahoots their whole lives and that they always would be.

"*My* fault?"

They were seated side by side on the edge of her unmade bed, waiting for a wheelchair. Though she'd been formally released from the hospital, patients were not permitted to leave under their own power. A chair had been requested half an hour ago, but it still hadn't arrived.

She elbowed Raymer playfully. "You promised me you wouldn't do too good a job."

His figuring out the identity of the hanged man, she meant. Which, okay, *was* good work.

"Franklin was amazed by how you pieced it all together."

He sighed mightily. "I never should've told you what was going on."

He'd wanted to wait until morning. After all, what possible good could come of waking her up to share upsetting news after such a punishing day? Indeed, he wouldn't have except that Jerome had assured him that his sister *wasn't* asleep. Despite the sedative she'd been given earlier, she'd awakened around midnight and been unable to get back to sleep. "I just got off the phone with her, Dawg. Call her. We promised to keep her in the loop."

Unconvinced, Raymer had texted instead: *Some breaking news on the BlackBerry. It'll wait till morning tho.*

Ten seconds later his phone rang. "Tell me," she said.

"Like I said . . . it can wait—"

"It's somebody we know, isn't it."

"I'm sorry," he said, "but it's Gus."

The line went very quiet. "Gus Moynihan? You're sure?"

"Not one hundred percent, but yeah, pretty sure." He then told her about the telephone handset he finally remembered seeing on the floor of the Sans Souci's ballroom, how it had struck him as odd, though at the time he hadn't made the connection to Alice, Gus's troubled wife, who had brought just such a handset with her everywhere she went so she could carry on conversations with imaginary friends.

Alas, as with so many things in life, the answers you were searching for just led to more questions. In this case *who* transitioning naturally to *why* and *how*. How had Gus's decision to end his life come to him? Raymer wondered. All at once or in stages? Had he opened his desk drawer one morning and discovered that he still had a key to the Sans Souci from his days as mayor? Had he immediately seen the key's utility, that he could use it to let himself into the old hotel and do what he needed to without having to worry about anyone finding him and causing that person or persons trauma? Had he at some point opened the trunk of his car and noticed a length of rope peeking out from under the spare tire? Or had he made a special

trip to the hardware store? What made him choose that particular
day and not some other? (Raymer had a strong intuition here.) At
what point, Raymer also wondered, had the tragic chain of events
become irreversible? Why had no one seen it coming and tried to
intervene? Surely, there'd been signs? Hadn't Raymer glimpsed one
or two himself without grasping their import? How many times
had he seen the man sitting all by himself on a bench in Sans Souci
Park, staring off into space. He remembered stopping one afternoon to say hello, and Gus had feigned delight to see him, explaining that the bench he was sitting on was the one that he and Alice
had donated years ago. He'd even slid down so Raymer could read
the plaque with his and Alice's name on it. Despite his attempt at
good cheer, he'd seemed as utterly lost as Alice had been. Had he
returned to that same bench the day he decided he could bear his
life no longer? Had he perhaps left his parka there in the hopes
that some needy person would come along and take it? Had he
shivered in the cold as he climbed those ballroom stairs, or was he
numb, inside and out? Who had he called on his freshly scrubbed
cell phone before leaping from the balcony? Had he made some sort
of pact with himself—to leap or not—depending on the outcome of
that final call?

After hanging up with Charice last night, he'd called the same
number Gus had called back in January. Given the lateness of the
hour, he wasn't surprised when it went immediately to voice mail.
"Hi, this is Alan," said a lilting voice. "Leave a message." Raymer,
unable to think of one, had simply hung up. *Alan,* he thought.

First thing this morning, after a night of tossing and turning,
he'd called the hospital in Utica and learned that his intuition
about what had set events in motion was correct. Alice Moynihan
had died there in early January from complications of advanced
dementia. Gus had been duly notified and come to Utica to make
arrangements and to retrieve his wife's few personal belongings,
among these the cracked, pink handset she still used to talk to her
imaginary friends, including, of late, Gus himself. How devastating
must it have been for him to learn that Alice had finally admitted

him into her inner circle of confidants. The night when Raymer came upon him in the hospital parking lot, what had distressed him most was the fact that Alice never came to him for comfort. He was right there, but she'd preferred to talk to people in her head, using a phone that was really just a prop. And now, his wife gone, that same prop had made its cruel way back to him. Any remaining doubt that the handset Raymer remembered seeing on the ballroom floor was indeed Alice's was laid to rest when Jerome returned there that morning and found it right where Raymer said it would be. It was, beneath layers of accumulated dust, cracked and pink.

Raymer's instinct had also been correct about the man Gus had called just before jumping. Alan, it turned out, was a bartender at Infinitum, where Jerome had gone for drinks with Dr. Qadry the night before. He'd introduced himself, in fact, and had recommended a red wine that was on special. (Jerome sheepishly admitted that it wasn't just white women who fell hopelessly in love with him. Gay white men were often unable to resist his elegant plumage as well.) This morning, using Gus's BlackBerry, Raymer had again called Alan's number, and this time the man picked up right away. "Gus," he said, drawing the natural but incorrect inference. "I thought we agreed it's over." When Raymer explained who he was and how he happened to be calling on Gus's phone, the man had exploded into tears, crying "Oh my God! Oh my God!" over and over. Eventually he'd calmed down enough to confirm Raymer's hunch that, yes, they'd been together for a while, though the relationship had been fraught from the start. Alan was much younger and "out, out, *out*," Gus older and deeply closeted. "Why call *me*?" he wanted to know when Raymer explained that the BlackBerry had been wiped clean, that Alan's was the only number on its call log. "I mean, we hadn't even spoken since he headed south for the winter." Here, there was a pause, followed by a fresh round of *oh-my-God*s. "He never left, did he." Raymer attempted to say something soothing, but Alan was having none of it. "Oh my *God*," he remembered now. "I didn't pick up! I saw who was calling and didn't pick up! I'm such a bad, *bad* person!"

═══

FROM THE CORRIDOR came the sound of a squeaky wheelchair, but instead of entering the room, the chair, occupied by a frail, elderly woman and pushed by an orderly, rolled right on by.

"I just don't see what the hurry is," Raymer said, still hopeful he could change Charice's mind about resigning. "Why not give yourself a day or two to think it over?"

"I *have* thought it over," Charice assured him.

He shook his head, genuinely bewildered. "But this was your dream job," he said, the word reminding him of the Langston Hughes poem he'd read that morning before coming to the hospital—the one with "dream" in the title. (He'd gone on Google to look the poet up, even tried to commit a few lines to memory, but of course they'd fled. Apparently poetry, like therapy, was lost on him.) "And, unlike me, you were good at it, right from the start."

"I'm not saying I wasn't."

"What *are* you saying?"

"I'm not sure," she admitted. "Maybe that you can want the wrong thing? Or for the wrong reason?"

"But how was your wanting to be the first Black chief of police north of Albany wrong? Can you explain that to me?"

"I think what was wrong was that I've been trying to make police work be about justice."

"Isn't it?"

She shook her head. "It's about enforcing existing laws fairly. Justice is about crafting better laws. Jerome's been right all along. I should be in law school. And you belong here, running Schuyler's police department."

*Here,* Raymer thought. He belonged *here. She* belonged *there.* This was what she was trying to help him understand. That they were now on separate, distinct paths.

"Okay, I admit, you're prone to gaffes," she conceded, grinning. "And there are times when you need a keeper."

*I need you,* Raymer thought. *You're my keeper.*

"But you've always been good with people. They like you. They trust you. Alice Moynihan trusted you, remember?"

"Alice was crazy," he pointed out.

Charice ignored this. "And what about old Mr. Hynes?"

Raymer frowned. "Didn't you say I was wrong about him."

"Okay, but my point is that *he* wasn't wrong about *you.* He liked you. You *saw* the man. Listened to him. You never have an agenda with anybody. That's what the Schuyler job is going to require. Basic decency. And you really need to quit selling yourself short. Admit it. Your work last night was inspired. Even Jerome said so."

Was she right? *Was* he a better cop than he gave himself credit for? Possibly. And it might also be true that people generally liked and even trusted him. But so what? Charice could catalog his virtues all she wanted, but the fact remained: something, well, *ailed him.* He found himself thinking, yet again, about Miss Beryl, how back in eighth grade she'd tried to draw him out, writing over and over in the margins of his essays: *Who is this Douglas Raymer?* Why had he resisted her repeated invitations to reveal himself? Why had he hidden *Great Expectations,* her gift to him, in the dark, upper regions of his closet? At the time he'd believed it was because, if his mother found the book, she would think he stole it, but now he wasn't so sure. The old woman had hinted that Raymer would find *himself* somewhere in the book's pages, and this was what he'd really feared. It was himself, not the book, that he'd been trying to keep hidden, which suggested he wasn't so different from poor Gus Moynihan. Apparently, there was more than one way to be closeted.

What had really allowed him to become a better cop, he was pretty sure, was falling in love with Charice. Love had rewired his brain even more dramatically than being struck by lightning. Was this how love worked? Did it simply allow a man to get out of his own way, to get over himself? Because this, surely, had been the crux of the matter all along. What ailed Douglas Raymer had always been Douglas Raymer. Instead of taking in the world, he had watched that world take *him* in, and then register its disappointment. This was the dynamic that Charice had altered. She'd taken a good long look at him and liked him anyway. Then, even more incredibly, like had morphed into love, which had changed how he navigated the world.

Not that love had cured him, exactly, any more than it cured Jerome, who also believed that the women he fell for were good for what ailed him, freeing him not just from his debilitating rituals but from himself, really. Which was, in a nutshell, how Raymer had felt the whole time he and Charice were a couple and why, after they agreed to their time-out, he could feel himself start to regress, to become once again the clueless Douglas Raymer who'd wanted to reassure voters that he wouldn't be happy until they weren't happy, the version of himself that he was hoping he'd left behind for good.

It had been their working together these last few days, Charice's proximity, that had restored not just his confidence but his competence. Jerome, he had to admit, had also played a role. His crazy monologues about plumage and the difference between Black time and white time, his lectures on the Harlem Renaissance, they'd all distracted Raymer from his own narrow concerns, widening his field of vision, allowing others to come into sharper focus. No longer quite so fixated on his own failures, he'd been free to imagine the final days and hours of a man with whom he'd previously thought he had little in common. Which meant that it wasn't just Charice he stood to lose if he couldn't convince her not to resign. He would lose Jerome as well.

She took his hand. "Tell me what you're really thinking," she said.

"I think you've fallen out of love with me."

"Why would you think that?"

He shrugged. "Becka did." Which came out sounding beyond pitiful.

"I'm not Becka."

"Okay," he said, "but I'm still me. You think that when you go off to law school, I'll be able to rise to the occasion and do this job."

"And you will."

"No," he said. "I won't." He paused here, not wanting to say what came next. "Here's what you don't understand. The truth is, I'm not the same man without you. If you and Jerome head back to North Carolina—"

He paused here because Charice was now regarding him the way you would an idiot, which Raymer, being Raymer, actually took as a good sign. Clearly, he'd misunderstood something. Something important, perhaps? "Who said anything about North Carolina?" she wanted to know.

Raymer scrolled back through the conversation. Okay, it was true, nobody had actually said the words *North Carolina*. "But . . . you just said Jerome was right. That you belong in law school."

"They've got law schools here in New York," she pointed out.

Which, of course, was true. "You're saying you'd stay here?" His heart did a somersault in his chest.

"Of course," she said. "What did you think?"

The wrong thing, obviously, but wrong how, exactly? "What about Jerome?" he said, because he knew Charice would never leave her brother. Had she somehow convinced him to stay as well? This was what he was about to ask, when a voice said, "What *about* me?"

The voice, Raymer thought, bore a striking resemblance to Jerome's, but the figure that had materialized in the open doorway was that of a very tall woman with pendulous breasts that were astir beneath her long, flowing robe. Her face was hidden behind a terrifying African mask like the one Jerome had been searching for yesterday in the Sans Souci.

Spying this apparition, Charice leaped to her feet and clapped her hands. "Ooooh!" she squealed. "You found it?"

The terrifying woman nodded gravely.

"Can I see?"

Jerome, beaming, took off the mask and handed it to his sister for her inspection, then turned to Raymer, who had remained seated. "Dawg?" he said, his voice sounding far away.

Raymer opened his mouth, but nothing came out. Just that quickly he'd broken into a flop sweat.

"Dawg?" Jerome repeated. "You okay?"

*Not really,* Raymer thought. And then everything went dark.

=

"HERE," Charice said, handing him a paper cup full of water. "Drink this."

It had taken both her and her brother to lever Raymer back into a sitting position. When he fainted, he'd slumped sideways onto the spot Charice had just vacated when she stood up. Knowing where Jerome had gone and why, she hadn't been nearly as surprised as Raymer to look up and see an African witch doctor standing in the doorway.

When Raymer emptied the cup, Charice put a hand on his shoulder. "How do you feel?"

"Better," he admitted, though he was still a tad light-headed. "How long was I out?"

"Not long," said Jerome. He had taken off the flowing gown and was again, thankfully, boobless. Crouching in front of Raymer, he had a hand on his chest, apparently unwilling to risk Raymer passing out again and pitching forward onto the floor. "Just a few seconds. You gave us a scare, though."

"I gave *you* a scare?"

Jerome was beaming at him now, clearly delighted. "You would've made Posey proud, Dawg. Passing out like that from sheer fright? Exactly what that mask was designed to do."

In truth, Raymer was pretty sure it wasn't the mask that had caused him to faint. He'd actually passed out the moment Jerome took *off* the mask. Why? He couldn't say for certain, but what he'd felt in the moment wasn't so much fear as relief—that the phantasm in the doorway was only Jerome and not the physical embodiment of all his doubts and fears. Or maybe he'd realized just then that his congenital optimism, until now mostly misplaced, was finally about to pay dividends. That somehow, all would be well. How? Damned if he knew, but the details, he felt certain, would reveal themselves in the fullness of time. For now, they didn't matter. And if Jerome wanted to believe that he'd passed out from sheer fright, well, that didn't matter, either. If the incident worked best as yet another Douglas Raymer story that people would be laughing at till the end of time, fine, so long as Charice and, yes, Jerome were among those having fun at his expense.

"Where did you find it?" Raymer wondered, glancing over at the witch-doctor mask, which Charice had leaned up against the wall. "At the Sans Souci?"

"Nope," Jerome told him. "At a place called Grandpa Zack's Treasures."

Raymer knew of it, had driven by any number of times, but had never gone in. "What made you look there?"

"It was Pam's idea. She goes there all the time and she remembered seeing a mask like I was describing last night at the wine bar. Said if Posey Gold was anywhere around here, that's where she'd be."

"She'd heard of the Harlem Renaissance? Dr. Qadry?"

"Of course," he replied. "She's an educated woman, Dawg."

"Right," Raymer said. She could probably recite the entire Langston Hughes poem that Raymer couldn't even recall the title of.

"Anyhow," Jerome continued, "I figured it was a long shot, but just for the hell of it I called over there to see if they had anything that might be African. When I described the mask, the guy I was talking to said they had a big one that gave him the willies every time he walked past it. Said he'd take it as a personal favor if I purchased it."

"You think it's really a Posey Gold?"

"Got a little p.g. etched on the inside of the mask, Dawg."

Raymer smiled, surprised at how pleased all this made him. "Congratulations, Jerome. I'm happy for you."

Charice now put a warm hand on Raymer's forehead. "You're looking better," she said. "You've got some color back. Shall we see if you can stand up?"

"Let's," Raymer said, blinking away the last of the mental cobwebs.

Charice and Jerome each grabbed an elbow and eased him to his feet.

"Well?" Charice said. "How do you feel? We could call for another wheelchair."

"No," he said, "I think the day's already been sufficiently humiliating."

"Okay, then," Charice said. "Let's go home."

Here, actually, was one of the details he'd been hoping would become clear in the fullness of time. "When you say *home,* where do you mean exactly?" The place he was now sharing with Jerome? Her own flat across town, which Raymer had not that long ago also called home?

Brother and sister shared a conspiratorial look. "You didn't tell him about the plan?" Jerome said.

"Plan?" Raymer said.

Both twins turned to regard him.

"Do you think he's ready?" Charice said.

Jerome shrugged. "Gotta tell him sometime."

"Well, then," Charice said. "The plan is, first, we terminate the lease on my place."

"And then?"

"And then we make an offer on the house."

"Which house?" Raymer said. Also, which *we*? Her and Raymer? Her and Jerome?

"The one you're living in," she said. "The one with a FOR SALE sign on the lawn."

Raymer nodded, pretending to understand. "Just to be clear," he said. "Do I still get to live there?"

"Uh-huh," Charice said.

"With Jerome?"

"With me."

"As . . . a couple? No more time-out?" Because that's what

he wanted more than anything, far more than to be the Schuyler Springs chief of police.

"That could happen," she smiled, "if you play your cards right."

"And me, Dawg," said Jerome. "Don't forget me."

"Are we a couple, too?" Raymer said, getting into the spirit of things.

"Sort of," Jerome said seriously. "Bert thinks that if we have a white chief of police again, it might be good to have a senior Black officer to act as liaison with the North Side."

"And what would that senior Black officer's name be?" he said, teeing up Jerome's favorite line.

Which the other man dutifully whacked. "Bond," he said. "*Jerome* Bond."

"I assume you've shared this plan with . . . Pam?"

"She's on board, Dawg."

"How about you?" Charice said. "Are you on board? Or do you require more convincing?"

He did not. Another man might've demanded more say. Odious Dougie would surely disapprove. But the decision wasn't Dougie's, it was Raymer's, and he was more than happy with the future that was taking shape before his eyes. Double-teamed—no, triple-teamed (Pam!)—was how he would end up. Outnumbered. Outvoted. Outflanked. Outgunned. Outsmarted.

He couldn't wait.

He would own it all.

# Magic Slate

THE DUTY NURSE SMILED when Peter arrived on the ward. "Did you get my message?"

Peter told her no, he hadn't, explaining that he'd turned his phone off to teach his class and neglected to turn it back on again.

"Well, there's been a change," she said. "Your son has regained consciousness."

At this, Peter's knees nearly buckled, causing him to grab on to the nearby counter to steady himself. "Sorry," he said, embarrassed. "I guess I wasn't expecting good news."

"It's okay," she said, touching his elbow. "Take a minute."

"It *is* good news, right? He's out of danger?"

"Well, put it this way," she said. "Regaining consciousness is huge. He's pretty listless, though. Probably not all that surprising, given what he's been through."

By "what he's been through" she meant the last forty-eight hours. What she had no idea about, of course, was the rest of his life. Nor, except for a few paltry facts, did Peter. "Can I see him?"

"Of course. Try to keep your visit short, though. More than anything, he needs rest." He'd made it only a few steps down the corridor, when she called to him. "Gosh, I almost forgot. A young woman came by earlier. She said to give you this."

She was holding a tablet-like object. It was about an inch thick and had a gray, rectangular screen that was shiny and wrinkled. There was a plastic stylus attached. The thing looked vaguely familiar.

Seeing that he was at a loss, the nurse took it back from him and used the stylus to scribble a wavy line on the screen, then pulled up on the plastic sheet, which made the line disappear. "Ah," he said, remembering now. A Magic Slate.

"I didn't understand at first, either," she said, handing it back to him, "but when you think about it, it's kind of brilliant, right? A way to talk to somebody who can't talk back?"

Peter agreed. It was brilliant. Also intuitive and slightly off-kilter. "Any chance this young woman had a wandering eye?"

"Now that you mention it," she said.

═══

THE WORD the nurse had used to describe Thomas was *listless,* but to Peter his son just appeared defeated, as if every bit of fight had drained out of him. He glanced up briefly when Peter entered but then looked down again. Peter didn't immediately recognize the silver object that held his son's attention as Will's stopwatch, which Peter had left on Thomas's bedside table the night before. The expression on his son's face suggested dissatisfaction not just with the stopwatch but with how time worked. As if he would have preferred it to go faster, or backward, or maybe just stop altogether. "How are you feeling?" Peter said, taking a seat at the foot of the bed.

Thomas shrugged, as if the question bore no relevance. Like he didn't much care how he felt and doubted he ever would.

Peter decided to try a new tack. "Hey," he said, handing his son the Magic Slate. "Remember these? You and Will used to play tick-tacktoe by the hour on road trips."

Thomas returned the stopwatch to the bedside table and examined the tablet, even managing a wan smile. Picking up the stylus, he wrote: *He always won.*

"He was a year older," Peter said. "He always took the center square."

*Stabbed him with this once,* Thomas wrote, holding up the stylus. It wasn't clear to Peter how he felt about this memory, or if he felt anything at all.

"You know what?" Peter said. "According to the doctors, you're pretty lucky."

Their eyes met now. *Lucky?*

"They weren't sure you were going to wake up."

Thomas erased the old message and composed a new one: *Too bad I did?*

"That's not how I feel, Thomas. That's not how I feel at all."

Another wan smile. Another shrug. This time, instead of erasing the message, he put a small *x* through the question mark at the end of the sentence, thereby turning it into a statement.

Feeling his own spirits plummet, Peter said, "Okay, look. You've had a pretty rough couple of days, and you need rest. The worst is behind you, though, I promise." He placed a hand on his son's ankle. "But as soon as you get your strength back, we've got work to do."

At this, Thomas shook his head. Pulling up on the plastic sheet, he filled the entire screen with a two-letter word: *No.*

"I don't understand," Peter told him. "Why not?"

*Finished.*

"What's finished?"

*Me. Everything.*

"Of course, you aren't finished, Thomas," Peter told him, though, in fact, his son's eyes were as empty as the void. "Are you worried about the cop who did this to you? Because he's long gone. You're never going to see him again. I know you assaulted a police officer, but given what was done to you, I doubt he'll press charges. If he does, we'll hire a good lawyer." When Thomas offered no response, Peter could see that none of this was the cause of his desolation. If he'd given up, something else had caused him to. "I know you're angry," he continued, "and I have a pretty good idea of why you came all this way. I don't blame you. You have to believe that."

When he got no response to this either, Peter took back the Magic Slate and drew a ticktacktoe grid on the screen. "Here's what needs to happen," he said, turning the device around so Thomas could see. "I know it won't be easy, but this, right here, is what you and I need to do." When he was certain he had Thomas's attention, he lifted up the plastic sheet, disappearing the grid. "Fresh start," he said. "Clean slate. Do you understand?"

Thomas held out his hand for the slate. Reluctantly, Peter gave it back to him. What he wrote this time was: *Too late*.

"Too late for what, Thomas? What is it that can't be fixed?"

Again, his son pulled up the plastic sheet, erasing the words *too late* and replacing them with *Me*. But apparently this wasn't quite right either, because he disappeared *Me* and wrote: *Us*. His eyes, Peter saw, were suddenly full.

"Thomas," Peter said. "Look at me. By *us,* do you mean you and me? Or you and Andy?"

Thomas let out a low moan.

Peter squeezed his knee. "Look," he said. "As soon as you're well enough, the two of us will drive down to West Virginia. We'll bring him back with us."

Thomas regarded him hopelessly for a long beat, then wrote: *Her*.

"Right," Peter said. "Andrea." Last night, his Google search had turned up an article in a West Virginia newspaper about conversion therapy. Andy was one of the kids whose gender dysphoria they'd tried and failed to fix.

Thomas, tears running down his cheeks now, was scratching furiously at the slate, giving Peter only a second or two to read what he'd written before disappearing the words and scratching something else.

*He never stopped believing you'd come for us.*

*Take us to live with you and Will.*

*But you never did.*

"I know," Peter said. "I'm sorry."

*Tried to convince him to stop loving you.*

Up went the plastic sheet.

*But he couldn't.*

"How about you, Thomas? Did *you* stop?"

If his son heard this, he gave no sign.

*Didn't want me to come here.*

*Tried to talk me out of it.*

*I wouldn't listen.*

*And now . . .*

A louder howl somehow escaped his frozen jaw.

*All gone. Lost.*

The tablet clattered to the floor.

*Magic Slate,* Peter thought bitterly. A lie you tell children. *Look! The words were right there, and now they're gone. Magic!* As if words or deeds or even thoughts, for that matter, could be unuttered, undone, unthought. In reality, of course, they all landed, and many left a mark, as did the refusal to say, to do, to imagine. Of Peter's many mistakes as a father, his failure to more truly imagine the lives of the sons he'd left behind was the most confounding. He'd permitted himself to believe that what he and they had in common—an absent father; a bitter, angry mother—would be sufficient to bridge the chasm of their profoundly different life experiences. Two days earlier, as he showed Thomas around the Upper Main Street house, he'd actually suggested that he and his brother had had it comparatively easy, that his own father's proximity had resulted in more mental anguish than if he'd vanished entirely from Peter's young life. Unable to forget the man, Peter had been forced to reconcile, again and again, what could not be reconciled—what his mother expected of him (that he see his father as redundant, as serving no useful purpose) with how he really felt each time Sully unexpectedly reappeared, upending their lives and making him feel . . . what? At the time he didn't even know what to call that feeling. It wasn't love. At least he was pretty sure it wasn't. All he knew for certain was that he wasn't allowed to indulge it. Over time he would come to understand that it was simply longing, his unruly heart inclining in a way that embarrassed, even shamed, him. Back then, however, he would've given anything to make it go away. This was what he'd hoped Thomas would understand—that at least he'd spared him and Andy that terrible longing. Over time any feelings they'd had for him or their brother Will would turn to ashes. A gift, really.

Except they clearly *hadn't* been spared. Far from it. Where Ralph, Peter's stepfather, had treated him like a son, theirs had apparently made little effort to be a loving father. For all Peter knew, the man might have been cruel, possibly even abusive. And unlike Vera, Charlotte would never have told her boys that their father was redundant. She would have made plain to them that Peter was not only worth remembering but worth hating. She would have nurtured that hatred, tended it faithfully, believing, as Peter did, that any yearning Thomas and Andy felt for their father would eventually be extinguished. Except that hadn't happened. If what Thomas just told him was true, Andy had never stopped loving him, never given up hope that one day Peter would come for them. Thomas had tried but been unable to persuade him otherwise. And Thomas? How surprised he must have been on Saturday when he saw Peter and felt, in addition to the loathing his mother had cultivated, a completely unexpected flare-up of the yearning he had assumed had been smothered long ago, a yearning so powerful that it neutralized the rage he'd been counting on to carry out his dark purpose. No more able to reconcile the unreconcilable than Peter had been, he'd turned his anger inward, just as Ruth had deduced. Rage—against his father and life's fundamental unfairness—had kept him alive and fighting. Longing, even its recollection, had brought him to death's door.

And Peter himself? Well, he hadn't escaped unscathed, either. Time to admit that. His failures to reconcile hurt and anger with longing had taught him an emotional reticence that had shielded him from further injury. His education—the rhetorical sophistication that was education's inevitable byproduct—had only deepened that reticence. Ruth, seeing it for the cowardice that it was, had called him on it. So, in her own way, had Toby Roebuck. That's what her touching his chest with that bloodred fingernail and wondering out loud if there was a heart in there somewhere had been about. What would these two women think if they knew how spectacularly his reticence—the habit of a lifetime—had failed him over the last twenty-four hours.

Though there was no real magic in the Magic Slate, Peter retrieved the tablet from where it lay on the floor, relieved to see that it wasn't broken. It had been kind of Tina to imagine its practical use and to want to help. Having loved Will, and seeing Will in Thomas, she must have wondered if Thomas might be worth loving, too. He would have to find a way to thank her for that.

Thomas's final message—*All gone. Lost.*—was still on the screen. He'd stopped weeping now and was watching Peter carefully, perhaps to see if he would disappear his expression of heartfelt despair, which Peter had no intention of doing. "You're right," he said. "We've lost a lot. And we've made an awful mess of things. Both of us. But here we are, Son." He paused to let the undeniable fact of their continued existence resonate, along with the word that affirmed their relationship. Only when Thomas didn't object, did he add, "But what's left? That can all be fixed."

Thomas once again held out his hand for the Magic Slate. When Peter gave it to him, he studied the words he'd scratched there for a long beat before disappearing them. In their place he drew his own ticktacktoe grid, and in the center, he wrote a small three-letter word and turned it around so Peter could see. *How?*

"I don't know," Peter admitted. "We'll try something. And if that doesn't work, we'll try something else."

# Acknowledgments

The first of my "Fool" novels was edited by David Rosenthal, the second by Gary Fisketjon, this last one by Jordan Pavlin. I owe each of them more gratitude than I can possibly express.

When I started writing about Sully, I was channeling my father and thought of the character as belonging to me. By the time I returned to him, Paul Newman and I shared joint custody. The same is true of Doug Raymer, played in Robert Benton's wonderful film by a young Philip Seymour Hoffman. You don't have to look very hard to register their ghostly presence.

What every writer needs and relatively few get is stability. My literary agent, Nat Sobel, offered to represent me after reading a story of mine in a tiny literary journal roughly forty years ago and we've been together ever since. For almost that long my friends at Knopf have offered me a home that I've never felt I needed to question. Literary careers are built on such relationships. The name Richard Russo appears on the covers of my books. Think of all these other people, please, when you read that name.

I'm indebted as well to my regular Sunday night dinner crew, which includes Emily and Kate, my daughters, and Steve and Tom, my sons-in-law, all four of whom indulge me when I pose hypothetical subjects that in reality originate in some problem I'm trying to fix in whatever book I'm struggling with. And none of these books would exist without my wife, Barbara, who listens to my problems on the other six nights as well.

Thanks, finally, to Chris Lynch, who counseled me on what happens when unlucky towns get incorporated by lucky ones.

## A NOTE ABOUT THE AUTHOR

RICHARD RUSSO is the author of nine novels, most recently *Chances Are . . .*, *Everybody's Fool* and *That Old Cape Magic;* two collections of stories; and the memoir *Elsewhere.* In 2002 he received the Pulitzer Prize for *Empire Falls,* which was adapted into a multiple award-winning miniseries; in 2017, he received France's Grand Prix de Littérature Américaine. He lives in Portland, Maine.

## A NOTE ON THE TYPE

This book was set in Granjon, a type named in compliment to Robert Granjon, a type cutter and printer active in Antwerp, Lyons, Rome, and Paris from 1523 to 1590. Granjon, the boldest and most original designer of his time, was one of the first to practice the trade of typefounder apart from that of printer.

Linotype Granjon was designed by George W. Jones, who based his drawings on a face used by Claude Garamond (ca. 1480–1561) in his beautiful French books. Granjon more closely resembles Garamond's own type than do any of the various modern faces that bear his name.

*Typeset by Scribe,*
*Philadelphia, Pennsylvania*

*Printed and bound by Friesens,*
*Altona, Manitoba*

*Designed by Cassandra J. Pappas*